"WHAT'S THE DATE? AND THE YEAR?"

"June twelfth, 1968, hon. Listen, can I get you something cold to drink? That heat outside is a bitch."

Mira squeezed her eyes shut. *Can't be. Impossible. No way.*

She rubbed her hands over her face and looked at Jake, now seated beside her on a stool, smoking. "May I see your driver's license, Jake?"

"My license? Sure." He dug out his wallet. "But what for?"

"Because you look to be in your early thirties."

"Thirty-two. So?"

"So when were you born?"

"Nineteen thirty-six."

"Then you'd be sixty-six years old."

He seemed really amused by this. "Not by any math that I know. But hey, look for yourself." He handed her his license and there, right next to his name, Jake Romano, was his date of birth: May 13, 1936.

"Jesus," she whispered. "It's true."

RFK had been dead for a week.

All four Beatles were not only alive, but still together.

The war in Vietnam was raging.

The Democratic Convention in Chicago was two months away.

Easy Rider wouldn't premier until next year.

Ken Kesey, Janis Joplin, and Jimi Hendrix were still alive.

Neal Armstrong would walk on the moon next summer.

BOOK YOUR PLACE ON OUR WEBSITE AND MAKE THE READING CONNECTION!

We've created a customized website just for our very special readers, where you can get the inside scoop on everything that's going on with Zebra, Pinnacle and Kensington books.

When you come online, you'll have the exciting opportunity to:

- View covers of upcoming books
- Read sample chapters
- Learn about our future publishing schedule (listed by publication month *and author*)
- Find out when your favorite authors will be visiting a city near you
- Search for and order backlist books from our online catalog
- Check out author bios and background information
- Send e-mail to your favorite authors
- Meet the Kensington staff online
- Join us in weekly chats with authors, readers and other guests
- Get writing guidelines
- AND MUCH MORE!

**Visit our website at
http://www.kensingtonbooks.com**

BLACK WATER

T.J. MacGregor

PINNACLE BOOKS
Kensington Publishing Corp.
http://www.kensingtonbooks.com

For Kate Duffy, who made it possible,
and for Rob,
who reminded me what the sixties were really about

ACKNOWLEDGMENTS

A special thanks to Al Zuckerman,
the best agent there is,
and to my daughter, Megan,
who never complained when I said I had
to get back to the book.

Part One
The Corridor

"The universe is not just a collection of separate points. It is what it is according to the observer and what he or she does."

—Fred Alan Wolf,
Taking the Quantum Leap

One

The fading afternoon light clung to the western horizon like blood to cloth. Mira Morales snapped two more photos of her daughter, a silhouette against the exquisite June light, as she moved along the beach, collecting another bucket of shells to take home.

"Hey, Annie," she called. "Let's start packing up the boat."

"Five more minutes, Mom," Annie called back.

Five more minutes, not right now, I'm not ready yet: the litanies of a thirteen-year-old always smacked of procrastination. But they had fifteen miles of open water to cross between Little Horse Key, an uninhabited spit of land in the Gulf of Mexico where they had spent the day, and Tango Key, where they lived. The thought of crossing it in the dark, in a puny skiff with an even punier outboard motor, made Mira distinctly uncomfortable.

She moved quickly, gathering up towels, umbrellas, suntan lotion, paperbacks, and the rest of the stuff strewn around the cooler and the boat. It looked as if they had come for several weeks rather than a day. She doubted she would ever master the art of packing lightly. But how could she possibly leave home without plenty of bottled water, food, snacks, her cell phone and Pocket PC? And it wasn't possible to go to the beach without something to read, preferably a choice

of books from the dozens of advance reading copies
that her bookstore got every week. She'd also brought
along a new tarot deck that a distributor had sent her,
this one with a motif from *Lord of the Rings*. The digital
camera that Shep had given her last Christmas had
come with her, too.

Annie bounded across the sand to show Mira the
shells she'd collected, her exuberance over something
so simple a refreshing change from the glumness that
had shadowed her for the past year. Although she'd
made a few friends since they'd moved to Tango three
years ago, she didn't have a single close friend, no one
who called her up every night to gossip or with whom
she could share her deepest secrets. At thirteen, the ab-
sence of a close friend left a mighty big void.

The few times Mira had tried to tune in on Annie,
she couldn't get beyond the waves of utter loneliness
and isolation. Years ago, Mira's grandmother, Nadine,
had warned her never to read someone she loved because the truth would shock her. *In our heart of hearts,
most of us are strangers to each other.* At the time, Mira considered the remark to be cynical. Now she realized that
what Nadine had really been saying was that some
things had to be lived through alone. Mira could be
there for Annie, supportive and offering guidance, but
she couldn't banish her daughter's pain. She couldn't
live adolescence for her. All of which was why she had
spent a day on a little island, swimming and sunbathing
with her daughter. Mom, the substitute companion.

"I saw a lot of dead crabs on the beach, Mom." Annie
poured her newest shells into a smaller cooler. "You
think it has something to do with that black water mass
out there?"

"I doubt it. The mass is fifty miles offshore."

The mass that Annie referred to had been reported
about eight months ago by commercial fishermen.

They described it as a large area of blackish-colored water with gelatinous globs floating on the surface of it. Fishermen who had been plying the gulf waters for fifty years claimed never to have seen anything like it. Although the mass didn't leave a trail of dead fish, as red tide did, no live fish were found in the black waters, either. Initially, satellite photos showed that the black waters covered a 750-square-mile area roughly the size of Lake Okeechobee.

Even though the mass had started breaking up into smaller pieces, environmentalists were concerned about its impact on marine life and on the coral reef, the only living barrier reef in the U.S. Marine biologists from all over Florida had been taking samples of the stuff ever since it appeared and had a host of theories. One theory said that the black water phenomenon was due to pollutants. Other theories attributed it to some sort of underwater explosion of algae or plankton, to a spike in ocean temperatures or salinity, or to a runoff of nitrogen from sugarcane fields in South Florida. But so far, no one had determined exactly what it was or what had caused it.

"Last week it was fifty miles offshore," Annie said. "On the news this morning, I heard the biggest piece of it is just a few miles south of here."

When Annie spoke with such authority, she reminded Mira of her father, the same passion in her dark eyes, the same flare to her nostrils, that proud lift to her chin. She was an extraordinarily pretty girl—not that Annie believed it—with her Cuban father's beautiful skin and high cheekbones. Tom was killed on Annie's third birthday, and at moments like this Mira ached inside for the life that she, Tom, and Annie would never have together.

Get over it and move on, she thought. *It happened ten years ago.*

"There haven't been any reports of dead fish in that mass," Mira said. "Hey, get on the other side of the boat so I can snap one more picture of you before we leave."

"You know, it's okay if it's dark when we head back to Tango, Mom. We're not going to capsize and drown or anything."

"I didn't say we were."

"But that's what you're thinking."

Annie flashed a mischievous grin and sprang over the skiff. She thrust out her right hip, planted one hand against it, and with the other hand flicked her long, dark hair off her shoulders, and Mira snapped a couple of pictures. Her daughter always joked that Mira's fear of being on the water after dark probably went back to a life in which she'd drowned at night. Mira usually laughed when she said it, but suspected she was probably right. One of the problems with raising an intuitive daughter was that Annie's intuition often surpassed her own.

For generations back, all of the firstborn women in the family had been born with the Sight. Mira rarely referred to it that way out loud because it sounded so antiquated. But it was the best word to describe an ability that had been a part of her life as far back as she remembered. Because of it, she had foreseen her husband's death several years before it had happened. The Sight hadn't prevented Tom's murder, but five years after it had happened, it had enabled her to provide Wayne Sheppard, who was then a Fort Lauderdale cop, with enough clues about the killer to find him. The ability was her livelihood, her passion, her greatest curse, and her most profound gift. It was as intrinsic to who she was as her own flesh and blood. But there were many times when the ability spoke to her that she wished it would shut up and leave her alone. Like right now.

For several moments, she had been aware of a growing discomfort just below her sternum, an intense heat that spread like melting wax. When she focused on the feeling to clarify it, the heat deepened, but no images came to mind. Maybe it was just indigestion from all the junk food she and Annie had consumed on the beach.

"Okay, now let me get some pictures of you, Mom."

They traded places and while Annie was deciding whether to crouch or to frame the photos vertically or horizontally, Mira punched out Shep's cell number. His cell was always on. It was the only phone he owned.

"Agent Sheppard."

"Psychic Morales."

He laughed. "Are you two on your way back?"

"In a few minutes. We're taking some more pictures. Where're you?"

"Nadine and I are sitting in the kitchen, having a beer. She's got a shrimp casserole in the oven."

"We should be there in under an hour."

"You feel like taking in a movie?"

"Only if I get to eat first. What'd you have in mind?"

"A video at my place."

"Sounds good."

A night alone with Sheppard sounded very good. She couldn't have said that two years ago. Shortly after the end of the investigation that had brought them together, Sheppard had inherited money from an aunt, quit his job at the sheriff's department, and had taken off for six months, satisfying a deep itch to travel. When he'd returned, she was living on Tango and their relationship had been erratic, unsettled, and complicated by distance. He was trying to figure out the next step in his life and she was trying to figure out if he would fit into her life at all. Then he had gotten a job offer from his former boss at the FBI, where he had worked for five years before he'd joined the Broward County Sheriff's Department. So Sheppard had joined the bureau for the second time, moved to Tango, and their relationship had flourished ever since.

"Oh, Nadine says to tell you that Annie got a call from that girl down the street," Sheppard went on. "She wants to know if Annie can spend the night."

"Hey, Annie," Mira said, covering the mouthpiece. "Christina called and wants to know if you can spend the night."

If she was hoping the news would cheer Annie up, she'd been grossly mistaken. Her daughter shrugged— *whatever*—which perfectly expressed her angst these days.

"Christina's a pain in the butt, Mom."

"I take it that's a no."

"I'll call her when I get home. C'mon, move a little to the left."

"Got to run. Georgia O'Keefe is going to take a picture of me. We'll see you in a while," Mira said to Sheppard.

"Hey, tell Annie she's got three cats who love her," he said.

"I don't think that's much comfort right now, but I'll pass on the message. See you soon."

She disconnected and Annie said, "Okay, hand on your hip."

Mira put her hand on her hip and Annie took a couple of photos. "So is dinner on?"

"Shrimp casserole."

Annie wrinkled her nose. "I hate shrimp, Mom."

"You can have salad and cold chicken."

Annie, Little Ms. Picky. She hated shrimp, but loved fish. She had never eaten a hamburger or had a soft drink, but she consumed Dannon coffee yogurt with all the relish of a true caffeine addict.

"Uh, Mom?" Annie said, lowering the camera. "There's a guy coming up the beach."

Mira glanced around, shading her eyes against the glare of the setting sun. The man was pulling a small boat onto the sand and seemed to be struggling with it. She saw that one of his arms was in a cast. He crouched over the outboard engine and banged on it with something, the clatter echoing along the beach. "If he needs help, he'll ask. C'mon, let's get our stuff together, hon. We need to get going."

They started loading their belongings in the boat. The sun shimmered as it began its descent into the gulf, its light burning against the surface of the water. A slight breeze had risen, the air swelled with the scent of salt and sand, a wilderness of water. Just offshore, a school of fish leaped up, a glistening silver mass in the light, then splashed down again. Mira realized the clatter had stopped and looked down the beach again. The man was trudging through the sand and now he waved.

"Hey, hello," he called. "My engine conked out. Can you give me a hand?"

Mira waved back. She didn't want to be held up any longer, but she couldn't refuse to help someone stranded out here, either. "Let's see what this guy needs." She walked away from her boat to meet the man halfway.

The discomfort she'd felt earlier just below her sternum now returned. She pressed two fingers against it, rubbing gently. It definitely wasn't indigestion. This feeling, she thought, was all about her fear of getting caught out on the water in the dark, which now looked like a distinct possibility.

"I'm really sorry to intrude like this," the man said, and waved his cast at his boat. A forearm cast. "The damn engine died on me about three hundred yards from shore and I don't have any tools or a cell phone."

"I've got a few tools. You're welcome to look through them."

"Thanks so much. The idea of having to row fifteen miles to shore, in the dark, isn't especially appealing."

She smiled. "Yeah, I know what you mean."

He was roguishly handsome, with a weathered face that said he spent a lot of time in the sun, and eyes the same color as the water at dusk, lead ringed with a dark blue. The sun had streaked his hair blond and he kept drawing his fingers through it as if to get rid of the salt and the elements. He carried a backpack slung over his right shoulder.

"I started having trouble with the engine when I was fishing. It kept sputtering. I should've turned back then, I guess."

They were walking toward Annie, who waited by the boat. "You live on Tango?" she asked.

"Key West. You?"

"Tango."

"You just out here boating?"

"My daughter and I came out here for the day."

"My name's Pete," he said.

"I'm Mira. That's Annie."

"Hi," Annie said. "Mom, you've got to lift this cooler into the boat. It's too heavy for me."

"Yeah, okay. Let me dig out the tools for Pete. He's having engine problems."

She flipped open the lid on the fishing tackle box and brought out a pack of tools. "I hope there's something in there you can use. Can I call someone for you?"

"I hate to bother friends." He opened the pack of tools, nodding to himself. "It's a long way out here."

The discomfort she'd been feeling now exploded into a full-blown pain that caused her to catch her breath. "Keep the tools, Pete. We need to shove off and get back across the water before it's completely dark. You sure you don't want me to call someone en route?"

"Thanks, I'm sure."

Then he raised his eyes from the tools and a second explosion of pain nearly drove to her to her knees. In an instant of utter horror, she realized that *he* was the source of the pain. She took a step back, tried to smile, to hide her terror.

"Good luck. Grab the rope, Annie. I'll get the coo—"

He rose up, still smiling, and slammed his cast against the side of her head. Agony detonated in her bones, stars blew up in her eyes, blood pounded in her ears. She stumbled sideways, shaking her head to clear it, the metallic taste of blood filling her mouth, and shrieked, *"Run, Annie, ru—"*

The second blow struck her in the back of the head. She heard the cast cracking, heard Annie screaming. The ocean thundered in her skull. Even as she was toppling forward, her arms shooting out to break her fall, her vision darkening, he threw himself into her and she crashed to the beach.

Sand flew up her nostrils, got sucked into her mouth. She spat and rolled onto her back, jackknifed her legs, and her bare feet sank into his stomach. He staggered, but didn't fall. As she scrambled to her feet, the beach, the light, the water, everything rolled to the right. She hurled herself at him, but she was so clumsy, so weak, that he merely leaped to the left and she lurched forward like a drunk, her vision swimming with blackness.

Then he hit her again. As she went down, she knew she would be unconscious before she struck the ground.

Two

The instant her mother shrieked for her to run, Annie took off down the beach, sand flying up and biting her heels, arms tucked in tightly at her sides. She looked back only once and saw her mother's final fall, the way she sprawled in the sand and didn't get up. And then the man tore after her, his long legs eating up the distance between them.

Annie cut sharply toward the trees, a few tall pines and a mangrove swamp. Her terror, so pure and powerful, filled her like helium, and she ran for her life, air and sobs exploding from her mouth.

It was nearly dark now. If she could make it into the trees, he would never find her. She would disappear. She would swim back to Tango if she had to. *Without my mom?*

Never.

Oh God, oh God. . . . Faster.

She blinked sweat from her eyes. Her leg muscles felt as tight as piano strings. She didn't think she could maintain this pace much longer.

The dark clump of mangroves loomed in front of her. *I can make it, I can, I can. . . .*

Annie stole another look back. Big mistake. He was closing in on her, moving like the wind. Seconds later, she plunged into the mangroves and promptly tripped on something, a protruding root, a branch, she couldn't tell exactly what it was, and lost her balance. She went down on her hands and knees. Her hands sank into the gunk up to her wrists—thick, deep mud, rotting leaves, dead things. The gunk squished up under her fingernails, between her toes, releasing a stink like rotten eggs.

She wrenched her hands back, shot upward, but the mud sucked at her feet, trapping them. Panicked, she twisted violently to the side, grappling in the darkness for something to grab, to use for leverage. Her fingers caught a branch and she grasped it and pulled her left foot out of the mud and the branch snapped and she stumbled forward. She heard him now, a giant crashing into the mangroves, breathing hard.

Then he was on her, his powerful arms closing around her, lifting her out of the mud as if she were as light as a branch. Annie screamed, kicked, writhed, and sank her teeth into the back of his hand. She held on, biting deeper, tasting blood. He made a low, terrible animal sound and for seconds his hold on her loosened just enough for her to slam her elbow back. She didn't know where she hit him, but it must have been exactly the right spot because he suddenly let her go.

Annie tore forward, the mud sucking at her feet, branches clawing at her face and arms, bugs scampering up her legs. She reeled to the left, the right, the left again, trying to make herself a more difficult target, but it was so dark in here she couldn't see a thing. She ran into a tree and tumbled back, the entire right side of her face burning with pain. He grabbed her again and they fell sideways and hit the water. Her head went under, the stink and the mud rushed up her nose, panic exploded inside her.

He yanked her upward by the hair, grabbed the back of her shirt, and carried her out of the mangrove by the back of her shirt, like a piece of luggage. She screamed and kicked, trying to get loose. He jerked on her hair and she nearly passed out from the pain. "Look," he said, his voice strangely soft, even. "If you struggle, you'll make me hurt you. I don't want to hurt you."

She didn't say anything. She stopped struggling. He carried her so that she faced the ground. It made her dizzy and she shut her eyes. He eased the pressure on her hair, and moments later they reached the beach, the dry sand. He dropped her on her butt, but didn't release his hold on her hair. If she moved her head, if she moved at all, she knew he would tear out a clump of her hair at the roots.

Talk to him. Wasn't that what you were supposed to do in a situation like this? *Think, Annie, use your stupid brain.* "What . . . what do you want?" *Establish a connection. That'll make it harder for him to kill you.*

"I want you to get up nice and easily and we're going to walk down the beach." He snapped a handcuff around her wrist; the other end was connected to his wrist.

Annie noticed he no longer wore the cast on his arm. "Is my mother . . ."

"She's alive."

"The cast was fake."

"Yes."

"To trick us."

"To make me seem unthreatening."

"Ted Bundy did that."

"You're absolutely right." He sounded surprised. "You're a smart kid. I bet you have straight As in school."

"I'm in a gifted program."

"I knew you were intelligent."

"How the hell would you know that?"

"Don't swear."

Hardness in his voice now. It scared her.

"I don't like hearing kids swear. That's the first rule."

Rules? What's he mean by that? Keep him talking. She would keep him talking and look for an opportunity to kick him in the balls. "Okay." She would tell him exactly what he wanted to hear. "How do you know whether I'm intelligent or stupid?"

"I've watched you."

Her arms erupted with goose bumps. *Don't go there.* But even as she thought this, her mind twitched, leaped around. When had he watched her? When? As she walked to or from school? *Find out everything you can.*

He pulled a flashlight from his back pocket, turned it on. The beam of light found her mother, still lying in the sand. She looked like she was sleeping. Annie could barely speak around the lump in her throat. "Is . . . is she breathing?"

"Of course she is. Touch the side of her neck. You'll feel her pulse."

He seemed to understand how important this was to her; he crouched so that she could crouch, too. She touched two fingers to her mother's neck, to the carotid, and felt a strong, steady pulse. She also felt the warmth of her mother's skin and inhaled her scent, a mixture of salt, sunburn, sweat, and something else, something pleasant, almost sweet, that she couldn't identify. "Mommy," she whispered.

"Nope. She has to sleep."

He stood quickly and the cuff bit into her wrist, forcing her to her feet, too. "Please," she whispered, and started to cry, pressing her knuckles hard against her eyes. "Please, let me stay here with my mom." Her hands dropped away from her eyes. "I . . . I promise not to say anything about any of this. I . . . I promise. . . ."

"I'm afraid that isn't possible. C'mon, let's get down to my boat."

He started walking really fast up the beach, forcing her to keep up with him. She stumbled, went down, and grabbed a handful of sand. The instant he jerked her to her feet again, she hurled sand into his face and kicked him in the balls. He shrieked, a different animal sound this time, a more terrifying sound, and doubled over, grasping for breath, and wiping frantically at his eyes. He fell to his knees in the sand and Annie desperately tried to reach the flashlight, which he had dropped. She could pummel him with it, knock him out, and then find the key to the handcuffs.

But the cuff cut into the soft underside of her wrist and now the man—Peter, his name was Peter—wasn't shrieking anymore. He was still groaning, but not shrieking. She strained, her fingers nearly reaching the flashlight, almost able to touch it; then the man yanked on the cuff and it felt as if her hand were nearly cut off at the wrist.

Annie screamed, twisted around, and kicked him hard in the chest. He grabbed one of her bare feet and then the other and pulled her toward him through the sand. She kept kicking and screaming and scooped up another handful of sand. She threw it, but must have missed his face because he didn't stop pulling on her feet, dragging her through the sand. And when she was right up next to him, he hissed, "That was really bad, Annie," and shoved her down against the sand, pinning her arms with his body. "I just want you to be part of my family. That's not evil. It's not bad. But your behavior is very bad. Bad behavior requires a sacrifice."

Then he slapped something wet over her nose and mouth and she recognized the smell, the same sweet odor that she had smelled on her mom, the same smell she'd inhaled when she'd had her tonsils removed. *Chloroform, oh God, no. Don't breathe. Go still. Make him think you're out of it.*

But she finally couldn't hold her breath any longer and had to breathe, to pull air into her lungs, and the odor rushed into her mouth, down her throat, and into her lungs, and she slid away into a soft, velvet darkness.

Three

Patrick Wheaton lifted the girl in his arms, marveling at how light she was. Her long hair fell over his forearm, a dark, tangled cascade, and her face looked strangely peaceful. She really was a pretty little thing, a looker just like her mother.

He wanted to touch the curls plastered to the sides of her face, trace the shapes with the tip of his finger . . .

Like Evie's hair in the summer, when the heat made her blond hair frizz. Evie, Evie, please don't leave me. . . .

Wheaton shook off the memory and glanced down at the handcuff, still locked around Annie's wrist. It dangled from her hand like an extra appendage. He would have to cuff her to the boat in a little while, but he didn't want to think about that just yet. About the trip back through the corridor. Every trip was progressively more difficult and more physically wearing.

He carried Annie across the sand, toward the skiff, regretting that he'd had to chloroform her. He'd hoped she would be more compliant, more accepting of the situation. But maybe her feistiness boded well for her surviving the aftermath of the trip through the corridor. He hoped so. Out of the four children he had brought through so far, only one had survived.

Wheaton set Annie carefully in the sand, put the cloth over her nose and mouth again so she wouldn't wake up, then scooped up her mother's cell phone and hurled it into the water. "Ring away," he murmured, and considered doing the same thing with the camera, but decided against it. They hadn't taken any photos of him and perhaps these last photos of Annie romping on the beach would bring Mira and her grandmother some measure of solace in the days ahead. He wasn't entirely without compassion, after all.

He pulled a kerchief from his back pocket and used it to lift the lid on the cooler. There wasn't much left, a few apples, several bottles of water, a sandwich in a Baggie. He stuffed an apple in the pocket of his shorts and drank down half a bottle of the water. He splashed the rest of it on his face, then twisted the bottle down into the sand and wiped it clean of prints. Let the cops figure it out.

The last of the light hugged the western sky, turning it a dove gray struck through with deep yellow. He needed to get moving. He picked up the girl, the cloth still covering her nose and mouth, and hurried down the beach to his boat. It wasn't anything fancy, his little vessel, but that was the point. Fancy boats attracted attention. The engine, however, was fast and new and would get him to where he wanted to go.

The many months of planning had paid off, he had what he'd come for. Months, he thought, in which he had watched her on the school grounds, riding her bike, and watched her at the bookstore, putting away stock, helping out customers. He had watched in his many disguises—as a man with dark hair, gray hair, blond hair, bearded and unbearded, with and without glasses. He had learned her school schedule and, since

classes had ended, had learned her recreational schedule. He had learned that she didn't have many friends,
that she was a loner.

She was also something of a renegade, this Annie
Morales, who rejected the usual trendy fashions in
favor of shorts or jeans that she wore with sandals and
cotton shirts. An independent thinker. While none of
these traits would ensure her survival, all of them
would give her the edge she would need and made her
worthy for his purposes.

Even though several more weeks of fine-tuning lay
ahead and he would have to play things with the ut-
most caution, this was an excellent beginning.

He set the girl down on the quilt he'd spread out on
the floor of the boat and locked the other end of the
handcuff to the metal handhold on the inner left wall.
If she came to during the trip, which she probably
would, she wouldn't be able to do too much damage
with just a single free hand. But she might try to kick
him, so he secured her ankles with a length of rope
and tied the end to the bench where he would be sitting. He didn't blindfold her, but decided he'd better
gag her. He removed the chloroform cloth from her
face, dropped it onto the sand, then pulled a Baggie
from his back pocket and pulled out the kerchief inside. He tied it over her mouth and worked it between
her lips, tight but not too tight.

The kerchief, of course, was scrupulously clean,
bleached, ironed, sealed. *Germless.* It was so clean that
Wheaton wouldn't hesitate to put it in his own mouth.
Nothing less would do.

He slipped a small pillow under her head to make
her more comfortable. The cooler just beyond her
head was built into the boat, so he didn't have to worry
about it shifting or tipping over during the trip. But
since the crown of her head pressed against it, he put

a folded towel between it and the top of her skull. He placed the paddles lengthwise in the boat, along both sides, then pushed the boat back into the water and got in.

He took a compass reading, cranked up the engine, and turned south, away from Little Horse Key and toward the black water mass that awaited him.

The boat had a searchlight mounted at the front, but he didn't turn it on. Instead, he turned on the running lights, glowing blue orbs along the sides of the boat, and dropped his head back, watching the stars pop out overhead. The moon wouldn't rise for another hour, but the stars provided enough illumination to navigate.

Out here in the silence, his worries crowded in around him. Had he forgotten anything? Overlooked some important detail? Would he make it into the corridor in time? Even a well-laid plan didn't necessarily mean he would succeed.

When he had arrived in March, he had docked his boat at a marina on Tango, walked into town, and taken a taxi across the bridge to Key West. There, he walked to the post office, where he had a PO box in the name of Peter Wheat. In the box was an updated driver's license and his second credit card in Wheat's name that he'd applied for the last time he was here. Armed with the license and the credit card, he rented a car and checked into a fleabag motel in Key West. Since 1997, he'd had a checking account in Wheat's name and he wrote a couple of checks when he was here just to keep the account active. But the ATM card was what he used the most.

Every morning for the last ten weeks, he had driven across the bridge, parked his rental car at the pier, gotten out his bike, and begun his surveillance of Annie Morales. He had first seen her last fall, when he had been here on a buying trip, and had stopped in at One

World Books, her mother's bookstore. Annie had been stocking inventory, a busy little bee who was exactly the right age, at the edge of puberty. Right then and there he'd known he had found his next target.

During the last several months, Wheaton had left only three times to check on things at home. These trips and many others through the corridor had taken a physical toll, he could feel it within himself, but he didn't know the exact extent of the damage this time. Tissues? Cells? Organs? Blood? All of the above? He knew these journeys often leeched iron and calcium from his body, but thought that the fatigue he'd been feeling lately was something new. Or maybe he was just more paranoid now that he'd turned fifty.

He couldn't worry about it now, though. The girl was stirring, coming awake. He cut the engine back to idle and turned the flashlight toward her so that he could see her better. Eyes wide open, staring at him, terrified. Free hand jerking the gag from her mouth. Now she screamed. The scream echoed in the silence and steadily rose in pitch until it collapsed into a full-blown shriek. He just sat there, watching her, waiting. Still screaming and now thrashing as well, jerking on the cuff, clawing at the ropes around her ankles. When she realized she couldn't get free and that no one was around to hear her cries, she shut up.

"Finished?" he asked. "Or do I need to restrain your free hand and gag you again?"

"I won't scream anymore," she said quickly. "Look, if it's money you're after, my mother isn't rich or anything. She just owns a bookstore and—"

"It's not about money."

"Then what?" she whispered.

"You'll understand in time."

"You're . . . you're a goddamn pervert, that's the only other explanation."

He hated the way that curse word rolled off her tongue so easily, so casually. Eventually, he would have to make her understand the rules, and rule one was *No swearing.* "I'm not going to hurt you. This isn't about money or sex."

"If you're not a sexual pervert, then what . . . what kind of pervert are you?"

"You use that word too loosely."

"Look, you . . . you can just drop me off on Tango Key. I . . . I swear I won't tell anyone . . . I won't describe you or anything . . . I swear. I always keep my word."

"No, I can't do that."

She started crying, soft, pathetic sobs that were muffled when she turned her head into the pillow. Wheaton touched her foot. "Listen, in another few minutes, the engine is going to conk out and the air is going to feel strange to you. Tight. Heavy. Oppressive. It's important that you relax as much as possible and—"

"*Relax?*" she burst out, and bolted forward, the cuff rattling. "How the hell can I relax when I'm handcuffed and my feet are tied up and I've just been kidnapped?"

"You're screaming."

"*Damn right I'm screaming,*" and started shrieking again.

Wheaton stood it for about ten seconds, her screams echoing through the darkness, grating on his nerves. Then he reached into his backpack and pulled out another pair of cuffs and snapped one end around her right wrist and the other end to the handhold on the right side of the boat. This shut her up instantly.

"If the boat tipped over, I'd drown," she said.

"We're not going to tip over. But if you keep screaming, I'll gag you again. Understood?"

He didn't hear her response. He opened the engine

up as far as it would go and the din drowned out the sound of her voice.

2

Pain sliced into Mira's awareness.

It was a hot, crippling pain that seemed to be everywhere and nowhere, like a point of light that darted randomly about. If she remained very still, the pain receded and she returned to a soft, comforting memory of the day she and Tom had brought Annie home from the hospital.

She was a tiny little thing, barely six pounds, bald as a radish. Instead of buckling her into the car seat, Mira had held her during the ride from the hospital and she and Tom talked about how beautiful she was, with her ten perfect fingers and her ten perfect toes and skin as smooth and pale as a pearl.

We have to teach her everything, how to brush her teeth and comb her hair and how to toss a baseball, he said, the awe in his voice so powerful that they both started laughing.

And in that moment, it had struck her that they knew absolutely nothing about being parents. Even though they had read books on pregnancy, gone to Lamaze classes, talked about how to raise their daughter, they were essentially clueless. Nothing prepared you for parenthood.

Within three days, Annie was on a bottle and suffering terrible bouts of colic because nursing didn't work the way the books said it was supposed to. Annie cried a lot, didn't sleep well, and by the end of the first month, Mira and Tom were so sleep-deprived that they were arguing with each other over the smallest things.

During the second month of Annie's life, Nadine

saved them by moving in for a while. She got up with Annie during the night, cooked their meals, and watched Annie during the day so Mira could get back to the bookstore and Tom could continue the practice of law without nodding off at his desk. By the third month, they started to get the hang of it. They learned to make room in their relationship for another person and from then on, they were a tightly knit unit and jokingly referred to themselves as the three musketeers. And that was how it had remained until Tom's death on . . .

No, don't go there . . .

The pain returned with a vengeance, clawing through the bones in her face, radiating up and down the right side of her body. She sucked air in through her teeth and inhaled a mouthful of sand and started coughing, a violent spasm that forced her to push up, to rock back on her heels. The instant she opened her eyes, she doubled over and vomited.

It all rushed back then, the man on the beach, the way he'd struck her with the cast, Annie running away, the whole terrible nightmare, and she started to sob.

Annie, sweet Christ, where's Annie? Where had he taken her?

She threw up again and realized he had chloroformed her. *You didn't pay attention, Mira. You didn't pay attention to what you were feeling.* The signs had been there, that burning discomfort just below her sternum that she'd wanted to believe was indigestion or fear of crossing the open water in the dark. Sure. Right. *Oh Christ, oh God. Get up, get moving. Find the cell phone, call Shep.*

She managed to get to her feet. A faint gray strip of light remained in the sky, just enough for her to make out the vague shapes of the cooler, the boat. She weaved toward them, dropped to her knees next to the cooler, raised the lid, brought out a bottle of water. She spun the cap and drank. She patted around inside the cooler until she found the bottle of papaya enzymes that she took everywhere and shook some into her hand. Five, six, who cared?

Mira chewed them all, praying they would settle her stomach. *Think. Focus.*

The cell phone. Where had she put the cell phone? The flashlight?

Light first. She opened the toolbox, which he apparently dropped or never picked up, and dug out one of the two flashlights inside. She shone it around inside the skiff, looking for her cell phone. It wasn't in the boat, the cooler, or clipped to her belt. *He took it.* She pressed her hands against the edge of the skiff, pushed to her feet again. She felt dizzy, nauseated, not here.

Okay, no cell phone.

But who had stuck a half-finished bottle of water in the sand? She turned slowly in place, shining the flashlight around the immediate vicinity. She shouted Annie's name. *Did he kill her? Is it as bad as that?* She let the questions move through her—and beyond her. Somewhere distant, she *felt* Annie, *felt* her daughter, her flesh and blood. The connection seemed pathetically weak, as if Annie were almost out of her range.

Or drugged. Chloroformed. Of course. He had slapped that wet cloth over Annie's nose and mouth and taken her.

Helplessness overwhelmed her and she started to cry again, sobbing into her hands, unable to think beyond this incomprehensible act. Some stranger had asked for her help and she had ignored her feelings about him, had been taken in by his rugged good looks and that cast on his arm, and now her daughter was gone. Her worst nightmare had happened and it was her own fault.

The side of her face ached and throbbed. She scooped out a handful of ice from the cooler, wrapped it in a towel, held the towel to the side of her face. The coldness relieved the ache and snapped her back into the moment. *This* moment. She couldn't go back, couldn't change what had happened. Her point of power lay in the present. *Use what you have.*

Mira sat down in the sand. It was dark now and she set the flashlight on the cooler, its beam aimed toward the sky, so the light dispersed over the sand. She picked up the bottle, held it between both hands. An image surfaced of the man, standing in the twilight, gulping from the bottle. She released it and slapped her hands against her shorts, trying to rid herself of the feel of him, of his energy, his *evil.*

She took a deep breath, hesitated, gathering her strength, then picked up the bottle again and shut her eyes. *Where're you taking her? Which direction?*

The image that surfaced was of Cuba. A neat little mental map of Cuba. Ninety miles south. She tossed the bottle in the skiff, her one fragile but tangible link to Annie, grabbed her flashlight, and pushed the skiff toward the water, her resolve now so strong and focused that even her connection to Annie felt stronger. Once the skiff bobbed in the breaking surf, she tipped the engine down into the water and slipped the compass out of her shorts pocket. South, she had to maintain a heading directly south, she thought, and turned on the engine.

She held the flashlight and compass in one hand and steered with the other. The narrow beam of light comforted her, made the darkness seem less threatening, until she glanced to the right and the darkness loomed around her like some vast, empty cave. She quickly looked down at the compass to be sure she was still headed south, and switched off the flashlight.

Terror instantly claimed her, rolling through her in

huge, crippling waves. Shudders tore her apart, she began to shake, her teeth chattered. Her connection to Annie started to fray and she struggled to shove her fear aside, to compartmentalize it, seal it off from the rest of her. She set the compass on the floor of the boat, next to her foot, and picked up the bottle again.

Feisty little thing . . .

His energy was so thick, so dark and viscous, it was like treading through a snake-infested swamp in the middle of the night. She nearly hurled the bottle out into the dark, but didn't dare. It was her link to the man—*Peter, say his name, identify the evil*—and, through him, to Annie.

Headed south to the black waters . . .

What the hell did *that* mean?

She turned on the flashlight again, checked her heading. South, good, she was still headed south. She shone the flashlight at the water and thought that it looked darker now, murkier, as if she were in the midst of an oil spill. She turned the flashlight off and forced herself to look upward, into the star strewn belly of the sky. The moon hadn't risen yet, but as her eyes became accustomed to the starlight, she found that she could actually see pretty well without the flashlight on. She also found a switch on the back of the compass that lit up the face so she didn't have to turn on the flashlight every time she wanted to take a compass reading.

Even though she still clutched the bottle, her link to Annie felt frailer now, like some weak radio signal she might lose at any second. She considered turning toward Tango and calling Sheppard from the public phone at the marina. But it would take her at least forty minutes to get there and more time for Sheppard to obtain a seaplane or a boat. She didn't have any idea how long she had been unconscious on the beach, how much of a head start he had, and knew that she couldn't lose any more time. The man and her daughter were out here somewhere and as long as she maintained her connection to Annie, she would find them.

Gripping the bottle in both hands again, she tested the inner connection again. Fading faster now. *Dear God, please, please . . . .*

A bank of clouds drifted across the stars. She glanced down at the compass again. The needle swung wildly from one side to the other, like a pendulum. She shook it. "C'mon, don't do this, please," she hissed, and shook it again.

The needle kept spinning. Impossible, she thought. The compass was brand-new.

Then the engine sputtered and died.

Gas? Was she out of gas?

Mira turned on the flashlight, checked the gauge. She still had half a tank. How many gallons? She couldn't remember. Her brain had emptied of nonessential details. She pressed the starter switch again. And again. And again. She slammed the heel of her hand against the engine. *"Start,"* she screamed, and banged the handle of the screwdriver against it.

The clatter echoed through the silent darkness and reminded her of the man—*Peter*—banging on his boat's engine with something. What kind of boat was it? She didn't know, hadn't noticed, couldn't remember. But she clearly remembered his face, the cast on his arm, and she knew she would remember the sound of his voice for the rest of her life.

I hate to bother friends. It's a long way out here.

The current nudged the skiff along. Water lapped at the sides. She tried the engine again and this time it coughed and started. Even the compass was working now, the heading at 81W0508, 24N5008. She was south of Tango Key now, but not south of Key West.

She gripped the bottle again. *Annie? You still with me?*

Annie? She felt the link, very weak now, almost gone. *Stay with me, Annie. Stay with me.*

Mira made a slight adjustment in her heading and the engine died once more, the face of the compass refused to light. She tilted it to catch the starlight and suddenly realized there was no starlight. She dropped her head back and saw only blackness. It wasn't a cloud cover, it didn't smell like rain. She didn't see a single star, not even a pale ghost light that suggested a star. This darkness was absolute, as if she'd been swallowed by a whale.

"What the hell?" She pressed the switch on the flashlight to turn it on, but nothing happened. "Matches, somewhere in here I've got matches."

She pawed through her backpack, found a box of kitchen matches, struck one. The flame flared, such a tiny bit of light. She stared at it until it filled her eyes, her skull. Wrong, something was very wrong. The flame didn't flicker, didn't move at all. It stood straight and motionless, a little soldier at full attention. What happened to the breeze? It wasn't this still moments ago, was it?

Mira held the match out over the water and the light spilled onto the surface of the water. It looked as utterly black as the sky. Terror crept up on her again and she dropped the match, grabbed the paddles off the floor of the boat, plunged them into the water. She knew she wasn't out of gas, so that meant the engine had worked at a certain heading. How far had she drifted from that heading? She paddled for a few moments, then tried the flashlight. It came on. She pressed the starter button on the engine and it roared to life.

She took a compass reading—81W0509, 24N5009. The engine had worked when both coordinates had ended in 08 and now it worked at 09. She had no idea what this meant, if anything, but reasoned that if she remained within this range of coordinates, she would get the hell out of here.

Wherever *here* was.

Keep moving.

The air now felt oppressively hot, heavy, not a breath of air. Yet, she could feel the current getting stronger and she checked her heading to make sure she wasn't drifting off course again. Her ears began to ring, a hard, relentless pounding that traveled upward from the back of her neck and swept in over the top of her head. A crippling pain bit into the back of her skull, her bones turned to rubber, the soles of her feet felt as if they had been plunged into hot tar.

A tidal wave of agony burned upward through her body. Her skin tightened and pressed in against her skeleton as if to crush her bones, pulverize them, and then she felt as if she were being flayed alive, the skin sliced away with a sharp, hot blade. The pain drove her to her knees, the skiff pitched violently to the left, the right, the left again. Water washed over the sides. She tried to reach the navigating stick, but her arms refused to move. The air tightened around her like wet leather and was now plastered to her forehead and across her nose and mouth, robbing her of air.

Every time she tried to breathe in, the invisible thing that covered her mouth and nose was sucked into her air passages. And when there was no more air to breathe, she sank like a stone into darkness.

Four

Tick-tock. Tick-tick-tock. Tick.

To Wayne Sheppard the noise of the art deco wall clock sounded like the beginning of a Grimm brothers' nursery rhyme that would end badly. He especially disliked the final *tick* at the end, just hanging there, waiting. It was 8:17. In another thirteen minutes, it would be dark.

According to the time recorded on his cell phone, he had spoken to Mira about an hour and a half ago. He knew she didn't like crossing open water at night and that she intended to leave early enough to get back here by dark. But neither she nor Annie had walked through the door yet.

He pushed away from the kitchen table, aware that Nadine was still on the phone in the other room, calling everyone she knew to find out if anyone had seen Mira. He already knew her attempts were futile. Mira would not have stopped anywhere, not when she was hungry, tired, and sunburned. She would be thinking of food, a shower, and the evening they had planned. But Nadine was the sort of woman who had to exhaust all the avenues before she allowed herself to think the unthinkable.

He was already thinking the unthinkable, a professional hazard, the result of too many years in law enforcement and the specific result of the cases he'd been working on since he'd joined the bureau for the second time and moved to Tango—missing children. *A child doesn't come home from school and the parents are frantic with worry.* That was how it usually started. Nine times out of ten, the kid stopped at a friend's or stayed after school or went to the ice cream store. Nine times out of ten, there was a rational explanation.

And this time it's a mother and a kid and there's probably a rational explanation, something I'm just not seeing.

She stopped at the grocery store.

She would've called.

She had car trouble.

She would've called.

She had trouble getting the canoe on top of the van.

She would've called.

Unless her cell phone had died.

She always carries an extra battery.

"Stop it," he muttered, and went over to the picture window.

During the day, it provided a spectacular view of the gulf and the beach. At the moment the glass swam with darkness, and his own reflection stared back at him. An ordinary face, all things considered. Bearded, threads of gray showing through. He still had most of his hair, but it had begun to pale at the temples. Good eyes, great teeth. That was about it. No matter how hard he tried, he'd never been able to glimpse in his own face any trace of the Englishman who Mira said he had been several centuries ago. In that life, she said, he had left her.

Even though he was fascinated by the British Isles and had spent six weeks just in Scotland during his trip more than two years ago, that didn't mean that he had had a life in that country. Even though he had known the Edinburgh streets as intimately as he now knew the streets of Tango Key, that didn't necessarily point to a former life in that city. He wanted to believe because Mira's beliefs in this area were so strong, so powerful, but somehow he always maintained his skepticism about such things.

He leaned closer to the window and cupped his hands at the sides of his face, trying to see anything down below. The house, a vintage three-bedroom cottage built in the early sixties, occupied a prime spot about three hundred feet above the gulf. The place had been in foreclosure when Mira and Nadine had bought it two and a half years ago and had been abandoned and neglected for several years before that. Over a period of six months, they had enlarged the family room, redone the kitchen, enclosed the back porch, added a second bathroom, and laid down tile. Nadine had landscaped the backyard, creating a lush little Walden that was as comfortable as the rest of the house. All told, Sheppard figured the place was now worth four or five times what they'd paid for it.

His own place, three miles southeast as the crow flew, was considerably smaller and didn't have the view that Mira's house did. It was perfectly adequate for himself and his cat, but he would trade it all in a heartbeat if Mira would marry him. Even though she denied it, Sheppard knew he was competing with the ghost of her dead husband and that, in some way, he didn't quite make the grade.

Ten years ago, on Annie's third birthday, Tom Morales had been in the wrong place at the wrong time, in a convenience store that was robbed by a masked assailant who had gotten away. Five years later, a homicide had brought Mira into Sheppard's life and that investigation had led them to a man named Hal Bennet, who was responsible not only for the crimes that Sheppard had been investigating, but for the death of Mira's husband as well.

The publicity surrounding that case, which entailed a government mind-control experiment in which Bennet had played an intricate part, had chased Mira and her family out of Lauderdale and nearly had unraveled their relationship. Things between them had been fine ever since he'd moved here, except for this single thorny issue.

Let's get married, Mira.

Aren't you happy with the way things are now, Shep?

Sure, I'm happy. But I'd be happier if we were married.

It's so complicated. Nadine would insist on living somewhere else, we'd have to sell both houses and get a bigger place . . .

And on and on she would go, an endlessly litany of details that left him exhausted and regretful that he'd brought it up.

"No one has seen her and the cell phone either isn't working or isn't on," Nadine announced as she returned to the kitchen. She was winding the end of her long, salt-and-pepper hair around her hand, something she did when she was nervous, and now she twisted it up and clipped it at the nape of her neck. "Something's happened, Shep."

He didn't argue. "I'll get us a seaplane." It was faster, they could see more from the air. He called John Gutierrez at home. Goot was the first man Sheppard had hired for the Tango Key field office, a thirty-three-year-old Cuban American with the instincts of a hunter and a nose for the kind of cases they were assigned. "Hey, man, it's me. How fast can we get hold of a seaplane?"

"Five minutes. Why?"

Sheppard quickly explained what was going on.

"I'll meet you down at Tango Sea and Air as soon as you can get there. Hey, should we alert the local cops?"

"Not yet," Sheppard replied. "We don't know what's happened."

"Yeah, I'm sure it's something simple. Stalled car, dead cell phone, you know how it goes. Have Nadine forward the calls to a cell."

"See you in ten."

Something simple.

In 1997, a twelve-year-old boy named Rusty Everett from Marathon, in the Middle Keys, left school at 3:00 P.M., walking home like he usually did, and was never seen again. No ransom note, no body, no trace of him at all. The only thing that was found along the path that he walked was a cloth that had been soaked with chloroform.

Two years later, an eleven-year-old girl, Becky Sawyer, was playing in her neighborhood in Key Largo and disappeared. No ransom note, no body, no trace of her at all. The only pieces of evidence were her shoe and a cloth that had been soaked in chloroform.

Six weeks ago, another child had vanished, a nine-year-old Latino kid who lived on Tango, but was taken from Sugarloaf, where his mother worked as a domestic. Same MO—nothing except the cloth.

So far, Sheppard and Goot had no suspects. John Walsh had run the stories on his TV show, with computerized renditions the forensics lab had created that showed how Rusty Everett and Becky Sawyer might look now. Even this hadn't yielded a single lead.

Simple. Yeah.

"I'm coming with you," Nadine said, slinging her purse over her shoulder. "I'm an asset, Shep." She jerked open a drawer, pulled out a map. "I can read things on a map that other people can't see."

"I'm already a fan, Nadine. You don't have to convince me."

She smiled at that, a quick flash of mirth in her eyes

that reminded him of Mira. "Well, I'm glad we agree on something."

She scribbled a note to Mira just in case she and Annie returned, put the phone on call-forwarding, grabbed her cell phone. Despite the fact that Nadine was in her eighties, she moved with the spryness of a much younger woman. She claimed that decades of yoga had kept her body flexible and fit, but Sheppard suspected that good genes had a lot to do with it, too. She'd outlived two husbands and two of her five children. Except for Mira, her children and grandchildren were scattered across the U.S. and there didn't seem to be much contact among them. Mira was her oldest granddaughter, and since Mira had been very young the two had been unusually close. Intrinsic to that closeness was what Nadine referred to as their "genetic predisposition for gathering information in nonordinary ways," a fancy phrase for their psychic abilities.

During the brief drive to the cove where seaplanes were kept, Nadine smoothed the map open on her thighs and rubbed her hands together vigorously. Then she moved her left hand slowly clockwise, fingers slightly splayed, over the map. He knew she was looking for a *trail*, the tendrils of a psychic residue for her granddaughter and great-granddaughter. Sheppard had a vague idea how this worked. Most cops who were cops for any length of time got hunches. But what Nadine did, what Mira did, even what he had seen Annie do on occasion, went well beyond hunches. It spilled into the realm of the weird and the strange, the permanently incomprehensible.

"I lose them," she said softly. "One moment their trails are there, the next moment, nothing."

The *way* she said it scared him far worse than what she said. He heard puzzlement in her voice, astonishment. "What do you mean exactly?"

"I mean that there are two trails, both leading away from the same place. I lose them in roughly the same vicinity."

Sheppard passed her a pen. "Circle the area, Nadine."

"There's something else, Shep. I feel the presence of a third person. A man. I don't like his energy. I feel . . ." She paused and quickly folded up the map. "I don't know. I don't know what the hell I feel."

He *really* didn't like that.

Tango Key was famous for its regulatory contradictions. In some areas, the island was like some last frontier, a wilderness without rules and regulations. But in other areas, the rules and restrictions were so numerous that entire departments in the island's regulatory hierarchy were devoted exclusively to transcribing and interpreting them. Tango Sea and Air fell into the latter category.

It had been in the bureaucratic works for five years before it finally opened eight months ago, thanks in large part to a wealthy local builder, Ross Blake. He had paid the enormous fees to the island for the right to build the tie-down area and fought the bureaucrats in court. The island had imposed strict regulations governing everything from how many seaplanes could be accommodated to the flight paths into and away from the island to the hours of operation. Even the structure and color of the office building and the types of docks were regulated. The office was blue and white, with top-grade hurricane shutters and shatterproof windows. The docks, three of them, formed a square to the shore and each segment rested on concrete pilings two feet thick.

They met up with Goot on the outermost dock, which ran parallel to the shore. He paced restlessly, a cell phone pressed to his ear. When he saw them, he waved, ended his call, and hurried over. "Nadine, *un placer,*" he said, and they did that Cuban kissy, kissy thing on both cheeks. "Shep didn't mention that you were going to be helping out."

Nadine smiled. "He didn't know until I insisted. Your pilot has to start at Little Horse and fly south, very low to the water. Fifty to a hundred feet up."

Goot didn't ask how she knew this. His family came from what Sheppard thought of as the Cuban mystics, the *santeros* who believed that the cosmos was composed of a hierarchy of saints or *santos* who helped direct life on the planet by intervention and communication with human beings. It wasn't a stretch for him—not in theory. But when Nadine had helped him and Sheppard locate a young woman who had gone missing in Miami—the victim of amnesia—Goot had become a full-fledged believer in Nadine's talents. All the mystical shit had become quite specific.

"Why would they head south?" Goot asked.

Nadine shook her head. "I don't know. I just know that they did. And you need to search the island."

Goot studied the map for a few moments, nodding to himself, intrigued by something. "This is interesting," he said finally. "You know that black water mass they've been talking about for months?"

"Yeah, what about it?" Sheppard asked.

"This evening around seven, a large piece of it was reported to be just southwest of Tango."

"Reported by whom?"

"Satellite photos," Goot replied, as though satellites were the ultimate proof of everything.

"So?" Sheppard said. "What's your point?"

Goot grinned and slung his arm around Sheppard's shoulders. "I don't know. I'm just mentioning it. Maybe there's a connection, maybe it's just horseshit. But let's keep it in mind."

Sheppard suddenly longed for the days when an investigation meant that you gathered evidence and narrowed your leads and got to the bottom of it all. You moved from A to Z in an organized, rational fashion. Life was simpler then. What Goot was suggesting went back, he thought, to that worldview held by Mira and her grandmother, that worldview in which the universe was a living entity whose energy responded to man's own.

Earthquakes in Afghanistan? Hey, no surprise, Mira would say. The earthquakes were just a reflection of the human turmoil in that part of the world. 9-11? On a deeper level, it happened to unify the world. Global warming? Mutant frogs? Vanishing coastlines? The planet had AIDS. *Correct the energy and the universe responds.*

"This isn't an *X-File*, Goot." Sheppard smiled as he said it, but the lightness in his voice sounded phony and they both knew he meant the exact opposite. He was suddenly terrified that the woman he loved and the little girl whom he considered his adopted daughter were in a very bad fix.

They flew low over the water just south of Little Horse, the plane's searchlights spilling across Florida Bay. But it was quickly apparent to Sheppard that it was like searching for the proverbial needle in the haystack, mile after mile of dark water. Now and then, way out in the gulf, they spotted the lights of a fishing boat or a sailboat, but that was it.

They landed in the area that Nadine had circled on the map and Sheppard and Goot took the Zodiac raft out a ways, their hurricane lamps blazing. Sheppard shouted for Mira and Annie, but his voice simply echoed through the darkness. The only thing they discovered was that the water was strangely dark. Sheppard suddenly wondered if they were in the black water mass and Goot, as if reading his mind, said, "Hey, I bet we're in the mass."

A few moments later, the engine on the Zodiac died and their lamps went out. Sheppard quickly lit a couple of matches, holding them up against the darkness. He and Goot just looked at each other, neither of them voicing the deep discomfort that Sheppard knew they both felt. "Let's get back to the plane," Sheppard said, and passed Goot a paddle.

Neither of them spoke on the way back to the plane, but they paddled like crazy, faster and faster, both of them so spooked that it was better not to discuss it aloud.

"What happened out there?" Nadine asked as they climbed back on board.

"The engine conked out," Goot replied. "Maybe it was flooded."

Sheppard noticed that Goot didn't say anything about the hurricane lamps going out. They removed the engine from the raft, set it inside the plane, then deflated the raft and pulled it inside.

"Let's head to the island," Sheppard called to the pilot.

As they flew low over Little Horse a few minutes later, Sheppard spotted something on the beach at the western edge of the island. The pilot landed about a hundred yards from shore, inflated the raft, and they paddled to shore. Sheppard didn't think the object on the beach was a body, but the ball of dread in the pit of his stomach grew larger and hotter.

The tide was out and bars of sand poked up from the water, making it impossible to paddle to the beach. About a hundred feet from shore, they got out and walked through shin-deep water, pulling the Zodiac behind them. As they neared, the powerful illumination from their hurricane lamps exposed a cooler, just sitting out there on the sand, abandoned.

Sheppard reached it first and for long moments, just stood there, staring down at it, the ball of dread now so huge it threatened to choke him. On top of it rested the digital camera he'd given Mira last Christmas. A beach towel lay next to the cooler. The markings and footprints in the sand told a story, but it would take them a while to decipher it.

They set their lamps on the sand and also turned on flashlights to provide extra illumination. "Christ," Goot whispered. "Where should we start?"

Habit kicked in for Sheppard. "Let's video the area."

He handed Nadine a pair of Latex gloves and worked a pair onto his own hands. Sheppard slipped the digital camera into an evidence bag, labeled it, then moved on to the towel. He examined it first, looking for traces of blood. He didn't find any. He smelled it; suntan lotion, salt, the beach, nothing more.

Sheppard and Nadine held their lamps above their heads so that Goot would have more light while he videotaped. "We have at least three sets of footprints," he said. "A child's and two adults. Shep, we need casts for all three."

"I'm on it."

"May I touch the cooler?" Nadine asked.

"Not just yet," Sheppard said. "Let's finish with the forensics and videotaping in this area first."

She nodded, her eyes on the ground, following something. "Shep, this is strange. Two sets of footprints head away from this area, but one set of prints comes toward it."

Goot walked slowly and carefully down the beach, videotaping the prints, and Sheppard came along behind him, taking impressions. He tried not to think about the story the footprints told, not yet, but he couldn't help it. The story seemed pretty obvious. Mira and Annie had been joined on the island by a third person with large feet.

Sheppard removed one of his shoes and set it next to the largest footprint. He wore a size eleven and this print was about that. So the person was at least six feet and weighed maybe twenty pounds less than Sheppard. Had to be a man, he thought. Few women had feet as large as his. And Nadine had mentioned the presence of a third person, a man.

He walked off toward the mangroves, where two more sets of footprints told another story. His dread deepened considerably. The first set of prints was smaller than the others and had to be Annie's. She'd been running, that was obvious by the depth and irregularity of the prints. The second set of prints belonged to the large person, the man. Both sets went into the pines and mangroves, but only one set emerged. *She's in there, dead.*

Then, about twenty feet from the trees, the smaller prints appeared again. Sheppard crouched, set his lamp on the ground, and studied the story. Here, a scuffle. There, the smaller prints seemed to be shorter. Perhaps Annie had been hurrying to keep up with the large person. Goot joined him, videotaping everything, then crouched beside him. "I don't like what I'm seeing here," he said softly, then pulled out an evidence bag with a cloth inside. "It smelled of chloroform. I found it back there." He stabbed his thumb over his shoulder. "The same fucker, Shep."

Sheppard went numb. It seemed to be a long time before his vocal cords worked, his tongue moved, before he could form words. "Nadine doesn't need to know anything about the connection to our other cases."

"I agree. But we both know that if we don't tell her, she'll find out anyhow."

"Let's finish up and get the camera back to the lab."

As they turned, Sheppard saw Nadine sitting next to the cooler, her upper body folded over the top of it, as though she had passed out. He and Goot broke into a run and reached her at the same moment. She was conscious, but weeping. He immediately knew that as soon as she had touched the cooler, she had absorbed details about what had happened here.

Sheppard knelt beside her. "Nadine?"

She raised her head and looked at him, the despair in her face as vivid as the despair in his own heart. He put his arm around her shoulder and pulled her close to him. "He surprised them," she said softly. "He seemed so unthreatening." She pointed down the beach. "His boat was down there. I . . . I could hear clanging, like he was banging on the engine. I think he pretended to have engine trouble and she . . . she offered to help and he . . . hit her with something. Then Annie . . ." She paused, shaking her head as if to rid herself of some vivid internal image. " . . . ran. I tasted something sweet. Strangely sweet. He may have drugged them with something. . . . Mira went after them and . . . beyond that, I don't know. I . . . I don't feel either of them around." She covered her face with her hands, her narrow shoulders trembling. "All day I felt . . . really uncomfortable about them being out here and I didn't tell her, Shep."

"You can't blame yourself for any of this, Nadine. We'll find them. There may be photos on the camera that will provide leads."

But even as he said the words, the lack of conviction in his own voice terrified him.

Five

Sheppard and the pilot were airborne as the sun rose. They followed roughly the same path as last night, but in reverse, over Little Horse Key first, then south, along the same coordinates where the engine in the Zodiac had conked out. They flew low over the open water, at about fifty feet, close enough to see wreckage, if there was any, and high enough to be able to distinguish the black water masses from the rest of the water.

The stuff looked strange, Sheppard thought, like dozens of small oil spills. The largest mass hadn't moved much since they'd gone into it last night in the Zodiac, but it appeared to have split off into at least two pieces, with the biggest mass covering perhaps two square miles. Sheppard wanted to see it up close, in the light, and asked the pilot to land nearby. Then he inflated the Zodiac and, rather than using the outboard, paddled out into the mass.

Up close like this, it didn't look much different than murky water anywhere along the coast. But unlike murky ocean water, this didn't have seaweed or any other stuff floating in it. He leaned over the side of the raft and sniffed it. Odorless. He touched his fingers to it, rubbed the tips together. It didn't feel oily. It just felt wet. He brought a bottle out of the tool kit, dipped it into the water, filled it. He doubted that the lab would find anything. After all, dozens of marine biologists had been studying the mass for months and still didn't have any idea what the hell it was. But he desperately needed to believe he was moving forward in his search for Mira and Annie.

It seemed he'd spent most of the night tossing and turning, chasing phantoms in his dreams and setting out strategy as he'd lain awake. He'd tried techniques that he'd learned from Mira—putting himself into a light hypnosis and allowing his senses to *stretch* beyond himself, beyond his own body and world, and reaching for her and Annie. But it had given him a headache and he'd finally gotten up. The only *techniques* he understood were investigative techniques: culling as much information as possible, then following one lead to another, one clue to another. Even if A didn't always lead to Z, even though it sometimes backtracked to F or L and then leaped to C, it always possessed *logic*.

As he paddled back to the seaplane, his cell phone rang. Goot's number came up in the caller ID. "I hope you've got news," Sheppard said without preface.

"Yeah, and it's good news. The techs at the lab think they've got something tangible on the photos from Mira's camera."

Something very much like hope surged in Sheppard's blood. "What kind of tangible something?"

"Richmond didn't specify. She just said to get our butts to the lab."

"I'll be there in thirty minutes."

The Tango forensics lab was a fraction of the size of the bureau's main lab in Quantico, Virginia, fifteen thousand square feet as compared to 145,000 square feet. Annually, the big boys in Virginia handled more

than twenty thousand cases, received in excess of
170,000 pieces of evidence, and carried out more than
a million examinations. It employed five hundred tech-
nicians and was considered to be the best forensics lab
in the world. The Tango lab couldn't even begin to
compete in terms of scope or personnel. But for speed,
precision, and sheer efficiency, it was tops in Sheppard's book. Its units included DNA analysis, trace
evidence, computer/Internet fraud, and latent prints,
which handled photographic analysis.

The latent print unit was headed by Tina Richmond,
an M.D. who hailed from northern Minnesota and
kept the temp in her third floor unit at about sixty-
two degrees. "Jesus, Tina. It's going to snow in here,"
Goot griped.

She winked at Sheppard. "Dead giveaway that he's
got Cuban genes."

Tina was in her late forties, physically striking, with
a tall, angular body that she tended to with the same
diligence that was evident in her work. She had been
happily married for fifteen years to a local attorney, but
had probably broken a few hearts in her lifetime. Like
Sheppard, she was a runner and he knew that at the
heart of it she ran for the same reason he did: not so
much for health or for longevity, but out of some
deeper need for solitude and reflection.

"I've got no need for anything cooler than seventy-
five degrees," Goot said, indignant at the suggestion
that he was a wimp.

"I've got a water sample I'd like you to run tests on,"
Sheppard said.

"Right now?" Tina asked.

"When you can get to it."

"Yeah, right now," she murmured, and led them
through a lab, a maze of computers, and into her office. She shut the door, gestured at the chairs in front

of her computer. "These photos tell a rather compelling story." She took the center chair in front of the screen. "And then we'll get to the cloth you guys found." Her fingers played the keyboard, bringing up a line of photographs, each one labeled with the time and date. But even without the time, the shadows against the beach and the position of the sun told him it was late afternoon.

Here, Annie playing to the camera. Mira clowning. There, a shot of the beach and the canoe, the cooler, Mira's backpack, and the setting sun. Then a long shot of the beach and a figure in the distance. Then a closer shot of the figure. And now Tina did her magic, framing the figure and another object, enlarging them, cropping them, and enlarging and cropping them again and again.

"So this guy suddenly shows up about half a mile down the beach. His boat looks basic. It has an outboard engine, nothing too high tech. Note the fishing rod sticking up over the side. Now. The man himself."

More keyboard stuff. More magic. The image of the man was incredibly grainy, useless, Sheppard thought. But then Tina did something, he couldn't tell exactly what, and suddenly the man was clearer—not his face, but his height, his bulk, and the shadow on his right arm.

No, not a shadow. A cast. It was definitely a cast.

Sheppard and Goot exchanged a glance and he knew they were both thinking the same thing: a fake cast. A pity ploy.

Years ago when Sheppard had barhopped in search of women, he had known a man who used a similar but benign prop, a bird he had carried around on his shoulder, an Amazon parrot with an impressive vocabulary. It had been an ice breaker with women.

"Now let me show you the clearest image we've got of this guy's face," Tina said.

Moments later, the kidnapper's face came up on the screen. It wasn't the clearest image Sheppard had ever seen, but considering what Tina had to work with, it was impressive. Sheppard flipped through his mental file of faces, but came up with a blank.

"Any idea who this guy is?" he asked.

"Actually, we have several possibilities," Tina explained. "We've got a new piece of software that takes a photo like this one and searches the bureau's database for certain matching facial characteristics." The printer spat out two dozen photographs, with a brief bio for each one. "These are the top twenty-four matches." She pushed away from the computer and they moved over to the conference table, where she lined the photos up side by side. "It's up to us to whittle them down based on the bio profiles."

"A pair of bank robbers from Illinois," Sheppard said, and drew two photos out of the lineup. He compared the pictures to the photo of the kidnapper and shook his head. "Neither of these looks like our man."

"My gut says this guy lives in South Florida," Goot remarked.

In moments, they had eliminated all but six of the photos. Of these, four of the men bore a shocking resemblance to the kidnapper. "Those are the same four I chose," Tina said.

Sheppard felt sick. "A pedophile, a convicted rapist who violated parole, a guy wanted for eight B-and-Es, and a missing marine biologist accused of stealing half a million bucks from his wife."

"A fine selection of our best citizens," Tina said drolly. "All four are from Miami or south."

Sheppard set the photo of the kidnapper in the

center of the table and arranged the other photos around it. "It's eerie how similar they look."

"That's what the software does," Tina said with a trace of pride in her voice. "I downloaded everything we have on these four men." She opened a drawer in the conference table and brought out two CDs. She handed one to Sheppard, the other to Goot. "There's more information on the Internet, but the CDs have the essentials.

"Now, about the cloth. I know you weren't with the bureau when Rusty Everett and Becky Sawyer were abducted, Shep. But you and I have talked about how difficult it was to lift latent prints from that cloth found when the little Latino kid disappeared six weeks ago. We may have a breakthrough on this one. I sprayed the cloth with Ninhydrin and it looks like some partial prints are developing. It's only been about eight hours and I want the prints to continue developing for at least twenty-four hours."

Ninhydrin, Sheppard knew, was a substance that worked well on porous materials like paper, wood, and cloth for developing latent prints. It reacted to amino acids, which were sweated out through the skin, rather than to fat, the reaction component of iodine, another substance used to bring out latent prints. "You tried Ninhydrin on the cloth we found six weeks ago, but nothing came up. What makes this cloth different?"

"Probably the fact that you found it relatively soon after it was discarded and it hadn't been disturbed. Also, this cloth didn't have any dyes in it, so it didn't run when I sprayed it."

"This guy who pulled the B-and-Es was a bug freak," Goot said. "I'd say a bug freak might need chloroform to knock out the bugs he catches, right? Or do they use something else these days?"

"I imagine they use other products, but chloroform is easy to make on your own." Tina pointed at the photo of the marine biologist. "Marine biologists probably have a need for chloroform, too."

"Then let's start with these two guys," Sheppard said.

"I want to show you one more thing," Tina said, and moved over to another computer. "You know how much I hate riddles. It really bothers me that two people—three, if we count the abductor—just seemed to vanish off the face of the planet and there's no boat, not even a shred of debris. So I took a look at the satellite photos for Florida Bay last night between six-thirty—shortly before you talked to Mira—and nine o'clock. Get a load of this."

She brought up satellite images of the bay taken fifteen minutes apart over the two-and-a-half-hour period. The black water mass was stained red, an elongated shape that began a mile or two south of Little Horse Key and stretched for maybe six miles. It was shaped so erratically that it looked, Sheppard thought, like a corridor or hallway built by someone stoned on speed.

Tina superimposed a longitude and latitude grid over each of the images. "What I found especially odd about this mass," she went on, "is that it follows a precise longitude and latitude and despite the currents, it hardly deviates at all from those coordinates."

The superimposed grid made it easy to see what she meant. Over a period of two hours, the mass remained between 81W5001, 24N5001 to 81W5010, 24N5010. "See?" Goot said, looking at Sheppard. "I knew there was something weird about this mass."

"Where is it now?" Sheppard asked Tina.

"Here's what it looked like at sunrise." Tina brought up another satellite image, the coordinate grid superimposed over it.

"It broke into two pieces," Goot remarked.

"I was in the smaller piece at sunrise," Sheppard said. "It's got slightly different coordinates, but it's close enough to last night's mass. Maybe you're on to something here, Tina."

"Beats the hell out of me. I'm a doctor, not a marine biologist. It's just one of those curiosities that you toss in the pot and see if it stirs up anything. While you two figure it out, I'll get your water sample down to the science lab, Shep. Oh, by the way, are you planning on bringing the local cops into this?"

"They'll have to be informed," Sheppard said. "But right now, we don't need their help."

And with any luck at all, they wouldn't need their help in the near future, either.

2

Patrick Wheaton stood under the hot spray of the shower for a very long time, letting the water wash away all traces of the filth on his body.

There had been a time when the caress of salt water against his skin had felt like paradise; now the salt merely felt sticky, dirty, and deeply unpleasant. In addition to the salt, Annie had thrown up on him while they were still in the raft and the stink now clung to his skin, to the hairs on his arms, to the creases on the backs of his hands. The stink of it drifted toward him from the pile of his soiled clothes on the bath mat. It drifted through the steam in the shower stall and he finally couldn't stand it anymore. He stepped out of the shower, dripping water all over the mat and the floor, picked up the clothes as though they harbored a nest of vipers, and dumped them in the hamper against the wall.

It would do for now, he thought, stepping back

into the shower. But when he was clean, when his skin squeaked, he would have to dump the clothes. Get rid of them. Maybe burn them. He couldn't stand the thought of these vomit-soiled clothes in his house. He had a place out back where he burned soiled things. A graveyard for germs, that was how he thought of it. The clothes would go there.

Over the years, he had burned shoes, shirts, pants, socks, underwear, hairbrushes, sheets, pillows, towels, dishrags, sponges. He had burned soiled things that contained germs, that held them the way a mirror holds sunlight. And when the fire was nothing but ashes, he had gathered up the parts that wouldn't burn and taken them to the dump.

Sometimes, germs could be eradicated with Clorox. But more frequently, only fire would do the trick.

He hadn't always been like this. He could remember when his life was like any other man's life, a mixture of chaos and order, of passions and indifferences, an ordinary life with an ordinary job, with a wife, responsibilities, and garbage to take out on Monday nights. He could remember all this. But the memories grew dimmer by the years and some days, he knew, he couldn't conjure any of the details of that life.

The corridor had divided his life between *Before* and *After*. And the division, he thought as he soaped himself hard, relentlessly, was entirely neat and perfect, like the splitting of an apple with a very large knife. Before, he had been normal. Now he knew that he was anything but.

Don't think about it. Get the germs off.

A long time later, he turned off the water, stepped out of the steaming shower stall, and stood on the mat toweling himself dry. The towel was free of germs. It had been washed with bleach and draped over a rack that had been sterilized with alcohol. He pressed it against his face and inhaled the sweet cleanliness, the beauty of it. He rubbed his hair with it, wrapped it around his waist, and padded out into his bedroom.

He sat down on the bed and stared at the phone. Would she be awake?

He stands over her on a cool December evening, and watches her sleep. Her soft, pale hair fans across the pillow. She has kicked off the covers and her long, perfectly sculpted legs lay motionless in a wedge of moonlight. He wants desperately to touch her, to run his hand over her calves, her thighs, the sharp blade of her hip.

Instead, he leans forward and brushes his mouth against her cheek. She stirs, and he quickly steps back, into the shadows.

* * *

He picked up the receiver, dialed the number. She answered on the fourth ring, her voice soft, husky. "Hello?"

Wheaton squeezed his eyes shut, absorbing the sound of her voice, the music, the familiarity. *Evie, it won't be long.*

"Hello? Who's there?"

Your past, Evie.

Then he hung up the receiver.

3

One World Books stood on a pine-shrouded corner, a block north of the Tango pier at the south end of the island. It was a one-story concrete block building the color of ripened mangos, with dark wooden shutters at the sides of each of the many windows. Just inside the gate, the yard exploded with color—bougainvillea vines with small, delicate flowers the color of blood; Mexican heather bushes with rich, purple buds; firecracker plants with bright orange tips. A light breeze strummed the wind chimes that hung along the front porch. The welcome mat featured a pair of kissing frogs.

Even though it was still very early, Nadine's aging Mercedes was parked in the driveway. It didn't surprise Sheppard; he figured she'd had a bad night, too. "You sure it's okay if we work here?" Goot asked. "It doesn't look like Nadine has opened up yet."

"It's fine."

He rang the doorbell, turned the knob, and he and Goot stepped inside. For a moment, Sheppard just stood there, inhaling everything that was Mira, and knew this was exactly where he needed to be right now. Her presence permeated every molecule of air, every square inch of space. From the selection of books on the shelves to the choice of coffee and food in the café to the tropical plants and the Mexican tile floors, the bookstore was like the inside of Mira's head. Or, at least, a part of Mira's head. There were other parts of her head, of her being, that were completely unknown to him, dark rooms that he couldn't enter, windows he couldn't open, doors that remained shut to him, mysteries he couldn't penetrate.

"Nadine?" he called.

"C'mon in, Shep," she called. "I'm making coffee."

She was behind the counter in the café, dressed in black yoga pants and a T-shirt with a yoga posture on the front and, under it, the words *Celebrate the yoga journey*. Her salt-and-pepper hair was drawn back in a ponytail, exposing the sharp angles of her cheekbones, the regal squareness of her jaw, and the anxiety and fatigue that pinched the corners of her dark eyes. "Juanito," she exclaimed when she saw Goot, and hurried out from behind the counter to hug him hello. *"Cómo andas, mí amor?"*

They acted as if they hadn't seen each other last night, Sheppard thought, and suddenly realized they were linked, these two, by their Cuban blood, a circle that couldn't be penetrated by outsiders, even by Sheppard himself. Never mind that he spoke the language as well as they did, that he had traveled in every South American country except Brazil, that his passions were more closely linked to things Hispanic than to things from the gringo world. None of that counted because his parents were gringos who just happened to be living in Venezuela when he made his entrance into the world. He was, as Nadine had once remarked, an accidental Latino. To Sheppard, that meant that he would never measure up in her eyes to Mira's husband, a full-blown Cuban born in Havana, one of the many refugees who had made it to the U.S. in 1959.

He had known this for a long time, of course, but feeling this way right now only reinforced his suspicion that Mira wouldn't marry him because she felt the same way. *Why're you a cop?* she asked him once. *Why not practice law instead?*

I felt like a whore when I practiced law.

But you didn't have to carry a gun when you were a lawyer.

The gun, he thought. Part of it was about the fact that he carried a gun and she detested them. *If you carry a weapon, you attract the circumstances in which you have to use it.*

It annoyed him, saddened him, angered him at a level so ridiculously extreme that he suddenly moved away from them, over to one of the tables where he could set up his laptop.

Leave them to their Cuban dance, he thought, and

popped in the CD that Tina Richmond had given him, loaded it onto his computer, and began to read.

In 1994, Patrick Wheaton was a forty-one-year-old marine biologist working at the Tango Marine Lab, outside Pirate's Cove, the town at the north end of the island. He had been there for nine years and oversaw the scientific analysis lab. He was the resident expert on leatherback sea turtles and dolphins and every summer for nine years had run a camp for teens on marine biology.

He had been married for ten years to a woman from a very wealthy Key West family. They didn't have any children and, according to Wheaton's coworkers, didn't have much in common, so it was no surprise to anyone when the marriage began to unravel.

In early 1994, a black water mass formed off the coast of Big Pine Key, and Wheaton and several assistants spent hours out in the mass, collecting samples of water, plankton, and marine life, seeking answers to what the mass was. Then, as now, dozens of marine biologists from around the state had convened in the keys to study the water formation. Then, as now, no one knew what it was but everyone had a theory.

In March 1994, Wheaton had gone out into the mass late at night to take samples and didn't return. The local police were notified and within twenty-four hours a massive search ensued. No trace of his boat was found, no debris, nothing. It was as if he—like Mira and Annie, Sheppard thought—had vanished off the face of the planet.

A week later, he showed up. He claimed that while following a pod of dolphins, his engine had conked out, his radio had died, and that he had drifted for several days in the Gulf of Mexico, sick and unable to do much of anything to help himself. He eventually got better and was able to fix the engine and get back to shore. By then, he was off the northwest Florida coast. He left the boat at a marina in Cedar Key, rented a car, and drove back to Tango. That part of his story had checked out.

After that, though, his job performance suffered. He began calling in sick to work. By April, his supervisor had put him on a probational status, he had moved out of his home, and his wife had filed for divorce. On May 14, his wife apparently discovered a major discrepancy in her bank accounts and contacted her accountant. Two days later, Wheaton was charged with grand theft; his wife claimed he had siphoned half a million bucks from her accounts over the past three months. But when the local police went to Wheaton's apartment, they found that the place had been cleaned out and Wheaton was gone.

The police report and subsequent investigation didn't tell Sheppard much. The detective who investigated the case for the next two years had been thorough, pursuing every lead, no matter how trivial, and backtracked through Wheaton's life with the nose of a hound. In 1996, the detective suffered a heart attack and was forced to retire. The case had been relegated to the cold cases division.

"Breakfast," said Nadine, and set down a steaming cup of *café con leche*, a platter filled with cheese *arepas* and vegetarian sausages, some empty plates, and silverware. She pulled out one chair, Goot pulled out the other, and no reference was made to Sheppard's earlier exclusion. He doubted if they were even aware of it.

"Anything useful on the disk?" Goot asked.

"Yeah, quite a bit." But before he got into it, he brought up an image of Wheaton and turned the laptop so that Nadine could see the screen. "Do you pick up anything on this guy, Nadine?"

She leaned closer to the screen, frowning, then slowly lowered her fork to her plate. She touched a hand to either side of the laptop's screen, staring at the image. When she finally spoke, her voice sounded choked. "This is the man I saw when I . . . I was touching the cooler. I couldn't have described him to you then in concrete terms, Shep, but this is him. This is the man who took Annie."

Six

Mira felt a light pressure that moved from her navel to her chest, a soft touch against her lower lip, then a shrill wolf whistle tore into her ears. Her eyes snapped open, her head whipped upright. A small green bird with a bluish crown wandered around on her chest. It cocked its head, peering at her with lovely amber eyes, and made an odd trilling deep in its throat.

"Who're you?" Mira croaked.

"Hello," the bird said in an old woman's crackling voice.

"You're a dusky conure."

"Dusty, Dusty," the bird said, then fluttered upward and landed on the sand to her right.

She lifted up on her elbows, blinking hard against the brutal sunlight, the endless blue sky, and saw nothing but sand and water around her. The tide was low and her canoe was beached about two hundred yards down the sand. She sat all the way up, found her pack beside her, and pulled it into her lap. Hugged it against her. *Where the hell am I? Is this Tango?*

She stretched out her legs, felt the sand stuck to the backs of her knees, to her calves, her ankles. She felt sand in her hair, against the side of her face. her calves. *Annie, Jesus, Annie.* Hours had passed. An entire night. What time was it? Her watch had stopped at 8:38 and there wasn't a tree or a bush in sight, nothing that cast shadows that would provide a hint of the time. The beach was completely empty.

"Dusty," squawked the conure.

"Water," Mira croaked back. She unzipped the pack and brought out one of the bottles of water that she'd put inside before she'd fled from Little Horse last night to find Annie. The stuff was warm but it soothed her parched throat. The bird waddled over, jumped up onto her leg, and tried to tear the label off the water bottle. Mira poured some water into the cap and held it out. "You're thirsty, too."

Dusty drank in small, delicate sips until the water was gone. Mira poured some more water into the cap, set it in the sand, propped the bottle between her legs. She reached into her pack again, rifling around for food. She had to eat before she could move, before she could think. She came out with a packet of crackers, an apple, and one of Annie's T-shirts. Her eyes flooded with tears.

Stop, that won't find her. Move forward, remember?

She rubbed the T-shirt over her face, wiping off the sand and salt, then set it on top of her backpack and tore open the peanut butter crackers. She snapped one in half, held it out to the bird, and Dusty took it, holding it with her feet, eyes fixed on Mira. The bird obviously had been someone's pet and had gotten away. Its situation perfectly reflected her own—hunger, thirst, confusion.

Mira bit off a sizable chunk of the apple and set it in the water cap for the bird, then consumed the rest of it in a kind of frenzy. It helped. It helped a lot. She drank more water, ate two more crackers, shared the rest with the bird, then finally picked up Annie's T-shirt again and pressed it against her cheek.

The familiar scent of Surf detergent and a faint fragrance of Dove soap inundated her senses. She altered her breathing, slowing it down, deepening it, and allowed herself to move into that familiar space between two thoughts, that timeless void where she had spent so much of her life. She was vaguely aware of the heat that poured over her, the sand that baked around her, the bird squawking, munching, very much at home beside her.

And suddenly, everything but the smells faded away and she drifted in the olfactory slipstream of detergent and soap. Images surfaced, quick glimpses of a room, of toes peeking out from under the edge of a blanket or quilt. Then these images faded.

More, give me more, she begged, and bunched the T-shirt up against her chest, the beat of her heart. Blood to blood, mother to daughter, the bond that no one and nothing could break. But she realized that whatever she'd seen probably related to the past. And she felt nothing more, no nudges, no connections.

No good, she thought. It was no good. Her own physical discomforts, the sharp pain in her side, the bruises and pulled muscles she was now beginning to feel, everything distracted her. She needed Nadine, Sheppard, professional help.

She stuffed the T-shirt back into her pack and dug around inside, looking for anything else that belonged to Annie. A pair of shorts, a pair of sandals, the change of clothes that Annie always took to the beach with her. But cloth wasn't a good conductor of psychic energy. She needed something plastic or metallic, Annie's watch or that ring Nadine had given her or the peace symbol she wore around her neck. Or that discarded bottle the man had held. Was it still in the canoe or had she lost it last night when . . .

What happened to me out there in the darkness?

This thought shut down everything else and filled her with such profound terror that for moments she just sat there in the hot sand, arms locked around her legs, chin pressed to her knees, and tried to remember, to bring it back. The raft. The engine dying. The odd coordinates and the engine starting up again. Then the suffocating air. And blackness. Now here she was, hours later, on a deserted beach. She had no idea where the hell she was—Tango? Key West? Big Pine? How far had she drifted last night? Christ, could she be in Cuba?

Ninety miles? No way. Not in a canoe, in a single night.

She pushed her fists against her eyes, admonishing herself to stay calm, to breathe through whatever this was. *Fuck breathing through it. This is major.*

Okay. She would get up now. She would head over to the canoe and pull it way up the beach where the rising tide wouldn't whisk it away. If the bottle was still inside, she would read it, get what she could from it, and then she would start walking. Up the sand, over the dune of sea oats behind her to the road. Surely a road would be there. Of course it was. This was Tango Key, it *felt* like Tango—

—but a little off, something not quite right—

The sun. Okay, the sun was behind her and the shadow her hand cast when she held it up was short, truncated. She guessed that it was morning and that she was either on the west or southwestern side of Tango. That meant that if she went over the dunes and reached a road, she would turn right to get to the village of Tango, where her bookstore was. And long before she reached town, she would come upon a public phone.

She dug into her pack again, found her wallet, and checked her cash. She had $227 and change. In the event that her geographic calculations were off and it turned out that she was on Big Pine and couldn't get ahold of either Sheppard or Nadine, she definitely had enough money for a cab or a bus or even to rent a car.

Start walkin, babe.

She got to her feet, felt as unsteady as a toddler taking those first few steps to freedom, and the bird cried out, "Dusty, hello, Dusty, pretty bird, hello," and waddled after her through the sand.

"I can't take you," she said impatiently. "I can't. I don't even know what *I'm* doing, okay?"

The conure stopped, cocked her head, and let out a piercing whistle so mournful, so incredibly tragic and alone, that Mira couldn't just keep on walking. "I must be nuts," she muttered, and crouched, extending her finger.

Dusty hurried over to her, almost tripping over her own feet in her eagerness for companionship, and climbed onto Mira's finger. "If you bite me, if you misbehave, you're gone, we clear on that?"

The bird touched her beak to the side of Mira's cheek and stroked it, making that soft, low trilling noise in her throat, the bird equivalent of a purr, and nearly reduced Mira to tears. She put the bird on her shoulder. "That's my problem. It really is. I'm a sucker for a sob story."

The man, Peter, had a sob story . . . And that cast on his arm . . .

Move forward.

The canoe looked battered. Her tool packet had gotten saturated by the four inches of water inside and had sunk to the floor, a blade on the engine had snapped off, her thongs floated. A bottle floated at the front of the canoe. She didn't know if it was the same bottle the man had drunk from, and she hesitated. Then she plucked it up, held it briefly in her hands. Nothing.

It wasn't the same bottle.

She dropped the bottle in her pack and retrieved a twenty-dollar bill that had somehow made the journey from her wallet, deep inside her pack, to the seat of the canoe. She rescued her thongs, slid the paddles onto the floor, and flipped the canoe over, draining out most of the water. She flipped it back over and pulled it way up the beach, away from the water, and left it under a low, squat sea grape tree.

Mira slipped on her thongs, put the tool packet into her pack, and unzipped the heavy canvas bag that held her Pocket PC. She was relieved to see that it hadn't gotten wet and the batteries hadn't run down. She returned it to her pack and headed for the dunes.

A slight breeze rustled through the sea oats that covered the dunes. Definitely morning, she thought, noting the shadows that the sea oats cast. Definitely the western end of the island. *An* island. She wasn't convinced yet that she was on Tango Key. Even though the beach seemed familiar to her, she hadn't seen a single thing yet that screamed, *Yes, this is Tango.*

On Tango's western beaches, for instance, there were hard-core sunbathers from morning to dusk, most of them sweet young things whose butts and boobs spilled out of their string bikinis. They had boom boxes, coolers filled with Evian water and expensive imported beers. But this beach remained deserted. And the western beach she knew didn't have sea oats or dunes and the sea grape trees were massive formations with twisted, complex braches; these trees were barely more than low hedges.

"Hello," Dusty said.

"I'm Mira. Can you say that? Can you say Mira?"

The bird made that low, trilling noise in her throat and rubbed her beak against Mira's cheek again.

Limited vocabulary, but hey, it was better than talking to herself.

She followed a worn path over the dunes and through the trees. In the paltry shade of a palm, she stopped and pulled out the bottle. She clutched it in both hands, shut her eyes, and *stretched* her inner senses, seeking the man and, through him, Annie.

But nothing happened.

Forget it for now, she thought. She needed to get help.

Mira started walking again and reached a road. A dirt road. She glanced right, left, right again. The compass, she thought, of course, how stupid of her. She dug it out of her pack. She was headed east, and the village of Tango—*if* that was where she was—was to her right. But if she was on Tango, then this road would be paved.

The compass worked just fine now, no weird spinning, and she started walking south, her thongs slapping against the bottom of her feet. The bird moved to the backpack's strap, then tucked her head under Mira's hair, where it was probably cooler. Mira unzipped the pack and brought out a second bottle of water. Like the first, it was horribly warm, but the bird drank the water that she poured into the cap and she took several long swigs, then capped the bottle again.

Before she could zip the pack completely shut, Dusty climbed down inside and wrestled with Annie's T-shirt, trying to pull it around her. Mira knew exactly how the bird felt, understood her need for darkness, something soft, a cocoon of safety. She left the top of the pack open and kept walking.

Pretty soon, the trees thinned and the road widened. Just ahead, she saw a motel on the left side that looked as if it were closed for the summer and a bar on the right, a dozen motorcycles out front. TANGO RUM RUNNER'S, flashed the neon sign. She'd never heard of the place, but at least she now knew she was on Tango.

It would have a phone and a rest room where she

could wash up and change clothes. She was still wearing her bathing suit under her shorts and T-shirt and she had never felt so grimy, so desperately in need of a shower. Her hair, filled with salt from the beach, had frizzed completely. Its shadow against the road looked like a retro atrocity, totally wild, untamed. She ran her fingers through it, trying to make herself look more presentable, but it was a lost cause. She'd slept in the clothes she was wearing, on a beach, hadn't brushed her teeth or showered, and felt pretty much like a throwback, a cave woman.

Music pumped from the open door of the bar, Mick Jagger belting out a tune from one of his very early albums. As Mira went up the steps, three bikers stumbled out the screen door, laughing. One of them took a second glance at Mira and let out a soft wolf whistle. The bird suddenly popped up out of the backpack and returned the whistle—not once, but twice, the whistle so shrill that Mira winced. The bikers all looked at her, then at the bird, who now climbed up her arm to her shoulder and sat there, whistling twice more.

The bikers erupted in collective laughter. "Hey, that's a good trick," one of them called out.

The bird fluttered up from Mira's shoulder and flew off, squawking and whistling. Mira watched it for a moment, then hurried into the bar.

The music assaulted her. A bluish cloud of smoke hung in the air. The Florida Clean Air Act obviously wasn't enforced *here*, she thought, and she probably would be hard of hearing for hours. The whole place, in fact, was a shameless homage to the sixties. Day-Glo peace symbols in various shapes and colors covered one wall and on the others hung numerous posters that depicted sixties icons—Marilyn Monroe with her skirt flying up, JFK and Jackie, Jimi Hendrix and Janis Joplin, The Beatles, Mick Jagger, Eric Clapton and Mama Cass,

Abbie Hoffman, Jack Kerouac, Jane Fonda, Peter, Paul, and Mary.

Mira went over to the bar, tasting salt, bits of sand stuck to her lower lip. She wiped her hand across her mouth and glanced at the round clock over the line of booze bottles: 9:09. *Nines, too many nines,* she thought. Nines meant beginnings and endings. "Is that time right?" she asked.

"Yes, ma'am."

"A glass of cold water and some coffee, please. And where's your phone?"

"Back there," the bartender replied, thumbing the air behind him. He looked as retro as the rest of the bar, long hair pulled back into a ponytail, a peace symbol around his neck, a T-shirt with a slogan that read *Hell no, I won't go!* His mustache was a bush, his eyes a bloodshot road map to nowhere.

He set her coffee and a glass filled with iced water in front of her. Mira gulped down the water so fast that the cold gave her a brain chill. The coffee definitely wasn't Cuban, but it would do.

She picked up the cup and went into a hallway that smelled of mold, dampness, stale smoke. Even the phone booth looked retro, an old-fashioned wooden booth with doors that shut and a little wooden seat. She slipped inside, shut the door, sat down—and didn't move. Couldn't move. Her entire body ached and throbbed, her stomach cramped with hunger, her blood seemed sluggish and thick, like syrup. She tried to breathe through her discomfort and finally forced herself to sip some coffee. She set the cup down and fished out her wallet. Change, she needed change.

She picked out a quarter, fed it into the slot, and dialed—*dialed,* no buttons to punch in *this* authentically retro booth—Sheppard's cell number. Fifteen cents in change dropped into the coin-return slot and she heard a click on the line.

Incredible, she thought. A local call for a dime. More retro authenticity. How'd the bar arrange that with the phone company, anyway?

"Operator. Your number, please?"

"Five-nine-two, sixty-two eighty-four."

"Five-nine-two isn't an exchange in the keys, ma'am."

"It's a cell phone."

"A what?"

"A cellular phone."

"I, uh, don't understand, ma'am."

What the hell's going on?

"Is there another number you'd like to call, ma'am?"

Another number. Sure, her home number. Or the store. Given the fact that she and Annie were missing, would Nadine have opened the store? Home number first. She rattled it off. A brief silence, then the operator said: "I'm sorry, ma'am. That number isn't in service. Is there some other way I can help you this morning?"

A ball of panic surged into Mira's gullet and lodged there. She could barely speak around it. "Information, I'd like information, can you connect me?"

"I handle that. What listing?"

"One World Books, Tango Key. Fourteen thirty-eight Mango Lane."

"One moment, please."

Throughout their conversation, Mira kept hearing other voices. It sounded as if some sort of telephone marathon were going on in the background. And she hadn't heard a single tap of a computer key.

"I'm, uh, sorry, but there's no such listing."

White noise exploded in her head. She slammed down the receiver, pressed her balled fists against her eyes. *What's happening?*

A dime dropped into the coin return.

A gag, she thought. Sure. This was some sort of gag for a new TV show, some new and improved version of *Candid Camera* or a reality show. That would fit with all the retro stuff in here. But as soon as she thought this, she sensed it wasn't true, that the situation was, in fact, vastly more complex than that.

Okay, maybe there was a glitch with Sheppard's cell phone. She would call him at work. She ignored the niggling little voice inside that reminded her that her home number "wasn't in service" and that the bookstore had no listing in information.

She picked up the receiver again and dialed the operator. A different woman answered this time. "Number, please."

"I'd like the number for the FBI's Tango Key office."

"Just a minute, please."

Finally.

"The closest FBI office is Miami, ma'am."

"That's impossible. There's been a bureau branch here for at least two years."

"I'm sorry, but the only listing I have is for a Miami number."

"Then may I have the number for the local police department?"

"Of course. I can connect you. Please hold."

Clicks. The number rang. "Tango Police Department. Lieutenant Holmes."

"My name is Mira Morales, Lieutenant. I've been missing for at least twenty-four hours and my daughter was kidnapped yesterday from Little Horse Key. I—"

"Slow down, ma'am. Start over. Your name again?"

"Mira Morales. I own One World Books on Mango Lane. My daughter and I were out on Little Horse Key yesterday and . . ." She went through an abbreviated version of what had happened.

"I'm sorry, ma'am, but we haven't gotten any reports like that. We—"

Mira slammed the receiver down. He didn't have a clue. The Tango PD wasn't very large and a kidnapping and disappearance would be big news on the island, big enough for the local cops to know about it.

Something is very wrong with this picture. She squeezed the bridge of her nose. She felt like the protagonist in *Nowhere Man*, a short-lived TV series whose premise had intrigued her. *Man is having dinner with his wife. He gets up to use the rest room, and when he comes back, his wife is gone and other people are sitting at his table. No one recognizes him. Other people are living in his house.*

She would get to town, to the bookstore, and everything would make sense again. Mira scooped up her wallet, dropped it into her pack. She threw open the phone booth door and went into the rest room to wash up and change clothes. Things would make more sense once she was out of her bathing suit and had washed her face. But the longer she stayed in the rest room, the *less* sense everything made.

Ten minutes later, Mira hurried out of the rest room. She felt unsteady, strange, *unhinged,* and the music blasting from the Wurlitzer—Jimi Hendrix's "Purple Haze"—didn't help. She made it to the bar, gripped the edge, and eased her aching body onto a stool. Her hand trembled, her vision blurred, sweat covered her face. *Heart attack, I'm having a heart attack.*

"You okay?"

Okayokayokay: the man's voice bounced back and forth inside her skull, each echo louder than the one before it until her entire head felt as though it might explode, the crown blowing off like a lid on a kettle. A hand touched her shoulder. "Sip this," the voice said, and she felt something cool against her lips.

She sipped. The liquid tasted sweet and cold and immediately revived her. She opened her eyes to the bartender's face. Features that moments ago had struck her as retro now seemed kind, concerned, helpful.

"Thanks," she murmured.

"Fresh herbal tea with a spot of honey," he said. "I keep it around here for customers who're drunk or hungover. Works for just about anything else, too. But my guess is you need to eat."

I need answers.

"We've got scrambled eggs, bacon, wheat toast."

"That'd be great, thanks. How far is it to the village of Tango from here?"

"Three miles, give or take."

"Three miles," she repeated, and knew that she couldn't walk it. "Could you call me a cab?"

"Cabs don't run out here in the summer. You don't have a car?"

"I was in a boat. Had trouble with it." *Went through suffocating air, guy. Passed out. Woke up on a beach. And that was while I was chasing the fuck who kidnapped my daughter.* "I need to get into town."

"I can take you in a few minutes, as soon as my partner arrives."

"That would be great. I'd be glad to pay you."

"Don't be ridiculous. It's three miles, not three hundred." He stuck out his hand. "I'm Jake."

"Mira."

"So what happened to your boat?"

"The engine died. Do you have today's *Miami Herald?*"

"Nope, just the Key West rag."

"That's fine."

He reached under the bar, brought out a newspaper, set it down next to her, and hurried off to finish making her breakfast. Mira unfolded it to the front page, expecting to see her and Annie's photos. Instead, there were three photos: of Robert Kennedy, bleeding on the kitchen floor of the Ambassador Hotel in San Francisco; of Martin Luther King, Jr. at the Lorraine Hotel in Memphis, right after he was shot; and a final photo of JFK, right after he was shot in Dallas. Beneath these three photos were the words that Robert Kennedy delivered in an extemporaneous eulogy after hearing about King's assassination: . . . *tame the savageness of man and make gentle the life of this world* . . .

Mira stared at the photos and the words, certain again that they were all part of some new reality show. Even the date on the paper supported this: June 12, 1968. She slapped the paper shut and called Jake over.

"Listen, this is going to sound like a nutty question," she said.

He laughed. "Hey, I get nutty questions all day long. Shoot."

"Is all this a ruse?"

He frowned. "All of what?"

"This." She threw her arms out at her sides. "The bar, the decorations, the music . . ." She pushed the newspaper toward him. "This."

"What do you mean by ruse?"

"A gag. A joke. Like for a reality show."

"What's a reality show?"

"*Survivor.* Like *Survivor.*"

"Never heard of it."

Okay, so he'd been living on the moon for the last few years. A pulse now beat hard and fast in her throat. "What's the date today, Jake?"

"June twelfth."

"What year?"

"1968."

She burst out laughing. "Yeah, right."

Mira gestured toward the small TV set mounted on a shelf in the corner behind the bar. "Could you turn on the TV?"

"Sure, but nothing's on."

"CNN is always on."

"What's CNN?"

Shit, I'm going to scream, I'm going to lose it big time. "Just turn it on, Jake. Please."

He shrugged. "Sure. But we barely get Miami."

He turned on the small TV. Snow filled the screen. He slammed his fist against the side of it, then reached behind the TV and brought out a pair of rabbit ears, the likes of which she hadn't seen since she was about three years old. The rabbit ears didn't clear up the reception. Alarmed, Mira spun around, scrutinizing the people in the bar, the tough guys playing pool, the tall, skinny woman at the jukebox, a cigarette burning between her fingers. *They might be a part of it, too.* But the two men now entering the bar couldn't be part of *it*, could they?

Mira hurried over to them, not entirely clear what *it* might be. "Excuse me," she said to the man closest to her. Long hair, tattoos, a gold tooth that flashed when he grinned. "What's the date?"

"The date? I dunno. June something."

"June twelfth," his companion said. "Yeah, Wednesday, June twelfth."

"What year?" she asked.

Both men laughed. "Hey, got any more of that weed you're smoking?" the first guy said. "It's 1968."

They walked off, still laughing, and Mira stood there, her body threatening to cave in on itself, her knees so rubbery she wasn't sure she could walk, her head roaring. She managed to back away from the doorway and collapsed on one of the stools.

"You okay, hon?" asked a waitress on her way to a table, a tray balanced on one hand.

"Please," Mira said in a choked, desperate voice. "What's the date? And the year?"

"June twelfth, 1968, hon. Listen, can I get you something cold to drink? That heat outside is a bitch."

Mira squeezed her eyes shut. *Can't be. Impossible. No way.*

"You still interested in that ride? And in breakfast?"

She rubbed her hands over her face and looked at Jake, now seated beside her on a stool, smoking. "May I see your driver's license, Jake?"

"My license? Sure." He dug out his wallet. "But what for?"

"Because you look to be in your early thirties."

"Thirty-two. So?"

"So when were you born?"

"Nineteen thirty-six."

"Then you'd be sixty-six years old."

He seemed really amused by this. "Not by any math that I know. But hey, look for yourself." He handed her his license and there, right next to his name, Jake Romano, was his date of birth: May 13, 1936.

"Jesus," she whispered. "It's true."

RFK had been dead for a week.

All four Beatles were not only alive, but still together.

The war in Vietnam was raging.

The Democratic Convention in Chicago was two months away.

Easy Rider wouldn't premier until next year.

Ken Kesey, Janis Joplin, and Jimi Hendrix were still alive.

Neal Armstrong would walk on the moon next summer.

The ERA amendment wouldn't pass Congress for another four years.

Segregation wouldn't end until next year, when the Supreme Court decreed it.

Watergate hadn't happened yet.

Bill Gates was just a kid and Bill Clinton was in his twenties.

Neither Bush had made it to the White House.

The Berlin Wall hadn't fallen.

Women were still burning bras, the gay liberation was in its infancy, Three Mile Island hadn't happened yet. There were no cell phones, no VCRs, no personal computers, no Palm Pilots, no Internet, no e-mail.

September 11 was thirty-five years in the future.

And her dead husband, Tom Morales, was a teenager living in the keys.

Part Two
Purple Haze

"'Scuse me while I kiss the sky. . . ."
—Jimi Hendrix

Seven

Annie kept hearing the same sound, a soft, comforting *swoosh*, like the echo of the ocean in a shell. But it wasn't the ocean. It was the dust bunnies that leaped around her as she crawled across the floor. It was the cat, her mommy's shoes, the noise of her daddy's breath. It was the sound of her heart swelling with joy.

Annie, sweetheart, come this way, her daddy called. And when she scampered toward him, he rocked back on his heels and clapped his hands as if she had done the most wonderful thing he had ever seen. Sometimes, her mommy was there on the floor, too, the three of them crawling around like bugs, darting toward each other and away, playing a game with rules she didn't really understand. Her mommy would call her, then her daddy would call and she would have to decide whom she wanted to go to most of all.

She liked it best when they both crawled toward her at the same time and they scooped her up and swept her around the room as if she were an airplane. She smacked her lips together, making airplane sounds, and when she felt brave she even threw her arms straight out at her sides, like wings, and they zoomed her around the house.

Swoosh, went her heart.

She threw her arms back and became a bullet, a speeding train, Superman. Now she moved her legs like a swimming frog and her daddy grinned and came toward her on his tummy, moving his arms and legs as if he were swimming, too. In his dark eyes, she saw herself, impossibly small and happy.

Then everything got turned around and she was in her car seat in the back of the car, half asleep. She heard her daddy's voice. *Do we need anything else, hon?*

Just the milk and bread, her mommy replied.

Be back in a jiffy.

The car door opened and shut, and the smell of the night filled Annie, a warm, still smell. It was the night of her third birthday, the woo-la-la was on, music playing, and her mommy hummed along and Annie started to drift away again. But something was very wrong with the way her mommy hummed. It was the way she hummed when she was nervous or scared, when she got *feelings*. And suddenly her mommy hissed, "No, Christ, no," and threw open the door.

Annie came instantly awake, kicked her legs, and pushed her feet down against the seat, trying to see where her mommy had gone, what was going on, why she'd left her alone in the car. But she couldn't see anything, she couldn't push herself up far enough, and she started to cry, to sob, to wail. And then she began to scream . . .

And her eyes opened.

She was huddled on her side, legs drawn almost to her chest, her body on fire. She groped for the quilt tangled around her feet and pulled it up over her waist, her shoulders, and shivered beneath it. *Fever, I'm sick, really sick. Flu? Bronchitis? Something worse?*

Then it all came back to her and she knew it was worse than sickness, worse than the worst illness she'd ever had, when her appendix had nearly burst. *I'm in deep shit.*

She rolled onto her back, pushed up on her elbows,

looked around. She was on a large couch in a small room. Light filtered through the Venetian blinds that covered two windows, giving off enough illumination so she would see there wasn't a TV, CD player, VCR, or computer in sight. Posters decorated the walls—musicians, from the looks of them, all of them from the sixties. She had posters like these on the walls of her bedroom at home.

The room suddenly spun and she sat straight up and leaned over the side of the couch and threw up. She fell back, her head sinking down into the feather pillow, down into the past again, where she crawled around on the floor with the cat and the dust bunnies and her daddy.

When she came to again, she hurt everywhere and she was still burning up. Her mouth tasted of deserts, sand, such a terrible dryness that the skin of her lips had split open. She heard moaning and realized it was coming from her.

"Hey, don't move too much," said a voice at her side, and someone pressed a cold, moist towel to her forehead. "Can you sip a little water?"

Annie wanted to open her eyes, to look at the face connected to the voice, but her eyelids wouldn't cooperate. They felt gummed together, scaled with hot wax. She lifted her right arm, but the effort nearly exhausted her. Her hand touched the wet cloth and she brought it to her mouth, her cheeks, her eyes. Her tongue moved over her lips, wetting them. "Advil." Her voice sounded like the croak of a hundred frogs. "I need Advil for the fever."

"Can you swallow?" the voice asked.

"I think so."

Her eyelids parted, she turned her head to the right, and saw Brad Pitt with long hair. "You're Brad Pitt," she said. "You had long hair in *Twelve Monkeys*."

"I'm Rusty," he said with a laugh, and slid a hand under her head, lifting it so that she could sip from a straw, one of those hospital straws that bent just right. He touched two pills to her lips and she rolled them into her mouth and sipped again.

The pills went down. Even though her body still burned, she knew she would feel a lot better in an hour. Advil always worked for her. He slipped his hand out from under her head and it sank into the feather pillow again. Her eyes felt so weighted, so horribly heavy that she shut them. He pulled the blanket up around her neck, tucking her in. Had Brad Pitt done this for Julia Roberts in *The Mexican?* No, no, wrong movie.

I'm Rusty.

But who was Rusty?

He pressed the cloth to her forehead once more. She didn't think she said anything or asked anything, she didn't have the strength. But he was talking to her, speaking in a low, quiet voice, his mouth close to the side of her head.

"Listen, you've got to stay awake a little longer. There's some stuff you need to know. He'll be coming in here to see you pretty soon. He'll have homemade soup. That's what he always does with the ones he brings through the corridor. You won't feel like eating for a while, but you have to eat. The soup will help you. Hey, are you listening?"

The ones he brings through the corridor: she had gotten stuck on that. What was the corridor? Who were "the ones"?

"You're going to think he's a terrible man, but he isn't. He means well. He really does. It's just that he's kind of off in the head. Follow his rules, that's important. If you don't, you'll have to sacrifice something. That's how it works around here. Once, when I broke a rule, he burned my collection of books. And these were great books, okay? *Treasure Island. The Count of Monte Cristo. The Shining.* Another time, he took all my Jimi Hendrix CDs, CDs he'd brought through the corridor for me, and broke them in half and buried them. I have this dog, Sunny, and deep down inside, when I was younger, I was terrified that he would do something to Sunny if I broke a rule. But I don't think he would hurt an animal." His laugh was sharp as glass. "Well, maybe he would. One time we had a frog in the house, a little thing, you know? And I saw him trap it under a glass and then he . . . he tore its legs off and threw it outside. He said it was infected with germs. Yeah, that's another thing about him. This obsession with germs. You know what he does before he eats? He cleans his utensils with alcohol."

Annie faded in and out as he spoke, but she caught the high points. And those high points didn't do much to change her original opinion of Peter. "I feel like shit," she murmured.

"Never say that to him. Never say shit. Or damn. Or fuck. He goes ballistic when he hears the F word. I say it to him a lot now, hoping he'll lose it, that he'll give me an excuse to punch him in the mouth. But I'm as tall as he is now and I'm stronger. I work out. I run. When I say fuck, he doesn't know how to deal with it."

This was all mixed up. First he told her that Peter wasn't such a bad guy, just fucked in the head, and now he was describing a monster. "Is he a cannibal, like Lechter? Is he that bad?"

"Who's Lechter?"

"Anthony Hopkins." Or was it Perkins? No, that was *Psycho.* But she couldn't remember the name of the movie Hopkins had been in. That was bad. That was serious. She clearly remembered that she, her mother, Shep, and Nadine had watched the movie together one night, on video, at home. She remembered that her semifriend Nicki had been spending the night and that *her* mother wouldn't let her watch R-rated movies, something she hadn't mentioned until after the movie was over. But she couldn't remember the name of the stupid movie.

"Listen, I've got a high fever," she told Brad Pitt. "It's taking away some of my memories."

"That's probably the corridor, not your fever. Pete's memory is sort of fucked up from the corridor."

"What's the corridor?"

Brad Pitt pressed the cool cloth to her forehead again, gave her a sip of water. "I'll tell you about it later."

"I need a doctor. I really think I need a doctor."

"Look, if you aren't better soon, he'll get Lydia. She's better than any doctor. She'll have medicine. She saved me. She can save you, too, if you take what she gives you. I'm going to leave a puke pot by the side of the couch in case you get sick again. The bathroom is off to the right. Just follow his rules and everything will be fine. But don't tell him I told you any of this stuff, okay?"

Okayokayokay . . .

Annie fell into that echo and was suddenly crawling around on the floor again with her daddy, her mommy, her Nadine.

When she came to, Brad Pitt was leaning over her, wiping her forehead with that cool cloth again, and a dog was licking her face. Was this part of the dream? It hurt to open her eyes, to move, but she did both, her arm reaching out, her fingers sliding through fur like silk. *This is real.* The dog panted and licked her face again.

"This is Sunny," said Brad Pitt. "I figure he's about six years old. I found him by the side of the road one day on my way home from school about two years after Pete brought me through the corridor. We've been together ever since. We protect each other. He'll protect you while you're in here."

"Protect," she murmured, and patted the couch, inviting the dog to come up.

The dog jumped up onto the couch and settled alongside her. Annie slid her fingers through the dog's silky fur.

Brad Pitt was speaking again and she forced herself to pay attention. It wasn't every day that Brad Pitt spoke to mortals. "Tell me about your life," he said.

"Sucks."

"Why?"

"Mom. Sees things. Won't marry Shep."

"What's she see? Who's Shep?"

Too complicated. And she was too tired. Annie turned on her side, her fingers resting in the dog's silky fur.

"Who won the election?" he asked.

Huh? She made her eyes open. "What're you talking about?"

"The presidential election in 2000? Who won? Pete refused to tell me."

Oh. She got it now. He was in Argentina filming that movie about the Dalai Lama in 2000. Sure. She giggled. "Right."

"Who's president?"

"The Bushes."

"Bush? Holy shit."

"The Supreme Court," she said.

"What's that mean? Here, take another sip of water. You need to keep drinking water."

They had CNN in Argentina, didn't they? Maybe he'd been filming a movie on the moon during the election. She sipped. Her neck ached and now she was seeing two

Brad Pitts, double your fun, double your enjoyment, oh shit, she was going to get sick. "I need papaya, Brad."

"I'll get you some. Tell me what that means, about the Supreme Court."

She tried to explain, but the words got garbled. The election, like her life, was too complicated to explain right now. She drifted away and when she came back, he was wiping her face with the cloth, speaking softly to her, saying her name over and over again. She thought she heard music. Sixties tunes. "Me and Bobby McGee."

"Janis, that's Janis," Annie muttered.

"You like sixties music?"

"Better than 'NSync and Britney."

He laughed at that, Brad did, and for a few seconds Annie thought she felt a whole better. "Janis, Jimi, Jefferson Airplane."

Janis and the Mercedes Benz. Jimi and the purple haze. Jefferson Airplane and the white rabbit. Yes, yes, she was running away with the white rabbit now, sliding down that hole into some other place, some other world. "Sleep," she whispered.

"No, you can't sleep." He grabbed her by the shoulders, shook her. "You can't. The others slept and never woke up. Please. Don't go to sleep. Talk to me. Talk. Christ, you have to *talk*."

Her head seemed to come unscrewed from her neck and fell onto the pillow. The rest of her body trembled, shuddered, shook, and she bolted to the side of the couch and threw up again.

"It's okay," Brad Pitt whispered, holding her head so it didn't roll into the puke bowl. "It's okay. This is the sickness. But there's no blood. You're okay. You'll be okay."

He eased her head back onto the pillow, wiped off her mouth, gave her a cube of ice to suck on. "Where's your dad?" he asked. "You haven't mentioned him once."

"Dead. Shot."

"You live just with your mom?"

"And great-grandmother."

"You said your mom sees things. What did that mean?"

Shitshitshit. He asked so many questions and all she wanted to do was sleep. "Psychic."

"Cool."

"No."

"Only psychic I ever met was this half-blind old woman who lived in our apartment building. She told me I was going to live someplace so far away from my birth family that my old man would never be able to find me." That hard, sharp laugh again. "Well, hey, that sure happened. Here I am. Here the fuck I am."

A wet warmth against her arm. The dog's tongue. And that silken fur. Paradise. "Not cool, not cool."

"So if your mother is psychic, then she may know where you are, right?"

"Dunno."

And she went away again, the dog still stretched out beside her, that fur like a long, soft rug, and Brad Pitt talking, talking, his voice following her into the purple haze of the music, and the white rabbit racing past her, laughing, *Follow me, follow me.*

How bad could any of it be?

Plenty bad, as it turned out.

Eight

Patrick Wheaton's home in 1968 stood on three wooded acres in the northeast corner of the island, a two-story A-frame with three bedrooms and a loft. The broadest part of the A was all glass and overlooked the water between Tango and Key West. In the twenty-first century, the view alone would be worth millions. But the entire parcel, including the five acres of pastures and fields across the dirt road, had cost him a pittance and he'd paid cash for it. There was a lot to be said for the cost of living in the sixties.

In the fields across the road lived free-range chickens. They provided him and Rusty with fresh eggs and the freshest chicken on the island. He had used one of them to make the pot of soup that he stirred now. No antibiotics, no hormones, nothing but the best grain for his chickens. He had added herbs that he grew and vitamins and immune boosters, courtesy of his native time, the same recipe he'd fed Rusty when he'd brought him through. Anything to give her an edge to survive the time sickness.

He heard Sunny barking outside. The dog and Rusty were returning from the field, where Rusty rode his bike every morning during the summer to feed the chickens and let them out for the day. Wheaton went over to the side window to watch him, just as he had many times in the last six years.

Rusty whipped a rag out of the leather bag under the seat and wiped down the bike, removing dust and bits of grass from the field. He took the same meticulous care of his 1955 Chevy and his room. However, he didn't share Wheaton's fanaticism about germs. His laundry usually piled up in the hamper and when he cooked he left food out, crumbs scattered across the counter, and dirty dishes encrusted with food in the sink. The dog's dish got washed only when Wheaton did it. Otherwise, Rusty dumped new food in the crusted bowl and the dog, not knowing the difference, just gobbled it down.

Three months after Wheaton had taken Rusty, when they had reached a kind of tenuous trust, he had explained the household rules to him. *No swearing, be tidy and organized, tell the truth, clean up after yourself.* He was twelve at the time, old enough to understand the rules, but frequently forgetful about abiding by them. Every time Rusty had forgotten, Wheaton had sacrificed something of his so that he would learn that every action had consequences and that the rules had to be followed.

Those days, though, were long gone. Rusty would turn eighteen at the end of June, and was now Wheaton's height, six feet, outweighed him by twenty pounds, and was all brawn and muscle. Not a kid who could be easily frightened or swayed by loss of freedoms and threats that something would be sacrificed. He wouldn't dare touch Rusty's books or CDs now.

In the beginning, Wheaton had worried that Rusty might confide in one of his teachers or in a friend about his situation, something along the lines of: *Pete kidnapped me from the future.* But Rusty had realized that his life with Wheaton was far better than his life with his own family in 1997. As long as he followed the rules, few things were denied him. He never brought friends home, however, because they might see the computers, the CD player, the VCR, the DVDs, and all the other toys Wheaton had brought him from his own time.

When he was fifteen, there was a Close Call. Rusty had a girlfriend who got a little too inquisitive and he, perhaps hoping to impress her, had brought her to the house one day when Wheaton was out and shown her his electronic toys. Wheaton happened to come home while they were still at the house, realized what Rusty had done, and a week later he made the girl disappear. He felt bad about it, but he couldn't risk her blabbing to someone else. She became a necessary sacrifice and he made it clear that computers and other items from the future stayed upstairs, either in Rusty's bedroom or in Wheaton's den.

Rusty never came out and accused Wheaton of killing the girl, but deep down, he understood what sacrifice meant and there was never another close call. Rusty had had other girlfriends, but none of them ever came here.

Wheaton watched Rusty deposit the rag in a plastic container outside the door and retrieve the egg cartons into which he put the fresh eggs every morning. He moved away from the window to tend to his soup.

A few minutes later, Rusty and the dog came in, the screen door banging shut behind them. He shut the main door so the AC wouldn't escape and slipped off his shoes and left them on the mat. Neither of them wore shoes in the house. Shoes tracked in germs.

"Nearly two dozen eggs this morning," he announced, setting the carton on the counter. "There's a hole in the coop fence that I'll fix later today."

"You have breakfast yet?"

"Yeah."

"Something bothering you, Rusty?"

Rusty looked at him as though he were nuts to even ask and laughed. "No, nothing at all, Pete. Unless you mean the kid in the shed. She's—what? Thirteen? Fourteen? And which time zone did she come from? You didn't bother mentioning that when you brought her in yesterday. You didn't bother mentioning much of anything. That's what you've been doing the last three or four months, isn't it?"

"That and buying supplies and other things to bring back. There's a box of stuff in your room, music, books, movies . . ."

"Yeah, I saw them. Thanks. You didn't tell me how old she is, Pete."

"Thirteen."

"Well, she was out there puking. I left her a puke pot."

"How much did she vomit?"

"I didn't stick around to find out."

"The mess is still *there*?"

"This is your gig, not mine. If they puke, you clean it up. If they die, you bury them. I don't want any part of it."

Wheaton cringed. Vomit on the floor. No telling what kinds of microbes were loose in the shed now.

"Does she have a fever?"

"She's burning up. I gave her some Advil."

Advil, which didn't exist in 1968. It had come from his native time, like so many other things in the house. He'd been so busy buying up DVDs, CDs, software, computer supplies, and all the other things that made life in 1968 somewhat easier, that he'd forgotten about the simplest item: Advil.

"I'll take the soup down to her in a few minutes."

"Yeah. Whatever." He started to turn away, then said, "So when're you taking *me* through the corridor, Pete?"

"You want to get sick again?"

"You don't get sick every time you go through."

"The damage isn't visible." He'd been sterile since his first trip through, his lungs were scarred from repeated respiratory infections, his germ phobia had begun after his fifth or sixth trip, and now there was a new problem, the aches in his joints. But it was true that Rusty would never get the time sickness again. You got it once, like chicken pox or measles, and then you were immune. "You nearly didn't make it your first time through. I don't know what would happen if you went through again."

"What bullshit," Rusty muttered. "You just don't trust me to go through. You think I won't come back."

"That's not true."

"Right."

"I know you're happy here." Happier, at any rate, than he had been with his dysfunctional family in 1997. Happier because the mind could adapt to almost anything once it got used to the parameters. "You've got everything you want here."

Rusty leaned forward, elbows on the counter. "And what about you, Pete? Do you have everything you want here?"

"Sure." *Except for Evie.* He began spooning soup from the pot into a bowl for Annie.

"Then why do you keep snatching kids from other time zones and bringing them through? Why do you do that, Pete?"

A vein pulsed at Wheaton's temple, he put the top back onto the pot, turned the burner to simmer. He didn't want to talk about this. Not now. Not ever. But he knew that unless he gave Rusty an answer that satisfied him, he would keep questioning him, prodding him, digging for answers. "You need a sibling."

"You're such a fucking liar." Rusty straightened up, shook his head, and walked off.

Moments later, music blasted from his room. It was

a relief for Wheaton to get out of the house, away from the relentless pounding of the music. He carried his medical bag and a tray down the path toward the shed. The soup. Crackers. A box of Gatorade, courtesy of 2003. For now, it was important that Annie think she was in her own time.

He had worried about Annie throughout the night and had gone down to the shed several times to check on her, but she hadn't seemed that sick. She had shouted at him, sworn at him, resisted his help. And that was okay. He preferred that to passivity. The ones who had been passive, who had whined and cried for their mommies, hadn't made it. Rusty was his successful prototype. He had resisted fiercely and he had survived. Wheaton felt hopeful and optimistic about Annie.

She was the fifth child he had brought through the corridor and a year older than Rusty had been when Wheaton had brought him through. So far, she had done better than the others, but he knew how devious the sickness could be, how insidiously it could lie in wait. If she survived the next forty-eight hours, that would support his theory that children at the brink of adolescence stood a better chance than those who were younger or older. Of course, if she survived, he wouldn't need any other children.

When Rusty had survived, Wheaton had thought he wouldn't need any more children. But he had grown fond of Rusty, had realized how much he enjoyed having a kid around the house, and so his search had started again. But that wouldn't happen with Annie. There wouldn't be time to grow fond of her.

The pines thickened and the branches fractured the morning light, creating shadowed mosaics against the bed of needles that cushioned his footsteps. A quarter of a mile later, he reached the shed. It wasn't a typical shed. No tin or metal for *this* baby. The building was solid concrete block with about six hundred square feet of living space. It had been on the property when Wheaton had bought the land. It had survived hurricanes and even a fire that had leveled most of the property back in 1942. It had a small bathroom with a shower and a basic kitchen.

Above the doorway was a wood carving of a leatherback turtle, a reminder of his former life as a marine biologist. He still had a deep fondness for these giants of marine turtles and, during the summer, often walked the beaches where they came ashore to lay their eggs. Sea turtles weren't endangered in 1968; that wouldn't happen for another two years. But concerned biologists already had begun to cordon off the turtle nests with wire mesh to protect them from people, something that would become a common practice from about the mid-seventies forward.

The carving over the doorway even had a name, Poseidon, a tribute to the leatherback's immense size, as much as fifteen hundred pounds, its vast range—from the Atlantic to the Pacific and Indian Oceans—and its ability to dive to depths of over 3,300 feet. Poseidon was the leatherback who had led him into the corridor in 1994.

He set the tray on the weathered wooden table outside the door and unhooked the set of keys that hung from his belt. He had a lot of keys. He was a big believer in locks. The shed, for instance, had a heavy metal door with a padlock, a dead bolt controlled only from the outside, and a chain. The windows were bolted shut, the glass was unbreakable. The temperature inside was carefully controlled by a thermostat with a lockbox over it and the power was controlled from the main house. Right now the temp was set at seventy-eight degrees. Once she got over the sickness with the high fever and the chills, he would put it at whatever she deemed to be most comfortable.

If she really gave him problems, if her resistance proved to be as bad as or worse than Rusty's, then he would cut off the power. He disliked resorting to such tactics, but that had broken Rusty's resistance.

He unlocked the padlocks, the dead bolt, removed the chain, picked up the tray, and went inside. Even though he shut the door again, he immediately knew he didn't have to. Annie Morales would not be getting up for a while. She looked bad, her skin ashen, her lips parched and cracked. He set his medical bag and the tray on the coffee table, unlocked the storage closet door, wheeled out a cart filled with cleaning supplies. He opened a pack of Latex gloves, snapped them on.

Puke bowl first.

He detested the sickness and his anxiety over whether the child would survive. One of the kids he'd brought through the corridor had started vomiting blood within twelve hours and he'd had to bring in Lydia, a black Cuban healer who had helped pull Rusty through. But with the child who had vomited blood, Lydia had told him right off that she didn't think she could do anything, that the child's immune system was already compromised. Even though Lydia had treated the child, she had died fourteen hours later. Wheaton had buried her in the cemetery in the woods, behind the shed, with his other failures.

There was no blood that he could see in this puke pan, though, so that was a good sign. He hoped that she hadn't vomited the Advil that Rusty had given her. It would bring the fever down. He had some penicillin he could give her if he had to, in the event that she was developing some secondary infection, but he wouldn't give it to her until she could keep food in her stomach.

He washed out the pan, scrubbed it well with

Clorox, then washed the sink with Clorox, too. He took the pan back into the main room.

"I'll take care of you, Evie. Let me slide a pillow under your head."

"I feel like shit, Patty Cakes."

He's so happy that he has her all to himself that he doesn't even care if she calls him by that horrible nickname. She's got the flu, nothing life-threatening, but while she's sick she is all his.

He caresses her face. He reads her poetry by Edna St. Vincent Millay, and she lets him stretch out alongside her, holding her while she sleeps.

Wheaton set the pan on the cleaning cart, then proceeded to clean up the mess on the floor next to the couch. Soap and water, mop, Clorox, more mopping, then a sound rubbing with rags. When the floor was finally so clean you could eat off of it, he stripped the gloves off his hands, tossed them in a bag with the rags, and washed up.

From the shelves of the storage closet, he brought down a blanket and pillow sealed in a plastic bag so bacteria and dust wouldn't get to it. He drew the blanket over Annie, and slipped the pillow, with a clean case on it, under her head so that she could breathe more easily. He pulled a chair over to the bed and opened his medical case.

He could tell just by looking at her that the Advil hadn't kicked in yet; the fever still raged through her. He removed the digital ear thermometer from its case, one of the many technological wonders he'd brought back with him. He turned it on, touched the tip of it just inside her ear. Seconds later, it beeped, and a chill swept through him: 104.2.

Two of the children he'd brought through the corridor had died when their fevers had hit 104.

Wheaton ran into the bathroom and filled the tub with tepid water. As long as it was cooler than her body temp, it would help bring her fever down. She wasn't going to like this, but he had no other choice. He hurried back into the living room, sat her up. The blankets fell away from her. She moaned, her head rolled to the left, she tried to push him away but didn't have the strength.

"It's okay," he said gently. "This is going to make the fever go down, I promise."

She was still wearing her bathing suit with a pair of shorts and a T-shirt over it, so he stripped off the shirt and shorts, lifted her, and carried her into the bathroom. When he set her down into the tub of water, her eyes flew open and she bolted forward, grappling for the faucet, the shower curtain, anything within her reach that she could use to pull herself out of the water. Wheaton gripped her shoulder, pushed her back.

"You'll feel better in a few minutes, Annie."

He grabbed a plastic cup from the side of the tub, filled it with water, poured it over her shoulders. She flinched, then wrenched free of his grasp, and grabbed the cup from him. Being put in the tub, he thought, had revived her spit and passion, her insolence.

"Do it myself," she said, her words slurring. "Don't watch me."

With that, she jerked the shower curtain shut and Wheaton rocked back on his heels, listening to the splashes, to the cup scraping against the side of the bottom of the tub. Minutes ticked by.

"How long am I supposed to stay in here?" she asked, her words no longer slurred.

"Until the fever goes down."

"Rusty gave me some Advil."

"Which you may have thrown up."

"Do you have a thermometer?"

"I'll take your temperature."

She jerked the curtain open and looked out at him. Beads of water were suspended at the tips of her thick, dark lashes. Her hair, a waterfall as black as coal, was plastered to the sides of her neck. "I'm thirteen years old. I know how to take my own temperature. And if you're worried about my cheating or something, why would I do that? I don't like feeling like shit, okay?"

"Hey, first rule. No swearing."

They always needed to be reminded about Rule One.

"You'd be swearing, too, if you felt like I do."

"Here's the thermometer." He handed it to her. "You know how to use that kind?"

She rolled her eyes as if to say that was one of the stupidest questions she'd heard yet. "Yes." She touched the tip just inside her ear and seconds later, glanced at the readout. "A hundred and three point one."

"Good, it's gone down almost a degree. Add more water to the tub."

"I'd like my backpack. It's got clean clothes inside."

"I'll get it. There're also clothes in the closet and in the bureau."

"I don't wear other people's clothes. It's like absorbing their psychic garbage."

"These are new clothes. Your size."

Her bravado faltered and he suddenly realized that although she talked tough, she was just a young, frightened teenager. "Yeah? Who bought them? You?"

"Yes."

Silence. More splashing. Now she turned the faucet on full blast and he understood that the pounding of the water served the same purpose as loud music in Rusty's room; it blocked him out. When she finally turned it off, the pipes clattered and clanked. She pulled the curtain back again. "I wasn't sick yesterday. Why am I so sick now?"

"I don't know."

She stared at him for so long that he began to feel deeply uncomfortable. "You're a lousy liar. You just don't want to tell me the truth." She yanked the curtain shut again. "I should take my temp again."

Wheaton, disturbed by what had just happened, passed the thermometer between the curtain and the wall. She snatched it away and seconds later, held it out again, so he could see the digital readout: 101.1.

"Good. You can get out now. I've brought you some food and I think it'd be a good idea if you eat it. There're Popsicles in the freezer and plenty of bottled water. You need to keep drinking liquids so you don't get dehydrated. Rusty or I will check on you from time to time."

"And what am I supposed to do while I lie out there on the couch? There's no TV. I haven't seen a single book. And I'm not tired right now."

"I'll bring you some books."

"I'd like my clothes, please. And a toothbrush and toothpaste and some shampoo and a hairbrush and hair dryer."

He stood, opened the wall cabinet, picked up the shampoo he'd bought. He set a toothbrush and a tube of toothpaste on the back of the sink. He put a fluffy towel on the back of the toilet. "Shampoo," he said, and set it on the edge of the tub. "I'll get your clothes."

"Excuse me," she said, opening the curtain again. "I think you should know something. My mother isn't rich, okay? She and my great-grandmother own a bookstore. Independent bookstore owners are notoriously *not* wealthy. I mean, we live okay, but we're not rich. So if this is about money, you kidnapped the wrong kid."

"We already had this conversation," he reminded her, and wondered if the corridor had swallowed that memory. It happened sometimes. "And my answer is the same. This isn't about money. And I'm not a pedophile."

"Then what's it about?"

Wheaton was already on his way out of the bathroom as she asked this and he didn't stop, didn't look back, didn't reply.

"Hey," she shouted. "What is it you want?"

"All in due time. Right now, my only goal is to get you better."

"Great. Then let me go home."

"I can't."

He turned and saw that her lower lip quivered and her eyes filled with tears. "My mom will find me. You don't know how she is."

"Actually, I know quite a bit about your mother, Annie. And about you." He stood at the bathroom door. He realized that in the physical scheme of things, the distance between them seemed hardly significant. But at a deeper level, it was as if they were speaking to each other across an impassable ocean. "Mira's closest to her grandmother, Nadine Cantrell. She rarely sees her own parents. She and your father and Nadine bought the property for her bookstore in Lauderdale when she was twenty-seven and pregnant with you. She owned it for nearly ten years.

"On your third birthday, your father went into a convenience store where a robbery was taking place. He was shot and killed." *And he's alive now, Annie, living on Marathon.* "Five years later, your mother picked up psychic information on the murder of a prominent psychiatrist, whose killer turned out to have been the same man who murdered your father. The publicity surrounding that case drove your family out of Fort Lauderdale and—"

"All that stuff's on the Internet. In newspapers," she snapped. "I'm not impressed."

"You just finished eighth grade. You'll be going to Tango High in the fall. You've been riding your bike to and from school, unless you catch a ride with your mom or Nadine or, sometimes, that guy your mother is dating. He's a cop."

"His name's Shep and he's an FBI agent and right this second he's looking for your ass, mister. So get to your goddamn point, okay?"

"Rule One. *Do not swear.*" He stepped over to the tub and leaned down and grabbed her head between his massive hands, his eyes boring into hers. "You are *not* to swear in my presence, is that understood? If you swear, if you break the rules, it will require a sacrifice. That's how it is."

He could tell that he terrified her, but even terror didn't mitigate her rage. *"Fuck you, fuck, you, fuck you!"* she shrieked.

And in that instant, Wheaton came very close to hitting her. Instead, he conquered the impulse toward violence by pushing her away, by stepping back. He clasped his fingers together and cracked his knuckles. "You may think your mother is the greatest psychic since Nostradamus, but I've got news for you, kid. She will *not* find you because where you are is impenetrable. Your food is on the end table. Someone will be in to check on you later."

He slammed the door on his way out.

A while later, he heard her crying softly in the bathroom and he thought, *Good. Get it out. It'll help you accept the situation and then we can get on with why you're here.*

Nine

Jake's 1966 black Beetle chugged along the dirt road, the tires kicking up gravel that pinged against the sides of the car. It was like riding in a tin can. The radio was on, Jose Feliciano singing "Light my Fire." The music sounded tinny to Mira, who had a CD player and quadraphonic sound in her car. The first hadn't been invented yet and she didn't know about the second. Jake kept fiddling with the knob, changing stations until he finally turned it off. She knew that she should say something to him, thank him again for the ride, for the breakfast that she'd neither eaten nor paid for. But social conversation was beyond her ability right now. She was still mute with incredulity and worried about what she was going to do for money. The cash she had from her own time looked like Monopoly money.

"There're shorter ways to get into town," Jake said.

"I just need to see something," she managed to say. "It can't be much farther."

The bright light seemed to pierce her eyes. It hurt to look too closely at things because no matter where she looked she saw vast differences. Fields instead of houses. No strip shopping centers. No convenience stores. Only two gas stations so far. The sheer lushness of this undeveloped island, circa 1968, overpowered her.

Then the VW came out of the vital turn, the turn that would convince her once and for all that it wasn't a gag, a commercial, or some new reality show. The bridge between Tango Key and the rest of the keys had been completed in 1985, a twelve-mile miracle of engineering. Until then, boats, car ferries, and small planes had been Tango Key's only link with the rest of the country.

"Keep going?" he asked.

She nodded and leaned forward, straining to see.

Now, on her left, through the parade of banyan trees and pines, she glimpsed water. Florida Bay. The bridge wasn't far from here, she thought, as the road straightened out.

They cleared the trees. Mira didn't realize she'd been holding her breath until she saw the gaping emptiness that loomed between the eastern shore of Tango Key and Key West, twelve miles distant. Her breath rushed out of her, a sound so sharp, so loud, so raw, that Jake pulled off to the side of the road and stopped. She threw open the door and stumbled out, Jake calling, "Hey, where're you going?"

She lurched forward, sounds exploding from her mouth, a huge and terrible weight lodged dead center in her chest. *No, no, no, it's true, something happened out there in the darkness, something impossible.*

At the edge of the steep slope, Mira dropped to her knees in the soft grass and stared. Her fingers gripped her thighs, sobs surged up her throat. No bridge. Nothing but water. And there, way in the distance, the shape of Key West. Two ferries moved in opposite directions across the bay, ferries built by the same company that had constructed the ferries that went to and from Martha's Vineyard, car ferries, ferries loaded down with people and supplies.

It's true.

"Uh, Mira?"

She felt Jake crouch beside her.

"Look, I don't know what kind of weird shit you're involved in, but if I can help in some way, just say so."

She felt shaky inside, as if she'd held a particular yoga position for so long that it had strained all her muscles. She kept staring across the bay, struggling with the reality of *no bridge*. "Do you know what Yahoo dot com is?"

"No."

"Do you know what the Internet is?"

"Nope."

"Ever heard of Bill Gates?"

"Don't think so. Who is he?"

Now *what* had been the point of *that?* Was she prepared to trust this guy just because he had been kind to her? She tried to put herself in his shoes, to imagine how she might react if he told her he was from 2036. She would distance herself immediately or call 911 or both, right?

Ha. She would be too curious for that. She would ask for proof. Or she would try to read him.

"Jake, I'm in a real jam." *Uh-huh, and now what? What lie?* "My ex-husband is . . . is following me. That's why I was on a boat. I was fleeing. Then . . . these guys came aboard the boat . . . stole my money . . . left me on the beach and . . . and took off in the boat. I . . . I can't go to the police. My ex is a cop, he has a lot of friends who are cops. He'll find out where I am. I need a place to stay and until I can get a hold of a friend who can wire me money. I'm broke."

"Jesus," he murmured, and reached into his pocket. He brought out his wallet, reached inside, pulled out a wad of bills. "Take this. It's probably a hundred bucks."

He held the money out and she suddenly felt so guilty about taking it that she nearly blurted the truth. She dug a piece of paper and a pen out of her bag and wrote him an IOU. "Take this."

"Don't worry about it. Rum Runners is doing really good now. I've got extra cash."

"Please take it."

She pressed it into his hand and he folded the money and set it on top of her backpack. "Okay, we're even. And I know a place you can stay. The artists' colony up in the hills rents cabins during the summer. It's private, your ex would never find you there. I can get you a good price, too."

The artists' colony. It had to be the same one that existed in her time, she thought, way up in the northeast hills. "What's a good price?"

"Forty to fifty a week if you do your own wash and cooking. Most of the cabins have kitchens."

It sounded way too cheap. "That'd be great." She slung her pack over her shoulder and got to her feet. "Can you drop me off there? I've taken up too much of your time already."

"Hey, it's not every day some pretty woman drops into my life with as much mysterious baggage as you've got." His eyes followed her up. "And when you have some time, I'd like to know more about Yahoo dot com, the Internet, and Bill Gates. Deal?"

"Deal," she replied.

The artists' colony looked somewhat different than it did in her own time—fewer buildings, fewer people, and much more land. If memory served her, the colony in her time owned about fifty acres; Jake claimed it covered more than twice that.

The main road, a two-laner that was barely paved, twisted through a pine forest so green that it was as if she could smell that color in the air. Here and there through the trees, she glimpsed paths, people in electric carts, on bikes, or on foot. Off to her left in a clearing, a yoga class was in progress, which in 1968 was still considered odd. Farther up the road, a group of men and women were constructing several more buildings.

"More cabins," said Jake. "The colony has twenty so far."

"You sure there are openings?"

"Yeah."

"Who owns it?"

"A rich northern couple, patrons of the arts. Their son and daughter run the place and they're pretty cool. About the only rule they've got is no drugs. To live here year-round, as an artist, you have to audition and a committee makes the final decision. Once you're in, you get room and board." He pulled up in front of an L-shaped building. "I'll be right back. Let me see who's on duty in the office."

As soon as he got out of the car, Mira rubbed her hands slowly over her face. Her hands were real, her face was real, her skin was real. She was here. That was real, too. She didn't have any idea yet how she'd gotten *here,* what miracle or aberration of nature had enabled this to happen. But she knew Annie was here as well, that in following her daughter's faint psychic trail, she had gone through the same portal where the monster had taken her daughter.

And who the hell is this guy?

Her only insight into the monster had come when she'd held the bottle he had touched. She had felt *soiled,* felt that he was *evil,* but what mother *wouldn't* feel that? You didn't have to be psychic to know that the man who snatched your kid was evil. She needed more than that. She needed the why, the what, the motive, the *story.* This guy had a mother, a father, a childhood, a history. He also had an agenda.

Mira started feeling nauseated and realized she hadn't eaten anything since—when? Yesterday? Or in thirty-five years? How was she supposed to measure stuff like that? What kind of jet lag happened in time travel?

She laughed, then her eyes flooded with tears, and she turned her head toward the window, knuckles pressed against her mouth. In the glass, she saw Annie as an infant, a baby, a toddler, a little kid with opinions. The day she had started kindergarten, Mira had driven her to school and parked in the lot and walked her up to the building. She was more nervous than Annie had been.

"You think it's okay if I walk into the building with you?" Mira had asked.

It sounded like a question about school rules and bureaucracy, but what she was really asking was if Annie wanted company into the building. And Annie had stood there for a few moments, her hand clutching Mira's, then finally had shaken her head. Her grip on Mira's hand had begun to ease up. "I bet it's not allowed, Mommy. But I think we should break the rules just for today."

"I think you're right," Mira replied, and they walked into the building together, but Annie wasn't holding her hand.

Afterward, she had sat in her car for a while, staring at the building. It wasn't so much about learning your ABCs. It was Annie's first step into the bigger world. She had invited Mira to share it, but not to hold her hand. *This is my journey, but company would be okay, too.* And for the last eight years, that was exactly what their relationship had been. They were close, they communicated well. But they were also mother and daughter and in the *please clean your room* department they didn't do very well.

Annie tended to talk a lot at night right before she went to sleep. Even when she was small she had been like that. When Mira sat at the edge of her bed and tickled her back or read to her, Annie talked about school, her friends, her world, and Mira advised her—not as a psychic or a mother, but as a friend. The day on Little Horse Key had been a lot like those bedtime moments. They had hunted for shells, watched little crabs discard one home and scurry to find another, they had gone swimming and sunbathed, and through it all, they had talked.

Sheppard, she knew, had wanted to join them that day, but she'd made it clear that it was her and Annie's day. If he had come along, would the kidnapping have happened?

Maybe not.

Men like the monster might not be so brazen with another man in the picture. This kind of thinking was exactly the sort of thing that sent feminists ballistic and it galled her to even go there. After all, gender hadn't saved her husband when he'd walked into a convenience store in 1992 and another man had shot him.

In those horrible moments when she had realized that the man on the beach, asking for her help, was the source of her unease, her and Annie's vulnerability had terrified her. Her instinct had been to flee. She was a woman alone with her daughter on a deserted beach. She was not armed. She didn't have a black belt in karate, she didn't even have a can of pepper spray.

Sheppard would have gone for his gun.

And Sheppard might be dead.

Mira rubbed her hands over her face and when she looked up, Jake was returning to the car. "Diego's not in the office," he said. "He's probably in one of the cabins. He's one of the colony poets and works part-time in the office."

"You know everyone here?"

He slid behind the wheel, shut the door, started the car. "I'm sort of a part-time resident here. My thing is photography, but the bar pays the bills. Every so often I come here for a week or two just to do photography and darkroom stuff."

Mira thought of her digital camera and realized she'd left it on the cooler, on the beach, back in 2003. She hoped that Sheppard would find it, hoped that an image of the man might be visible in the background of the photos Annie had snapped of her. But even if he found the camera and discovered an image in one of the photos, what good would it do? Thirty-five years separated him from the man, from her, from Annie.

The reality of her situation crashed over her again and pressed her back against the seat with the weight of excessive gravity. Her nausea returned, she felt light-headed. A humming started way down inside her eyes, then suddenly filled her skull and spread like hot, liquefied wax over the crown of her head and down into her neck and shoulders. A sensation like an electric current shot down the nerves in her face, swept into her shoulders, and raced down her arms and into her fingertips. Her entire body felt as though it were lit up, glowing as brightly as a radioactive heap, and humming like a tuning fork.

The humming grew in pitch and intensity and she grabbed the sides of her head, pressing the heels of her hands against her temples. But the pressure only made the humming worse. Now it sounded like the shrieks of a thousand terrified birds. Hot nails were being driven into her skull. Her chest exploded with heat, she couldn't catch her breath, and she snapped forward, gasping, hands grappling for the dashboard. Just when she didn't think she could stand it anymore, when blackness seeped into her peripheral vision, the agonizing shrieks in her head stopped and a soft but tolerable humming settled through her skull.

The car had stopped, Jake had gotten out, and now Mira threw open the door and stumbled into the warm, fresh air. Her skin felt extremely sensitized, as if the pores had blown open. She had no idea what had happened just then, but her skin still felt strange, *electrified*.

Jake and a black woman came out of one of the cabins and he gestured toward his car. The woman, holding a bucket in one hand and a broom in the other, hesitated, then shrugged, set her things down, and fell into step beside him.

Mira walked over to them and Jake introduced them. "Mira, this is Lydia. Lydia, Mira."

"Hey," Lydia said. "Jake tells me you need a place to stay."

"Just for a week or so."

"It's fifty a week, furnished, with linens. Jake says Diego's not in the office, so we'll get you checked in later. I know for a fact that cabin eleven is free. I'll take you down there now."

"Let me get my stuff out of the car."

"I need to get back to work," Jake said as he handed Mira her pack. "I'll be back to look in on you. Oh, the colony grocery store is down the main path and then right. If you need anything else, just give a holler, okay?"

"I can't thank you enough, Jake." She gave him a quick hug and, in those brief moments of physical contact, felt his acute unease, his urgent need to get away. She spooked him. Mira quickly stepped back. "See you soon."

"Take good care of her, Lydia."

They stood there, the two of them, watching Jake drive off in his VW, dust flying up behind him. "He's a nice guy," Mira remarked.

"He's a good white boy who's always asking for favors and doing stuff for other people, when he needs to be spending more time doing his darkroom magic and taking pictures. But hey, his bar is the moneymaker. Cabin eleven is down here a ways."

They walked silently along the path, past ancient trees,

the pack growing increasingly heavier on Mira's shoulder, her body still tingling. "So what's your specialty?" Lydia asked.

"My specialty?"

"Yeah, you know. Painting, sculpture, photography . . ."

"I need a specialty to rent a cabin?"

"Well, no. But the renters usually have an interest in some artistic area."

"I'm a psychic. Does that count?"

"You mean, like a fortune-teller?"

"If that's what you want to call it."

"So tell me my fortune," Lydia said with a smile.

"Here?"

"Hon, I'm a sculptress. I can sculpt anywhere. I figure it should work that way with fortune-telling, too, right?"

All she wanted to do was shower, find some food, and fall into a bed, but Lydia was starting to piss her off. "Give me your hand."

"You're gonna read my palm?"

"I need to touch you. That's how I work."

"Oh." She gave a nervous laugh and extended her hand, palm upward.

Mira cupped her own hand under it and started to run her thumb over Lydia's palm, but she never got that far.

She is small, hiding in the bushes with her mommy, terrified that if she moves, if she breathes too hard, the bad men in the clearing will find her and her mommy. The men in white hooded robes are shouting, dragging her granddaddy through the clearing and out to the big old tree where only yesterday she was climbing through the branches.

One of the men tosses a rope over some branches. Others bring a ladder over to where her granddaddy stands, his face swollen, his chest bare, his back whipped and bleeding. Lydia

*squeezes her eyes shut and buries her face in her mother's arm.
But her mother grabs her chin and hisses, "You watch and
remember what white men do to us. You watch, Lydia."*

*She whimpers, tears burn her eyes, she wants to run and
run and keep on running. But her mother holds her hand so
tightly that she can't move. Her breath refuses to rise up from
her lungs, the air is stuck down there, and now the men are
shouting and laughing and forcing her granddaddy to step
up onto the ladder. Now they drop the noose around his neck
and the breath rushes from her lungs and her mother's arms
close around her, her cries muffled against Lydia's hair.*

*And then the men kick the ladder away and her grand-
daddy hangs, his entire body twitching, twitching, twitching,
and then going still and . . .*

Lydia wrenched her hand away from Mira's. "Jesus
God, woman, what the hell *are* you?"

Mira didn't realize she'd been talking the entire
time, describing the events that she was seeing. Even
now, she was still in that clearing, staring at the black
man swinging from the tree, the rope creaking softly
against the branches. She rubbed her eyes and the images dissolved. "You fled after that with your mother
and another woman . . ."

"My . . . my grandmother."

"Where did the hanging happen?"

"Alabama. I was four, just got there from Cuba. They
said my grandfather raped a white woman. It was a lie.
We fled and moved to Orlando. How . . . how can you
see all that, girl?"

I don't know. Her ability had never been this pure,
this undiluted, this raw, and it frightened her. "Your
energy is strong, that makes it easier." Behind those
primal images, Mira had seen and felt other details of
Lydia's life, about her marriage to a man who had

been active in the civil rights movement, but they were too remote from her now to even recall them.

"Well, you're no Gypsy fortune-teller, that's for sure. You see the future like you see the past?"

"Sometimes. One thing I do know is that where I come from, they would call you a woman of power."

Lydia laughed. "Power? Shit. I'm a black woman. On top of it, I'm a black Cuban woman. That means my power doesn't amount to a pile of dog shit. But I if you're in need of cash, I can sure as hell find you clients."

"Right now I'm pretty wiped out. And I need to buy some food."

"Let's get you settled in. If you need a way to get around, the office rents electric carts for a buck a day."

Fifty bucks for the room, seven bucks for the cart, more money for food, and she needed a few clothes. Jake's loan, she thought, was going to be gone in five minutes.

The cabin was basic but certainly adequate as a base of operation. The kitchen, though small, had pots and pans and a few dishes and glasses. She could save money by cooking her own food. She set her pack on the bed and turned on the window AC unit. It gasped, sputtered, clattered, and finally pumped out tiny breaths of cool air.

"That's all the luggage you got?" Lydia asked.

"I was robbed," Mira said, perpetuating the lie now. "This is what they didn't take."

"*Robbed?* Did you go to the cops?"

Mira shook her head and told Lydia the same lie that she'd told Jake. Then she changed the subject. "Can you show me where the grocery store is?"

"Sure thing. Then I need you to fill out a registration card and get a check."

"They stole my checks. Will the office take cash?"

"Even better."

Mira's nausea increased once they were outside in the

extreme heat again. The strange humming in her head escalated in pitch and intensity as if it were seeking its ideal range. She felt consistently more light-headed and distracted and sensed it wasn't just hunger or the strangeness of everything. She was getting sick. It made a kind of terrible sense. Travelers to any foreign country were inoculated first against diseases prevalent in that region; no telling what sort of diseases a time traveler might pick up. What diseases or illnesses had been prevalent in the sixties? Smallpox hadn't been eradicated, people still got polio, but what else? She couldn't remember, couldn't seem to think straight.

"You feeling okay?" Lydia asked her outside the store.

"Not really."

"C'mon, I'll go in with you. They sell some herbs and stuff that'll help."

The store was small and cramped and the aisles so narrow it was difficult to push a cart through them without knocking something over. The shelves were jammed with items. She grabbed a couple of cans of soup, eggs, a loaf of bread, cheese, vegetables, and fruit. In her own time, an entire aisle of her grocery store held nothing but bottled water, but there was no such creature in this store. Maybe no such creature at all in the sixties. She opted, instead, for a container of ginger ale, which would at least settle her stomach.

She couldn't find any Advil and had to settle for plain aspirin. The only orange juice she could find was frozen. No vegetarian products, no fresh fish. Even if she had been inclined to eat chicken or meat, everything was frozen. The milk came in two varieties: whole or powdered. She grabbed a box of powdered milk, a container of peanut butter, then weaved her way toward beach supplies, the air so blurred now that she wasn't sure she would make it out the door, much less back to her cabin. She stood for a few minutes in front of the

beach supplies, trying to focus her vision and finally settled on a couple of T-shirts, two pairs of shorts, and a
pair of thong sandals. Hardly a fashion statement.

Lydia caught up with her at the register and added
fresh herbs to her cart. There were no scanners, no
setup for ATM or credit cards, no computerized regis-
ters. Everything was done the old-fashioned way, with
the cashier ringing up each item by hand. She expected the total to hit forty bucks and nearly fell over
when the cashier said that the total was $16.18.

By the time she and Lydia carried the groceries back
to the cabin, Mira was stumbling along, her body on
fire, her ears ringing, the humming back with a
vengeance. She tripped as she went into the cabin and
Lydia caught her arm.

"You're burning up, girl. Take some of those aspirins
and change into something comfortable. I'll put your
groceries away and make you a Lydia Powerhouse
Drink."

When Mira emerged from the bathroom a while
later, a cold, wet cloth pressed to her head, she
dropped back onto the bed, pulled the top cover over
herself, and Lydia brought her a plate of scrambled
eggs, toast, and a tall glass filled with something that
looked like a power smoothie. "Eat and drink and then
sleep. That drink has got all sorts of stuff in it—rose
hips, chamomile, oranges and strawberries, and some
immune boosters."

"I can't thank you enough, Lydia."

"It's the only way I can pay you for that reading, hon.
I'll be checking in on you."

Mira finished the food and the drink and then she
let her head drop back to the pillow and sank into a
sleep like death.

Ten

The inside of the office at the Sugarloaf Marina looked as if a bomb had hit it. Papers were strewn across the counter, a dismantled engine rested on the floor to the side of the main counter, a carton filled with containers of engine oil had been pushed to the side of the register and held a bottle of Coke. Wheaton inhaled the stink of oil and gas, and had a very bad moment when the old man behind the counter glanced up at him and seemed to do a double take. As if he'd recognized him.

It was clearly impossible. He was more than thirty years older than the Patrick Wheaton whom the old man knew and had gone to great lengths to disguise himself. He had darkened his hair, wore granny glasses, and was dressed like a professor on summer break.

"Mr. Hanes, I'm Pete Smith. I called you a couple of days ago about reserving a boat for use some time between June twenty-sixth and July first?"

"Right. You're the fellow who wants a boat that's fast and has a small cabin."

"I'd like to make a deposit. I anticipate that I won't be able to pick the boat up until after you've closed for the day."

"You know exactly which day yet?"

"No."

"Well, not a problem. Just need to see your license

and a five-hundred-dollar deposit. It'll be returned when you return the boat."

Wheaton showed him his license—one of several he had for this time—and paid him in fifties and hundreds. "Where will the key be?"

"Out back. I'll show you the spot."

Wheaton followed the old guy through the rickety front door and around to the back of the building. Two docks jutted out like tongues into the painted water, six or eight boats tied up alongside them. Wheaton listened to the old man's explanation about the boat, but his gaze wandered to the house across the canal.

She's in there. Right this second.

He forced himself to look away from the house and back at Hanes.

"You figure you'll have the boat how long?" the old man asked.

"About five days."

"Key'll be right here." Hanes touched his hand to a wooden post and pointed up under the edge of the metal roof. "Top peg."

"Got it."

"You want me to show you how the nav equipment works? Radio? All that?"

"I know how to use it, thanks." He stuck out his hand. "I'll be here between the twenty-sixth and the first, Mr. Hanes."

As soon as Hanes headed off toward the docks, Wheaton walked quickly away from the canal, struggling against the nearly overpowering urge to glance back, to take one last look at the house. He knew he would see lights coming on in the upstairs windows, that he might even glimpse her shadow as she moved past the blinds.

Move faster, don't look back. . . .

He knew that her parents weren't home, that she was alone in the house, either listening to music or talking to that prick Billy Macon on the phone. He knew he could walk up to the house, ring the bell, and take her now.

But the timing was wrong.

In the car. Back up. Get out of here.

Moments later, he sped away from the Sugarloaf Key Marina, slammed across the wooden bridge, and didn't stop until he reached the Key West ferry.

2

Brad Pitt was back, tending to her, making her comfortable, keeping her company, talking to her.

"See, my old man was nuts and my mother was on her way to being the same way, so Pete actually did me a favor by taking me out of that situation. That's what I have to keep remembering. I owe him, you know what I mean? I feel a certain loyalty to him. And he's treated me really well these last six years. He bought me a car as soon as I turned fifteen and he's always bringing me stuff when he comes back through the corridor. Music, videotapes, my computer . . . But he only brings what *he* thinks I should have, see? He's a control freak like that. And because of the Close Call a few years back, I have to, uh, keep everything out of sight. Come to think of it, he's pretty controlling all the time. I don't notice it as much now, though, because I don't spend all that much time here. Got some friends in town, I spend a lot of time there. Don't tell them much, though. Can't risk it."

"But you're here now," she said.

"What was that?"

He leaned closer and she realized that she either

hadn't spoken or hadn't spoken clearly enough or loudly enough. But it was getting increasingly more difficult to make her tongue work. "You're here now."

"Yeah. You need someone here more than he's willing to be here. I can't just let you . . . be all alone. You're a fighter, like I am, and I figure I can make your fight easier by keeping you company. Here, take a bite of this. It's a piece of chilled mango."

He held it to her lips and Annie sucked on it like ice, then nibbled and sucked some more. "Good," she murmured.

"Lydia says it's one of the most perfect foods. I don't know about that, but it was one of the foods she fed me that helped me through the sickness."

"What's the name of this sickness?"

"I don't know if it has a name."

"Tell me about your life," she said, and so he did, his voice moving through her like soothing music. But the life he described didn't sound like anything she knew about Brad Pitt's life. It sounded like a nightmare— chaotic, abusive, a life where social services or the cops or both intervened every few months.

"But that's changed since I came here. Pete and me used to do a lot of stuff together the first couple years I was here. He taught me to fish and to drive, and once he got his pilot's license we'd fly up to Miami for dinner or over to the west coast of Florida to go houseboating. Shit like that. He tried hard to be a father to me. But as he took more and more trips through the corridor and kept bringing children through . . . I don't know, everything changed. Ever since the Close Call, I've been planning to move out as soon as I turn eighteen."

"Children? Where're the children?" The dog started licking her hands and face and jumped up onto the couch with her. "Brad?"

"Still here."

"I'm going to be sick."

He helped her sit up and she opened her eyes and the world swirled and she vomited and gagged and vomited again and felt as if she lost half her stomach. "I need a doctor," she whispered.

"You . . ." He stopped. "Jesus," he hissed. "Annie, I'll be right back. Just don't move, okay?" He set her head back on the pillow. "Just shut your eyes and don't move, please. Promise me."

"Promise," she murmured, and fell back into a dream.

3

It was dark when Wheaton pulled in alongside Rusty's old Chevy. He was exhausted but exhilarated. He had resisted the ultimate temptation, to intervene too soon, before all the preparations were in place. Later this week, he would head up to Miami to begin decorating his new home. He would start lining up people to tile the floors, redo the swimming pool, paint the walls. He would shop for furniture, hire a landscaper, the place would be perfect by July first.

He got out of the car, his thoughts still back on Sugarloaf, and suddenly Rusty came tearing up the path from the shed, Sunny racing alongside him. "Pete, get down there fast! She's burning up, puking. It's bad, really bad. I saw blood in the puke. I'm going to get Lydia."

Christ, oh Christ. "Tell her it's an emergency. I'll pay her when she gets here."

"Right." He leaped into his car, the dog jumped in behind him, and he peeled out of the driveway.

Wheaton ran into the house, grabbed his medical bag from the downstairs pantry, and tore down the path to the shed. The door stood open and as soon as he went in, the stink of sickness nearly made him gag. Annie was on her hands and knees, trying to crawl somewhere—*for the door? To escape?* She had vomit smeared on the front of her shirt, her hair and eyes were wild, her face was bright red.

Wheaton dropped his bag on the coffee table and approached her cautiously, as though she were a wild beast, and kept his voice low and soft as he spoke to her. "Annie, let me help you up and—"

"Get away from me," she shrieked, and reared up, her arms flying upward. *"You did something to me, this is your fault, you fuck!"*

If she used that kind of language when she wasn't sick, she would discover the consequences. But because she was out of her mind, he ignored it and caught her gently at the wrists. "C'mon, let's get you onto the couch. This is just part of the sickness."

She tried to wrench her arms free but was far too weak, and he lifted her off the floor. She got one hand free and struck out blindly, her nails raking the side of his face like claws. *Germs.* He gasped and dropped her on the couch and she shot to her feet and raced with shocking speed toward the open door. Wheaton didn't understand where her energy came from, how she had the strength to move, much less to take off like a bullet. He hurled himself at her, grabbed her around the waist, and they crashed to the floor, his body cushioning her fall.

The air rushed from his lungs, his head spun, and even before he could get his bearings, she twisted savagely in his arms—and sank her teeth into the back of his hand. *Disease.* Then she was on her feet again, weaving toward the door. Wheaton caught her before she got very far and carried her, a writhing, savage beast whose body was burning up, over to the couch. He ran back to the door, slammed it shut, opened his medical bag.

He brought out damp wipes that wouldn't be available for a number of years and rubbed them gently over Annie's face and mouth, then tried to clean the puke off her shirt. She needed to change clothes, but it wasn't a proper thing for him to do. Lydia would do it. Lydia would see to it. He paid her to do those kinds of things. She knew what caused the sickness, of course, he'd had to confide in her so that she could treat Rusty when he had been so ill. And he compensated her well for her silence in that regard, too. But it frightened him that Annie had taken such a bad turn when he'd believed she was recovering.

He dropped the cloth in the puke pan, pulled the quilt over her again, then took the pan into the bathroom to rinse it out. No time to bring the cleaning cart out now, to sterilize anything.

Wheaton tried not to look at the specks of blood, tried not to think further ahead than sixty seconds. *Please don't die, kid.* His hand bled from where she'd bitten him and his face felt raw where she'd scratched him. He scrubbed his hands, rinsed them, lathered the soap in his hands and cleaned the bite wound and the scratch. Not enough. He would have to use antibiotic ointments later.

Rusty, the dog, and Lydia swept into the shed moments later. She was a tall, striking, large-boned woman with skin the color of rich chocolate. Her black currant eyes took one look around the room, zeroing right in on the girl. The look she gave Wheaton could cut glass. "Jesus Christ, Pete. You gone and done this shit again. How old is she?"

"Thirteen," he replied. "She's been sick like this for—"

"Shut up and get out of here. Both of you. Leave the dog. And close the door on your way out."

"Can you help her?" Wheaton asked anxiously.

"You know I'll do what I can. But I got nothing to promise. I'll come up to the house when I'm done and it's going to be late."

Wheaton and Rusty left, the beams of their flashlights barely making a dent in the darkness. Wheaton's bowels felt watery, his stomach churned, his head had started to ache. He desperately wanted to stay and observe, to assist if she needed assistance. But in all these years, Lydia had never called on him to help her in any way. Her healing techniques remained steeped in secrecy, a mystery so arcane that to even attempt to penetrate it would be a violation of their own tenuous and unspoken agreement.

"Pete?"

"Yeah?"

"Is she going to make it?" Rusty asked.

"I think she has a good chance."

Rusty nodded, his eyes on the rocky path. "She better make it. Or you're to blame, Pete." He jammed his hands in the pockets of his shorts and hurried on ahead of Wheaton.

Wheaton stared at Rusty's receding back. A broad back. Muscular arms. In the six years since Wheaton had brought him through the corridor, his hair had gotten longer and darker and his daily workouts at the gym had sculpted his lean body into a landscape of muscle and sinew. In the fall, he would be going to the University of Miami, an opportunity that his own dysfunctional family could not have provided.

It worried him that Rusty now stood up to him, sometimes refusing to do what he asked. Wheaton couldn't threaten him anymore. He would just have to wait this out, see where it led, and in the meantime, there was the girl.

He suddenly veered away from the path and made

his way into the pines, circling back behind the shed, perilously close to where the land dropped a hundred feet to the rocks below. Waves crashed against them, an echoing din that he could hear even before he reached the small clearing. A milky light spilled through the thick pines, revealing the uneven ground where he had buried the other children, the ones who didn't survive the trip through the corridor.

There, with a cluster of purple flowers marking her grave, lay Becky Sawyer, a pretty little blonde from Key Largo who was eleven when he took her. And over there, begonias marking his grave, lay Antonio Pantello, a nine-year-old Latino boy from Tango Key. And there, between them, his grave covered in Mexican heather, lay Morgan Washington, an African-American boy from Miami who was twelve when Wheaton had taken him. Two eleven-year-olds, one nine-year-old, one twelve-year-old, and now a thirteen-year-old girl. He had tried different ages, different races, different nationalities. Maybe, in the end, it all came down to nothing more than gene pools and which pool could withstand the crippling effects of the corridor.

In 1994, while he was investigating a black water mass that formed off the coast of Big Pine Key, a leatherback turtle had led him into an area of utter blackness—what he now knew was the corridor. The engine on his boat had died, his compass had gone berserk, he'd lost all his navigational equipment, his radio. The blackness he had entered was so profound that even the moon and the stars hadn't shone through it.

Even now, he could taste the suffocating air, feel it pressed against this mouth and nose. He could feel the terrible weight against his chest, the top of his head, could feel his leaden feet. He could still feel every painful sensation as the corridor had closed in around him, as though his bones, his very skeleton, were being compressed, crushed, annihilated. He had come to on his boat, just off the Tango pier. Once he'd gone ashore, it had taken him about ten minutes to realize he was no longer in his own time.

He'd spent ten days in September 1962 and for several days he'd been holed up in a motel room, sicker than he'd ever been in his life. He'd survived the sickness—and still didn't know how or why—and then he'd begun piecing together what had happened and how he might be able to return to his own time. It had taken three attempts and when it finally had happened it wasn't as terrible or painful. He hadn't even lost consciousness.

He supposed his plan about stealing money from the woman who was then his wife had been born as he'd headed toward shore, his mind racing, stitching together an alibi for where he had been. *Got lost at sea.* Who could dispute it?

Over the next few weeks, he had culled everything he could find on when the mass had existed in the past. He had pinpointed dates, times, the size of the mass, the coordinates, and had begun to formulate a theory that the black water mass was Mother Nature's wormhole, a corridor through time. An anomaly. Time travel had been speculated about for years in scientific circles and was now accepted to be theoretically possible by some physicists. But for these scientists, time travel for a human being was still eons in the future.

Wheaton believed that whenever the mass formed at the same coordinates in the past and the present, a wormhole was created. His research revealed that the mass had appeared in places other than Florida Bay— off the Greek Isles, the Canary Islands, the Galapagos Islands, Easter Island, and between New Zealand and Australia. It had been sighted near Manaus, Brazil, off Cape Cod, and in the South China Sea. It had also been sighted in the Bermuda Triangle, that area in the Atlantic that Charles Berlitz had made a household name after the publication of his book by the same name.

In some of these places, the mass had a history that went back decades and an oral tradition that dated back centuries. In many instances, though, its size had been too small to be noticed by any great number of people or it had occurred close to Third World countries for whom ocean ecology was at the bottom of the list of Important Things. He was sure the mass accounted for many instances of lost boats and ships. It was possible that the mass might also explain the disappearance of certain marine species.

His theory about how the black water mass actually functioned had taken him years to work out and the turning point had come when, during one of his forays into his own time, he had run across a scientific paper on paracrystalline vesicular grids in the human brain. These grids were so tiny that there were billions of them in the brain, found at the ends of nerve synapses. As Wheaton understood it, the fact that these crystalline structures existed at all in the brain suggested that they followed the laws of quantum physics. In essence, these grids created a quantum physical probability field that interacted with human consciousness to create events.

He believed that place of utter darkness within the black water mass—what he had called the corridor—was a vast probability field analogous to the paracrystalline vesicular grids in the brain. When he entered the corridor through particular coordinates, the grid in his brain and the probability field present within the mass interacted and the mind became a kind of time machine. As a result of observation—his presence in the corridor— the quantum wave function collapsed and he was carried through the corridor to the place in the past where the black hole also existed.

The pull of a person's natal time line was very strong and the more often he returned to his own time, the deeper the groove in the corridor, and the easier it was to do. The trick was to be precise in either direction and that was where the coordinates came in. He was still mapping the many possibilities.

Back in 1994, he studied the tides, currents, and general weather conditions to determine when the mass in the present would be at the same coordinates where it had been in June 1964. Then, one night in March 1994, he had embarked on his second journey through the corridor. This time, he stayed away only for twelve hours, long enough to do what he needed to do, but not so long that he roused suspicion. Two days after that second trip, he had begun siphoning money from his wife's accounts.

In all, he had siphoned nearly half a million, pocket change to her, and over a period of several months, had converted the money into jewelry, had taken it back to the sixties and sold it. Yes, he had taken something of a loss when the jewels were converted into the sixties' equivalent of their worth. But it was less expensive to live in this time and besides, the cash was *sixties* cash. He had opened bank accounts under several different names, in various cities, and then proceeded to establish a life for himself as Peter Wheat.

With his knowledge of his own time, making money in the sixties was a no-brainer. He knew which stocks to buy, which properties would surge in value, which companies he should watch. He bought several rental properties that provided a tidy monthly income and when they had doubled in value he sold them and bought other properties. Since he knew which artistic trends would be hot, he dabbled in art and now had quite a nice collection of original Andy Warhol pieces.

From time to time, some of the technological wiz-

ardry that he brought back through the corridor went
to people who would understand what to do with it.
Only last year, he had flown to the northwest, to the
neighborhood where a very young Bill Gates lived, and
had given him a laptop computer. *Here, kid, figure it out.*
Two years ago, he had tracked down Douglas Engelbart and given him a computer mouse and laptop.
This year, he knew, Engelbart would invent the computer mouse. He meddled and he always did it in small
ways that held the potential for vast and profound
change.

But he didn't try to save lives or to warn public figures of potential danger. He didn't seek out Lennon.
He didn't whisper anything in Ronald Reagan's ear. He
never warned Warhol to stay clear of the crazy woman
who had nearly killed him two weeks ago. That kind of
thing would draw attention and attention was the last
thing that Wheaton wanted. There was only one life
that he intended to save.

He stood there for a while in the little graveyard,
thinking about where he had been and where he was
going. And while he thought, he talked to each of the
children, offering up his thanks and his regrets to
them. He had done his best to save them. What more
could be done?

Wheaton was so wrapped up in his own thoughts
that he failed to see the car in his driveway until he'd
nearly reached the house. By then, it was too late to
turn around. The sheriff had seen him.

"Evening, Pete," he called, waving.

"Hey, Joe Bob. Got some coffee on." *Herd him toward
the house. Keep him away from the shed. Jesus God. What the
hell's he doing here?* "I was just about to start dinner. You
staying?"

"Can't stay that long. Wife's got some veal for tonight.
But I'll take some coffee, for sure." Joe Bob Fontaine

hooked a thumb over his shoulder. "Saw Rusty takin on outta here like the devil was on his tail."

"Teens," Wheaton said with a roll of his eyes, and Fontaine laughed.

"Yeah, I know all about it."

Fontaine had three teenagers, two boys and a girl, and a fat wife who sat around in the house most of the day, watching the tube and consuming chocolate bonbons. Fontaine himself wasn't exactly slender; he liked his beer in the evening and it showed. He was going bald, he had bad teeth. But pity the fools who mistook Fontaine for a bumbling cop. He had the instincts of a hunter, he knew his job, and he did not make social visits.

They went inside the house and Wheaton started a pot of coffee and put on another pot of water for spaghetti. His mind raced, calculating the odds that Lydia would finish up with the girl in the next ten or fifteen minutes and head up for the house. His only hope was to get Fontaine out of here as quickly as possible, but without causing suspicion.

The sheriff made himself right at home at the kitchen table, one of the main reasons Wheaton kept the electronics upstairs. He lit one of his stinking cigars and chatted on about the difficulties of parenthood. And all the time, his eyes moved restlessly around the kitchen, as though he were looking for a specific something.

"Hey, where's that gorgeous dog of Rusty's?"

"He probably took her with him. How's Stephanie doing? I heard she had the flu."

And on it went, the innocuous exchange, the way they circled each other over the seemingly casual conversation. Then, the crux of it, the reason for Fontaine's visit: "You know, Pete, I don't give a good goddamn what a man does in his own life. But this island is a hive of bullshit and gossip and the gossip now is that you're carryin on with a nigger."

That word shocked Wheaton. He hadn't heard it for decades and he had never heard it in his own home, when he was minding his own business. "Excuse me?" he managed to say.

"Me, I don't call 'em that, what with the new laws and all, but we've got people here on the island who aren't so, well, open-minded. Just thought I should pass that along."

"And who's this *black* person supposed to be?"

"Dunno. I'm just passing on what I've heard. Seems there's some concern, what with Rusty living here, what kinda example does that set for him and on and on . . ." He rolled his eyes toward the ceiling to show that he didn't buy into that small-time racial thinking.

But, of course he did. Fontaine was a small-town southern racist, the kind who maybe wore a white sheet at night and burned crosses on lawns.

"Frankly, Joe Bob, I haven't met a woman yet, black, white, blue, or green, who compares to my ex-wife."

Fontaine, like everyone else around here, believed that Wheaton's wife had divorced him a decade ago to marry her younger lover. He also believed that Rusty was his nephew. "Like I said, Pete, what a man does in his private life's no concern of mine. I just wanted to pass this on so you know what folks are saying."

"I appreciate it, Joe Bob." *Now just move along.* Wheaton pushed away from the table, ostensibly to get the coffeepot, and stole a look through the window. No Lydia. *Stay in the shed.* "You need a refill on that coffee, Joe Bob?"

"No, thanks. I'd best be pushing off. Stop in at the house some night soon and we'll have a couple beers."

"Sounds good, Joe Bob."

Wheaton walked him outside to his car. Even at dusk, the heat was extreme and seemed to drip through the branches of the pines and banyans on either side of the long, winding driveway. The air was so still that each breath felt as if he were inhaling cotton. He tried to see the property from Fontaine's point of view, the towering trees, the tidy front yard blooming with anything colorful that would grow in the summer heat, the A-frame house. He noticed that Fontaine's eyes kept darting toward the path that twisted down through the woods to the shed and felt a gnawing anxiety that Fontaine's visit had a purpose other than to pass on gossip and hearsay.

The sheriff clipped his shades to his shirt, shades right out of *Deliverance*, which in 1968 hadn't become a movie yet, hooked his thumbs in his belt, and hoisted his trousers. "You tell that boy of yours that if he's still interested in earning some extra money this summer, I need someone to cut my lawn and do some handy work around the house."

The anxiety in the pit of Wheaton's stomach bit a little more deeply. "I sure will, Joe Bob."

Fontaine got into his car and drove off down the road, past the woods. Wheaton stood in the driveway, waving, questions crashing around him. When had Rusty spoken to Fontaine about earning extra money? Why hadn't he mentioned it to Wheaton? But, even more to the point, why would Rusty seek out the sheriff at all?

Eleven

Annie knew she had slid down a rabbit's hole, that she was in Wonderland, and the white rabbit was now giving her the tour of the place. But it was the caterpillar who whispered, *Eat this, drink that.* The caterpillar didn't look quite right, though. Its face was dark, it wasn't smoking a hooka, and it had a human body.

Now she nibbled at the edge of a mushroom and suddenly began to grow and grow. In seconds, she seemed to be ten feet tall and she could hear music, someone singing about the white rabbit. *Go ask Alice. She's ten feet tall.* Way up where she was, she could see someone lying on a couch below, a girl, definitely a girl, she could see the girl's hair fanned out against the pillow. A large black woman tended to the girl, soaking her feet in wet cloths, lifting her head, and urging her to sip from a cup. Now and then, the black woman sang and puffed on a cigar, blowing smoke up and down the girl's body.

Annie suddenly shrank and floated up, up, up toward the ceiling, and hovered there, watching the black woman at the stove. She picked up one container after another, shook some of the contents into the pot, stirred, sniffed, stirred, and shook some more. She floated down closer to the girl on the couch and saw her own face, her own body, and suddenly she was inside that body again, unable to focus her eyes.

"Alice?" she murmured. "Are you Alice?"

"No, hon, I'm Lydia. And I need you to help me get you better, okay? Sip a little of this."

And the woman's hand slid under Annie's head, lifting it. She tasted something warm and sweet and it tasted so good as it went down her parched throat that she begged for more. More. The woman held the cup to her lips again and Annie drank. "That's enough for right now. It'll break that fever and get you back on your feet."

Annie loved the sound of this woman's voice—*her name? What's her name? Alice or Lydia? Or something else?*—and started to follow it somewhere. But she was afraid that if she followed the woman's voice, she would be defenseless again and the man would come back.

"Listen," she said hoarsely, and groped for the woman's hand. She held on tightly, terrified that she was a dream or a ghost. "Are you real?"

"Oh, yes."

"Find my mom, please. That man . . . he kidnapped me right off the beach where my mom and I were—"

"Ssshh, little one. You've got the fever bad and you're—"

"No, listen," Annie hissed and grabbed on to the woman's arm, pulling herself to a seated position. The room rocked like a boat, her breath caught in her throat, and for a moment she thought she would choke. Then the words came out in a rushing tide. "He came up the beach with a cast on his arm and said his engine had died and did we have any tools and my mom couldn't just turn him away and he hit her with that fake cast and I started running and he chased me and and and . . . and I know she'll find me 'cause she and I are connected and she always knows when something's happened to me and . . ."

Annie fell back against the pillow, exhausted. The dog stuck her head under Annie's arm, licked her face, her arm, her face again.

"You must promise me something." The black woman leaned close to Annie. "Don't do anything to make him angry. I'll do what I can to help you. Rusty is trustworthy and you can always get a message to me through him. He's not happy with the situation. He's on our side. But I must do this carefully, without endangering Rusty. Do you understand what I'm saying?"

"Yes." Did she speak or did she just imagine it? Maybe she was dreaming, maybe it was all a dream. "Am I dreaming?"

"You're dreaming awake, little one."

"Don't leave me, please."

"I have all night, *mi amor.*"

Spanish, this woman spoke Spanish, just like her mom did. Like her father had. Like Nadine.

"Take another sip of this and then try to sleep," the dream voice said.

Annie sipped, then the woman touched her hand to Annie's forehead and drew it down over her eyes, shutting them.

"I'm going now," Annie said, and away she went, walking around the room, moving through it like a breeze.

The dog saw her and trotted after her, across the room to the windows, the door. Annie pressed her hands to the door and suddenly found herself on the other side of it, the dog barking in the room behind her. Annie turned and stuck her head through the door and saw the woman—*Lydia*—staring at the door. "What is it, Sunny?" Lydia asked, rising from the couch.

Sunny barked again and Lydia hurried over to the

door, opened it, looked outside. "Nothing there, girl. Just the darkness. The trees."

And me! Annie shouted.

The woman didn't seem to hear her, but the dog did. Sunny barked and leaped up and her paws went through Annie. It felt weird, as if a warm breeze had just passed through her.

"The girl's ghost-walking, right, Sunny?" Lydia said.

A ghost? I'm not a ghost. I'm alive, I'm moving, breathing . . .

She wanted to explore the woods, to see where she was, and abruptly found herself in the middle of it, in the darkness. She heard the crash of waves, saw the stars, the lonely moon. Owls hooted, crickets chirred, she didn't like it, she wanted light, safety, she wanted her mom.

She felt a sharp tug at the back of her head and abruptly snapped back into fever, pain, the horror.

"Sleep, little one," the woman whispered.

2

Her fever broke around four that morning, sweat streaming from her pores, the stink of the sickness permeating the room.

Lydia filled a large metal bowl with warm water and sponged the girl's face, her arms and legs and feet. She stripped off her soiled clothes and dressed her in a clean T-shirt and soft cotton shorts, then lifted her head and brushed her wet hair into a loose ponytail. She covered Annie with a clean sheet and went into the kitchen to prepare one more bit of magic, a recipe that her grandmother had given her in the last months of her life.

La penúltima brujería, her grandmother had called

it. The penultimate witchery. Sooner or later, every soul making a journey through physical life reached this critical point, whether to release the body or to press on through physical life. This spiritual essence helped link body and soul to make that critical decision. She had used it on Rusty and he had lived. She had given it to Becky Sawyer and she had died. Antonio Pantello also had died and so had the boy from Miami. Either way, the soul chose. If the soul chose life, as Rusty's soul had, then the body used this concoction to give it the edge it needed to conquer the time sickness.

The history of this potion went back centuries, perhaps even thousands of years, to Nigeria, where Lydia's ancestors were born. She didn't pretend to know how it worked, she only knew that it followed the desires of the soul. And in a battle like this one, she thought, it was the final arbiter between life and death.

The recipe was complex but unwritten. Her grandmother had recited it to her word by word, just as her grandmother had before her and so on down through the centuries. Some of the ingredients were found only on the African continent and Lydia obtained them through a specialty shop in Miami, at a hideous expense. Other ingredients were common and some of them she grew herself.

The unspoken law in her family was that the recipe and its administration were to be passed on to the firstborn female in each generation, but Lydia had no heirs. Her husband, Enrique, had been shot down during a civil rights protest five years into their marriage, in 1964, and they hadn't had children. Lydia doubted that she would marry again. There were men that she dated, men with whom she slept, but no men whom she loved as she had loved Enrique.

After he had died, she had moved from Miami to the

keys, the end of the line, as far south as she could get without returning to Cuba. And here she was, a part-time sculptress, a part-time cleaning woman, a part-time healer, living out her part-time life.

Until her passion for art went somewhere, she needed Peter Wheat and what he paid her to treat his time orphans. For every child she treated, he paid her a thousand in cash. For every visit she made to his miserable little shed, he paid her five hundred more.

Her art had never come close to paying her that much. She couldn't afford to break her silence. But even whores had their limits and she had reached hers.

Lydia heard the first twitters of birds outside. It would be dawn soon and the next twenty-four to forty-eight hours would determine whether this child would live or die.

She put ice in the pot, cooling the concoction, and when it was tepid, poured it into a glass pitcher. She put more ice into a cup, stuck a straw into it, and filled a glass. She put the container in the fridge and carried the glass over to the coffee table. She kneeled beside the couch, slipped her hand under the girl's head, and woke her. "Drink this," she said, and coaxed the straw between her lips. The girl sipped and sipped until half the glass was gone.

No promises, child. But she felt good about what she had done here tonight. Good, except for Peter.

She gathered up her things, stuck the girl's soiled clothes in her bag, whistled softly for Sunny. The dog, tail wagging, followed her outside. She didn't bother locking the door. That was Peter's job, not hers.

Granddaddy would be proud of the healing and ashamed of the blood money I take. Thinking of her grandfather brought back the strange woman at the colony who had read her as though her entire past were transparent. A spooky woman. Lydia refused to think about her right now.

As she approached the house, she saw Rusty's old car in the driveway, next to Peter's truck. Neither the screen door nor the wood door was locked. She stepped into the silent, dark kitchen, and listened. Listened hard. Not a sound. Sunny's claws made ticking sounds against the floor. The dog ate from her bowl, lapped water, and these sounds followed Lydia through the kitchen and into the hallway. She paused at the bottom of the stairs, listening again.

She slipped off her shoes, set her bag on the floor, and went up the stairs. She passed Rusty's room, where the door was shut, and continued to the end of the hall, where the door to Peter's bedroom stood ajar. She went inside, her bare feet moving silently across the old wooden floors, and paused at the side of his bed. It suddenly occurred to her that she could pick up one of the potted plants in the nearby windowsill and smash it down over his head, ending this nightmare. But she was no killer. She reached out and turned on the lamp.

Peter raised himself up on his elbows, blinking against the light. "Will she make it?" he asked, his voice hoarse with sleep.

Lydia took hold of his stubbly chin, squeezing it, the bones like sponge beneath her powerful fingers. "You are no better than the white men who hung my grandfather, Pete. It stops here. With this child. The next time you call for help, I won't come. Do you understand me?"

He pushed her hand away and sat all the way up. *"Will she make it?"* he repeated.

"The next twenty-four to forty-eight hours will tell."

He swung his skinny legs over the side of the bed,

opened the nightstand drawer, removed a thick envelope.

"You can take your next child to the ER," she said.

"You know I can't do that."

She grabbed one of the potted plants and slammed it down against the corner of the nightstand. He wrenched back, glanced down at the mess on the floor, then up at her. Their eyes locked, and in his she saw madness and rage and something else, something unspeakable. The silence stretched so tightly she could hear him breathing.

"I don't know why you feel you must steal other people's children, Pete, but I will no longer be a part of this." She snatched the envelope from his hand. "I will see the child once more to make sure she is cured, but after that you will not buy my silence."

She dropped the envelope into her bag and headed for the door.

"Lydia," he said, "the sheriff stopped by right after you'd gotten here. I hope your car is parked in the field across the street."

"Fontaine?" She turned around. "What'd he want?"

"I don't know about his real reason for stopping by, but what he said was that there was some gossip circulating that I was involved with a black woman. But that's not the word he used."

Lydia laughed. "Honey, to a man like Fontaine, if you've got a good suntan, you're a nigger. And that's all he wanted?"

"So he said."

She shrugged. "Maybe he knows something, maybe he's just poking around. Either way, he's no nigger lover, Pete, and me and mine stay clear of the man. And considering what you've been doing up here, you'd best do the same."

"You're as guilty as I am, Lydia."

"I'm here because of the children."

"You're here because I pay you well."

Her eyes didn't just bore through him; they pierced him to the core, forcing him to look away. Then she turned and left the room, the house, the sick madness of the white man's world.

Twelve

The Tango Key Bridge, completed in 1985, spanned twelve miles of open water across Florida Bay, an engineering feat that staggered Sheppard's imagination every time he crossed the damn thing. It rose forty feet above the water, a maze of cables, struts, and steel, supported at either end and at the midway point by concrete pilings two feet thick. It had taken six years to build and pieces of it had been assembled elsewhere and shipped to the site on barges. The only time he felt any sort of vertigo on the bridge was when the traffic stalled, as it had done moments ago, stranding him six miles from land in either direction.

He lowered his window and stuck his head out, trying to see what the holdup was. But there were too many trucks ahead of him, heavy trucks, he thought, and wondered how much weight the bridge could hold. At this very moment, the struts overhead might be straining, fraying, getting ready to snap. Scenes of collapsing bridges from a dozen movies came to mind, cars plunging, cables collapsing, chunks of concrete and steel falling, people screaming . . .

Sheppard knuckled his aching eyes. The traffic jam seemed to be a fitting metaphor for this investigation. They were closing in on the four-day marker and he still didn't have a single solid lead on Patrick Wheaton's location. But at least Wheaton's ex-wife was back in town and had agreed to speak to him. She and her present husband lived on an estate outside of Key West and, if the traffic would just get moving, he would get there on time.

At Nadine's invitation, he had moved into the spare bedroom with his cat and some of his clothes and had spent the last two nights there. He had set up a work area in the dining room, where he had laid out a time line, files on Wheaton, the black water mass, and on the other abductions. The dining room table now looked like a giant case board, a visual rendition of the investigation. And so far, it all led to a big fat question mark.

From the very beginning, Sheppard had been looking for a strategy in these abductions, for something tangible that linked the victims. But other than the fact that all had lived in the keys, there were no apparent similarities among them. Different ages, different races, different genders. Yesterday, however, he had discovered a fifth abduction case, Morgan Washington, an Afro-American kid from Miami, that had happened two years ago. He had called the investigating agent and found out that although no chloroform cloth had been uncovered, the general MO fit the other cases.

Rusty Everett, twelve, dark-haired, Marathon. Taken in 1997. Lived in a trailer park with his dysfunctional family, an alcoholic father and bipolar mother and two younger siblings. Social Services had made home visits. Nabbed as he walked home from middle school. The cloth had been found a day later in some bushes, long after the chloroform had evaporated, but forensics had pulled off a miracle and tagged the substance that had been on the cloth.

Becky Sawyer, eleven, Key Largo. Taken in 1999 while she played in her own neighborhood. No witnesses. Blue-collar neighborhood. Her father was a pastor in a local church, her mother was a homemaker and Sunday school teacher, both of them hellfire and brimstone Bible thumpers. Four other kids in the household. According to neighbors and the observations of the detective who had initially investigated the case, the Sawyers ran a very tight, strict ship. Becky had few friends and even fewer liberties.

Antonio Pantello, nine. He lived on Tango, but was taken from Sugarloaf Key six weeks ago, while playing down near the water of an estate where his Cuban mother worked as a maid. His Mexican father, a mechanic who owned his own business, had taken out a loan against the business to post a reward, which the mother's employer then doubled. There were three other siblings in the family, all younger.

The Pantello family was unusual in several ways. Although they were staunch Catholics, the mother was a renowned practitioner of Santería, who knew Goot's grandmother, also a *santera*. During one of Sheppard's early interviews with the family, he had commented on the altar in the living room, where fresh honey and sweets had been left as an offering to one of the saints, in the hopes that the saint would intervene in the affairs of man and bring Carlos home.

"Eloggua?" he had asked the mother.

She'd given him an odd look, shocked that an American cop would know enough to name any saint in the vast pantheon that she worshipped, and had finally nodded. Then she addressed him in the ancient language of Santería, in the Yoruba dialect from the heart of Africa, where Santería had been born, and he had responded in that dialect, uttering the few words that he knew. The mother had started to cry and insisted that he accompany her to the shed out back, where she conducted her mystical work.

And there, she had read her mysterious cards, relating things about his life that she couldn't possibly have known. She had cleansed his energy with smoke and incantations, and by the time she was done he felt as if he had just traveled into the deepest heart of ancient man.

"If you can do all this," he'd said to her, "then surely you can see where your son is."

"He is dead," she had whispered, and began to sob. "He is buried on a hill that overlooks the sea. His spirit comes to me, but I cannot hear his voice. The man who took him is of this time, but not of this time, guided by things we cannot understand. I do not know any more than that."

Morgan Washington, nine, Miami. He was taken in March 2001, while biking to a friend's house. According to the investigating agent in Miami, the Washington family had its own dysfunctional signature. Washington's mother was a single parent with four other kids to raise, all of them by different fathers. She'd been on welfare for most of the boy's life. His father was doing time for armed robbery.

And then there was Annie. Nabbed two days ago on Little Horse Key. Family? Unusual by the standards of consensus reality. Father murdered when she was three. Lived with her mother and great-grandmother, both of them psychics. Fled the publicity after the case in Lauderdale.

Sheppard reached for the tape recorder on the passenger seat, clicked it on. "The thread that ties all these abductions together is dysfunctional or unusual families. Abuse, alcoholism, mental illness, religious fanaticism, the weirdness of Santería, psychics, and an atypical family structure. Does he see himself as their savior? Does he think he's rescuing them? Is that it, you miserable fuck? And then what? What do you do with them afterward?"

Don't go there.

But he already had gone there hundreds of times, speculating on the vast and terrifying possibilities. Torture. Pedophilia. Perversions.

"Wheaton has never demanded a ransom. He apparently watches the children for a time, learning about their families, their routines and habits. Annie's kidnapping was the first in which he has taken a child in the presence of an adult. Does that mean he's getting more daring? Or more desperate? In the Pantello case, where the boy was nabbed while he was outside, the mother was nearby, but in the house. The chloroform cloth was found in all the abductions except for that of Morgan Washington."

Sheppard turned off the recorder and reached for one of the yellow notepads where he'd taken notes on the black water mass. Did it fit into this picture? If so, how?

The first documented instance of the mass appearing off the Florida coast dated back sixty years, to 1942, when it formed off Pensacola, in the northwestern part of the state. From then through 2003, he had counted eighteen other instances. But there didn't seem to be any pattern to the formations, no particular time intervals, no one season that predominated. The sizes of the masses varied from a half mile square to the largest mass that had formed eight months ago, which covered about 750 square miles. It had formed on the Atlantic side of the state just twice, off Jacksonville in 1989 and off Fort Pierce in 2001. On the west side of the state, the formations had ranged from Pensacola to the keys, with the water around the keys taking the prize for the most formations: 1952, 1962, 1964, 1968, 1983, 1994, 1997, 1999, 2003.

It bothered him that the last four times the mass had

formed somewhere in the keys, someone had disappeared. In 1994, it was Wheaton. In 1997, the Everett kid had been abducted. In 1999, Becky Sawyer had been taken. And this year, just six weeks apart, the Pantello kid and Annie.

It was as if the pattern began with Wheaton's disappearance in 1994. Even if that were true, what did the black water masses have to do with any of it? Granted, no one knew where Wheaton had gone. He might have perished at sea or he might be living a high life overseas on the money he'd stolen from his ex-wife. But they had a positive ID for his presence on the beach shortly after Sheppard had spoken to Mira and they'd found the chloroform cloth, the only link among the abductions. If Sheppard was correct that Wheaton's motives had something to do with each child's family life, then he had to be living close enough to the keys to be able to observe the kids, study them, get a sense of their lives.

And if he'd been observing them, then surely someone would have recognized him. Unless he'd disguised himself somehow.

But none of that provided a connection to the mass.

Sheppard's cell phone rang. He glanced at the caller ID and considered not taking the call. But if he didn't take the call, relentless Leo Dillard would just keep after him or would go through Goot to reach him.

"Hey, Leo. What's up?"

"Looks like you've got a serial kidnapper on your hands."

Dillard's voice instantly conjured his face, plump as a full moon, with a crooked nose and a mole on the curve of his jaw and thick white hair that was his greatest vanity. It was no secret that Dillard had resented Sheppard since his first day on board, but it had taken him a few months to realize the animosity stemmed from the fact that Dillard had wanted the job that Sheppard had landed. Even though it would have been a demotion for Dillard, who was second in command of the southeast division, Sheppard knew he viewed Tango as the living manifestation of a Jimmy Buffet song. A hammock beneath palm trees. Ice-cold beers and margaritas served by sweet young babes in string bikinis. A permanent vacation while drawing a paycheck. All that aside, Tango was a more desirable place to live than Birmingham, Alabama.

"And your point is?" Sheppard asked.

"I'm in town and I'd like to see everything you and Goot have on this case."

Why, Leo? So you get can the publicity when we crack the sucker? "Right now, we don't have much." He sure as hell wasn't going to tell Dillard about the black water. "We've put out an APB on our primary suspect, Patrick Wheaton."

"The man vanished in 1994, Shep. How can he be the primary suspect?"

"Photographic evidence." He quickly explained about Mira's digital camera.

"Let's get together this afternoon."

Let's not. "Goot and I can meet you wherever you're staying."

"The Hilltop Inn. Six o'clock."

"See you then."

Sheppard disconnected before Dillard could say anything else. The fact that he was already on Tango worried Sheppard. The only time Dillard left Birmingham to go out into the field was when he believed it would further his own ambitions. To maintain control over this investigation, he and Goot would have to play this in a circumspect manner, giving Dillard only the bare minimum. And in the meantime, Sheppard would call the big boss, Baker Jernan, the man who had hired him, and ask him to keep Dillard out of the investigation.

Traffic began to inch forward and Sheppard dropped the notepad on the passenger seat and turned on the recorder again. "I did a Web search for Wheaton and found several articles about his disappearance, but most of the stuff was about the marine summer camp he started for teens on Tango and about his parents. They were molecular biologists, Nobel nominees. The mother committed suicide in 1968, his only sibling, a stepsister, died in a car accident that same year, the father died a few years later. Wheaton would've been about sixteen when his mother and sister died, young enough for scars."

But would those deaths have scarred him deeply enough to turn him into a child abductor?

Granted, the line between sanity and madness was a fine one. Even Bundy, despite his perversions, had been able to function in a normal society at times. True-crime writer Ann Rule, for instance, had gotten to know him in the newsroom of the paper where they both worked. So it was possible that the marine summer camps that Wheaton had run for teens had been a way for him to target his victims.

The quagmire finally broke and traffic picked up speed. Sheppard called his assistant at the office and asked her to find out if Rusty Everett had attended the Tango Marine Lab summer camp between 1991, when he would have been old enough to attend, and 1993, the last summer before Wheaton's disappearance. He wasn't sure what this would prove if it turned out to be true. Probably nothing. But it would be personally satisfying to Sheppard. It would mean he had made some sort of connection. And right now, any connection was better than nothing.

Five minutes later, he drew up behind Goot's navy

blue Jeep, parked at the curb in front of the Lenier estate. Goot got out, hurried over to Sheppard's car, and got in the passenger side. "Drive on through the gates, James. The lady has spoken over the intercom."

"Yeah? And we peons have been called for an audience?"

"Actually, her exact words were, 'Ring the bell and the gate will open. Take the first left turn and keep driving until you see the stable.'"

"The stable," Sheppard repeated.

"Yeah. How many private stables you figure there are in and around Key West?"

"Just this one."

"How much is she worth again?" Goot asked.

"I don't know about now. But for fifty years, the Leniers were *the* largest citrus growers in the state. Then in the late eighties, a conglomerate bought them out for around eighty million. She remarried about five years ago, guy named Steven Nymes. His net worth surpasses hers. He was a childhood friend. Summers on the Vineyard and in Europe, you know, all the stuff F. Scott wrote about."

"Shit, man, I don't have to read Fitzgerald to know the very rich and I have zip in common."

A kind of hunger claimed Goot's face as he surveyed the grounds, a lush and private paradise of fruit trees, banyans and pines and palms, and grass the color of Oz. Bougainvillea vines climbed the massive trunks of the banyans and spilled over the tidy white fence that surrounded a swimming pool. Sheppard glimpsed the house through the trees, a two-story sprawl with huge picture windows.

Sheppard took the first left and followed a winding dirt road through the trees. The sweetness of the air wafted through the open windows. It felt like the kiss of wealth against his cheek. The island had its share of money, but Sheppard didn't think there were many people in *this* particular league.

"By the way, Dillard is in town," Sheppard said. "We're supposed to meet him at the Hilltop Inn at six."

"Shit, that means dinner. I don't feel like breaking bread with that asshole."

"We'll tell him five and we give him next to nothing on this investigation. Agreed?"

"Absolutely."

A quarter of a mile later, Sheppard parked between two electric carts in front of a concrete stable that looked to be about as large as his entire house. Beyond it lay paddocks and fenced pastures where horses grazed.

Goot whistled softly. "Why would Wheaton want to leave all this?"

"The marriage sucked?"

"C'mon, when there's this much money, amigo, you make it work. It's amazing he only stole half a million from her."

As they got out, an impeccably dressed man in riding clothes stood in the wide, arched doorway of the stable, watching them, and tapping a riding crop against his open palm. He smelled of prep schools and Ivy League colleges and when he spoke, his tone suggested that Sheppard and Goot were on a par with the hired help.

"I assume you're from the FBI?"

"You're Steven Nymes?"

"Yes."

"I'm Agent Sheppard, this is Agent Gutierrez."

"I thought this business with Wheaton was put to bed years ago."

Interesting choice of words, Sheppard thought. "Nothing's been *put to bed*, Mr. Nymes. The case is still open and some new information has surfaced."

"Such as?"

"We'd like to discuss it with your wife," Goot said.

He peered down his regal nose at them. "Who will discuss it with me, gentlemen."

Sheppard wasn't in the mood for this horse's ass. "We'll find her ourselves." He swept past Nymes, who looked startled that the hired help would dare to be so presumptuous, and Goot fell into step beside him.

"She's in the office," Nymes called after them.

"Fucking control freak," Goot muttered.

Odors reached Sheppard—the rank stink of horse manure and the sweeter smell of hay and something else, something that ran through the other smells like a current, a scent he couldn't identify. But as they entered the office, it struck him; it was Julia Lenier's perfume and it smelled expensive.

She was an absolute knockout, a natural blonde with the complexion of an angel and the kind of body you dreamed about when your testosterone was racing. She was on the phone and gestured at the chairs in front of her desk. Sheppard and Goot exchanged a glance; they both knew this ploy. They had used it themselves. The person behind the desk held the power. They both remained standing. Goot, in fact, moved restlessly around the office, inspecting the photographs, the plaques, the horse *stuff*. Sheppard studied the woman and summed her up in a single word: class.

"Sorry about that." She hung up the receiver, flashed a smile that could light up the darkest corners of any room, and stood, extending her beautiful hand. "I'm Julia Lenier."

"Agent Wayne Sheppard. And this is Agent Gutierrez."

Her grip was strong, her hand soft and cool. Maybe, he thought, he and Goot were mistaken about the desk and the chairs as a power ploy. They all sat down and he reached into a zippered pocket of his laptop's carrying case and turned on his tape recorder. He also brought out the photos of Wheaton and set these on his lap.

"You mentioned over the phone that there's news about Patrick."

Sheppard got right to the point. "He's implicated in a series of kidnappings."

Julia Lenier looked shocked. "He's *alive?*" She barely breathed the words.

Sheppard set the photos on her desk. "These were taken three days ago, shortly before he abducted a thirteen-year-old girl."

She took the photos and went through them slowly. "This is him. Older, but definitely Patrick. But you're saying he *kidnapped* a girl? I find that impossible to believe. Patrick loved kids, that's why he ran a marine camp every summer."

"It's not just one girl," Goot said. "He's implicated in three, possibly four other kidnappings."

"If he loved kids so much," Sheppard said, "why didn't you two have any children?"

"I didn't want kids. Then in early 1994, I guess it was, when I realized our marriage was falling apart, I got this ridiculous idea that kids would save our marriage. I tried to get pregnant and discovered that Patrick was sterile."

"Was that when he was investigating the black water mass?"

Her expression darkened and she leaned forward and spoke quietly. "I don't have any idea how much either of you know about Patrick. But he never *investigated* that mass. He *courted* it, *obsessed* over it. It became his passion. He was gone so much that I thought he was having an affair and hired a detective to follow him. He said that Patrick was spending twelve, thirteen, sometimes fourteen hours a day out in that mass. The night he allegedly got lost out there—and was gone for a week, do you know about that?"

Sheppard and Goot nodded.

"Well, the detective was following him. He claims that Patrick literally disappeared into a blackness so profound that it was like the blackness swallowed him."

"We didn't see any reports to that effect in the file," Goot remarked.

Color now rushed up the sides of her pale neck, a vein throbbed at her temple. "Of course not. I didn't tell that to the police or to the FBI. It sounded so . . . so ludicrous. But what I am telling you is that something very strange was happening in that mass. And when Patrick took off with my money, that's where he went. Into the mass. I'm sure of it. I don't know what the hell that thing is out there, but it's not just black water." She paused, looked at each of them, shook her head. "I can tell you don't believe a word I'm saying."

"Right now, Ms. Lenier, we're just gathering facts," Sheppard replied. But he happened to agree with her that something odd might be happening out there. "Was there something unusually traumatic that happened in Mr. Wheaton's childhood?"

"Traumatic?" She laughed, but it was a sharp, biting sound. "You mean, besides the fact that his mother committed suicide and that he was, if you'll pardon my crassness, screwing his stepsister?"

Sheppard knew about the mother, but not the stepsister. "You know that for a fact about the stepsister?"

"Here's the picture. Imagine it. Patrick's mother was divorced from his father when he was just two. A year later, she meets Dan Wheaton, widowed, with a three-year-old daughter. They're both scientists, researchers, have everything in common. They get married, Wheaton adopts Patrick, now they're one big happy family.

"Flash forward. Times are good. The Wheatons are both professors of molecular biology at MIT, Nobel material. They're never home. It's just Patrick and Eva, together all the time. Eva was seducing him when mom and dad weren't home and he never told anyone because he was in love with her. Two years into the whole perverted thing, she was killed in a car accident. She was with another guy, they were both drinking. To make matters worse the autopsy reveals that she was pregnant. Guess whose child it was? The mother ended up killing herself, the father drank himself into an early grave, and Patrick went into therapy—and was eventually committed."

"Committed where?" Goot asked.

"Therapy with whom?" Sheppard asked simultaneously.

"They had a second home on Sugarloaf where they went holidays and summers. I think the psychiatrist was in Miami and so was the hospital where he was committed for six or seven months."

"How old was he when his relationship with Eva started?" Sheppard asked.

"Fourteen. She was fifteen. But at some level, it started long before that. You won't find anything about the commitment in any record, Mr. Sheppard. The medical records were sealed because of his age and later expunged."

Sheppard, an attorney, had never heard of medical records being expunged and immediately suspected that someone had been paid off. "Did you know all this before your marriage started disintegrating?"

"No. I learned all this two weeks before he split."

"He told you about it?" Goot asked.

"Hardly. Patrick never volunteered information about himself. The detective I hired uncovered it and then I confronted Patrick. He said it was all true and so what? It had happened a long time ago. Somewhere in here . . ." She opened a drawer in her desk, rummaged, opened another drawer. ". . . I have some old newspaper clippings and things that Ted George—the detective—collected. He died a couple of years ago and his daughter brought me the files and stuff before she left." She brought a thick manila folder out of the drawer, unfastened the clasp, and slipped out papers, notebooks, photos, a gold mine of material. "You can take all this. But just return it when you're finished with it."

Nymes stepped through the doorway. "Julia, your instructor's here."

"I'll be along in a few minutes."

"He's already been here ten minutes." Nymes looked pointedly at Sheppard and Goot, as if he expected them to say they were just leaving. Sheppard refused to play his game and he and Goot remained silent.

"I said, I'll be finished in a few minutes," Julia repeated.

"Suit yourself," he snapped, and left.

"I apologize for my husband. He never liked Patrick and can't stand the fact that he was part of my past." Then she stood, signaling that she was finished. "I really need to get to my riding lesson. But if I can do anything else to help you, please let me know."

"I have one more question," Sheppard said as the three of them walked out of the office. "How did you discover that Patrick had stolen money?"

"My accountant discovered it. We had several money markets in both our names. Over a period of three or four months, Patrick apparently had been withdrawing twenty-five here, forty there. Some of the withdrawals were electronic and traceable. They were deposited in an account in Miami in the name of Peter Wheat."

Nymes had come up behind them as they were talking and now he butted in. "All of this is in the police records."

"Actually, Mr. Nymes," said Sheppard, "this is the first

thing I've heard of Peter Wheat. So please shut up and let your wife finish."

Color rose in Nymes's neck, just as it had in his wife's, an emotional barometer, and when he spoke, his voice shook with anger. "I think it's time you gentlemen left. Now."

Goot whirled around, his Latin temper getting the best of him. "And I think it's time that *you* learned some manners. Wheaton's most recent abduction is the daughter of Agent Sheppard's fiancée. So knock it off and let us finish our business. *Sir.*"

Nymes looked like he was on the verge of a stroke, Goot's fists were clenched, and the air between them crackled with tension. "Jesus, Steven," Julia Lenier said, her voice tight, barely controlled. "Leave us alone."

He had the good sense to walk off, but whacked his riding crop against everything within reach, making it clear that no one had heard the last of it. Julia Lenier then continued without apologizing for her husband this time. "It took us a while to trace the money and Patrick was gone by then and the account only had a thousand dollars or so in it." She paused and regarded Sheppard with genuine compassion. "I'm truly sorry about your fiancée's daughter, Mr. Sheppard."

Minutes later, Sheppard and Goot headed back up the winding dirt road with the manila envelope jammed with notes and photos and newspaper clippings and a name that they could run through every database available to them. Finally, Sheppard thought, they had a lead that might amount to something.

Thirteen

Mira measured the passage of time by the rising and setting of the sun. This proved to be flawed, though, because sometimes when she woke, it was dark and she didn't know if she had slept around the clock or for only a few hours.

In her more lucid moments, Mira knew that her body raged with fever and nothing helped—not cool baths, not ice packs, not even the Bayer aspirin she'd bought her first evening here, at the colony's small grocery store. She stayed in the cabin, sucking on ice, shivering under a blanket, nibbling periodically at one of the mangos she'd bought, and trying not to think of Annie, as alone and lost as she was. She forced herself to get up every so often to shower, use the bathroom, and make a few notes on her Pocket PC, describing how she felt. She didn't know why she bothered, but thought it might be important later.

Mira also struggled with the horrendous noise in her head. Sometimes, it was like white noise, annoying but tolerable. She called the white noise level one. Other times, it was the humming she'd experienced before, which varied from a soft almost melodic sound—level two—to the painful shriek that she'd heard when she had read Lydia, level three.

Occasionally, the noise became something else altogether, indescribable and physically agonizing, as if her skull were about to implode. That was level four. When these episodes happened they lasted from ten to twenty minutes and, afterward, her entire body felt as if it were in the throes of some huge upheaval. She vomited everything she ate or drank, her legs felt rubbery and unsteady when she walked, her head spun, and she was too weak to do anything except sleep. This part of it lasted for untold hours in which she alternated between deep, dreamless sleep and sleep chopped up by dreams, visions, voices. At these times, her fever spiked into delirium, wiping her memory clean of everything.

She suspected that the source of this noise phenomenon was a result of whatever had happened to her out there in the darkness of the gulf, the impossible thing that had taken her thirty-five years back in time. It had done something to her psychically, blown open all her circuits, allowing her to see things in detail that hadn't been available to her before. She was beginning to understand the nuances of whatever this was, but still hadn't found a way to control it.

The physical manifestations and its repercussions worried her most of all. Not only was she sick and alone, but she was displaced in time and didn't know anyone whom she could trust about her situation. It was worse than being alone and sick in a foreign country. She couldn't just get herself to an airport and fly home; she didn't have any idea how the hell she had gotten here or how to get back to her own time, and even if she did she wouldn't leave without Annie.

Her daughter was somewhere on the island and still alive, she had sensed that much. And if she was here, then so was the bastard who had taken her. Since Mira already had decided she couldn't go to the police, it meant that when she got well she would be completely alone in her search. To find Annie, she would need all of her intuitive skills and, quite frankly, she doubted if her skills, even in a heightened state, were good enough to locate her daughter. She didn't know where to begin, didn't know who the man was or what motivated him, and the longer she lay here, trying to regain her strength, the more likely it became that the man would move Annie. Or hurt her. Or worse.

In her darker moments, and there were plenty of them, she worried about what would happen to Annie if she herself died. No one would know Annie was here. Even if Sheppard figured it out, it didn't mean he would be able to do anything about it. But at least three people had gone back in time, so didn't that mean Sheppard might be able to do it, too?

When she woke on what she believed was the fourth day, she realized she had turned a crucial corner—her fever had broken, she was ravenous, the white noise was gone. She lay there for several minutes, wiggling her toes, her fingers, testing her limbs, her body. She knew she had lost weight, maybe eight to ten pounds, because her hipbones were like blades. The loss of weight worried her a lot less than whether she was in remission or permanently cured.

Whatever it was, she intended to take advantage of it. She didn't have the luxury of time.

Forty minutes later, she walked over to the front office, her pack slung over her shoulder. In the office, music played on a record player, music that she recognized from her childhood, music her mother and Nadine used to listen to: Sergio Mendez and Brazil 66. Tom, she thought, used to talk about how his Cuban parents had listened to Sergio Mendez. Tom, alive right now, a thirteen-year-old kid living out his teen years on Marathon. This was the summer he would become interested in girls, that he would kiss his first girlfriend in the haunted house at a local fair. She knew the texture of his childhood. They had shared such things and she hadn't forgotten a word of it.

"You compare me to your dead husband, Mira," Sheppard had said to her on many occasions.

And it was true. True and unfair, but there you had it. As hokey as it might sound, Tom had been the song of her soul, her missing half. She figured you found that kind of relationship only once in your life.

So here she was, thirty-five years in the past, at a juncture in time where she could intervene not only in her personal history, but in national history, world history. But even if she could get people to listen to her, would it change anything? If John Lennon were forewarned, would he vacate the Dakota in December 1980? Would Janis Joplin or Jimi Hendrix knock off the heavy-duty drugs? Would Nelson Mandela's long stint in prison be any easier if he knew he would one day become president of South Africa? Would a thirteen-year-old Bill Clinton remember to ignore a woman named Monica?

Would Tom Morales remember not to walk into a convenience store on the eve of this daughter's third birthday in 1992?

Forget it. A door slammed shut in her mind.

She stopped at the desk. A young man with long black hair came dancing out to the desk, snapping his fingers in time to the music. "Hey, cabin eleven," he said. "I'm Diego. What can I do for you, Ms. Morales?"

"Lydia mentioned that the electric carts are for rent."

"A buck a day, the best deal on the island. We only ask that you plug it in every evening. There's an outlet pole outside your cabin."

He spoke very fast, she noticed, as if he were pressed for time and needed to get everything said before he went on to the next thing, whatever that might be. "Should I pay you now?"

"End of the week. I assume you've got a driver's license?"

"It got stolen along with my other things. I'm applying for another one."

"Forget it. Just give me the number when you get the license."

"I will, thanks."

"The bikes are for rent, too. And here's a map of the island, with important things like the grocery store and the Laundromat clearly marked, and the schedule for the ferry."

"Great."

"Oh, Jake left you a phone message two days ago. He asked if you could call him. Here's the number." He turned, retrieved a piece of paper from cabin 11's slot, and handed it to her. "Lydia said she looked in on you, that you were sick. You okay now?"

"Better, thanks."

He leaned forward, elbows against the counter. "Lydia said you're a psychic."

Shit, not now, please. She was afraid that if she read for anyone, the white noise would return, and then the humming and the shrieking, and before she knew it she would be back in bed again. "And Jake tells me you're a poet," she replied.

He shrugged. "Wanna-be poet. I've gotten a few things published in local magazines, nothing major yet."

"That'll change."

He flashed that engaging smile again. "Is that a psychic prediction?"

He wasn't going to leave it alone. And sooner or later, she would have to test herself, to find out if she was in remission or if the auditory horrors would return and, with them, the physical malaise. As soon as she thought this—as she gave herself permission—light appeared around him. An egg of light, shimmering with colors. His energy field. Within it, she saw information.

"Up here," she said softly, pointing at his right temple, "is your father. And over here"—her finger now pointed at his left temple—"is your mother. They were very young when you were born and didn't have a clue what it meant to be parents. When you left, your sister took the brunt of their anger and she wasn't ever able to forgive them. She . . ."

She's dead, his sister is dead, drug overdose, some seedy apartment after a concert . . . And he knows about it.

". . . died from a drug overdose."

Now a part of her reached into that cocoon of color just an inch or two above the crown of his head, and a new block of information dropped into place. About his future.

"Within a month, you'll get an offer. It has something to do with why you're here, in the colony."

And suddenly two paths opened in her mind, both equally viable, equally possible, at this very instant. On the left fork, she saw the towering buildings of Manhattan and the display window of a Barnes & Noble and understood that on this path, he would became a major poet. But when she moved down the right path, she found herself surrounded by cops in full riot gear and saw him hit in the head by something that killed him.

Where? When? What good is this if I can't see where and when?

The answer came to her immediately. Chicago, August. The Democratic National Convention. Sweet Christ, what was she supposed to do with this?

The right thing.

His energy field shimmered now from violet to dark red to navy blue and then to a soft, celery green. "Don't go to Chicago in August. Who's Carla? Don't listen to her. She'll pressure you about Chicago. *Do not go.* If you can do that, people will be reading your poetry well into the twenty-first century."

Just like that, the information dried up, the colors vanished, and Diego stood there in a kind of shock, eyes wide, the color bleeding from his face. "No one . . . no one knows about my sister," he finally said.

"Look, what happened to her isn't your fault. You made your choices, she made hers. You need to focus on the present—and on not going to Chicago in August."

Before he could ask her anything else, Mira said she had to get going and hurried for the door, grateful that there had been no white noise, no humming, no levels three and four. Although she'd seen energy fields before, she'd never seen any field as vividly, with such personal information. And the path with the two possible futures, both paths so vivid—that was new, too.

But the only thing she cared about was how she could use this heightened state to locate Annie.

She drove out of the colony and turned right, following the Old Post Road. It was less built up than in her own time, with tall, gorgeous trees on one side and rolling pastures on the other. Horses and cows grazed in the fields. One Saturday shortly after they had moved here, she and Annie had biked Old Post, following the paved path that didn't exist in 1968. They had packed a picnic lunch and stopped at a scenic spot that overlooked Florida Bay and the bridge and the ferries that churned back and forth between Tango and Key West. There, they had talked about Tom's life and death, the events that had chased them out of Lauderdale, and Annie's hopes and dreams for the future. She had many memories like this one, perfect moments in perfect days, and she wouldn't settle for anything less than that in the future.

You grabbed the wrong child.

Mira suddenly pulled off to the side of the road, in the shade, and opened the map that Diego had given her. The island was the same shape as it was in her time, a cat's head with major proportion problems. The artists' colony was located slightly below the cat's right ear, about a mile or so from the Wilderness Preserve, which was considerably larger than it was in 2003. The town of Pirate's Cove was between the cat's ears, and the town of Tango, where her bookstore was located in her time, was south, near the cat's neck. The Old Post Road ran around the periphery of the island, so that hadn't changed in thirty-five years. But other things were vastly different.

In her time, a number of roads, including a two-lane highway, ran from east to west across Tango; that road wasn't on this map. It, like the bridge, apparently hadn't been built yet. There were roads that cut into the middle of the island, but not a single road that crossed it in 1968.

She unzipped her pack and dug around inside until she found the chain with the peace symbol on it that Annie wore. She pressed the symbol between her hands and waited. Nothing happened. She altered her breathing to deepen her concentration.

The only thing she experienced was a definite sense that Annie was still alive and still on the island.

Give me more, she thought, and tried again.

Zip.

Mira wound the chain once around her hand to shorten it, then steadied her arm by placing her elbow on her knee. She held the peace symbol over the center of the map. "Is Annie in the middle of the island?"

The peace symbol began to swing slowly, very slowly, from right to left, left to right, then swung in wide, uneven circles over the heart of the island, as if searching for Annie's energy. It finally slowed and went still, having told her nothing at all. When she'd seen Nadine do this, whatever object she used as a pendulum nearly always provided some kind of information. She obviously didn't have the knack.

She transferred the chain and peace symbol to her left hand, held it in her fist, and brought her right hand, palm downward, over the map, just an inch or so above it. "Show me," she said quietly, and focused her attention on the map again. She realized it was too small for her to use her entire hand. She extended three fingers just an inch above the map and shut her eyes.

Gradually, she felt a sensation of heat. Rather than question its source, a sure way to shut down the process, she allowed the heat to guide her. As the heat increased, she opened her eyes. The greatest sensation of heat seemed to be around the preserve, not far from the colony. But this map was too small to pinpoint it any closer than that.

Frustrated, she grabbed the map off her lap, crumpled it, threw it to the floor, and pressed the heels of her hands against her eyes. She struggled not to give in to futility, despair, and an overwhelming sense of terror that Annie was not within her ability to find.

What bullshit. You've been at it for all of five minutes.

She started the electric cart and swerved back onto the road.

The strip shopping center seemed familiar to her, probably because it looked like a hundred other strip shopping centers in her own time. A ma-and-pa grocery store, a pet store, a drugstore, and—the lost anachronism of the sixties—a head shop. But as she pulled the electric cart into a parking spot, she realized that in her own time, a Publix supermarket stood here, a building that local residents had resisted, but which the county approved because it would provide jobs and boost the county's coffers. She liked it better like this, streamlined, simpler.

She took inventory of her finances. With the fifty the cabin had cost her, seven reserved for the cart for a week, and the sixteen and change she had spent on groceries, she had about twenty-six dollars left from the hundred that Jake had lent her. Her only hope was that Lydia or Diego would recommend her to their friends at the colony so she might pick up some cash for readings.

As she got out of the cart and really paid attention to where she was, culture shock lay everywhere—in the hippie panhandlers outside the store, in the ever-present sixties music, in the VW Bugs that chugged into and out of the parking lot, and in the grocery store itself. The place was larger than the colony's store, but there was still a paucity of the things she took for granted in her own time.

Where was the Dannon coffee yogurt that Annie loved so much? Where were the peaches from Georgia? The Advil? Where were the Fuji apples from New Zealand? The papaya from Costa Rica? The freshly baked rye bread? The vegetarian section? The soy milk? The organic fruits and vegetables? Where the hell was everything that constituted her diet at home?

At home: yes, that was the whole thing, wasn't it? She really was in a foreign country, a stranger in a strange land, born into the sixties, but never really a part of the whole movement because she had been too young. Perhaps, because of that, the decade held a weird fascination for her that had bled over into Annie's interests. Annie knew the sixties the way kids in her own time knew about McDonald's. She knew it as if she'd lived it.

And she is. She's here and she's living it. But in what context?

The humming came on her suddenly, unexpectedly, and it wasn't the soft, melodic version. This was a level three, a shrieking banshee that came at her out of nowhere, driving her to her knees while her hands still clutched the handle on the cart. The cart started to roll and her hands refused to let go so she got dragged forward, down the aisle, her knees moving in staccato jerks to keep up with the cart. Her pack slipped off her shoulder and banged against her hip, the floor.

Mira's fingers slipped off the handle and she sprawled gracelessly on the floor and the cart kept on rolling until it crashed into a shelf. Cans and cookies and boxes tumbled to the floor. Someone helped Mira up and she rocked back onto her heels and looked up at the man. The shrieking in her head stopped. The transition from the incessant, painful noise to complete silence happened so abruptly that it took her brain a few moments to process what had happened, to catch up. She blinked, rubbed her hands against her legs, stood, and stammered her thanks.

She knew the sudden cessation of the noise was significant and that it was connected specifically to the man who helped her.

"You okay, ma'am?" he asked in a rolling southern droll.

"Yes, thanks. I guess I stumbled."

A skinny guy whose name tag read *Manager* hurried into the aisle, eyeing the mess with dismay. "Just what's going on here, Sheriff Fontaine?" The manager's prissy mouth pursed with disapproval.

A cop, great, he's a cop and I'm busted.

"Your floor's slippery, Henry. The young lady tripped and the wheel on that damned cart came off." He pointed at the cart, now at the end of the aisle, one of its wheels gone.

"Well, the floor's *really* slippery now," the manager observed. "Them jars busted open."

He strutted past them without saying another word. He apparently hadn't heard about customer relations, Mira thought, and started down the aisle to get her cart, but the cop—Fontaine—got it for her. "Ignore Henry," he confided. "He hates his job. C'mon, I'll help you get that stuff out to your car."

As he touched her elbow, an image took shape behind her eyes: the face of the man who had taken Annie. Fontaine knew him.

Fontaine insisted on carrying her groceries out to the car. She didn't know whether he felt personally responsible for the manager's behavior or whether this was just part of his human relations duties as a cop. Either way, it struck her as odd.

"I haven't seen you around the island before," Fontaine said. "Where're you from?"

"Lauderdale."

"Tango's quite a bit different than Lauderdale."

"Much different. Here's my car." She gestured toward the electric cart.

He glanced at the license plate. "You're staying at the artists' colony?"

"Just temporarily, while my boat's being repaired."

He set her groceries in the backseat of the cart. "How'd you hear about the cabins at the colony?"

"From Jake Romano. At—"

"Sure, I know Jake. Known him for years. He's got quite an eye with that camera of his. Nice young man. I didn't catch your name," he added.

"Mira."

He frowned. "Unusual name. Spanish, isn't it?"

"It can be. I don't know that my parents intended it that way."

"Funny, but several days ago, one of my lieutenants took a frantic call from a woman named Mira Morales who said she'd been missing and her daughter had been snatched off Little Horse Key."

And guess what? You know the guy who did it. "How awful," she exclaimed. A pulse beat hard and fast at her temple. She turned her head away from Fontaine just in case her lie showed on her face. "I didn't hear anything about it in the news."

"Well, that's the strange part. The lieutenant says they got disconnected and she never called back. Your last name isn't Morales, is it?"

"Nope. Piper. Mira Piper."

"Terrible thing. The kidnapper asks for a ransom and warns the parents not to get in touch with the police, so the parents get spooked. Understandable. But my God, the police are here to help, you know what I'm saying?"

She understood his reasoning: just how many women named Mira could be on the island during the slowest tourist season of the year? Everything he said was directed at her and she nearly blurted it all, probably would have except that she touched his arm . . .

And finds herself in a small windowless room, her arms and legs strapped to a table, an IV drip snaking into her arm. People fire questions at her—cops, doctors, FBI agents—and she can't lie, whatever they're pumping into her won't let her lie. She hears herself saying things—Microsoft, e-mail, Bill Gates, Bill Clinton, the George Bushes, Yahoo, Watergate, Reagan, 9-11, the dot com revolution, Enron, WorldCom, Pocket PCs, moon walks . . .

In the next scene, she's in a locked psychiatric ward, something straight out of One Flew Over the Cuckoo's Nest, *and Big Nurse is holding her down on a table, inserting something between her teeth, and telling her it won't hurt, not to worry, the shock treatments will cure her.*

Mira jerked her hand away from Fontaine's arm. "Thanks so much for your help, Chief Fontaine."

"You give me a call any time, Mira." He handed her a piece of paper with a couple of phone numbers jotted on it.

As she putted off in the electric cart, he was still standing in the parking lot, gazing after her, his good intentions as potentially lethal to her as a .357 fired at point-blank range.

Fourteen

The Hilltop Inn reminded Sheppard of a movie set. Painted in tropical pastels, it curved like a pair of arms reaching out to embrace the Tango reservoir just below it. The sprawling fifteen-acre estate had grass greener than emeralds, and everyone looked as if they had come from central casting—the same Colgate white smiles, the same perfect hair, perfect bodies, and chirpy voices.

Even in the off-season, the rooms were a bit pricey for a government employee like Dillard. Sheppard wondered how he would justify it as an expense.

"So Dillard has a trust fund no one knows about?" Goot muttered as they entered the massive lobby.

"Yeah, it's called the taxpayers' till."

"We show him the Wheaton photos and tell him about how Wheaton siphoned money from his ex-wife's accounts. That's it, right?"

"He doesn't even deserve that much."

"Does he know about your relationship with Mira?"

"If he does, he hasn't mentioned it and I'd just as soon not bring it up."

Sheppard spotted Dillard as soon as they entered the bar. He was seated at a window table with Tango's chief of police, Doug Emison, a southern cracker from the school called *I'll scratch your back and you scratch mine.* Sheppard had had several run-ins with Emison in the past, mostly over the sometimes thin line between federal and local investigations. He wasn't cut from the same soiled cloth as Dillard, but the fact that he was here at all made it clear that Dillard believed he needed local allies.

"Shep, John, I think you know Doug Emison." Dillard smiled broadly as he said this, but it was a strange smile, his teeth gritted as though he were constipated. "He'll be sitting in on this meeting."

They greeted Emison and sat down across from him and Dillard. Sheppard wasn't in the mood for casual conversation, so he opened the file and removed the photos that Tina Richmond had given him. "This is why we know Patrick Wheaton is behind the abductions. A chloroform cloth was found at the scene and that's the one item that connects these kidnappings."

Dillard, in his usual dilatory way, studied the photos, passing each one to Emison when he was finished with it. "That sure does look like the Wheaton I remember," Emison said. "'Cept he didn't have blond hair when I knew him. You shoulda called us, Shep. We could've had planes and boats searching that area around Little Horse."

"We did a thorough search the night they vanished and the next morning. We didn't even find debris. Nothing."

"You're making it sound damn mysterious." Dillard leaned forward and smiled again, that broad, teeth-gritting grin. "You figure this is an *X-File*, Mulder?"

"Fuck off, Leo."

Dillard slapped his hand against the table and laughed, a loud, lonely echo. The instant he realized he was the only person laughing, he shut up. Emison, to his credit, looked embarrassed by Dillard's outburst. "The department rents about half a dozen planes from developer Ross Blake," Emison said, trying to be help-

ful. "All you have to do is say the word, Shep, and we'll
be out there. We can search the islands close to Little
Horse as well."

"I'll take you up on that, Doug. How about starting
tomorrow morning?"

"Will do. You've spoken to Wheaton's ex?"

"Today," Goot replied. "She finds it hard to believe
that he's implicated in a series of kidnappings. Says
he loved kids."

"Yeah, and the Boston Strangler loved nurses," Dillard replied. "She provide any useful leads?"

"Nope," Goot said.

"Have you circulated photos of the woman and her
kid?" Dillard asked.

The question irritated Sheppard; Dillard was imply-
ing that Sheppard and Goot didn't know the protocol.
"Of course we have. And her name is Mira Morales,
Leo, and the girl's name is Annie."

Dillard put up his hands. "Hey, man, calm down. I'm
just trying to get a sense of what you two have done so
far."

"Everything we're supposed to do," Sheppard
snapped. "In fact, we need to shove off. We've got a lot
of ground to cover tonight." With that said, Sheppard
stood and Goot got hastily to his feet. "Nice seeing you,
Doug, and keep me posted. If anything new crops up,
Leo, I'll call."

"Hold on a goddamn minute." Dillard rose. "We
aren't finished here."

Sheppard stared at the twitch in the corner of Dillard's mouth, then looked him in the eyes. "You have
something else to say, Leo?" *O great asshole of assholes.*
"Any nuggets of wisdom from your vast experience as
a paper pusher?"

Dillard, who stood about five-ten and half a foot
shorter than Sheppard, drew himself up to his full

height and sank his bony index finger into Sheppard's chest. "Let's get something straight here. I'm in charge of this investigation and you, my friend, are—"

Sheppard took hold of Dillard's finger, clutching it, twisting it. "I know you smell publicity and good PR for the bureau, Leo. But that doesn't entitle you to butt in. If you've got a problem with that, call Jernan." Then he released Dillard's finger and gave him a little shove to send him on his way.

He stumbled back, holding his finger, wincing, making quite a show of it. He sat down hard in his chair and as Sheppard and Goot turned away, he shouted, *"You're off this case, Sheppard."*

Sheppard didn't bother stopping or glancing around. He shot him the bird and kept on moving.

They ended up at Nadine's. She had a yoga class and wouldn't be home until later, so they had the place to themselves. They ordered wings and a pizza and went to work, sifting through the information that Julia Lenier had given them.

The first interesting item Sheppard uncovered was a newspaper article from the *Key West Courier* dated September 10, 1968.

PROFESSOR'S SUICIDE
by Nivia Jones
Key West Courier Staff Writer

MARATHON—It was raining the night of September 4, when Katherine Baylor Wheaton, 42, sat down on the edge of her bed in a darkened room and slipped the barrel of a rifle into her mouth. Perhaps she hesitated a few seconds before her finger twitched against the trigger.

Perhaps she thought about her husband, her son, the stepdaughter she had lost on July 1 in a car accident on Big Pine. Or maybe nothing went through her mind. We'll never know. She left no suicide note.

Dr. Wheaton's résumé reads like a Who's Who of the academic world: full professorship at MIT, a Nobel nomination last year that she shared with her husband, Dr. Dan Wheaton, professional accolades, author and lecturer. But there was a dark side to Katherine Wheaton's life.

"She was being treated for depression," says Dr. David Ring, a psychiatrist on the staff of Mt. Sinai Hospital in Miami who has been treating her since the death of her 17-year-old stepdaughter Eva, in a car accident two months ago. "But she never gave me any reason to believe she would take her own life."

Police, based on the coroner's report, are calling her death a suicide. "We have found nothing to indicate otherwise," says Lt. Thomas.

Her body was discovered around nine P.M. by her son, Patrick, 16, who had just gotten home from his swim team practice at the YMCA. A memorial service was held on September 7.

David Ring, Mt. Sinai Hospital. Sheppard pulled out his cell phone and called information. A few minutes later, he paced across the kitchen, Goot watching him, and spoke to a clerk, who connected him to another clerk and another. Finally, on the fifth transfer, he reached someone who informed him that Dr. Ring had gone home for the evening. She gave Sheppard the number for his answering service. Another call, another faceless woman.

Sheppard went through his spiel. "Tell him this

concerns Patrick and Katherine Wheaton. That Wheaton is being implicated in a series of abductions and that it's urgent that I speak to him tonight."

"So this is an emergency?"

"That's right."

"He should be calling in within thirty minutes."

Sheppard left his number, rang off, and returned to the table. Goot passed him an article from the *Miami Herald* about Eva Wheaton's death.

On the night she died, she and a friend, Billy Macon, had gone to a party on Big Pine Key. Around two that morning, she was driving Macon's Mustang when it slammed into an abandoned gas station doing sixty-five miles an hour. She was hurled out of the car and died of massive injuries. The vehicle caught fire and Macon was burned over sixty percent of his body and was airlifted to Jackson Memorial Hospital. He died several weeks later without ever regaining consciousness. Their blood alcohol levels indicated they'd consumed the equivalence of two bottles of wine.

"Nothing here about her being pregnant," Goot said.

"Not too surprising. It wasn't the sort of thing to be made public back in 1968, at least not in those circles."

Sheppard's cell rang and he reached for it. "Agent Sheppard."

"This is Dr. Ring. I understand you're looking for information about Patrick Wheaton?"

"I'm looking for information about the whole mess," Sheppard said.

"The physician/patient confidentiality exists even when the patients are dead, Agent Sheppard."

"Wheaton's not dead. He's just missing."

"But Katherine is dead."

"Is a pact with the dead more important than what you might be able to do for the living?"

The doctor didn't have a snappy reply. In fact, he didn't say anything for so long that Sheppard wasn't sure he was still on the line. "Dr. Ring?"

"You mentioned the abduction of children. Tell me about that."

So Sheppard did. And he spared no details. It sounded as sordid and heartbreaking as it was. Then he ended with a question: "Was Eva Wheaton pregnant with Patrick's child?"

"You seem to know a great deal about this, Agent Sheppard."

"Is that a yes?"

"Of course it's a yes. Patrick Wheaton, even at the age of sixteen, was a dangerous man. Extremely bright and completely without conscience."

"A psychopath, in other words."

"Not in the way we normally think of psychopaths. You see him in a crowd, you think he looks like an ordinary kid, going through the ordinary teen things. Then he says something and it hits you viscerally. *This kid belongs in a lifetime lockup ward.*"

"What did he say exactly?"

"Oh, many things, Agent Sheppard. Many things. One day, he described to me in detail what it was like to make love to his stepsister. Another time, he implied that he had been present when his mother had killed herself, that he had helped her slide the rifle barrel into her mouth. He never came out and said, *I'm responsible,* he was too clever for that. But there was always a big question in my mind about Katherine's death. I think that was the night that he told her Eva was pregnant with his child. Eva's car accident happened within eight to ten hours of her telling Patrick she intended to get an abortion. He wanted that child.

"That young man whose car she was driving? I later found out that he had a relative in the Bahamas who performed abortions. Remember, this was before Roe versus Wade, and desperate women took desperate measures. She had bought a ticket to Nassau and Patrick had found it. I think Patrick did something to Bill Macon's car. I think he intended to kill Macon. There wasn't enough left of the car to prove it, but in all these years I've never changed my opinion about him."

"Did he intend to kill Eva?" Sheppard asked.

"I doubt it. Just Macon."

Ring was describing a monster that lived within ordinary skin. "And how is it that his medical records were expunged, Dr. Ring?"

A note of indignation entered Ring's voice now. "I had nothing to do with that. Dan Wheaton was responsible. He was a bright, sensitive man, but he was so weak, a passive personality surrounded by aggressives. His wife, Patrick, Eva . . . I don't know how he stood it for as long as he did. These days, you hear about dysfunctional families, Agent Sheppard. It's coffee room conversation. But believe me, the Wheatons were paragons of the dysfunctional family. It's not the fault of any single person, it's the chemistry, the mix of these four particular people."

Sheppard knew what Mira's response to that would be: *karma*. "Did Wheaton ever impress you as a pedophile?"

"Absolutely not. That's not what he was about. If he abducted these children, then pedophilia has nothing to do with it."

"But you knew him over thirty years ago. People change."

"Let me put it this way, Agent Sheppard. Pedophilia is a psychiatric illness with roots that usually go way back. It's not a hobby. It's not an interest that comes over a person suddenly, without warning. If he abducted those children, then there's some grandiose scheme behind it that won't make sense to anyone else, some bigger picture that you and I won't see."

"Like rescuing kids he believes come from dysfunctional families?" Sheppard asked.

"That would fit. But it's only the trigger. There's something else going on, something deeper."

"After he was released from the hospital, did you see him again?"

"Only once. At his stepfather's funeral five or six years later. He was in college by then, trying to put his life together, or so he told me. He also told me he was pissed that his old man had drunk away whatever money he and his mother had. I wasn't surprised when I read about his marriage into the Lenier family. It's just the sort of stunt that Wheaton would pull to satisfy his greed. After all these years, I have come to the conclusion that greed was at the heart of Patrick's illness."

"Greed? That's it? He's the guy in *Wall Street?*"

"Greed isn't always about just money, Agent Sheppard, at least not from a psychiatric viewpoint. Patrick's greed was about what he felt that life owed him. And if life wasn't going to deliver, then by God he would just take what he wanted and screw the consequences." He paused, then added: "That last part is something he said to me at his father's funeral. 'Some day, Dr. Ring, you, too, will fuck the consequences.' I guess that's what I'm doing now."

Resignation: that was what Sheppard heard in the man's voice just then. "Where do you think he vanished to with half a million bucks? Where would a guy like this hide for nine years?"

"Some place where the rest of us wouldn't think of looking."

* * *

It was coal black outside now. Insects buzzed against the windows. Nadine had returned from her yoga class, made them all a large pot of Cuban coffee, and helped them sort through the information.

Sheppard went back into the original file that had been established on Wheaton and, buried in the dozens of pages, found a reference to Peter Wheat and his account at the Miami bank, and the Social Security number he had used. A check of the Social Security records indicated that the number belonged to a man born in 1919 who had died in 1960. The bank officials apparently hadn't bothered to check out the number and Wheaton hadn't deposited the money all at once. Maybe if he'd had the account longer than several months, the bureaucracy would have caught up to him before his wife had discovered that he'd stolen from her.

Sheppard went into ancestry.com, a genealogical site maintained by the Mormon church, and entered Wheat's name to see what came up. The site had all kinds of interesting links, message boards, and information on birth dates, marriages, and deaths. He wanted to verify Peter Wheat's date of death and find out if there were any other Wheats listed.

Six entries for *Wheat, Peter,* came up. The second one, born in January 1919, was the man whose name Wheaton had taken. His death was listed as April 4, 1960. Four other Wheats were considerably younger, still alive. The last entry, though, puzzled Sheppard. The DOB was the same as the first Wheat, January 4, 1919, but the date of death was listed as July 1, 1968, with cause of death listed as *unknown.* That Wheat died at the age of fifty, the same age that Patrick Wheaton, born in 1953, would be now.

Yeah? So? Wheaton had been sighted in 2003, not 1968.

Still, it nagged at Sheppard.

"Hey," Goot said suddenly, glancing up from his laptop. "I just found something weird. A Peter Wheat got a driver's license on April fifteenth, 1994—that'd be about a month before Wheaton vanished—and it was renewed in November 2002."

"Renewed where?"

"Miami. And I've got a home address." Goot ticked it off: 3130 Savoy Place, Tango Key.

Sheppard had never heard of Savoy Place. Nadine had heard of it, but didn't know where it was. She went over to Mira's kitchen junk drawer and rummaged through mounds of coupons, pencils, notepads, playing cards, and everything else that didn't have a proper place in the house, and finally found a map of Tango Key.

"Here, use this. It's a recent map," she said.

The cats—three that belonged to Mira and his cat, Powder—jumped onto the table one after another, to investigate the rustling of paper. Whiskers, Annie's black and white cat, plopped down at the north end of the map. Tiger Lily, Mira's baby, curled up at the south end. Demian, Nadine's Himalayan, claimed the east end, and Powder took up the western position. The humans all looked at each other.

"Now *that,*" Nadine said, "is significant. We're on the right track."

Sheppard nudged the cats away and drew his finger down the list of street names at the bottom of the map. "Here it is. C-seven and D-four. It's in the northeast hills. It borders the preserve area."

"I thought there were just old farms and ancient homesteads up there," Goot said.

"I've only been up there once." With Mira. They had hiked through the preserve, Sheppard remembered, and made love in a grove that looked like something out of Middle Earth. "Let's do a quick check with property records." He went on-line to the property appraiser's office and put in the Savoy address. A corporate name came up, Imagine, Inc. Sheppard clicked on the name and got a list of four corporate officers, all with Japanese or Hispanic names and a head office located in Hong Kong.

Absentee owners, he thought, but just to be sure, he called information and asked for the number for Imagine, Inc. There was no local listing, only an 800 number. Sheppard punched it out and got a recording that the number had been disconnected.

"They moved on," Nadine remarked.

"Let's go take a look," Sheppard said.

"You think we need backup?" Goot asked.

Sheppard considered it. The bureau's Tango office was small, just four men besides himself and Goot. Two were on vacation, one was in Miami, and the other was out with the flu. That would mean calling in Emison's people. It would mean a SWAT team, cruisers, choppers, the whole nine yards. If Wheaton was hiding Annie at 3130 Savoy, then protocol was not the way to go on this one.

"No. Just you and me."

Goot grinned. "I was hoping you would say that."

Fifteen

"Annie?"

His voice was like that of some angry god, booming, vengeful, terrifying. Her impulse was not to answer, to pretend that she hadn't heard him. But if she did that, she knew he would come over to the door and bang on it until she answered him. If she continued not to answer, he would break the door down. That's how it was in Peter's world. So although she apparently had survived whatever illness she'd had, her immediate circumstances hadn't changed. She was still his prisoner.

"I'm taking a shower," she called back, and stepped out of the shower quickly and listened hard, ear to the door.

She heard Peter moving around in the other room. She had pressed a towel up against the crack because she pegged him as the type who would look for her shadow to determine where she was standing.

"I've got some food here for you."

For which meal? Breakfast? Lunch? Dinner? She had no idea. It didn't matter. She had lost track of hours and days. "Just leave it on the table."

He rapped at the door now, startling her, and she wrenched back. "Do you need anything?" he asked. "Shampoo? Soap? Toothpaste?"

The god, pretending to be concerned. She turned

her head toward the shower so it would sound as though she were there and not here in front of the door. "No, you bought me everything." *Thanks for nothing.*

"We need to talk. I'll be back later."

She turned her head away from the door again and called, "Yeah, okay."

She heard him move away from the door, but didn't dare peek out. She kept the shower on a few minutes longer, letting the steam build up so that the wall tiles would be looser. She quickly dried off, dressed, and wrapped the towel around her head. She turned off the shower, pressed her ear to the door again. She didn't hear anything. She unlocked it, peered out.

No Peter. The front door—a heavy metal door, she had discovered—was shut again and undoubtedly locked up, sealed like some Egyptian tomb. Annie ducked back into the bathroom, locked the door again, and went over to the linen closet. She reached under the towels where she'd hidden a spatula knife that she'd found in a stack of wall tiles. In its normal state, it resembled a flattened spoon and Peter or Rusty probably had been using it to replace the loose tiles on the wall that decades of moisture had loosened. It was useless as a weapon, but she had bent it at either side so that now it looked like it was folded almost in half.

She climbed into the tub, popped six tiles loose, and tried to ignore the horrible pleas for help that other children had scrawled on this same moist wall: *Bad man. Help me. Find my mommy. Hurt. Sick.* With the point created by the fold in the metal, she finished carving her own message. She believed the man would move her now that she was better, and she hoped that Sheppard and her mother would find this place, wherever it was. And when they did, they would find the loose tiles and her message. *Mira Shep A here okay.*

When she finished, she opened the can of grout, scooped some onto the spatula, and put four of the six tiles back into place, but lightly. She left the other two off because that was how the wall had been since she first had noticed it. She hid the spatula behind the stack of tiles in the linen closet again, shut the door, and hurried out into the main room.

She tossed the towel on the couch, picked up her hairbrush, and glanced at the food platter he'd left her. Was the food drugged? She kind of doubted it; he seemed to want her to get better, not worse, that was why he'd sent the black woman. Lydia.

Who lied.

Lydia hadn't helped Annie and neither had Rusty, who seemed that he might, and her mother and Sheppard hadn't galloped in to rescue her. That meant that if she was going to escape from this place, she would have to do it on her own.

Peter had left her a peanut butter and jelly sandwich with slices of fresh strawberries and an apple on the side and a bowl of split pea soup. *Must be lunch,* she thought, and picked up the sandwich. She devoured it, gobbled down the strawberries, and stuck the apple in the pocket of her shorts, part of her stash of food in the event that some day he didn't show up with food.

Annie went over to the window and peered through the slats in the blinds, looking for the man or Rusty or the dog. The path into the woods was empty, but she knew Peter would be back. He said he would. And he always seemed to do what he said he would do.

She went into the bathroom and locked the door again, stepped up onto the edge of the tub, and worked the shower pole loose. It would make a very good weapon. Annie slid the curtain hooks off the pole, balled up the curtain, tossed it on the floor. Then she twisted one end of the rod, shortening it. When it was about three feet long, she ran into the living room and peered through the blinds again to check the path.

Still empty.

Annie clutched the shower rod like a bat and swung at the window closest to the door. The impact sent vibrations racing up her arms, into her bones, her teeth. The glass didn't break. Okay, so busting out the window wouldn't work. She would wait for him to return. She would wait against the wall so that when he opened the door, she would be hidden behind it. As soon as he stepped into the room, she would hit him from behind, in the backs of his knees.

But first, she shut the bathroom door. He would notice it as soon as he entered and turn in that direction, away from her; that was when she would hit him. And then she would run. She would run into the woods and keep on running until she reached a phone, people, a building.

Annie took up her position against the wall, to the right of the door. She practiced holding the rod, swinging it. She was only five-two, and both Peter and Rusty were at least six feet tall. She wouldn't be able to swing high enough to hit either of them in the head, so she would aim for the backs of their knees. She would have to hit hard enough so the knees would buckle.

She took practice swings that made the pole whistle as it sliced through the air. She *saw* the pole hitting the man or Rusty, saw it vividly, in detail, *saw* him stumbling forward and hitting the floor, and *saw* herself bolting for the door, for freedom.

If you can imagine it, her mother always said, *you can make it so.*

She heard whistling outside, a weird, toneless refrain the man had hummed at some point when she was sick, and pressed up against the wall, clutching the pole. Keys rattled. She forced herself to remain motionless, to barely breathe. Beads of sweat broke out on her forehead, her heart slammed around in her chest like a tennis ball.

The locks disengaged, the door opened, a wedge of sunlight spilled into the room and with it, the fragrance of summer heat and freedom. She saw him through the crack in the door, a tall, thin man with slightly stooped shoulders, a long nose, and more wrinkles than she remembered. He had short, graying hair. Had his hair always been gray? She didn't remember it that way. She thought his hair was blond. *Gray, blond, what difference does it make?*

He carried a small television and paused to shift it in his arms. *Move,* she screamed at him in her head. *Get in here.*

His head came up, almost as if he'd heard her, and he hurried through the door. "Annie?" he called, and kicked the door shut.

For the space of a heartbeat, her legs seized up, her feet rooted in the floor, she couldn't move. She just stood there, staring at his back, gripping the pole. Then she lunged forward, swinging. He apparently heard something because he had started to turn when her first blow struck him—not in the backs of his knees, not in the face, but across his arms and hands, which were wrapped around the TV.

His eyes bulged, the TV slipped out of his arms and crashed to the floor, the screen shattered. He didn't scream, he roared, a sound so huge and powerful that it was as if the blow had released decades of blind rage. Blood poured out of his fingers, he clutched one arm to his side, but he didn't stumble or fall. She swung again. The pole slammed into his ribs, his feet slid around on the broken glass from the TV screen, and he lost his balance and went down like some clumsy giant. When he slammed against the floor, she felt the vibrations through the soles of her bare feet.

Annie dropped the pole and tore toward the door, his roars and shouts eviscerating the air that she breathed, the surface against which she moved. She threw open the door, slammed it shut, and fumbled with the chain, locking him inside. She raced across the path, gulping at the fresh air, reveling in the warmth of sunlight against her face. She heard him shouting, pounding at the door, rattling it.

Then she plunged into the woods and ran, weaving between trees, stumbling over roots that protruded from the ground. She didn't have a clue where she was, how close to a road she might be, or how far the woods extended. She thought about climbing a tree and waiting until dark, but she didn't want to stop. If she kept running, she would eventually reach something or someone who could help her.

The woods ended abruptly and the land dropped down a hundred feet, to rocks, water. Florida Bay? The gulf? She didn't know, didn't recognize anything. She sighted a narrow beach just ahead, umbrellas dotting the sand, and ran along the edge of the cliff, hoping she might be able to catch the attention of a sunbather, a swimmer, a lifeguard, someone, anyone.

"Hey, Annie. Over here."

Her head snapped around. Rusty and the dog waited at the edge of the woods. He gestured for her to hurry up. "C'mon, quick, my car's parked down here."

Annie ran over to him, nearly sobbing with relief, and Rusty took hold of her arm and pulled her along through the woods, deeper into the trees, moving in the opposite direction now. "We don't have much time. He'll break outta there. I'll drive you into town, then you need to get lost."

"What . . . Why's he doing this?"

"He's sick. All the trips he made through the corridor twisted his head. He sees himself as a savior, thinks he's saving us. But there's something else, too, I just don't know what it is yet."

Corridor. He had talked a lot about the corridor when she was sick. Or someone had. Brad Pitt, she thought. "What corridor? What're you talking about?"

The expression on his face scared her. "Right. You still don't know. You—"

"Know what?"

"I'll explain in the car. Can you move any faster?"

They ran now, Rusty gripping her hand tightly, pine needles and stickers piercing her bare feet. They had circled around behind the shed, into a clearing. "This is where the other children are buried," he said. "Under the leaves and pine needles. Those flowers . . . they marked the graves."

The others. The ones who had written their desperate messages on the bathroom wall. *Help me, bad man, find my mommy . . .*

"The ones who didn't survive the corridor," he finished.

She wrenched her hand free of his grip now. "He's going to *kill* me?" she hissed. "And you . . . you've been a part of these . . . these other deaths? My God, you people are monsters, you're—"

"I'm not a goddamn monster," he snapped. "Six years ago, I was just like you. Scared shitless. Desperate. Imprisoned. But . . . oh Christ, c'mon, please, we have to hurry. We'll talk in the car. . . ."

More running. They reached a dirt road, where an old car was parked on the shoulder. Rusty threw open the passenger door and Sunny scrambled in, as if she thought she was going to be left behind. As Rusty coaxed the dog to move over and give Annie some room, a truck screeched to a stop, and Rusty spat, *"Oh shit, it's him, it's him."*

In the moment when his eyes connected with hers, she realized everything had suddenly changed, that Rusty's fear of Peter was greater than his compassion. Annie whipped around to run, but Rusty had read her eyes as correctly as she had read his, and he grabbed her by the back of the shirt. His hand slapped down over her mouth, his arm closed around her waist.

"Jesus, I'm so sorry, I really am. . . ."

She screamed against the rough, sweaty skin of his hand, kicked, tried to wrench free. But he held on, wrestling her to the ground. The shriek of brakes, then Peter's voice: "Good job, son. Hold her still."

Something wet slapped down over her mouth and nose. Chloroform again, she thought, and then the ground blurred, voices echoed and drifted away, and the world went completely dark.

2

"Help me get her into the truck," Wheaton said, picking up the girl's arms.

Rusty just stood there, staring at Annie, his dog licking the girl's face and whining. He seemed to be in a kind of shock.

"Grab her legs, Rusty."

He glanced up, a tall, muscular young man with a jaw that showed a five o'clock shadow. "What you're doing is wrong, Pete."

"So you've said before. Get her feet."

"No." He backed away from Wheaton, shaking his head, struggling with himself. "This is really wrong, Pete. It's not just illegal, it's . . . it's immoral."

Wheaton dropped the girl's arms and moved toward Rusty. "Was it *wrong* for me to get you away from that hellhole family you lived with for twelve years? Huh, Rusty? Was that *wrong?*" He didn't shout, didn't have to. He recognized the fear in Rusty's face, that vestige of fear from when he was younger. "Was it?"

Rusty didn't back away from him. He didn't look down at the ground as he used to, didn't clasp his hands behind his back, didn't pull his head down, as if to hide it within the muscles of his shoulders. He stood his ground. "I'm grateful to you for taking me out of that. I really am. But you were wrong to kidnap me. You did wrong when you took those other children. And you've done wrong with this girl. She's going to survive, Pete. She's like me in that way. She's strong. But you need to take her back to her own family."

"No." Wheaton turned away from him, determined to get the girl back into the shed. He lifted her by the arms and began to drag her through the pine needles, toward his truck. But she was a dead weight and he felt weak, used up, *old.*

Years ago, shortly after he'd stumbled into the corridor the first time and when things were still relatively okay between him and his wife, he had felt like this after lovemaking, used up, old, worn out, as dry and brittle as a twig. He remembered staring at the ceiling fan, the old paddle fan, some antique that had belonged to Julia's grandmother back in the days before air-conditioning. It turned with excruciating slowness and made a soft, clicking sound, as rhythmic as the tick of a clock. And in that moment he had realized that his life was finite, that at birth you were doled out a certain number of seconds, minutes, hours, days, months, and years, and his were ticking away, marching inexorably toward a black vacuum called death. Between that realization and the next breath, *relatively okay* ceased to

be enough for him. He committed himself fully to an
exploration of the corridor.

Now here he was, on the other side of the corridor,
dragging a young girl toward his truck, his adopted son
staring holes through his back, and he felt just like he
had that night long ago, Father Time breathing down
his neck.

"Patty Cakes, when're we going to start having some fun?"

*He and Evie are in the attic and she is on the mattress that
rests against the floor, just under the window. Her legs stretch
high into the air, her nimble fingers supporting the small of
her back, and now, as he watches, she allows her right leg to
fall forward toward her head, the leg still straight, the toes
slightly curled. As the toes of her right foot graze the floor, she
brings her left leg back. She is completely naked.*

*The soft, muted light coming through the dirty window
cups her beautiful ass, traces her lovely legs. Her head is
turned toward him but because of the way she is positioned,
her face is completely in shadow. He can't make out the details.
That terrifies him.*

*"Don't call me that," he snaps, and turns back to the book
that he was reading aloud to her, a battered and torn copy of*
Lolita *that he bought at school for five bucks.*

The clock was ticking, all right. July first was just
around the corner and he would have only one crack
at this.

He strained, pulling harder on the girl's arms, and
suddenly her legs lifted into the air. "You need a
shrink," Rusty said, hurrying forward with his powerful
hands clasped around the girl's ankles. "You need professional help, Pete."

"Shut up," Wheaton rasped. "Just shut up."

They got Annie into the back of the truck and the silence between them was so thick and terrible that Wheaton understood that something irreparable had just happened, something tragic. "It's for her own good," Wheaton said. "She was living in a dysfunctional family that—"

"That isn't why you took her. You want me to believe it is, but I know it isn't, Pete. So just stop telling me all these fucking lies."

"Don't swear."

"Go fuck yourself," he replied, and didn't flinch when Wheaton's fist flew up. Rusty's own arm jerked upward, an arm more powerful and muscular than Wheaton's own. "Don't make me hurt you, Pete."

Wheaton's arm dropped to his side. He turned without another word, got into his truck, and drove back toward the house, watching in the rearview mirror for Rusty's car. He felt an odd mixture of relief and satisfaction when it turned in behind him.

He pulled up onto the grass and took the truck as far into the trees as he could, and stopped. Rusty got out, Sunny stuck to him like paper to glue, and helped Wheaton get Annie out of the truck.

"How long will she be out?" Rusty asked.

"A few hours. I can get her from here."

"I'll help you," Rusty said, and moved backward down the path, holding Annie's shoulders.

Wheaton's legs ached where she'd smacked him and he stumbled once and nearly went down. "You okay?" Rusty asked.

"Fine, I'm fine."

"You don't look fine, Pete. You look tired."

And old. Rusty didn't say it, but Wheaton heard it in his voice. Every day, he felt increasingly older, more feeble.

The door to the shed still stood open and they carried

her inside and put her on the couch. Wheaton picked up the shower pole and hurled it outside. He unlocked the storage closet, brought out the cleaning cart. Then he and Rusty started sweeping up the shattered TV, Rusty with the broom, Wheaton holding the dustpan. The shed needed to be disinfected again, but he would get around to that later.

"We need to bring another TV down from the house. And magazines and that videotape I made. It's time she found out exactly where she is."

"I don't know if she's ready for that. I wasn't."

"She's strong, you said it yourself. The sooner she knows the true situation, the sooner we can get on with it."

"And what is *it*, Pete?"

Wheaton glanced at Rusty. In the shadowed room, the two of them less than three feet apart, Rusty suddenly looked like a formidable opponent. And yet, Wheaton knew that as much as Rusty disliked this business with the children, he wouldn't betray him. Rusty might not love him, but he felt indebted to him. "It doesn't have anything to do with you, Rusty."

"Then why did you bring me back, Pete?"

This conversation always ended in the same place. "Let's not go there again."

"Have you ever gone into the future, Pete?"

The abrupt change in conversation was a welcome respite. "Our time *is* the future."

"No, I mean beyond our time. Like, to 2020 or something."

"I've tried. But I can't seem to get there."

No, that wasn't quite right. Once, while fishing off the coast of Cancún, Mexico, he had emerged briefly in a place where the sky looked red and the air was so polluted he could barely breathe. He had gone to shore and discovered that the hotel where he was staying was gone—and so was every other hotel. The entire Cancún area was little more than rubble.

It had shaken him up so deeply that he had run back to his boat and headed straight for the nearest black water, a relatively small mass where he figured he had gone through. He had drifted in it for a long time, praying that the pull of his natal time line would kick in, struggling not to panic. Then he'd hit what he had come to think of as the wall, had passed out, and when he'd come to, he had seen the usual coastline of Cancún, hotels towering against the exquisite blue sky.

He still wasn't sure how it had happened.

"Do you think it's possible to go into a future beyond our own time?"

"Yes. I think once you've gone through the corridor, something in your DNA is altered. The paracrystalline grids in your brain are activated. But I also think it's more difficult and there's no way to gauge where you'll come out."

Rusty nodded, and for a few minutes they swept in silence. But Rusty couldn't leave it alone. "Why'd you bring me through the corridor, Pete?"

"I rescued you from a family that—"

"*Besides that,*" Rusty snapped. "Me and four other kids. Why?"

Wheaton's head now ached terribly. All he wanted to do was stretch out in the cool darkness of his bedroom at the house and shut his eyes for a while. It seemed so hopelessly complex, the entire strategy that he had planned so carefully for so long now.

"I can't go into it now."

"You *won't* go into it, that's what you really mean," Rusty shouted. "You won't because it's something . . . something sick and perverted, just like this is. Clean the place yourself." Rusty threw down the broom and hurried out of the shed.

Sunny hesitated, glancing back at Wheaton, then at Rusty, and ran after Rusty, barking loudly, as if shouting at the boy to wait up.

She writhes beneath him, her head thrown back, her lovely pale throat warm against his mouth, her hair fanned out against the pillow. Her skin releases a scent that will be with him for the rest of his life, the fragrance of jasmine on hot summer nights. . . .

Wheaton squeezed his eyes shut against a tidal wave of memories, then grabbed the broom off the floor and hurriedly swept up the rest of the mess.

Sixteen

Sheppard's first run with the bureau had ended because he refused to storm an encampment that easily could have become another Waco. From this experience, he had learned that weapons weren't necessarily what gave you an edge. Yes, they helped. Weapons, like money, were power. But any kind of power had to be wielded with discretion, a fine point that neither Janet Reno nor John Ashcroft, politicians at opposite ends of the political spectrum, understood. Fortunately, Reno and Ashcroft were absent from this scenario and lucky for him, he had complete freedom to decide what to take and what to leave behind.

So he and Goot kept things simple and brought the weapons they normally used. Goot's preference was a Beretta 92FS 0mm with a laser grip. Just grip the gun, the laser comes on, fire. He claimed he could shoot more accurately with this weapon. Sheppard's weapon of choice was the P226 Sig Sauer, hardly the most aesthetic weapon, but it was rugged, reliable, and accurate. It had a double-column magazine holding fifteen rounds of 9mm parabellum ammunition, measured 7.7 inches overall, and weighed just twenty-nine ounces without the magazine. It was the smoothest weapon he had ever shot and one of the most compact of the 9mm automatics, a premier combat weapon. In a situation like this, it would give him the edge.

They also brought along a Remington twelve-gauge shotgun, a repeating pump weapon with a tubular magazine and a modified choke barrel that Sheppard kept in the trunk of his car. It was a favorite weapon for riot control and urban warfare. Overkill, but what the hell.

Goot drove. His Jeep had four-wheel drive and negotiated the unpaved roads in the preserve with complete ease. They weaved through the preserve for a mile or so, then weaved out again and climbed into the hills along the perimeter. Suddenly, the land leveled out again and pasture and fields rolled away on their right. Here and there stood abandoned farmhouses and old citrus groves swallowed up by weeds. The road, once paved, had potholes and ruts in it where nature had begun to claim the crumbling asphalt.

They passed a scattering of homes—inhabited, by the looks of them—and just beyond them stood a small white church that marked their turnoff. Goot hung a right onto Savoy, a narrow country road, barely paved. Banyans lined either side of the road and they were so immense their branches twisted together overhead, forming a tunnel through which they drove. The headlights flashed across the huge, thick trunks and exposed the barbed-wire fences just behind them. Signs were posted along the fences: NO TRESPASSING, PRIVATE PROPERTY, FOR SALE. "Thirty-one thirty is just ahead," Sheppard said quietly. "Kill the headlights and pull off into the trees."

Moments later, they got out, and headed through the woods on foot. Their shoes crunched over dried branches, their feet sank into soft cushions of pine needles and decaying leaves. Sheppard's heartbeat sped up, his senses sharpened. The night sounds became identifiable—crickets, frogs, reptiles scurrying off into the brush. This was Longfellow's forest primeval, filled with trees that had stood here for centuries, as dark, dense, and mysterious as the Amazon.

Please let her be alive, he thought, and wondered to whom he was praying.

When they emerged from the woods, the moon still hadn't risen, but the starlight was so brilliant that their bodies cast shadows on the road in front of them. On the other side of the road, behind another barbed-wire fence posted with more signs, stood the ruins of what used to be an A-frame house. Only the steel girders remained, a perfect steeple in the starlight surrounded by the rubble from a fire.

"What the fuck?" Goot whispered.

"Let's go," Sheppard whispered back, and they darted, hunkered over, across the road to the barbed-wire fence.

Now that they were closer, Sheppard could see charred wood, scorched concrete, twisted metal. The fire wasn't recent; vegetation had sprouted in the center of the house, small trees, bushes, even flowers. Signs posted on the fence warned of danger from debris and threatened prosecution and fines for trespassing. He felt his heart breaking apart; Annie wasn't here, couldn't be here. There wasn't any place that someone could be hidden. But they'd come this far and Sheppard knew he had to go the distance, to get inside the fence, see what was here besides the burned house.

Goot tried to twist the bottom of the fence upward with his hands, gave up, and brought out his wire cutters. Moments later, they were inside the fence, moving along the perimeter of the burned house, shining their flashlights inside. Sheppard went in first, stepping over what remained of an exterior wall, and realized he was in what had once been a kitchen. Everything except the kitchen sink and the counters had been removed. He found pieces of what might have been a refrigerator, the lid of a stove, and two large pieces of what probably had been kitchen cabinet doors. Their flashlights flushed out rodents and reptiles and cockroaches that looked to be as large as his hand. Mutants, he thought, cavorting up here in the ruins.

As they made their way through the kitchen toward what remained of a staircase, a weird feeling came over Sheppard, a flush of heat followed by a chill and then a sudden, vivid sense of déjà vu. *I've been here before.* He stopped and looked to his right, his left. "Goot," he whispered.

"What?" Goot paused, glancing over at him. "What is it?"

"Over there was a den. And over here"—he pointed at the wall next to the partial staircase—"was a circuit breaker for . . ."

For what?

He pointed his flashlight at the place where the circuit breaker had been, but there was only empty space. "Jesus," he whispered. "This is eerie. I've been here."

"What the hell're you talking about?" Goot hurried over to him.

"I don't know."

"Don't go weirding out on me, Shep."

Right. Get grounded. And do it fast. "There's no one here. Let's see what else we can find."

They left the hulk of the house, crossed the remains of what had once been a driveway, and ventured into another wooded area. Sheppard realized how easy it would be to get lost in here, so he took a compass reading, then unzipped a side pocket in his pack and brought out a piece of colored chalk. Every few yards, he left a bright yellow X on the trunk of a tree.

He didn't expect to find anything or anyone here. But the puzzling déjà vu he'd experienced earlier kept him moving through the woods and a vague sense of familiarity still nagged at him, like vestiges of some dimly remembered dream. There was obviously something odd about this place, but damned if he knew what the hell it was.

Now the land sloped downward slightly, as if toward a ravine or a gulch, and their flashlights found what appeared to be an old path. They followed it, kicking aside the weeds, trampling the vegetation that had grown over it, exposing patches of gravel here and there. A quarter of a mile in, they reached a tangle of giant ivy that dropped from the branches of the trees and climbed over the walls and roof of what looked to be a small concrete building. Sheppard and Goot turned off their flashlights and crouched down, whispering.

"Looks deserted, but let's not take chances," Sheppard said.

Goot went first, moving swiftly through the truncated starlight, then plunging into the shadows to the right of the building. Sheppard followed directly behind him. They reached the right corner of the building and stopped. The vines that covered the walls had climbed upward from the ground, rooted in the porous concrete, and swept in over the roof of the building. While Goot covered him, Sheppard tore away vines with his hands, exposing a window with the glass still intact. No lights inside. Other than that, though, the glass was so filthy it was impossible to see anything inside. They ducked under the windows and Sheppard tore away more vines, exposing a door with three rusted locks, all of them engaged.

"FBI," Sheppard shouted, banging on the door with his fist.

"I have a feeling no one's been inside this place for years," Goot said, and touched the chain to slide it off. It fell apart in his hands.

As Sheppard touched the doorknob, it came off. A single blow from the handle of his gun smashed the rusted dead bolt. The door gave way, swinging inward, creaking and groaning until it finally fell off the lowest hinge.

Sheppard pulled an electric lantern from his pack, turned it on, and held it up so the illumination was cast throughout the room. A large room, with wooden beams running across it and eaves on both sides. A small kitchen was located on the far side of the room and there was a bathroom off to his right. The air smelled stale and old, but it was surprisingly dry and free of vegetation and bugs. Goot headed toward the kitchen and Sheppard moved toward the bathroom.

The old tub, sink, and toilet were crusted and stained, the closet was missing a door. Like Goot had said, this place probably hadn't been inhabited for years. Sheppard set the lantern on the edge of the sink and shone his flashlight into the dark corners. Tiles had come loose from the wall alongside and behind the tub and when he looked closely, he saw that letters had been carved in the bare concrete with something sharp. He climbed into the tub for a better look and shone his flashlight on the area. He made out the words *Help me.*

A chill licked its way up his spine.

He ran his fingers over other letters, but time had eroded them and he couldn't make them out. He dropped his pack on the floor, unzipped it, brought out a notepad and pencil. He tore a piece of paper off the pad, placed it against the wall and, using the side of the lead, moved the pencil back and forth across the paper until the letters began to take shape on the paper. Some words were missing letters, others came out clear and complete in their horror. He tried to shout for Goot, but his voice came out as a pathetic croak.

He scrambled out of the tub, grabbed his pack, and ran into the other room, the paper in his hand.

"You find any—Jesus, amigo, what is it?" Goot asked.

"On the wall," Sheppard managed to say. "In the bathroom." He held out the piece of paper and Goot aimed his flashlight at it.

"Jesus," Goot whispered.

Sheppard squeezed the bridge of his nose and briefly shut his eyes. The words scrolled across the screen of eyelids: *Help me. Bad man. Find my mommy. Hurt. Sick.* And then the clincher: *Mira Shep A here ok graves in woods.*

Deeply shaken, Sheppard waited outside the building while Goot videotaped and photographed the writing on the bathroom wall. He breathed in the warm summer night air, his head racing with questions that only raised more questions. He realized that at least one of those questions could be answered by the Tango fire department.

Five minutes later, he had his answer. The house at 3130 Savoy had burned down in the mid-nineties, before Sheppard, Goot, Nadine, and Annie and Mira had arrived on Tango. At the time, the property was owned by a Japanese conglomerate, which had planned to turn it into a resort or time-share or something. The fire was believed to have been accidental, the result of squatters building a campfire during a drought.

"Do you happen to know who sold the property to the conglomerate?" Sheppard asked.

"No, sir. I sure don't. My understanding is that the conglomerate owned the property since the mid-eighties and the county property records aren't computerized back that far yet. The property history records are at the county courthouse."

Goot appeared just as Sheppard thanked the man for his time and disconnected. "It's recorded, but I don't know how much will show up," Goot said. "We need to get forensics up here."

"Not yet. Once we do that, Dillard will get wind of it."

"I don't get any of this, Shep. How could Annie possibly have left a message here?"

"I don't know. C'mon, I want to check the woods."

For graves.

They searched the woods for more than an hour and the only thing they found was that the property ended at the edge of a steep dropoff. Way down below, waves crashed against rocks and the black surface of the water caught the reflection of the rising moon. No wonder the Japanese had considered turning the place into a resort or a time-share. Raze the trees and you would have a view worth millions.

"Shep, there's no cemetery here," Goot said.

"The message didn't say cemetery. It said *graves.*"

They were behind the shed now, working their way through dense vegetation. What they really needed, Sheppard thought, was a machete.

"Graves, cemetery, what the fuck's the dif?" Goot said. "Either way, it's like looking for a pimple on the ass of the planet. We can come back when it's light."

"Do you have a shovel and blower in the trunk of your car?"

"We need a tractor, not shovels and blowers. We're dealing with decades of pine needles and leaves."

"Does that mean yes?"

"You know I just mowed my girlfriend's lawn and that—"

"When you mow, you blow." Sheppard snickered. "So give me your keys."

"I'll get it," Goot snapped, and marched off toward the road.

Now that he was alone in the woods, Sheppard allowed himself to think the unthinkable. Wheaton had

brought Annie up here after he'd kidnapped her and
she had scratched those words into the bathroom wall.
It was an ideal hideout for a kidnapper, abandoned in
a sparsely settled part of the island, fenced, with no-
trespassing signs posted everywhere. Since Wheaton as
Peter Wheat had listed this place as his address, then
he knew the layout of the land, knew about the shed.

But the shed had burned down years ago and it sure
as hell didn't look like anyone had been kept inside it
any time recently. It didn't make sense. And in his experience, when things didn't make sense, it meant he
wasn't asking the right questions in the right way.

Shit, shit, shit, he thought, and suddenly stumbled
over something, a root, a rock, he couldn't tell what it
was, but he lost his balance and all six feet, four inches
of him went down. He landed on his left side, with his
backpack taking the brunt of the fall. He pushed up,
rolled onto his knees, let go of his flashlight, and dug
frantically through the decaying mulch of the decades,
looking for what had caused him to stumble.

And then he touched it and pushed the needles and
leaves aside and sat back on his heels, staring at a ce-
ramic cross about three inches high. He rocked back
on his heels and aimed the flashlight's beam at it,
aware that part of him had gone dead inside.

Goot appeared, took one look at Sheppard, at the
cross, and turned on the blower. For five or six minutes, he blew leaves and needles away from the little
cross, laying bare the ground in the immediate vicinity
of the cross, exposing three crosses in all.

Sheppard just sat there, hands pressed hard against
his thighs, fingers clenched, his heart shattering into a
million pieces.

Seventeen

Mira had spent most of the day driving around Tango Key in the electric cart, her psychic antenna twitching, but no signals coming in. Now it was late afternoon and she was tired and discouraged. She didn't understand how she could read strangers better than at any point in her life, yet she couldn't pick up anything on Annie. The anomaly, the aberration, whatever it was that had brought her here, was like some sort of unforgiving god. It had given her a gift beyond her wildest expectations but it didn't work for locating Annie.

She took the Old Post Road, the long way back to the colony, and suddenly realized she was close to the neighborhood where Nadine and her second husband, David, owned a vacation home. Mira used to visit them during the summers and over holidays and always remembered what an adventure it was to come to Tango by boat or small plane and settle into Nadine's world.

Her mother had been terrified of her immersion in the world of the unseen and had done everything she could to discourage it. When Mira had come home from school one day and told her mother that she'd seen her first grade teacher naked with the football coach, her mother had grounded her for lying. On other occasions, her mother's response to Mira's abilities was that she shouldn't talk about such things or, worse, that she was imagining it. Yet, when Mira had related the story about her first grade teacher and the football coach to Nadine, her grandmother had understood immediately that she referred to the Sight, not to a literal seeing, and told her not to worry about it, that she would see a lot of things like that in her lifetime.

As she turned down the road that would lead into the neighborhood, Mira heard a familiar screeching in the air and glanced up to see Dusty the conure sweeping in toward her. "Hey, where've you been?" Mira pulled to the shoulder of the road, stopped, and held out her finger. "Hop on."

The bird fluttered down to Mira's finger and cocked her head. "Mirror," Dusty said, and touched her beak to the side of Mira's finger, stroking it. "Hungry."

Mira laughed. "You're consistent, I'll give you that much."

She unzipped her pack and brought out a bag of sunflower seeds. The conure knew immediately what they were and helped her tear open the pack. She grabbed a seed in her beak, scampered up to the back of Mira's seat, and perched there on one leg while she held the seed in the claws of her other foot. "We're taking a little trip down memory lane."

"Hello," the bird said in between nibbles at the seed.

Mira started the cart and the bird remained where she was, finishing one seed and starting on another. Given the way her life usually worked—at least before she had ended up here—her environment often alerted her to where she should put her attention. If she took the cues, things generally unfolded more smoothly. Following that line of thought, the appearance of the conure was as significant as her acquaintance with Jake, Lydia, Diego, and Fontaine. Jake had lent her money and suggested a place for her to stay, Diego had allowed her to test her abilities after she'd been so sick, Lydia she wasn't sure about yet, and Fontaine knew the monster who had abducted Annie. So what did the conure mean?

In mythology, birds were often depicted as messengers between worlds and dimensions. She certainly had slipped between worlds and the conure was the first thing she'd seen after coming through the portal to the past. Dusty had reflected her own condition, seemingly as lost and confused as she was, and had accompanied her as far as Rum Runners, where she discovered where she actually was. So perhaps the first level of interpretation was that the conure represented a kind of guide for her in this time.

On a deeper level, the nature of the species might hold clues. She knew that in the wild, conures were family-oriented birds, with both parents feeding and caring for the young. Their nests were often year-round homes and the young sometimes returned to the nests to roost. *Family* and *parents* were the key words. She was here because of her daughter, was looking for her daughter, and was about to enter her grandmother's neighborhood.

Conures were also noisy mimics with strong beaks. *Communication,* Mira thought. Perhaps Dusty's appearance now indicated that she should talk to Nadine.

Or all of this was bullshit and she was really grasping for straws.

Mira turned into Nadine's neighborhood. The homes, most of them built in the fifties, created an easel of art deco pastels, the soft blues and pale sea greens so prevalent now on Miami's south beach. The yards were steeped in shade, the still air quivered with the summer heat.

The cottage came into view, a single-story concrete block house painted canary yellow. It was one of the few homes on the street with a garage instead of a car-port and had the most lushly landscaped property. A stone path twisted through the greenery, the flaming vines, the clusters of bright orange firecracker plants. Wind chimes hung from the branches of the trees and every now and then emitted soft, inviting notes as a breeze touched them. A navy blue Mercedes was parked in the driveway, the same car that had pulled into her parents' driveway in Miami at least once a month throughout much of her childhood. Into the Mercedes she would go and her real life would begin. Through the lens of memory, these visits now seemed like her initiation into some secret school.

She pulled the cart to the side of the road, suddenly uncertain about what to do. Ring the bell and intro-duce herself as Mira Piper? Tell Nadine the truth? Run?

Before she could make up her mind, the garage door came up and a slender woman wearing a floppy hat, shorts, and a sleeveless cotton shirt walked out. She was barefoot, carried gardening tools, and dragged a hose behind her. Mira couldn't see the woman's face, but she recognized Nadine by the graceful way she moved. She was in her late forties now, in the prime of her life, not much older than Mira.

Mira watched as Nadine dropped the hose, set her tools on the ground, crouched, and began to dig. She knew that Nadine was humming to herself or talking softly to her flowers as she dug up weeds and soil. She paused and fanned herself with her straw hat and sud-denly glanced out at the road, as if she sensed that someone watched her. Mira, heart hammering, looked down at her hands.

Decide. Fast. Leave or stay, but don't just sit here. She dug into her pack and brought out a pen and a pad of paper. *What to say?*

The truth. She would write the truth.

But the truth had to be written in a way that Nadine in 2003 would understand—if she ever saw it—but which wouldn't cause Nadine in 1968 to dismiss her as a nutcase. Mira wrote the note, phrasing her words carefully, then tore it off the pad, folded it into her hand, and got out of the cart, Dusty perched on her shoulder. She started toward the house, the steep driveway, those brilliant flowers, and toward the woman who was—or would become, depending on the time frame—the greatest influence on the course of her adult life. *You don't know me, but . . .*

Nadine got to her feet, slapped her hands against her shorts, and twisted her thick black hair into a tighter knot at the back of her head. "Hi," she called. "Can I help you with something?"

"I hope so."

The conure suddenly squawked, *"Hola, amigas,"* and Nadine laughed.

"She even got the gender right. Amig-*as* instead of amig-*os*. A dusky conure, right?"

"Yes."

Nadine spoke to the bird in Spanish, a language that Dusty seemed to understand, and when she held out her finger, the bird accepted the invitation, her wings fluttering, her feathers fluffing up. "There are flocks of wild birds on the island. Conures, green parrots, even a few macaws. You see them sometimes in the evening," Nadine said. "Around dusk." She touched her nail to Dusty's breast and moved it along her left wing, and Dusty spread it. "Her wings aren't clipped. But she doesn't fly away. That speaks well for you."

This was the Nadine Mira knew, the woman for whom a primary measure of other people was how they treated animals and how animals reacted to them. "Actually, she just appears from time to time. She found me on the beach the other day."

"The Cubans have a saying about animals who find *us,*" Nadine said, putting Dusty back on Mira's shoulder. "They are our beacons and our mentors. They choose to teach us something." She gave a small, self-conscious laugh. "I'm sorry, I'm rattling off and you had a question."

They stood only a few feet apart now and Mira suddenly couldn't speak around the lump rising in her throat. Her childhood memory of Nadine at this age didn't do her justice. Her beauty was shocking enough, but it was her voice—that soft, almost musical lilt to it—that touched Mira most deeply.

"You look so familiar to me," Nadine remarked, frowning. "Have we met?"

At some level, she recognizes me. "I don't think so. I'm actually lost and stopped to ask directions. I'm, uh, trying to get to Pirate's Cove."

It was the quickest lie she could think of.

"Just follow the road that brought you into the neighborhood and turn right at the first intersection. That road will take you north. The—"

The front door flew open and a young girl with pigtails bounded out, shouting, "*Nana, Nana Nadine, come quick. Lucy ate . . .*"

Mira didn't hear the rest. Noise roared into her skull, the light trembled, everything listed to one side. *It's me, that kid is me.* She felt as if she were watching a car in her rearview mirror that was speeding toward her and knew that if she didn't leap out of the way, it would mow her down. "I have to go," she murmured, and thrust the note into Nadine's hand and practically ran back to the street, to the cart.

The bird screeched, the noise kept roaring in her skull, her hands shook as she started the cart. She drove away from the house, drove as fast as the cart would go, and didn't look back. She went maybe half a mile before her emotions overwhelmed her and she pulled off the road.

She pressed her fists into her eyes, wishing desperately that she could have put her arms around that younger self and whispered some pearl of wisdom that she could carry with her into adulthood, something that would comfort her when Tom was murdered.

I can prevent that.

And I can prevent Annie's abduction. All I have to do is . . .

What? Tell her younger self not to move to Tango?

Every science fiction book she'd read, every time-travel movie she'd seen, and nearly every scientific theory she'd read about time travel mentioned the paradox of meddling in the past. Yet, her experiences as a psychic, especially since she'd come here, seemed to suggest that reality was multidimensional, rather like the many-worlds theory of quantum physics, with new possibilities and probabilities created with every decision that was made. In this view, there might be a reality where she had *not* pursued Annie and the monster and had sped back to Tango for help. There might be another reality in which she had fought with the abductor and one of them had been killed or a reality in which Annie had escaped or in which the abductor had been caught.

She wondered if her memories were different now.

As soon as she thought this, a memory surfaced of the afternoon in June 1968 when she had run outside Nadine's house, shouting about Lucy, the injured dove. It had started eating and she just had to tell her Nana Nadine. But Nana was talking to a lady with a bird on her shoulder and when the lady saw Mira, the blood rushed out of her face. She shoved something into Nadine's hand and hurried away, the bird squawking.

"Who was that lady, Nana?"

"She was lost, mí amor," Nana replies, staring after the electric cart as it drives away.

"What'd she give you?"

"I'm not sure."

Nadine unfolds the piece of paper in her hand. Mira watches how her expression changes, the lines between her eyes deepening, her dark eyes startled, concerned, mystified. "What is it, Nana?"

"Strange. How many people on Tango do you think there are named Mira?"

"Just me." She laughs.

"That lady's name is also Mira. In Spanish, whenever someone has the same name that you do, we call that person your tacayo.*"*

"What's the note say?"

Nana Nadine fans herself with the straw hat and slips an arm around Mira's shoulders as they walk over to the front steps. "I'll read it to you and you listen with your inner senses, mí amor."

"It's just a letter."

"I think it's quite a bit more than that, but let's see how it strikes you." They sit down on the shaded front steps and Nadine begins to read. Mira shuts her eyes, trying to listen in the way that Nadine has taught her.

Mira waits a moment, her eyes shut, then shakes her head and looks over at Nadine. "I don't understand it. What are coordinates? Who is Sheppard?"

"I don't know. What did you feel when you heard me reading the note?"

"That I should know what it's about."

Nadine hands her the piece of paper. "Hold it tightly between your palms. Close your eyes. Breathe the way I've taught you."

Mira sits quietly, the heat against her face, the paper pressed between her palms, and within her eyes images burst and burn like torches. A child, a woman, two men, books, and then a blackness so thick and impenetrable, so totally horrifying, that she drops the paper and shoots to her feet and runs into the house.

Mira sensed another new memory forming behind this one, but she couldn't seize it, couldn't bring it into her conscious mind to scrutinize it. Terrified that she would forget this experience or that it would replace another memory, she dug her Pocket PC and the portable keyboard out of her pack. She unfolded the keyboard on her lap, connected it to the Pocket PC, and quickly typed out everything that had happened.

For long moments, she felt as if she inhabited two worlds, dual realities that were equally valid, equally genuine. She hoped the same would be true for Nadine in 2003, that she had saved the note from the stranger in 1968, and that she would give it to Sheppard or mention it to him, and he would piece it all together and find his way through the darkness and back thirty-five years in time. She immediately recognized this for the absurdity it was.

Help wasn't going to come from her own time and she couldn't count on Nadine, in this time, to bail her out. She could give it her best shot, but the bottom line was glaringly simple: she was on her own.

As if to underscore that fact, the bird rubbed her beak against Mira's cheek, then flew off to join a flock of wild parrots and conures that flew by overhead, their cries echoing through the waning light.

2

When Annie came to, she didn't know how long she'd been out or what day it was. It was dark, but for all she knew it could be darkness of the next day.

And that day is . . . ?

She didn't know. Time had gotten away from her. She had no more reference points. But that was all part of what he intended for her. It was part of his brainwashing.

She sat up, swung her legs over the edge of the couch, rubbed her hands over her face. *Graves, there are graves out there in the woods,* she thought, and bolted off the couch. She ran into the bathroom and jerked open the linen closet door. They hadn't found the spatula knife hidden behind the stacks of tiles. She grabbed the spatula and climbed into the tub, loosened the tiles that hid the message she'd carved, and added: *graves in woods.*

She still felt disoriented from the chloroform and it seemed to take her a long time to carve those three words. But she knew that if Shep and her mother found this place, these three words would lead them to the graves, which might lead them to answers.

Annie put the tiles back in place, hid the knife behind the tiles again, and returned to the room. Now she noticed that Peter or Rusty had brought in a TV, a VCR, videotapes, a CD player, and stacks of CDs and magazines. Frowning, wondering what the trick was, she glanced through the magazines. *Look, Life, TV Guide, Time, Newsweek,* but all of them dated back to 1968. Nadine had stuff like this in the attic, but her magazines were yellowed with age. These looked new.

She looked through the CDs and found one of Jimi Hendrix's greatest hits. She popped it into the CD player, cranked the volume up, and listened to Hendrix belting out "Purple Haze."

'Scuse me while I kiss the sky . . .

She noticed that the power for the VCR was already on and when she turned on the TV, the tape began to run. She turned off the CD player and watched the first scene on the videotape unroll: the road sign for Mango Drive, where her mother's bookstore was located. "We're moving east now on Mango Drive." Peter's voice. He was in a car. She could hear the engine, the noise of the tires against the road, even the soft drone of music in the background.

Annie stepped back from the screen and folded her arms across her chest, as if to protect herself from his voice. "Some things are the same, like this coffee shop coming up on the left where you and your mother have eaten lunch a couple of times. It's a different color here, but I think you'll recognize it."

Antonio's, sure, she recognized it. The neon sign was there, a throwback to the fifties, but the building was sea green instead of yellow. And the landscaping looked new, with stunted bushes, small trees, and no flaming bougainvillea.

"Now we're approaching the corner where your mother's bookstore should be." The car pulled over to the curb and the camera paused on a vacant lot. "But, oops, no bookstore. How can that be? But I don't expect you to take *my* word for it. We're going to move on now, east toward the Tango bridge. Everything looks similar, but different."

Annie stepped back again, knuckles at her mouth as she watched the landscape unfold, familiar yet changed. An ice cream store where there should be a kids' clothing store. A restaurant where there should be a smoothie shop. "What the hell?" she murmured, and picked up the remote and paused the image.

At the bottom of the screen, a date appeared: June 18, 1968. Peter obviously didn't know how to program his videocamera, she thought, and leaned close to the screen, staring at the name of the restaurant. Ginny's Seafood. It seemed familiar, but she knew she'd never seen it. Then she remembered one of Nadine's stories about Tango in the early days and how she and her second husband, David Cantrell, used to eat at Ginny's Seafood every weekend. Nadine had told her that Ginny had died of a heart attack in the early seventies and the place had been sold.

How stupid did Peter think she was, anyway? This was just some old historical tape and he'd superimposed his voice over it. Even old home movies could be put on a videocassette these days. What was the point of all this? *What trick is he trying to pull on me now?* He was messing with her head. She'd read about stuff like this, brainwashing techniques used on POWs. But if she was a POW, where was the war?

It was Peter's private war.

"Now we're coming out of the turn so you'll be able to see Florida Bay and Key West in the distance," said Peter's voice.

As the car came out of the turn, Annie saw Florida Bay in all its breathtaking beauty, with Key West a dark spot in the distance, but no bridge connected them. She paused the image, looked more closely, and exploded with laughter. "C'mon, anyone can do this with splicing, you ass."

The voice said: "The bridge hasn't been built yet, Annie. It won't be built for another seventeen years."

"Yeah, right."

She heard the jingle of keys at the door, Sunny's bark, the locks being disengaged. Rusty walked in with a tray of food, the dog hurrying alongside him, and Peter right behind him.

"You've seen the tape?" Peter asked, shutting the door.

"Some of it." She refused to look at him or at Rusty. She still stood in front of the television, pressing the channel button, but nothing happened.

"The remote won't work for the TV stations," Peter said. "Channel surfing hasn't been invented yet."

"Just like the bridge hasn't been built, right?" She glanced at him then and caught the look that he and Rusty exchanged.

"I told you she wouldn't be convinced by a tape," Rusty said, and set the tray of food on the coffee table in front of the couch.

"Go through the channels the old-fashioned way." Peter again, the voice of authority. "You'll find stuff you've never seen before, not even on the endless reruns in your own time. When a show is in color, the *TV Guide* makes special mention of it. *Wild, Wild West*, for example, is in color. So is *Star Trek*—the original cast, Annie, with Captain Kirk and Spock."

"My mother's attic is filled with old magazines like those. . . ." She gestured toward the magazines. "And this stupid tape you made . . ." She grabbed it, tore it out of the container, and tossed it on the floor. ". . . doesn't prove anything. You're just a sick bastard who takes kids."

"Don't swear." Peter stepped forward for the first time, away from the door. Color rushed up his neck. "That's rule one. *No swearing.*"

"*Fuck you,*" Annie screamed, and kicked the spent videocassette.

It spun across the floor, spewing bits of broken plastic, and Peter looked down at it, following it with his eyes. Then those dark, evil eyes flicked to her face and she *felt* their touch, *felt* the evil, the madness, the rage. She flinched and suddenly the world went from swift, violent motion to a terrible slowness in which she perceived every detail—Peter lifting his arm, the back of his hand headed toward her face, her own arms rising upward in protection.

Just as suddenly, everything slammed into a kind of frenzy. Rusty leaped between her and Peter, grabbed his arm, shoved him back. Peter stumbled, but didn't fall.

"Don't."

That was all Rusty said, just a simple *Don't.* But he said it with such authority and power that Peter understood the implications. He glared at Rusty with the bottled rage of a man at the edge. His eyes narrowed to shiny daggers, the air burned with all that lay unspoken between them. Peter balled his fist and pressed it into his other hand, as if he were grinding glass with his knuckles. For a moment, Annie thought he would take a swing at Rusty. Rusty must have thought so, too, because in that same, low and threatening voice, he said, "I'm not twelve anymore, Pete."

Peter held Rusty's gaze, his lips pressed tightly together. "I'll be outside. Don't be long."

He slammed the door as he left. Annie bit at her knuckles to keep from screaming, to hold back sobs. Rusty touched her arm. "Everything he said is true, Annie." He spoke loudly and she realized he was doing it so that Peter would hear him, that Peter was probably standing just outside the door, listening. Rusty also gestured toward the CD player. "He brought you back in time. To 1968."

"Yeah, sure, right." She mouthed, *Please help me,* and hurried over to the CD player. "You're no better than he is. I don't want to listen to either of you," and she turned the volume high so that Hendrix's voice echoed throughout the room.

She and Rusty moved toward each other and he grasped her by the arms, leaning close to her so she could hear him. "I'll help you. I swear I will. But it has to be done carefully. There's something for you under the tray that will explain everything."

He started to turn away, but she caught his hand and spoke fast, urgently, emotion crackling in her voice. "Help me now. Both of us can take him, we can knock him out, you can drive me into town, leave me there. I won't tell. I just want to go home, I—"

"You're not listening." His hands swallowed hers, gripping tightly. "What he said is true. This is 1968 and I don't know how to get you back through the corridor. The most I can do is get you somewhere else on the island and hide you there until . . . until we can figure out how to get you home." He dropped her hand. "I have to go. He'll come in here if I don't get out there. Trust me, Annie. Just trust me." He cupped her face in his hand, his beautiful eyes swallowing hers, and kissed her quickly on the mouth.

Her insides lit up, her lips tingled, and then he was gone.

Even after the door shut, she stood there for a moment longer, her fingers touching her mouth. *He kissed me. My God, he kissed me.*

Then she shot toward the tray, picked it up, but didn't find anything under it. She lifted the tray higher and saw a sheet of paper taped securely to the bottom of it. Relief rushed through her. Relief, gratitude, hope. Annie removed everything from the tray, flipped it over, peeled the paper away, and fled for the bathroom.

This is 1968 . . .

Impossible, no way. But why would Rusty lie to her? What could he possibly gain by lying to her?

She locked the door, sat on the edge of the tub, and opened the envelope.

Here's the deal. He brought you through a weirdness that we call the corridor. It's like the wormhole in Deep

Space Nine, *but it's in the gulf and the oceans instead of space. He taped some of those episodes for me when he went back—and he goes back often—and I recognized the parallels. Maybe that's why he taped them. That's the kind of guy he is. If he does something that seems kind, then you know he has himself in mind. Do NOT forget that.*

You had the time sickness. It happened bad to me, too. It killed the other kids. It hits everyone differently. Peter is sterile because of it and I sometimes see sounds and hear colors. I know there's a word for it, like a medical term, but I don't know what it is.

He brought me here in 1997. He'd been watching me for a few months. He knew a lot about my messed-up family. He claimed he was saving me from them. I guess that part is true. But there's some deeper thing going on here.

I can't do this anymore, standing by and watching him do what he does. But right now, I have to find out what he's really up to and then, as soon as I turn 18 and am a legal adult, I can do something about him. I think that Lydia knows the truth, but she's too scared to do anything about it. Life for blacks in 1968 isn't a picnic and he pays her well. Very well. He's rich. I think he stole money from his wealthy wife back in 1994 and came back here and began setting up a life for himself.

That black water mass? That's where the corridor is. Been here six years and I still don't know the exact location of the corridor, but I'm working on that, too.

When I was in the shed, I nearly went crazy trying to figure out where I was. Once I knew the time frame, I started going crazy again trying to pinpoint the geography. Just in case things have changed on Tango in the years I've been here, I've drawn a map so you have a rough idea of where his property is in relation to other landmarks I remember from 1997.

*The color I hear for you, Annie, and the sounds I see
for you, are on that Jimi Hendrix CD, the song "Purple
Haze."*

Stay cool.

The sensation of his mouth against hers still lingered
against her skin and she kept touching her lips as she
read the note again. That part about the color he
heard for her, the sounds he saw for her, made her feel
as warm and strange inside as the kiss. *I am Purple Haze.*
He had come through the time sickness hearing colors
and seeing sounds, but what the hell did it do to her? *I
puke, I feel like shit, I'm scared all the time.*

Think, think. What would her mother do? What
would Shep do?

They would take different tactics. Shep would find
out everything he could about where he was, Peter's
motives, how he might escape from this room. Her
mother would turn inward first, looking for intuitive
information. Shep was left-brain to her mother's right-
brain. Annie knew that if she was going to get out of
here, she needed to be both left- and right-brain.

The map, okay, the map would tell her where on
Tango she was. The X that marked her location was in
the northeast hills, near the preserve. Rusty had given
her two landmarks from 1997 that still existed in 2003:
a church and a Publix supermarket. She shut her eyes,
trying to visualize the location, to see it in terms of bike
paths and her own life. And suddenly it hit her. She was
on property that had burned before she and her mom
and Nadine had moved to Tango.

She and her mother had passed the church one time
when they spent the day biking around the Old Post
Road. Its fences were covered with no-trespassing signs,
that was all she knew about it. But in this time, the land
thrived. She had run across it, through the deep woods.

She had seen the graves. If Sheppard were miraculously able to locate this place, would he explore what were ruins in his time?

Yes. He was thorough.

But none of that mattered. Thirty-five years separated her from her mother, Sheppard, Nadine, her cats, her life. No one was going to come back here to rescue her. Even Rusty had admitted he didn't know how Peter went through this thing called the corridor. And that meant she would have to find a way out of here and back to her own time by herself. She hoped that Rusty would help her, but perhaps, for now, he had done all that he could.

She tore the map to shreds and flushed the pieces of paper. She had to flush several times, the plumbing wasn't all that great here. And as she stood there, flushing the toilet repeatedly, it suddenly occurred to her that in June 1968, her father was alive, the same age that she was now, a teenager living in the keys.

Eighteen

Over the next three days, the media blitz that followed the discovery of the children's bodies crowded dozens of other stories out of the news and placed Sheppard squarely where he didn't want to be: in the limelight. But he understood that he needed the media now, that the more exposure the case got, the more likely it was that someone, somewhere, would spot Wheaton. He gave statements to the three networks, to CNN, to Fox News, and to a dozen local affiliates. Larry King interviewed him via satellite. He filmed a segment with John Walsh, and walked the Savoy property with Jane Pauley.

The lives of the children's parents and families were turned into a living nightmare, with reporters and broadcasters and camera crews camped out across the street from their homes and their places of employment. The bookstore had been closed since noon of the first day because Nadine's phone rang constantly and the media trucks made it difficult for customers to get into the store.

Sheppard checked with Tina Richmond regularly by phone or e-mail, hoping for news about the positive ID of the bodies. He knew it would take time for forensics to identify all the children's remains, but anxious parents were breathing down his neck, his cell phone rang nonstop, and he was wrestling with his own demons, his own questions about whether Annie's body was among those in the graves.

CNN had regular updates on the investigation and posted photographs of the five children, of Wheaton, of Mira. Julia Lenier, the ex-Mrs. Wheaton, had called several times, raging and blaming him for the media trucks that had made her a prisoner in her own home. Her husband, the arrogant Steven Nymes, called to inform Sheppard he was suing. Sheppard gave him the number for the bureau attorneys, then hung up on him.

This morning, Sheppard's cell phone was turned off and he was using a cell phone with prepaid minutes on it and no caller ID. Only three people had that number—Goot, Tina Richmond, and Nadine. So when it rang, he thought it was one of them. Instead, Chief of Police Doug Emison said, "Shep, John gave me your new number. I hope that's okay."

"Sure, what's up?"

"I know you're swamped right now. But could you meet me down at Tango Sea and Air?"

"I'm not far from there now. I can swing by. Did your search parties find something?"

"I'll fill you in when you get here."

Southern cracker, mystery man, Sheppard thought when they disconnected. He made a U-turn in the middle of the road and three minutes later, turned into the parking lot. Emison and another man were out on the dock, standing beside three red and blue seaplanes that looked spanking new.

His companion stood about six-two, was well built, with blond hair that was thinning and going gray. He had a handsome, weathered face and looked vaguely familiar to Sheppard. But these days, everyone seemed to look vaguely familiar to him. He wore casual chinos, a cotton shirt, moccasins.

"Shep, this is Ross Blake," said Emison.

The man who fought city hall. The man who owned Tango Sea and Air. "It's a pleasure, Mr. Blake," Sheppard said, and extended his hand.

Blake's smile was genuine, but quick, almost shy. "I've been following the media frenzy, Agent Sheppard, and I called Doug and asked what I can do to help."

"Our budget is straining at the seams," Emison explained. "I told Ross we need planes and pilots." Emison gestured toward the three seaplanes. "So these are ours to use for the search."

Sheppard immediately wondered what Blake's angle was, then chided himself for being so suspicious of other people's good intentions. "That's very generous, Mr. Blake. But the bureau leases their planes from you. You're going to lose money on this."

"Money really isn't the issue. News like this . . . involving children . . . on the island you call home . . ." He shook his head. "It does something to you."

Blake pulled two business cards from his shirt pocket. Sheppard realized that Blake had kept his left hand in the pocket of his khaki shorts the entire time they'd been standing here and wondered what, if anything, that was about.

"When you need the planes, call one of the numbers on the card. The pilots are all local and can be here in five minutes." He gave them each a card, emblazoned with the double gold Bs that were the logo for Blake Builders. "Any time, day or night." He paused. "Doug mentioned that the woman and her daughter are practically family for you, Agent Sheppard."

He nodded and wished that Emison had kept his mouth shut. "I've known them a long time, yes."

"Since that case in Lauderdale."

"Right." Sheppard felt increasingly uncomfortable and Blake must have sensed it.

"I wish you the best of luck in finding them." Blake turned to Emison. "Doug, you take care and call any time."

He strode toward a boat tied to the end of the dock, got in, untied it, and putted off, headed north. Emison grinned. "Fuckin' impressive, huh?"

"But why's he doing this?"

"He's divorced, has two kids, doesn't see them much. The ex is somewhere up north. You don't realize how cases like this hit people, Shep."

"Why didn't you get Leo down here?"

"Ross asked specifically for you, as the agent in charge of the investigation."

"Not according to Leo."

Emison wrinkled up his pudgy little nose. "Fuck Leo. Let him think what he wants."

Interesting, Sheppard thought. "Did your search parties find anything?"

"Not a damn thing. They've searched for a total of twenty or twenty-five hours and covered six hundred square miles of the gulf and the bay. And nothing. We're going out again today, into that black water mass."

"Be careful in there. When we took the Zodiac in, we lost radio and cell phones, compass, even the flashlights."

"Yeah, we've run into some of that already."

Sheppard's cell phone rang again. He thanked Emison, told him he needed to take the call, and hastened up the dock, the phone pressed to his ear. It was the archive librarian at the county courthouse. She said she'd gotten his number from Agent Gutierrez and hoped he didn't mind. She had tracked down some curious information about the ownership of the Savoy property and could he possibly get over to the courthouse?

It occurred to Sheppard that breaks in any investigation often seemed to come in threes. The discovery of the graves was the first break and perhaps the information about the Savoy property would be the second.

The librarian, Vicki Webber, was an attractive woman in her early fifties who definitely understood the strangeness of the situation and got right to the point. "There are gross inconsistencies in this information, Agent Sheppard, so I'll just give you what I have and let you figure it out."

They were in her quiet office at the back of the courthouse, her long oak desk strewn with CDs, microfiche, old deeds, and a huge book in which the ownership of property on the island before 1922 was recorded by hand. The air smelled of freshly brewed coffee and cigarette smoke. Sheppard realized he hadn't eaten anything since a bagel he'd wolfed down about five this morning and asked if he could have a cup of coffee.

"I'm running on empty," he admitted.

Vicki not only brought him a mug of strong Cuban coffee, but put a plate in front of him that held a Swiss cheese on rye, slices of apple, and two chocolate chip cookies. "You eat, I'll talk."

Sheppard turned on his tape recorder and let her talk. "The Savoy property, all ten acres of it, had been bought in July 1965 by Peter Wheat for eighty-five thousand. If Peter Wheat is Patrick Wheaton, then that's inconsistency number one because Wheaton was thirteen years old in 1965. I, uh, looked up Mr. Wheaton's bio on the Internet."

Sheppard nodded. His head ached, his throat felt parched, he desperately needed sleep, silence, and a rational world.

"He bought the property from Lucia Ray, firstborn daughter of a family on Tango that had owned a large portion of that area of the island since the eighteen hundreds. After Wheat's death in 1968, the property passed to his eighteen-year-old nephew, Rusty Everett."

"What?"

Vicki smiled. "I told you this was strange, Agent Sheppard. The Rusty Everett who was kidnapped in 1997 was born in 1985. So there're two people by that name or someone's played a huge joke here."

Or they're the same person. Impossible. Out of the question. "You said he's listed as Wheat's nephew?"

"That's how he's listed on the deed." She turned the papers so he could see them. "Everett sold it to the artists' colony in 1973 for a hundred and sixty-five thousand. They sold it to a Japanese conglomerate in 1985 for six hundred and fifty thousand. That company owns it now and the property has gone into foreclosure because they haven't paid taxes on it for the last two years. I printed out a history for you." She passed it to him. "With Mr. Everett's address as of 1973."

"Do you have a history for this address since 1973?"

She shook her head. "No. Up until ten years ago, most of these files were on microfiche or in folders, ledgers, and whatnot. Everything between 1975 and 1981 was destroyed in a fire. We've been piecing the records together ever since."

His cell phone rang—his new cell phone, the one with the prepaid minutes whose number was known to only a handful of people. Ha. Sheppard answered it with a wary "Hello?"

"Hey, amigo, it's me." Goot spoke in an urgent whisper. "Nadine and I are at the Savoy property."

"Why the hell did you take her *there*?"

"Because her place is surrounded by media. Because she wanted to see it, walk around. Shit, how can I refuse an eighty-two-year-old woman? Dillard's here, too, and he's demanding to see you."

"I'll be there in a while. If Nadine tries to read the property, make sure she's not anywhere near anyone but you."

"She refuses to read—and I quote—such an evil place. So what should I tell the boss?"

"I'll be there within the hour."

Sheppard left the county courthouse with the printout on the Savoy property and Rusty Everett's Tango address, circa 1973. It couldn't be the same Rusty Everett, that much was abundantly clear. But what a troubling coincidence that the abductee and this other Everett had the same name.

Too troubling.

On his way north, Sheppard called information and requested a listing for Rusty Everett. It didn't surprise him that there was no such listing on Tango or anywhere else in the keys. And he wasn't surprised when the elderly woman who answered the door at Everett's last known address told him that no one by that name lived in the house.

"How long have you lived here?" Sheppard asked, and held up his badge. "I'm asking in an official capacity."

"Oh. Oh dear. Well, let me think a moment. Reagan was in the White House. Early 1980."

"Who did you buy the house from?"

"Mrs. Foreman. Iris Foreman."

"Do you happen to have a phone number or an address for her?"

"It may be on the closing papers. I'll look, if you could wait a few minutes."

"Sure."

The door shut. Sheppard stood on the porch, waiting, and his new cell phone rang again. Who now, he wondered, and worried that Goot had given the boss his new number.

No, Goot wouldn't do that. He pressed the answer button. "Agent Sheppard."

"It's Tina. We won't have definitive IDs on these bodies for another day or so, at least not as far as the media and the families are concerned. But we've got dental record matches for two of them. Becky Sawyer and Antonio Pantello."

Sheppard shut his eyes against the memory of Antonio's mother's voice: *He is dead. He is buried on a hill that overlooks the sea.* "Any idea on the gender of the other one?"

"Male, Shep."

His relief was so extreme that his body went empty, like a balloon that suddenly loses all its air.

"Now here's an odd thing. Although Becky Sawyer was abducted three years ago, her remains suggest decay well beyond that."

"I don't understand."

Tina, nearly whispering now: "Shep, it's as if the body has been buried for *decades*, okay?"

"Decades." But this was no stranger than a boy selling a home before he was even born, a home he had inherited from the man who had abducted him. "What about Pantello's body? He vanished just six weeks ago."

"Same thing."

"Is there some scientific reason that could happen?"

"The bodies were buried just in the soil—no coffins, no boxes, no embalming. Deterioration would be quicker, but not like this, Shep."

He squeezed the bridge of his nose, wishing that at least one facet of this investigation would make sense. "How long can we keep this between us?"

"That depends on how pushy Dillard is."

"We both know the answer to that."

"Look, Dillard's interested in the media, not the specifics. I'll do what I can."

He leaned against the porch railing and was still leaning against it when the front door of the house opened again. "Tina, I'll call you back in a few minutes." He disconnected. "You found it?" he asked the woman.

"I believe so."

She handed him a stapled sheaf of yellowed papers. At the bottom of the top page was Iris Foreman's name, signature, Social Security number, a Gainesville, Florida address, and two phone numbers. Sheppard copied everything into his notepad, thanked the old woman, and hurried back to his car. As soon as he was inside, he called Iris Foreman's home phone number and reached an answering machine. He disconnected and called the work number.

He got a recorded menu, listened to it, punched a number, got another menu, punched another number, got another menu, and went through this process four more times before he pressed 0 and heard a human voice.

"Registrar's office," said a woman.

"Iris Foreman, please."

"She's in the language department, sir. This is the registrar's office. You'll have to call—"

Sheppard's blood pressure shot toward the moon. "I just went through six recorded menus. Please connect me to Ms. Foreman's office."

"I'll try, sir. If you lose the connection, call the main number and punch in extension fifty-three."

A click, a buzz; then the extension started to ring. And ring. Sheppard rubbed his dry, aching eyes and started the car. He adjusted the vents so that cool air blew directly into his face.

"Professor Foreman."

"Iris Foreman?"

"Yes, this is Iris Foreman."

"My name is Wayne Sheppard, ma'am. I'm a special agent with the FBI and I'd like to ask you a few questions about a house you owned on Tango Key before 1980. Do you have a few minutes?"

"Just because you say you're an agent with the FBI, Mr. Sheppard, doesn't mean that you are."

Good point, he thought, and liked her for that. "What sort of proof would you like?"

"Your badge number and an official phone number I can call to verify it."

"Call it in on another line," he said, "so I don't have to navigate all those recorded menus again." He gave her the information she asked for.

"Just a minute."

She didn't put him on hold; he could hear her speaking to the FBI office in Miami. When she picked up the receiver again, she said, "What would you like to know?"

"The address of the house, just for verification, when you bought it, and who the seller was."

"It was on Ruby Drive, I don't remember the exact address. It was the third house in from the corner. I bought it in 1976 as a weekend place from a young man named Everett. I don't recall his first name."

Time to believe the impossible. "What do you remember about him?"

"He was missing the little finger on his left hand. He was scrupulously polite, in his early to mid-twenties, and had a calm, quiet voice. I believe he was in the real estate business. Commercial real estate. That's all I can tell you, Agent Sheppard."

He asked her to get in touch with him if she recalled anything else and gave her his new cell number and e-mail address. He took one last look at the house and a chill snaked up his spine.

* * *

The police barricade around the Savoy property began at the church where he and Goot had turned the night before last and got heavier as he approached the burned-out house and the woods that had hidden the graves. Dillard spotted Sheppard as soon as he approached the shed and hurried over, a cell phone mashed to his ear. *Be with you in a second,* he mouthed.

The early afternoon light slanted through the branches of the tree under which they stood and settled against Dillard's face, exposing every line and wrinkle and imperfection. As usual, his thick white hair was perfectly coiffed. He probably visited the beauty salon at the Hilltop Inn and paid a small fortune for a stupid haircut. The money would be better spent on a membership for the gym; the guayabera shirt he wore didn't hide the roll of fat around his waistline.

"Excellent work here, Shep," said Dillard, as if the incident at the Hilltop had never happened. He pulled a monogrammed handkerchief from his back pocket and dabbed at his sweaty forehead. "The bureau's public opinion ratings have gone up several notches just since the story broke."

It was no secret that since September 11, the intelligence agencies—the FBI in particular—had come under attack for their failure to prevent the tragedy. And this story certainly made Dillard look good since Tango was part of his territory and he was Sheppard's and Goot's immediate boss. "I just heard from forensics that they have dental matches for two of the victims." There. That was all Dillard needed to know for right now.

"Have the families been notified?"

"Not yet. We're waiting for the third match. And we won't be releasing any statement to the press until the

DNA results are in. There're a lot of inconsistencies in this case."

"Yeah, Goot filled me in on some of the details. I didn't realize, however, that one of the missing children is the daughter of your fiancée."

"We're not actually engaged."

Dillard jammed his hands in the pockets of his slacks and studied the ground as though some sort of answer lay in the arrangement of pine needles. "But there's a personal connection between you and this child and you and her mother."

Sheppard had a very bad feeling about where this was headed. "Yeah, so? We're not married, they aren't blood relations."

Dillard looked at him then and Sheppard thought he saw glee in those dark currant eyes. "I don't make the policy, Shep."

"There isn't any official policy that covers personal connections to the victims, only marriage and blood connections."

"That's true. But ever since the Burns case in 1993, the unwritten policy in our office has been no personal connection whatsoever."

The Burns case that he referred to had involved an agent in Georgia who was living with a woman who was raped and murdered. The agent had hunted down the perps, killed them, then turned the gun on himself. "If I'm not mistaken, Leo, there have been exceptions to that unofficial policy."

"Left to the discretion of the supervisor in charge." Dillard rocked forward onto the balls of his feet. "That's me. And you, my friend"—he tapped his stubby finger against Sheppard's chest, exactly what he'd done that night at the Hilltop—"are under my jurisdiction."

Sheppard flicked his hand away. "Who the fuck do

you think you're kidding, Leo? You're going to remove me from the case so you can step in and claim the credit."

Color seeped into Dillard's cheeks, anger flared in his eyes, and right then he reminded Sheppard of a cornered rat. "You don't belong in this job, Sheppard. You never did. As of right now, you're off this investigation. And that means *off*—no use of airplanes, boats, or vehicles that the bureau owns or leases."

As soon as Sheppard pulled out his cell phone, Dillard guessed that he was going to call the big boss, Baker Jernan, head of the southeast division, because he said, "Don't bother. Jernan's in Europe on vacation. I told Goot I want everything on this case in my hotel room by five this afternoon."

In a pig's eye, Sheppard thought.

"And you're not to give any statement to the press."

"You don't have any idea what you're dealing with in this investigation, Leo. And you're not going to find it in any of the material we turn over to you."

With that, Sheppard turned away, but Dillard snapped, "Just a goddamned minute. I'm not finished." Dillard grabbed his arm.

Sheppard wrenched his arm free, whirled, and grabbed Dillard by the front of his shirt so quickly, so expertly, that Dillard didn't have a chance to even think about what was happening. "If any harm comes to Mira or Annie because of you, Leo, you're fucked."

"D-don't you d-dare thr-threaten me," he sputtered, trying to squirm free.

"It's not a threat, you shit. It's a promise." Sheppard shoved him away and walked off to find Goot and Nadine.

* * *

"We're off the case, right?" Goot said when Sheppard joined him and Nadine.

"Only in the world according to Dillard. Let's talk over there."

They crossed the road and stopped next to a fence that enclosed a pasture. Cows and horses grazed in the distance, their lives undisturbed by what was going on in the woods. Sheppard glanced at Nadine, who stood with her arms folded at her waist, her eyes gazing off in the distance.

"Nadine, have you picked up anything here?" Sheppard asked.

She didn't seem to hear him. She still gazed toward the pasture. Sheppard looked over at Goot, who shrugged as if to say that the vagaries of Nadine's mind were beyond his ability to understand. So they stood there silently, in the stifling heat. After a few minutes, Nadine raised her arm and pointed. "Over there. He raised chickens. He took pride in them, fed them wholesome grains, and used them in a special soup he made to boost the immune system."

"Wheaton? Are we talking about Wheaton?" Goot asked.

She nodded.

If she could see something that specific, then why couldn't she see where Annie and Mira were? "Where are they, Nadine?" he asked, his voice quiet.

"Here, but not here."

Antonio's mother had said something similar. "But what's that mean?" he asked.

"I don't know." She finally turned her head and slid her hands into the pockets of her yoga pants. "This is going to sound strange. But last night, I woke up with a new memory. Actually, I have two memories—the way this particular event happened once and the way it happened the second time. The original memory is this: it's June 1968, probably early June, right after school was out. Mira was staying with Dave and me for a few weeks. She often did during the summer and holidays. She must've been about six, I guess, and we found a baby dove that had fallen out of its nest. We took it in. I remember that I was out gardening one evening and Mira came tearing outside, shouting that Lucy, the dove, had started eating."

Yeah, so? Sheppard thought.

Goot must have been thinking the same thing because Nadine gave them both a dirty look. "Hey, that's a big deal, all right? Wild baby doves rarely survive falls from a nest."

"And the new memory?" Sheppard asked.

"June 1968. Mira was staying with us, just like before. I was out gardening, just like before. But in this memory, I noticed an electric cart parked at the side of the road near the house. There was a woman inside. As she got out of the cart, I saw a bird perched on her shoulder. The bird said, *Hola, amigas.* It was a dusky conure, friendly, I held it while we talked about birds. There was something disturbingly familiar about this woman. I felt like I'd met her. I recognized her face, but couldn't place her name. Anyway, she said she was lost and asked for directions to some place on the island. I gave her the directions and before I'd finished, little Mira ran out of the house, shouting about Lucy the dove.

"And the strangest look came over the woman's face. She grabbed my hand and pressed a piece of paper into it, then ran back to the cart and drove off." Nadine slipped her right hand out of her pocket now. It held a piece of paper, yellowed with age, brittle at the edges. "Here's what she gave me."

She held it out and Sheppard took it, unfolded it carefully.

June 16, 1968
Nadine,
*   I know this won't make much sense to you now, but
one day it will. Please tell Sheppard that the mass is a
bridge. To get across the bridge, I think he has to find the
right coordinates in an area within the mass that's completely dark. The last digits of the coordinates, for both
latitude and longitude, end in ten. Let him know that
I'm sure Annie is here, but I haven't found her yet.*
*   If you have any questions, I'm staying in cabin 11 at
the artists' colony.*
*   Thank you so much.*

*   Mira Morales*

Sheppard felt nearly overwhelmed by a torrent of
powerful, almost violent emotions. *How can this* not *be
true?* He handed the note to Goot and looked help-
lessly at Nadine. "You never mentioned that you had
this, Nadine. Not once in the years since we met."

"Mí amor." She spoke softly, her eyes locked onto his.
"Until last night, I never knew I *had* this note." She
stepped back, letting that sink in.

"Holy shit," Goot murmured.

"The day she gave me the note, young Mira wanted
to know what the lady with the bird had given me,"
Nadine continued. "I read her the note and asked her
to listen with her inner senses. It upset her and she ran
into the house."

"So what's this mean?" Goot asked. "I mean, what's
it *really* mean?"

"It means that I met Mira, as a grown woman, in 1968,"
Nadine said. "Clearly impossible. But it happened."

"It means it's one more anomaly," Sheppard replied.
"Nothing more, nothing less."

Nadine looked at him with something that closely resembled disgust or contempt or both. But it was anger

that brought a tightness to her voice. "You are one very stubborn gringo. If you want to find Mira and Annie—and I assume that you do—then you need to believe the impossible."

With that said, she walked on down the road where they had left their cars.

Nineteen

Word had gotten around the colony that the brunette in cabin 11 was psychic and suddenly Mira had people coming to her for readings. At first, it was the residents, then they brought friends who brought other friends and within six days, she had read for about fifty people and had made nearly two thousand dollars.

With money, she could repay Jake what she owed him and do what she did at home—pay her bills. But she could also begin thinking about better transportation, a faster way to get around the island looking for Annie. She needed a car. She couldn't rent or buy one without a driver's license, at least not from any legitimate place, so she began to ask around, hoping someone had one to sell for a couple of hundred bucks.

She had driven every road on this island in the electric cart. It had taken a lot of time and yielded nothing. Mira worried that the monster had moved Annie *or killed her, don't think like that, she's still alive, you know she is*—or that she herself was in the wrong time zone altogether. Wouldn't that be a hoot, zip on through a portal into the past only to find out that your daughter had never been here and you were actually in a mental hospital and the whole thing was the result of a massive misfiring of synapses?

On the morning of June 24, she was waiting for her first client to arrive, the door to her cabin half open, when someone knocked and said, "Mira? You got a few minutes?"

She glanced around to see Jake and a woman with wild hair. It sprang out from the sides of her head, the top smashed down by the fabric hat she wore. The second thing Mira noticed about her was everything else—the ankle-length psychedelic dress, the fingers laden with rings, the peace symbol around her neck, and the feathered boa that made Mira want to sneeze just looking at it. Her eyes were hidden behind very dark sunglasses.

"Hey, Jake. C'mon in. Coffee's hot."

Jake shut the door and strolled into the cabin, his pupils the size of half dollars. No question that he was stoned out of his mind, Mira thought, and wondered what he was on. "Mira," he said again, and exploded with laughter, doubling over to slap his hands on his thighs. "This is Pearl."

"Hi," the woman with the boa said, her husky voice a testament to cigarettes, fat spliffs, and long, drunken nights. "Sorry to barge in like this. Jake swore it would be okay."

"You're not barging in," Mira said. "In fact, I've got moola, Jake. What I owe you with interest. She opened a drawer and brought out four fifties paper-clipped together. "I can't thank you enough."

"Goddamn." He rubbed the cash between his thumb and index finger, as if testing the texture. "I say we use this to get your fortune told, Pearl. How about it? I mean, if Mira has the time."

"Sure, I've got time."

"I've been hearing how incredibly good you are at this," Jake gushed on. "And I was telling Pearl about it and she wondered if you'd be able to read for her."

They sat down side by side at the kitchen table together, Mira across from them. She asked Jake to put some distance between himself and Pearl so she didn't confuse their energies when she read for Pearl. Pearl, who seemed to be as stoned as Jake, leaned forward and extended her hand. "By the way, nice to meet you."

"You, too," Mira said, and grasped her hand.

Big mistake.

What she saw was the raw electricity of such profound creative talent that she couldn't process it, couldn't translate it. There was no language for this kind of talent, this kind of *drive*, and *energy*. The intensity of her talent would burn out someone else, but it was this woman's fuel. It didn't defeat her. It kept her going. And the voice would echo across time, a voice that pundits and critics and fans would critique, hate, and love. But love her or hate her, this woman's emotional power would speak to these people on a visceral level and it would speak for many years, into Mira's own time.

She would come to personify the rebellion of the sixties.

"So am I a blank slate or what?" the woman finally asked, and Mira realized she was gripping the woman's hand and hadn't uttered a word.

"I got lost. I . . ." She dropped the woman's hand, sat back. "Listen, I don't usually get this kind of stuff. You're famous. You're going to be famous for a long time. Your going to ascend into legend because . . ."

Why?

She dies. Drugs. LA. Hendrix. Woodstock. Smack. Good-bye.

Mira leaned forward and gently removed the woman's glasses. She knew that her breath changed, she felt it, the rush of air from her lungs. Her heart seemed to slam around in her chest. "You're Janis Joplin."

She didn't whisper it, didn't shout it. The words came out somewhere between.

"Wow, babe, that's good, that's really good," Jake exclaimed, looking over at Janis. "She didn't know you till the glasses were off."

"So do I stay with Big Brother?" she said.

Mira nearly laughed. "You *are* Big Brother."

"I *know* that. But do I ever leave them?"

"Yes, at the end of this year you play your last gig with them." These facts came from Annie, an expert on Joplin after she'd done a report on her for American history.

How is Joplin part of American history? her teacher had asked.

How is she not a part of it? Annie had responded.

"In August, the release of an album called *Cheap Thrills* cements your career."

"Not too many people outside of Colombia Records know that title," the woman said.

"At least two of the songs on that album become classics that people are still listening to in the twenty-first century."

Janis beamed. "Which ones?"

Mira noticed that Jake looked astounded by the specificity of the reading, so Mira toned it down. "One about the heart and another about summer."

"That'd be 'Pieces of My Heart' and 'Summertime.'"

"The album soars to the top of the charts and also brings in unimagined amounts of money and drugs. Tensions mount in the band. At a music festival at the end of August, you announce you'll be leaving Big Brother."

"Damn," she whispered. "You got all that just by holding my hand?"

No, I'm cheating. I'm reading from Annie's history paper. "Unless you quit heroin, you don't live long enough to enjoy that career."

She blurted it. She didn't mean to. Never in a million years would she discuss death with a client. But the history that she knew was written in a certain way and perhaps, by saying it, she could change it somehow, at least for this woman.

"I don't do that anymore," said the woman with the feathered boa who, in Mira's time line, would die of a heroin overdose in a little over two years.

"She's been clean awhile now," Jake added.

"You go on the *Dick Cavett Show* next year. He asks who you go see when you're up for really good music. You tell him about a black woman. Tina someone."

"Turner," said Janis. "Tina Turner."

"Cavett has never heard of her."

"Fuckin' figures. Ike's the band leader, Tina's the show." She thought a moment, eyes fixed on the table. "So what do I do after I leave Big Brother?"

"You form a new band. It's more oriented toward blues. In the summer of 1969, you play at a festival called Woodstock. It becomes the most famous festival of the twentieth century. In the fall of next year, your new group releases an album. Reviews are mixed here in the States, but they love you in Europe. Your drug and alcohol consumption increase dramatically, then you decide to quit. You form a third group and start working on an album called *Pearl*." And unless she stayed clean, Mira thought, that album would be released posthumously. "It soars. In fact, most of your music goes gold, platinum, and triple platinum. At least two movies are made of your life."

"That sounds like I die."

"If you don't kick heroin completely, it'll get you young."

"I *have* kicked it."

"But the craving is still there."

"The craving's always there." She spoke softly, her smoky voice dreamlike. "Heroin is paradise. The world slows way down. You drift into an incredible place and want to stay there forever. But it's all a fucking lie, see, because when you crash, you're in hell. Your life is collapsing around you. So you just want more of the paradise and you'll do anything to get it."

Then you're screwed. As soon as Mira thought this, two paths opened up in front of her. On the right path, Janis overcame her addictions, lived well into her seventies, and became one of the greatest pop artists of the twentieth century. On the left path, history unfolded in Technicolor: she shot up in a motel room in LA in October 1970 and passed on into legend. The right path was less clear than the left, fuzzy around the edges, and therefore much less probable.

"You're seeing something else, right?" Janis asked, frowning, her husky voice barely above a whisper. "Something not so good."

"I'm just saying that if you're not careful, heroin will do you in before your time."

"Ex-addicts say that all the time." She sat back, the feather boa across her lap now. "That part isn't psychic."

No shit. I'm reading out of the almanac of history here. "The choice is yours."

"So you see my death?" she persisted.

"No, that's not what I said."

"So I'm not going to die early."

Jake leaped in. "What she's saying is that you're master of your own destiny. Kick the smack and you live into a ripe old age."

"Exactly." Mira nodded.

"What can you tell me about my friend Grace? And her friend Jerry?"

"That's Grace Slick and Jerry Garcia," said Jake.

The Jerry Garcia, musical shaman? "He becomes famous beyond anyone's expectations, especially his own. He performs at Woodstock next year, along with you and Hendrix and everyone else in the musical universe. He has a drug problem that he never really licks. Grace Slick lives on, but stops performing and eventually becomes an animal rights activist."

"I should've taken notes," Janis remarked.

"Would you sign an autograph for my daughter?" Mira blurted.

"You have a *kid?*" Jake exclaimed.

"Annie's thirteen and she's a fan of Janis's."

"Cool." Janis dug into her bag, brought out a Rum Runners napkin, scribbled something on the back of it, and handed it to Mira.

It read: *Annie, hold on to the pieces of your heart. You can be anything you want to be. Your friend, Janis Joplin, 6/24/68.*

"Thanks so much," Mira said. "Annie's going to be thrilled."

"So Jake and I heard you need a car, Mira."

"Something cheap."

"You're going to hole up here awhile?" Jake asked.

"Safer," Mira replied.

"Her ex is after her," Jake explained to Janis, who was already on her feet.

"C'mon outside and take a look at my Mercedes Benz." Janis said it just as she would sing it on her *Pearl* album, and laughed.

"A Mercedes is a bit out of my league."

"Not *this* Mercedes," Janis assured her.

The three of them walked outside and there, parked in front of cabin 11, was Jake's VW and a second VW, all black except for a psychedelic-colored hood. "You can use it. The only time I need it is when I visit Jake."

"Let me rent it from you."

"How about if we do an exchange? You use the Bug in exchange for the reading."

"That'd be great, but it seems like I'm getting the better deal."

Janis waved the remark away, rolled onto the balls of her feet, brought her hand to her mouth as though she were holding a mike, and belted out a refrain from "Mercedes Benz."

"Now *that* would make a terrific song."

"I'll remember that." Janis grinned and handed Mira the keys. "So it's settled."

Jake quickly fetched his camera from his car and told them to get over closer to the psychedelic-colored Bug and snapped half a dozen photos of the two of them acting goofy, playing to the lens. "Have you ever photographed Janis for publication?" Mira suddenly asked.

"Hey, Jake-o, I like that idea," Janis said in her husky voice.

"And photograph her friends. Grace Slick. Jerry Garcia. Hendrix."

"Loving this idea, Jake-o," Janis said, and flicked the feathered boa over Mira's shoulder, jutted out her left hip, and Mira jutted out her right, and Jake snapped another photo.

"Is that your psychic impression?" Jake asked. "That I should do those kinds of photos?"

"Yes."

"What else do you pick up on Jake, Mira?"

They looked at each other and she sensed his reluctance about having her read him. "That he's not quite sure what I'm about."

Jake laughed. "True enough."

"That he doesn't want to know anything bad about his future."

"True, all of it true."

"That he's going to be a renowned photographer and it's all going to start with you, Janis."

Just then, several people came over and asked Janis for her autograph, and within minutes she was surrounded by fans. Mira and Jake moved out of the way. "That was pretty specific information you gave her," he remarked.

"That's how it comes through with some people."

"Excuse me, Mira, but I've met three-year-olds who lie better than you do."

Just then, the heat and the stillness seemed extreme. The humming had returned to her head and threatened to become something much worse, maybe even a level-four screaming banshee. "I can't tell you the whole truth." The humming receded slightly, a wave playing tag on a beach.

"Are you a *narc*? Is that it?"

"A *narc*?" She burst out laughing. She'd been called many things in her life—satanist, witch, wacko, mentally unbalanced, fake, fucked up, even evil. But no one had ever accused her of being a narc. This was the sixties, though, and in this world people like Janis and Jake were the revolutionaries, and for them drug use wasn't just rampant. It was what you did as soon as you got up in the morning. "No, I'm definitely not a narc."

"Then what the hell are you?"

"A psychic whose ex is pursuing her."

"Why'd you lie to Sheriff Fontaine about your last name?"

"My last name isn't any of his business."

He held her gaze for a moment longer, then shrugged. "Sorry. I'm a suspicious prick."

"I'd say you're entitled." She dug out the hundred bucks he'd given her for the reading and held it out. "Please take this. And do you have a piece of paper and a pen, Jake?"

He took the money and reached into his camera case for a notepad and pen. Mira thought a moment, then jotted down the names of a dozen musicians who would become prominent in the next five to ten years. "Watch for these people. All of them will become famous. Photograph them. Start your portfolio with Janis and her contacts. It will grow from there."

He put the notepad back in his pocket and held her eyes longer than necessary. Many feelings passed between them, but neither of them said anything. In her time, if he was still alive, he was sixty-seven.

"How do you know Janis?" she asked.

"We're from the same Port Arthur, Texas neighborhood. Our parents knew each other. She's good people." He paused, then added, "Like you."

"Jake-o," Janis said, hurrying over, "let's shove off. I've got a plane to catch."

"She's playing in California tonight," Jake said.

"I'm going to think about everything you said," Janis told her. "I like the idea of being alive in the twenty-first century."

"Good. And I can't thank you enough for the use of your car."

Janis whipped the feather boa over her shoulder, tugged her cap down over her hair, slipped on her shades. "We're outta here." She grabbed Jake's hand and they cut through the crowd around Jake's VW, hopped in, and sped away.

Mira took the psychedelic VW out at dusk, a time of day when her abilities were typically stronger and her impressions, clearer. Today had been a good day, so perhaps this evening would be even better. She had Annie's peace symbol, her beacon, clutched in her left hand. The hum that had been echoing in her head all day had receded again and her inner world felt strangely quiet without it.

The Bug drove well, but now and then she picked up flashes of insight into Joplin's life. When she tightened her hands on the steering wheel, for instance, she heard Janis and Jake laughing. When she opened the glove compartment, she had a sudden image of Janis doing the same thing and bringing out several joints. It distracted her.

She rolled down the windows and turned onto the Old Post Road. In her time, the road was lined with homes and town houses. Yes, they were tastefully built and lushly landscaped, but the wooded wilderness she saw here took her breath away. The pines seemed to reach all the way to heaven. The long, thick fronds on the palm trees clacked like castanets in a stray breeze.

In the distance, she could see the glittering blue of the bay—unbroken by the bridge that crossed it in her own time. Two ferries churned their way in opposite directions across the water and the long, mournful whistle of one of them reached her.

In her time, the ferries were mostly for tourists, but still hauled some heavy equipment back and forth between Tango and Key West. The first time she and Annie had ridden one of the ferries together, she had two close friends with her from their old Lauderdale neighborhood. The girls had visited again last summer. Annie had seen them once since, but the friendships were unraveling with time and Annie had no other friends close enough to replace them. The angst of middle school, Mira thought.

Maybe it was the reminiscence that did it, maybe it was the depth of her need, but the peace symbol suddenly felt like a scalding branding iron against the palm of Mira's hand. The tug that came moments later—and that was the only way she could describe it, a *tug*, as though invisible fingers had grabbed her hand and pulled—was to the right. But there was nothing on her right except a rolling pasture and, beyond it, brush and pines rising against the bruised sky.

Mira drove to the shoulder of the road, killed the headlights, stopped. She slid her fingers together, in an attitude of prayer, the peace symbol pressed between her palms, and shut her eyes. *Show me the way to Annie.*

The humming stayed constant, tolerable, unchanged. But the peace symbol grew noticeably hotter. Mira slung her pack over her shoulder, rolled the flashlight out from between the seats where she had put it earlier, and got out of the car. She wished, suddenly, that the funny little bird would sweep down out of nowhere and alight on her shoulder. But she didn't hear any squawks ripping through the twilight. She heard only the breeze, rustling through the trees behind her.

She pressed the symbol between her palms again, surprised that it was so cool now. She and Annie had experimented with this kind of thing numerous times and had concluded that sometimes the object actually heated up and that other times, the sensation of heat or cold was an illusion that the mind created. Either way, heat was a signal that meant *Follow me.*

The heat started gradually and she moved toward the fence that enclosed the pasture. When she was up next to it, she heard a low humming, not unlike the humming that filled her own skull. She realized the fence wasn't just four horizontal slats of wood; a pair of tiny electrified wires ran along the top of it.

Mira climbed between the two lowest slats, the peace symbol secure in her left hand now, and paused on the other side to orient herself. The symbol still felt warm, but didn't seem to be offering up any guidance about which direction she should move.

Her desperation slammed around inside her, an orphan without hope. But it changed something, too, molding her body into a kind of psychic lightning rod.

When the muscles in her legs and feet started to twitch, her brain understood and commanded them to move. And move they did, moved so fast that the rest of her had trouble keeping up with them.

Pretty soon, she was running through the field, past cows clustered together like daisies, through grass that got progressively taller, wilder. The night air caressed her cheeks, the smell of salt and sea stung her nostrils. In her left hand, the peace symbol burned and burned.

When she reached the brush beyond the pasture, her feet led the way, and she turned abruptly to the left. The lightning of her daughter's energy seared through her. She thought she heard Jimi Hendrix singing, *'Scuse me while I kiss the sky* . . . Then, suddenly, she tripped and pitched forward and sprawled, gracelessly, in the tall grass. Her lungs emptied of air. She lay there, fingers hooked like claws and digging through the grass, into the soil, as though Annie's energy came from somewhere six feet under.

Gone, it's gone.

The peace symbol had gotten knocked out of her hand, severing her connection with her daughter.

Mira pushed up on her hands and knees and, sobbing with frustration, crawled through the grass, searching for the peace symbol. She patted the ground, combed her fingers through the grass. She didn't know how long she wandered around in the field, sometimes walking, but most of the time on her hands and knees, looking for the peace symbol. At some point, she just couldn't go any farther and she sank to the ground and didn't move. She watched stars popping out in the eastern sky and listened to the orchestra of insects, a song as timeless now as it was in her own time.

Annie wasn't dead and she wasn't giving up or

surrendering; Mira felt that much. But she couldn't sense Annie's location, couldn't pinpoint her. The ability that she had taken for granted since she was old enough to understand it short-circuited when it came to finding her daughter. So what the hell good was it? Nadine would say that she was too close to it, that it didn't get any closer than blood. That might be true, but there was more to it than that.

The man who had taken Annie had acted by design, not whim, and Mira realized that her inability to find her daughter was mixed up, somehow, with *his* agenda.

The first inkling she had that she wasn't alone was the light. It darted, it danced, it skipped across the surface of the tall grass, touching down here, there, and then it paused on her. She felt it pinned to her shoulder blades and thought: *Oh shit. Pervert. Rapist. Killer.*

Her fingers dug down through the grass, into the earth, and worked loose a chunk.

"Ma'am?"

Christ. She recognized the lolling southern drawl.

"Ma'am, you all right?"

"Hi, Sheriff Fontaine."

"Miss Piper. Are you okay?"

"I hurt my foot," she lied. "I was just resting."

"But what're you doing way out here?" he asked, stopping beside her, his flashlight burning into her face.

"I lost something and was trying to find it." Mira turned her head to the left, away from the light, and lifted her hands. "Could you turn that off or away or something?"

"Oh, sure. Sorry." He turned it away, but not off. "What'd you lose?"

"A piece of jewelry. I'll never find it in the dark. I'll have to come back tomorrow."

"Can I help you up, ma'am?"

"Thanks, but I'm fine," she said, and got to her feet without touching Fontaine's outstretched hand. She was afraid of what she might see if she did. She also realized that she had better be friendly and as honest as possible to distract him from asking her for ID.

"I, uh, saw the car and was about to ticket it, when I remembered I'd seen it over at Rum Runners. Hard to forget that psychedelic hood. It belongs to that singer friend of Jake's."

"She's letting me use it while I'm here. In exchange for a reading I did for her."

"A reading? What kind of reading?"

"A, uh, psychic reading."

"Right," he said, nodding. "I remember Jake saying something about you being a fortune teller."

Given Jake's paranoia about narcs, Mira found this bit of information interesting. "How do you know him?"

"His old man was a cop at the Tango PD back when Jake was a teen. I stop in at Rum Runners for breakfast some mornings. Jake and I talk. Met some oddballs in there, for sure," he added with a laugh. "Beginning with that singer woman."

"She's talented."

"Guess that depends on your definition of talented." He slipped a pack of cigarettes from his shirt pocket, offered one to Mira. When she shook her head, he lit one with the relish of a man who truly enjoyed smoking. "Wife gets all over me for smoking. So I limit myself to five a day. Not too bad, huh?"

"Sounds reasonable." Either he was lonely, she decided, or he wanted something.

"So tell me about being a psychic. Wife believes in all that stuff. Me? I'm skeptical. How does it work? You read cards? Palms? Tea leaves? What?"

Oh shit. Best to keep him talking so she wouldn't

have to touch him. But maybe she needed to touch him to find the monster's name. Fontaine was in the lineup of clues, after all, right up there with Jake, Lydia, and the bird. "I pick up images, mental pictures, feelings. It varies."

"Pick up how?"

"Are you asking me to show you?"

He laughed, stabbed out his cigarette in the grass, shredded it. "Yeah, I guess I am."

Here goes. "Let's sit down."

They sat side by side on the moist, cool grass. "Extend your hand," she said.

"My hand?"

"Yes."

"Okay." He stretched out his arm and Mira cupped his hand in both of hers. "Don't tell me anything bad. Unless it's a warning that'll save my life or something."

He laughed nervously as he said it and the oddness of the whole situation, sitting out here in a field, beneath a star-strewn sky from another time, with a chief of police who was probably dead in her time, struck her fully. Then she began to relax into his energy and immediately felt a constriction in her chest and saw an infant connected to tubes, machines. She felt a stab in the small of her back. And felt the infant's release. "The death of an infant. A boy. He was on life support. He died." She felt a stab of pain in the small of her back. "Kidneys. His kidneys failed."

"Jesus God," Fontaine whispered, and drew his hand away. "That . . . that happened thirty years ago. I was twenty-two, we were living in Georgia. No one but our family knows about it."

Even though she no longer touched him, she was still connected to him, to his energy. "You have other children. But that boy was special. He was . . . not your wife's. Not your present wife's."

She couldn't see him, it was too dark now. But she felt him nod, felt him shudder, felt him clutching his knees to his chest, as if to ward off the ghosts of the distant past.

"What else?"

Mira touched his arm, reconnecting herself more fully. "You get the raise you've been hoping for. Your oldest son gets into the college of his choice and he does it on scholarships. My God, he's bright. It's a science scholarship of some sort. Your wife. She has high blood pressure, high cholesterol. She needs to get that taken care of . . . ." Before she could utter another word, a massive pain exploded through her chest and she gasped and doubled over, trying to catch her breath, to detach from whatever this was, to separate herself from it.

Shrieking filled her head, the noise at the screaming banshee level, tearing the inside of her skull apart. Just as abruptly, everything went silent and the pain in her chest ebbed away and Fontaine was saying, "Are you *okayokayokay?*"

The word echoed briefly, stopped, and she pulled air deeply into her lungs and realized she was flat on her back in the grass. When had she fallen back? *Why* had she fallen back? *Gunshot.* Mira pushed up on her elbows. Fontaine had turned on his flashlight and was shining it directly into her face. She pushed it away.

"What happened?" he asked, genuine concern in his voice. "Do you need a doctor? Should I call—"

"No." She pressed her fists against her chest. Not her injury. Definitely not hers. "Do you wear a bulletproof vest?"

"Sometimes. Depends on the situation."

"Wear one constantly. From this moment on, wear one all the time, Mr. Fontaine."

"Who . . . I get shot? Is that what you saw?"

"That's what I *felt*. I don't know who pulls the trigger, I don't know any of the details. I just know that it's going to happen and it's going to be soon and if you're not wearing the vest . . ."

"I'm dead."

"Or wishing that you were."

He sat beside her on the grass again, and for the longest time neither of them said anything. The sweet scents of the field enveloped them, lightning bugs darted about through the darkness. He had another smoke and Mira kept pressing her fists against her chest, trying to knead away the last vestiges of that crippling sensation. An explosion, then pain. It would happen fast. He would be dead before he hit the ground.

He walked her back to the road, his flashlight aimed at the ground, so they could see where they were going. They ducked between the slats of the fence and he paused long enough to show her the no-trespassing sign posted there.

"Guess we both broke the law," he said.

"Guess we did."

"I'm grateful to you, Mira. I'm going to take your advice."

He didn't offer his hand. He understood that the reading was finished, that she wouldn't see anything more. She wanted desperately to confide in him, to spill every detail of what had happened to her since she and Annie had gone to Little Horse Key, to describe the monster who had introduced himself as Peter. But there were probably hundreds of Peters on Tango Key, and for all she knew, the monster had changed his appearance, the color of his hair, and her description wouldn't fit any Peter that he knew.

"Take care, Mr. Fontaine."

He followed her out to the intersection and honked as she went right and he continued going straight on through the darkness.

Twenty

Sheppard regarded the note Nadine had shown him as a piece of evidence. Even though it supported a hypothesis that was clearly impossible—time travel—he would seek substantiating evidence. And if he found it, then he would have to consider the unthinkable as not only possible, but probable. The most likely place to see substantiation was at the artists' colony, where Mira had told Nadine that she was staying.

Cabin 11, June 16, 1968.

Sheppard's knowledge of the artists' colony had come primarily from the newsletter that was mailed out monthly to Mira's bookstore. The place had been founded on the premise that artistic ability of all kinds could be nurtured within an environment where creativity was honored rather than held suspect. To live here, artists were required to submit samples of their work and be voted in by a committee of their peers. Competition, however, was fierce, with five or six thousand applicants for about a hundred positions open annually.

Once they were accepted, they paid a nominal fee for the cabin or apartment and were entitled to many free activities—concerts, plays, workshops, and seminars taught by visiting artists in a variety of fields. They also were entitled to free professional critiques and had the opportunity to exhibit and sell their work in the gift shop and exhibition center.

The colony also catered to the public, which was how it made the bulk of its money. It had one of the best vegetarian restaurants on the island, an impressive gift shop, and charged admission for all its activities. It also published a bimonthly magazine that brought in revenue through advertising.

From Gina, the woman at the front desk, Sheppard learned that in the sixties, when the colony was just getting off the ground, some of the cabins were rented out during the summer to plump up the coffers. When he asked if he could look through the colony register of rentals for June 1968, she didn't ask to see his badge. She took him at his word that he worked for the FBI.

She brought out a large, dusty ledger book and set it on the desk. "This thing isn't in the best of shape. We're eventually going to have to scan it into a computer, but for now, this is all I've got. You said June 1968, right?"

"Yes."

Gina turned the yellowed pages carefully, her plump fingers moving across the top of each page. "They weren't very organized back then," she remarked. "They used residents here at the desk who were working off their room and board. But if memory serves me, Diego Muñoz was the resident in charge in the late sixties and he was pretty good about keeping the records up to date. Do you know his work?"

Sheppard shook his head. "I don't think so."

"He's a Cuban poet. Quite well known in the Latino community."

"How long have you been here, Gina?"

"Since 1971." She laughed. "Forever. Okay, here it is. June 1968. What was her name again?"

"Mira Morales."

"Here we go." She smiled and turned the book toward him. "June twelfth."

Sheppard stared, face-to-face with the incomprehensible. Every belief he had held about reality, about what was possible or impossible, went south. "Christ," he whispered.

"It's a shock?" Gina asked.

"It's . . ." He groped for the right word, then just shook his head. "Gina, here it says that she was checked in by Lydia Santos. Who's she?"

"One of the residents, a sculptress. She'd had a hard life, that one, saw her granddaddy hung up in Alabama when she was just a little thing, saw her husband killed during a civil rights march. But my God, that woman had talent even back then. She could sculpt like nobody's business. That's her sculpture over there." She pointed at an exquisite sculpture of an old woman and a young child, made entirely of copper wire. "Every resident donates at least one piece to the colony. Many of them have donated multiple pieces. Even after Lydia started making it big, she still came around every so often to talk to the residents, teach a workshop, whatever. Her artistic roots are here."

"She's still alive?"

"Oh, my, yes. Has a home here on Tango where she lives part of the year."

He noticed that Mira had billed groceries from the colony market and had rented an electric cart that was charged to the cabin. On June 19, she rented the cabin for another week and on the twenty-sixth, had rented it for a third week. There was no entry for cabin 11 for the fourth week. "Do you have a current address for Ms. Santos?"

Gina grinned. It sliced her face, as round as a pumpkin, in half. "You bet. Right on my Rolodex. If you have a few more minutes, I'll find it for you. Be back in a jiffy."

She disappeared through a door and Sheppard ran his fingers over the entries for Mira. *Here, but not here.* "Fuck," he murmured, and walked restlessly around the lobby, studying the displays of sculptures, art, photographs. One large photo collage caught his attention. At first, it seemed to be similar to an image that tested your perception, where one shape is contained within another. The right brain saw one thing, the left saw another, but when both halves of the brain worked in unison, the image was clear. And now he saw all of it: Jimi Hendrix, Grace Slick, Jerry Garcia, Jim Morrison, Peter, Paul, and Mary, Andy Warhol. Toward the bottom of the frame was a montage of two women standing in front of a VW with a psychedelic hood. It was Janis Joplin and Mira, her face superimposed over Janis's feathered boa.

How many more pieces of evidence do you need?

"Agent Sheppard, I—"

"Gina, who took these photos?"

"Jake Romano. Wonderful man, exceptional. He was always a good photographer," she explained, joining Sheppard in front of the collage. "But he really hit his stride when he started drawing on his contacts in the entertainment industry."

Sheppard pointed at Mira. "That's the woman who was in cabin eleven."

Her eyebrows shot up. "Really? How fascinating. Her identity has always been the sixty-four-thousand-dollar question around here. I asked Jake one day when he was in here, but he just winked and said I had to figure it out on my own."

"You have a current address for him?"

"Sure do. C'mon back to the desk."

She waddled back to the front desk and began flipping through the fattest, most tattered Rolodex that Sheppard had ever seen. She flipped to the Rs. "Okay,

Jake Romano. I've got three phone numbers, none of them with South Florida area codes. Course, nowadays, that doesn't mean much, does it? Let me jot them down."

"Any e-mail address?"

"Just through his Web site. I'll include it. There's also a post office box address in Asheville, North Carolina." She scribbled, then flipped to the Ss. "Santos, okay, here she is. I've got phone numbers for Tango, Manhattan, Seattle, and Jamaica."

"I'll take them all. And any kind of address, e-mail or otherwise."

She laughed. "I figured you were going to say that."

"Any idea where she's likely to be at this time of year?"

"Probably not here. Seattle would be my guess." She finished her list of numbers, handed it to him.

"Thanks, Gina, you're a doll."

"You come on back any time now, Agent Sheppard."

The moment he was inside his Jetta, the AC blasting into his face, he called the first Romano number on his list. It had been disconnected. Same thing for the second number. On the third number, he reached an answering machine. "You know the drill," said the voice on the recorded message. "I'll try to get back to you within twenty-four hours." *Beep.*

"My Name is Wayne Sheppard. I'd like to speak to you regarding Mira. She was staying in cabin eleven at the artists' colony on Tango Key in June 1968. You snapped a photo of her and Janis Joplin outside one of the cabins and included her in the photo collage that's hanging in the colony lobby. It's urgent. Thanks." He left his cell number, backed out of the parking space, and started in on the Santos numbers.

Tango: an answering machine. He left a message.

Manhattan: a maid. She didn't know when Ms. Santos

would be back in town and claimed she didn't have a forwarding number. He left his number, emphasized that it was urgent, and hung up.

Seattle: endless rings.

Jamaica: his cell phone didn't have international capabilities.

Seattle again: a woman answered.

"I'd like to speak to Lydia Santos, please."

"I'm sorry, sir. She isn't here. May I take a message?"

"Yes. My name is Wayne Sheppard. I'm an FBI agent in the Florida Keys and I need to speak to her regarding a psychic named Mira Morales, whom she checked into the artists' colony on Tango Key in June 1968." He gave her his number, she said would get the message to Ms. Santos, and he hung up.

Three separate pieces of evidence: the notes to Nadine, the registration, and the photo. The impossible wasn't just possible, it had happened. *But how?*

Sheppard headed toward the address in Pirate's Cove that Gina had given him for Santos. It was the most exclusive area on Tango, with the cheapest homes starting at about three-quarters of a million and the most expensive hovering around the five-million mark. The town was no stranger to celebrities. Julia Roberts, Mel Gibson, Carly Simon, and Tina Turner had homes here. At one time, Spielberg and Stephen King had homes on the same street.

The colony owned a couple of homes up here, too, where they housed their visiting speakers for workshops and seminars and for their annual book fair, which always involved One World Books. Just a few months ago, he and Mira had hosted a bookstore event for suspense writer Nancy Pickard, who had been staying in the colony's guest house in the cove. Last year, it had been Anne Rice. Tango, he thought, might not be big, but the people here were book lovers and many book-related events drew crowds from as far north as Daytona and Jacksonville.

He found Doubloon Drive easily enough, a private, tree-shrouded road with miniestates hidden behind black iron gates and fences. Number 14 was set back from the road and while it wasn't the grandest estate he'd passed, he figured the price tag probably stood at about a million and a half. Not bad for a woman who had seen her granddaddy hung back in Alabama.

He pulled up to the gate and peered through the slats. Two or three acres, he thought, a little kingdom on an island like Tango. And it was old, he could tell that much by the towering banyans that lined the driveway. A car stood at the end of the driveway, but no voice came through the intercom when he rang the bell. No guard dogs appeared, either.

Sheppard returned to his car and retrieved a pad of paper, a pen, and a roll of Scotch tape from the glove compartment. He scribbled a note, slipped it into his pocket, then climbed the iron gate and dropped onto the other side. He was now trespassing but didn't give a shit. He was so far beyond giving a shit that he darted into the trees, through the deep shade.

When he approached the front of the house, he could see the license plate on the Mercedes. He committed it to memory, then went the distance to the front door. He punched the bell and heard the melodic sound inside, echoing through what he imagined were spacious hallways and wide, still rooms. No one came to the door. He tore off a piece of tape from the roll and pressed the note to the front of the door.

As he left, he touched his hand to the hood of the Mercedes; it was still warm. He glanced up at the second-story windows and thought he glimpsed someone watching him from a corner window.

2

Lydia saw the tall white man run his fingers over the hood of her Mercedes and figured he knew someone was inside the house. She ducked back behind the window and hurried downstairs, her agitation so extreme that she felt her quickening heartbeat, the rushing of blood through her veins. She knew what this concerned, that the time had arrived, knew it but denied it until she finally opened the door a crack and snatched his note.

She walked back into the kitchen, sat down at the table, smoothed her fingers over the paper. "Just unfold it," she said irritably.

But she sensed that once she unfolded this piece of paper, she would be opening a Pandora's box to the past and everything that she thought had been put to rest would leap out and fly off into *this* time. She took a deep breath and unfolded the note.

On June 12, 1968, you checked a woman named Mira Morales into cabin 11 at the artists' colony. I need to speak to you about this. Please call me at any of the numbers listed below. This involves the abduction of five children and a man named Patrick Wheaton. Thank you.

Wayne Sheppard, FBI

Lydia pressed her knuckles into her eyes. *Now it begins again and ends once and for all.* She reached for the portable phone, punched out a number. The man on the other end picked up on the third ring.

"It's happening, isn't it?" he said without preface.

"Yes. An FBI agent was here, Rusty. I feel like I've met him."

"Hell, you probably have. Who knows? My memories are shifting hourly."

"Mine, too."

They discussed options. They argued. They discussed some more. When they finally hung up, she knew they had turned a vital corner into the past and that now the script would be rewritten.

Twenty-one

Annie woke in a sweat, her stomach rumbling with hunger. She sat up and swung her legs over the side of the couch, wondering how long she had slept, what time it was. Had she slept around the clock again? That had happened a couple of times and she suspected that Peter was putting something in her food to keep her doped up. But if it was still June 26, then no one had shown up at all today with a meal. No breakfast, no lunch, and from the looks of it, dinner was probably a lost cause, too.

She went over to the window to check the path. It looked like a winding trail in a fairy tale that emptied into a darkening woods. She guessed it was around 6:30, although the woods blocked the light and made it seem later. No one was in sight. Tiny flutters of panic started up in her chest. Maybe Rusty was dead, Peter had fled, and the world had ended. Maybe this was just another one of Peter's tricks, something to keep her off balance or to break her spirit. *No food*. Another small cruelty. If that didn't break her spirit, what would he try next? No bathroom privileges? No TV? No music or books?

She hit the wall switch; no lights. She tried the lamps; same thing. She listened for the hum of the AC, didn't hear it, and realized he had cut the power to the apartment. No food and now he would leave her in here at night without power, in the dark, sweltering.

For two weeks, Peter had stuck to his rigid routine as though it were his religion. Now, suddenly, the routine was broken. What did that mean? Nothing good, she thought. If he had decided he didn't have any use for her, then maybe he planned to just leave her here and let her die of starvation. She wanted to believe that Rusty wouldn't allow that to happen, but she hadn't seen Rusty in four or five days. She didn't know where he was, what he was doing. It occurred to her that Peter might have killed Rusty. In fact, the more she thought about it, the more likely it seemed. He probably buried him behind the shed with the other children. His other failures.

Well, she wouldn't starve for a while. She had a stash of fruit that she kept in the fridge, fresh water ran from the tap. Or it had the last time she'd washed her hands.

She ran over to the kitchen sink, turned on the faucets, and relief washed through her. Water poured from the tap. But suppose it was drugged? He probably had a well or a cistern for the property, she thought, and that would be easy enough to poison or drug. The more she thought about it, though, the less likely it seemed. If Peter was going to kill her, he would just put a bullet through her chest or her head and bury her. Poison or starvation would take too long and her dying body would leave too many germs.

She didn't find much comfort in this thought.

You're alive right this second. Make it count.

Annie looked slowly around the room, seeking something she could use as a weapon. But she had done this a thousand times in the days she had been here and already knew what there was: thirty-six small bathroom tiles, a spatula with a worn-down point that would only enrage him if she struck him with it, and a couple of pencils. The sharpened lead of a pencil could inflict serious damage to an eye or an ear, but her pencils were as worn down as the point on the spatula.

She eyed the storage closet door, went over to it, rapped her knuckles against it. Like the front door, it was metal, but the jamb around it was wooden. It had a regular key lock. If she could chip away at the wood with the worn end of the spatula, could she spring the locking mechanism somehow? It was worth a try. Inside the storage closet were mops and brooms, cleansers, all sorts of stuff she could use to defend herself.

She ran into the bathroom and got the spatula knife and ran back over to the storage closet. The light in the room was now dim and she didn't have a flashlight or matches or anything else. She would have to work by touch, in the dark, she thought, and would do this because she knew that if she didn't, she wasn't going to live much longer.

2

His longing was like some deep, terrible itch that he couldn't reach. It pursued him when he was awake, rattling around inside him until he could barely think. It sat with him at his meals. It taunted him when he took the girl her food, when he visited the graves of the other children, when he saw Rusty turn away from him with contempt in his eyes, the phantom of the Close Call flaming in his eyes, haunting him. It pursued Wheaton in dreams where he would see Eva in all her flaming, maddening beauty, her arms around Billy Macon as she whispered sweet nothings in his ear.

And when he couldn't stand it anymore, Wheaton broke. He bolted out of a nap that evening, sat there blinking against the shadows pooled in the corners of the room, and couldn't remember where he was, how old he was, what time zone he was in. It came to him only because his eyes fixed on a photograph of Rusty and his dog, taken only a few weeks ago as they were coming across the road from the pasture. Rusty had just fed the chickens and carried an empty bucket in one hand and a bag of feed in the other.

It's 1968. Evie's still alive. But not for long.

Wheaton showered, dressed, and went downstairs. Rusty wasn't around, his Chevy wasn't in the driveway. More and more often, he was elsewhere and Wheaton rarely saw him. He made sure the power to the shed was still off, as it had been since early this morning, and wondered how long it would take Annie to break.

In the kitchen, he plucked the shed keys off the hook and pocketed them. They were new, just like the locks on the shed. A precaution, just in case Rusty decided to do the noble thing and free Annie. If he took a hammer to the locks, he could destroy two of them, but the dead bolt, like the unbreakable windows, was from his own time, the strongest one made. He picked up his video-camera case and hurried out to his VW bus.

It was a 1967 model that he'd bought recently. It had a spanking-new red and white paint job, a spotless interior, and dark curtains on the windows. It was registered to Peter Wheat, all nice and legal. He had another bus identical to this one that he kept in his new place in Miami, snug in the garage, and that one was registered to Harvey O'Connor, the identity he would use in his new life. The life he would claim in just five days, on July first. Unless he decided to make his move a bit sooner, a distinct possibility.

The seven o'clock ferry was crowded, but that was fine with Wheaton. He spent most of the ride in the bus, fussing with the video-camera. It was a palm-size digital Panasonic, top of the line, something that wouldn't be seen for another thirty-five years. When he got home, he would dump the stream onto his laptop and study it until every detail was embedded in his mind.

This ferry was usually faster than the earlier ferries, but just to be sure, he timed it. He would be driving the bus that night, but only as far as the Sugarloaf Marina, then he and Evie would go the rest of the way in the boat he had reserved. The boat would take them right to his dock on one of Miami's many canals. By the time the old guy at the marina realized the boat was stolen, it would be too late. Peter Wheaton would have vanished without a trace.

He had toyed with the idea of attempting to move several years into the future. While that might still be the ultimate escape hatch, Wheaton was reluctant to try it. His experience off the Yucatan was still painfully vivid. He had no idea how that time slip had happened and didn't have a clue about how to control where he would end up. Too much would be left to chance.

The ferry docked exactly thirty-eight minutes later, and by 7:50 he was on the road, headed out of Key West. Traffic was light. He cruised along at an even fifty miles an hour and reached Sugarloaf at exactly 8:06. Just about perfect, he thought. It had to be absolutely dark outside for what he wanted to do, so he decided to kill some time over dinner and turned into the lot of the Sugarloaf Lodge and went inside.

The place didn't do much business in the summer of 1968. The lodge was mostly a spot where travelers en route to Key West and Tango stopped off for a bite to eat or to use the rest room. Some years into the future, the lodge's visitors would increase because of a dolphin named Sugar who would live for twenty years in a part of the lagoon that the lodge's owners fenced off.

He counted five diners, three of them hippies at a table next to the window, and a young couple who were studying maps. The hostess showed him to a window table, handed him a menu, and walked off. If memory served him, a few nights ago on the time line he already had lived, his younger self had caught Eva in the hammock . . .

He is in the kitchen, fixing himself a snack, alone in the house when he hears the laughter, soft and husky, intimate. That laughter drifts upward from the yard and he knows immediately that it's Evie's laughter, that she is with someone down there where the shadows are thickest and the hammock is strung. A terrible heat rushes through him, searing his heart. His head pounds, he can barely think.

He sets the knife, covered with peanut butter, in the sink. He removes his shoes. He opens the back door carefully, praying it won't squeak. He moves slowly down the steps, avoiding the spots where the old wood creaks and groans. His every movement is deliberate. His head pounds so hard now that the pain has spread across his eyes.

At the bottom of stairs, he pauses, listens. Laughter, a moan, the rustle of a breeze through the palm fronds. Then, Evie's voice, soft but not whispered, "Don't stop doing that, don't stop, Billy."

Billy Macon. Wild, rich boy from Manhattan. His parents have a cottage on Big Pine, on the water. He zips around in his snazzy convertible, Mr. Cool.

Patrick moves through the area under the house with the stealth of a thief. From the tool rack, he picks the hedge clippers. New hedge clippers. The blades are sharp and shiny, like mirrors. He darts silently to the other side of the house, through the darkness, to the twin palms where the hammock is strung. The hammock sways, its ropes creak, and through the netting he glimpses the pale beauty of Evie's naked skin. She and Billy are side by side, Evie is groaning, Billy is groaning.

Patrick moves quickly to the palm tree that is closest to him, raises the clippers, and cuts through the ropes. This end of the hammock plunges to the ground and they tumble with it, Evie shouting, Billy shouting, the two of them tangled in the hammock netting. Patrick smiles, walks calmly to the other tree, and cuts the rope here, too.

They scramble to their feet, struggling to get the netting off their bodies. Patrick remains where he is, watching, the hedge clippers glinting in the moonlight. Billy gets free of the netting first and then wraps part of it around his waist, covering himself.

"You fucking asshole," he shouts. "What the hell're you doing?"

"Giving you a warning, Bill. The next time you're anywhere on this property . . ." Patrick snaps the clippers in front of Billy's face and he wrenches back. ". . . I'll cut your cock clean off."

Then he turns and walks back into the dark area under the house, his heart shattering.

"May I take your order, sir?"

That voice. His head snapped up. It was her. Eva. She stood there in a tight blue uniform, a phony smile fixed in place, her thick blond hair gathered back in a tight bun that was covered with a thin net. His mind screamed, *What're you doing here? You never worked in this place.* The sight of her rendered him completely mute. He just stared, taking in her breathtaking beauty—that flawless, pale skin, the perfect curve of her jaw, and those eyes, soft blue pools in which he could lose himself forever. It had never occurred to him that her life had deviated much from the way she had lived it when he was a teen. Now he realized there were still many things he didn't know about the time lines—his, hers, everyone's.

"Sir, are you ready to order?"

"Uh, yes, thanks. Just the club sandwich and coffee."

"That'll do it," she said, then started to turn away, but stopped. "You look so familiar to me."

Familiar. He actually looked pretty much the same now as he had the day he had gone to the marina to reserve the boat. Like a professor. "I was just going to say the same thing about you. Do you go to the University of Miami?"

Her soft, coy laugh sent his blood racing. "I'm not in college yet. I just graduated a few weeks ago. Do you teach at U of M?"

He nodded. "Where're you going to college in the fall?"

"Probably Boston University. My parents work at MIT, so I wanted to stay in the Boston area."

"What're you going to major in?"

"Men," she said with a laugh, then hurried off to put in his order.

Men. It drove spikes into his heart.

He watched her, the sway to her hips, the grace with which she moved. She didn't look pregnant, but she was at least two months pregnant with his child now. Never mind that he, as an adult, didn't have anything to do with it. The child was still his, a miracle handed to him through the corridor.

She returned with a pot of coffee, and while she filled his cup he realized that he would have to revise his strategy somewhat, but it would be easier now that she'd met him as an adult and believed he was a professor. Academics were trustworthy, after all. Her own father and stepmother were academics.

"When did you start working here?" he asked. "I don't believe I've seen you here before."

"Just a couple weeks ago. Summer got boring."

Another spike went through his heart. How could

she say that when she and his younger self had spent so much time together?

"You sure we haven't met?"

"Positive. I'd remember. I'm Professor Harvey."

"I'm Eva Wheaton. Let me go get your sandwich, Professor."

Take her tonight.

No, he wasn't ready yet. He needed to do what he'd come here to do and then leave.

He ate in a hurry, left her a large tip, and slipped away without seeing her again.

It was dark now, Venus just visible above the horizon, a dove-gray strip of light to the west. He drove straight across the highway and onto the narrow road. He followed it over the bridge that led eventually to the marina, but turned on a dirt side street and nosed into the trees that covered a vacant lot.

This tiny peninsula of homes and vacant lots was shorter than the other fingers of land that jutted out into the lagoon and, therefore, less desirable from a home owner's point of view. But it afforded him an unimpeded view of the house, where the lights were on, and of the yard, where two people stood on the dock with flashlights, watching something in the canal. Fish, probably. His mother and stepfather always found the water ecology of the keys fascinating. He recalled how, when they had free time, they often sat on the dock, looking for schools of jumping fish and the occasional dolphin or manatee that wandered into the lagoon.

He turned on the videotape recorder and zoomed in on the two people on the dock. His mother's face came into view, the image so clear and so close it was as if he could extend his arm and touch her.

* * *

He stands beside his mother's bed, her hunched figure little more than a shadow. "Go ahead, Mom, slide the barrel into your mouth," he whispers. "It won't solve anything. Her baby is still my baby."

Wheaton shook the memory away and watched his mother and stepfather walk back toward the house, their arms around each other's waists. He switched to record, panning the entire length of the property, zooming in on the dock, the yard, the porch, the dock again. He pulled back and panned the area behind him—the canal, the marina, and its dock. He zoomed in on the house again, capturing the length of the. screen porch on the second level, the sliding glass doors, and the living room lights.

He turned off the camera and sat there for a long while, just watching, absorbing, listening, planning. It worried him that Eva had taken a job. What else had changed from when he had lived here as a teen? For all he knew, Bobby Macon might not be in the picture, and if he wasn't, then that meant Eva wouldn't die. *What if, maybe, could be . . .* He would drive himself crazy if he started in on all the possibilities. He simply had to stick to his plan and use whatever changes he knew about to his advantage.

He dug to the bottom of the bag and brought out a pair of binoculars, the ultimate tool for the voyeur. He focused on the porch again. His stepfather and Eva were visible now, both of them leaning against the wall, smoking. She was still wearing her uniform from work. Wheaton wondered what they were talking about. Eva's pregnancy? Probably not. He was almost certain that Dan Wheaton had found out about her pregnancy when she was autopsied.

Well, pretty soon it would be a moot point. Eva would

be among the missing and Wheaton's younger self would be spared all the terrible things he had gone through and maybe his own mother would live on for a while, her despair over her son's corruption and her stepdaughter's pregnancy no more than an unpleasant dream that hadn't happened.

He hoped so. All he wanted was Eva and his child. What could be simpler than that?

Twenty-two

"What's he doing?" Rusty whispered.

"How the hell should I know? You're the one who lives with him," Lydia replied.

Lydia and Rusty were crouched down behind a row of hedges that ran parallel to the marina seawall. They had followed Wheat in a truck that Lydia had borrowed, a vehicle he had never seen, and had left it on the far side of the marina, behind an old aluminum shed. "From where he is, he can see into the houses along the canal," Rusty whispered. "All four of them. We need to check it out before he leaves, Lydia. Let's take the bikes."

It was why they had put the bikes in the back of the truck, but now that Rusty had suggested using them, she got very cold feet. Peter Wheat terrified her. He terrified Rusty. And because of that, neither of them had done right by Annie. Rusty had said he could go to Joe Bob Fontaine and tell him about the children, show him the graves, but they both knew he couldn't do that because they would be arrested as accessories. There was only one choice—to free the girl themselves. They should be doing that right now, while Wheat was here, spying. But they wouldn't until they understood what Wheat was *really* up to. Maybe that was wrong, too, but before they made a move they had to *understand*.

And to begin to understand, they had to know which house interested Wheat so very much that he sat for hours, spying. They had to know who lived in that house and how they were connected to Wheat and what the girl, Annie, had to do with any of it. Hell, Lydia thought. She needed to know what any of the children he'd brought back had to do with whatever was cooking in his evil head.

They bicycled quickly through the dark, up over the creaking wooden bridge, down the other side, past the road where Wheat was, and onto the next side road. The moon hadn't risen yet, and since they were both dressed in black clothes they were practically invisible. Rusty had gone the extra mile by wearing a long-sleeve black shirt—hot as shit on a night as humid as this— and he'd rubbed black shoe polish on his face and the backs of his hands.

They checked the first three mailboxes, but none of the names meant anything. Oskin, Laker, Davidson. The last house, the one that occupied the tip of this particular finger of land, was enclosed on two sides by a tall wooden fence. The wooden mailbox was engraved with a name: *The Wheatons.*

"Jesus," Rusty whispered. "Wheat-Wheaton. I mean, c'mon, that's too big a coincidence, Lydia."

"It doesn't tell us anything. We need to go inside, take a look around, figure it out."

Rusty, his clear blue eyes ringed with black, looked like a startled raccoon. "He told me his family used to come to Sugarloaf on vacations."

"Yeah? So? Even if this is his family, what's that prove?"

"I don't know."

"Exactly."

They walked their bikes over to the bushes in the cul-de-sac and hid them. Lydia rang the bell outside the gate, waited, rang again. When no one answered, she pushed it open and she and Rusty slipped into the yard.

"We're crazy," he whispered.

"We gotta know. Once and for all, we gotta know."

The yard was large, beautifully landscaped, with several elegant palms reaching for the sky and surrounded by other thick tropical plants. The house was built on stilts, with a huge area underneath. Part of it had been decked and screened; the rest of it was for storage. A boat was tucked back in the shadows. Bikes leaned against the walls. Kayaks were stacked on a wall rack. No cars. No dogs, either.

Wheat/Wheaton, she thought.

They darted across the yard, under the house, and stopped behind the boat. Part of her mind shrieked, *Insanity, girl, they catch you here and your ass goes to jail and never passes go.* She was a black woman trespassing on a white family's property. Never mind that she was with a white boy who had a vested interest in uncovering the truth; the law would make up some sort of lie about that. Only thing worse would be if she were a black man. Or if they were both black men.

Rusty pointed at the narrow stairwell that led up to a door. She nodded and followed him. They moved swiftly up the stairs and, at the top, Rusty pressed his ear to the wood, listening. "Nothing," he said softly, and turned the knob.

Then they were inside. A kitchen. It was pure white. White everywhere. Like being in the center of a snowstorm. Even the floor was white linoleum, as ugly as a gnome's face and pitted with dirt, mold, old food.

The still air felt cool.

Nothing human was in here.

Dinner smells lingered. A light over the sink was turned on, exposing a sink filled with dirty dishes, dinner still crushed against them. A lone saucepan remained on a burner, the red sauce inside long since gone cold. The garbage can overflowed. Another bag of garbage stood against the trash can. The floor was filthy, mottled with stains, old food. These people, she thought, were pigs. If these Wheatons were Peter Wheat's actual birth family, then no wonder he had such a phobia about germs.

She touched Rusty's arm, pointed at his sneakers. He nodded and they removed their shoes but not their socks—no way were they going to walk barefoot on *this* floor—and she dropped them in her shoulder bag. It was a beautiful black canvas bag her husband had given her during their first Christmas together, and he had filled it with other gifts that they couldn't afford. Lydia tightened her grip on the strap and murmured a silent prayer to her husband, God rest his soul, asking for guidance, illumination, any goddamn thing he wished to impart, amen and thank you.

Now: in the living room. They kept to the wall, side-stepping along it like crabs on urgent business. Big place, nicely furnished, but messy. No one cleaned up around here. They crept along the bookshelves, studying the collection of family photos. Mom and dad together, a happy smiling couple. Mom, dad, daughter, and son, their arms around each other, one big happy family. Happy, happy, happy.

Except that beneath their smiles and their beautiful faces, they looked miserable as hell. And the son seemed familiar. Lydia picked up the photograph and held it under the gooseneck lamp. "Jesus God," she said softly, and rubbed her thumb over the son's face.

It was him. Peter Wheat. It was a much younger version, yes, but definitely him. She guessed he was fifteen or sixteen in this photo and since Wheat was pushing fifty now, this picture had been taken over thirty years ago. But thirty years in which time zone? The 1968 time zone or the twenty-first-century time zone?

"It's him," Rusty hissed, peering over her shoulder. "It's him." His nimble fingers removed the picture from the frame, turned it over. Scribbled in pencil was *Dan, Katherine, Eva, and Patrick, spring 1968.* "Shit, how can two versions of Pete exist in the same time?"

"You're asking me?"

"We need to get outta here," he said.

Rusty headed for the kitchen, the picture still clutched in his hand, the empty frame on the bookcase.

"You shouldn't have done that." She spoke to his back as they hastened back into the kitchen. "They'll see that it's missing."

"So fucking what?"

"We still don't know why they're of interest to him."

"Of course we know. They're his family." He sounded annoyed and scared, deeply scared. "He wants something from them. He's going to take something. That's what he does, Lydia. He *takes* what he wants. He's a sick fucking pervert who figures life owes him."

She happened to agree with his assessment. But that wasn't enough. She grabbed his arm. "We need to poke around some more."

Rusty wrenched his arm free, grabbed the pan of cold red tomato sauce, and scooped his fingers inside. He went over to the fridge and swept his fingers across the pale surface, making a big P, and then across the pale cabinets in a sweeping E and a sloppy R, and then to the pantry door for a simple V and a another E, and then to the table for the final glorious R and T followed by what looked like several dozen exclamation points. He did it so fast, with such deliberate intent, that by the time Lydia realized what he was doing, it was too late to stop him. As she came unrooted from the floor and lunged for him, he already had added water to the saucepan and was hurling it.

The wave of cold tomato sauce, now the consistency of weak tea, splattered against the white walls, the white appliances, the white sink and floor. Lydia grabbed the back of his shirt and wrenched as hard as she could and Rusty stumbled back, one hand still clutching the pan, the other clawing at the air. She yanked the pan out of his hand, dropped it in the sink, and groped behind her until she felt the knob. She threw open the door and down the stairs they went, part tumble, part fall, part *oh shit, what's happening.* Like a pair of tomcats locked in battle, they landed on their feet.

"You dumb fuckin' white boy." She shoved him forward and he fell, hands flying out, into the boat. He pushed himself back from it and spun around, black shoe polish smeared up over his ears now, into his eyebrows, thickening on the tips of his lashes. He looked pissed, but not crazy. He looked enraged, but not dangerous, at least not to her. Before he could utter a word, the huge wooden gate in the wooden fence began to squeak and complain and they realized it was opening, that a car was driving in.

They scrambled behind the boat, both of them crouched down, barely breathing. She heard the car as it drove in, heard the car door open and shut and shoes crunching over the gravel in the driveway. She heard the gate shut, the shoes across the gravel again, the door opening, the engine dying. Then she heard giggling, husky voices, laughter, and when she peeked out from the side of the boat, she saw them, young Peter Wheat/Wheaton, whatever his real name was, and the pretty white girl in the photo, running naked across the yard, through the starlight.

They were holding hands.

They paused at the edge of her range of view and

embraced. Then they ran out of her sight and Lydia looked at Rusty. *Fuck oh fuck,* he mouthed.

She would never be exactly sure how they got out without being seen, but she supposed that when you were a teenager and your hormones were raging and you were fucking your sister, stepsister, cousin, or whatever she was, the rest of the world disappeared.

Once they were on the road, they pulled their bikes out of the bushes and leaped on and rode. They rode so fast that her eyes teared and her hair flew all over the place. At the end of the street, she leaned into the right turn just as Rusty did and they both nearly collided with a VW bus as it came out of the next side street. She knew instantly that it was Wheat. He laid on the horn and it bleated like a wounded sheep, the noise echoing in the darkness.

She nearly wiped out, but caught herself and pedaled until her thigh muscles screeched and she was going like the wind. Had he recognized them? Was he following them? She knew Rusty was thinking the same thing, that their minds were locked in terror, because they both looked back at the same time.

Headlights bore down. Her breath burst from her, like a loud belch. She leaned forward, her legs working frantically at the pedals. The bridge loomed just ahead, the marina beyond it, not a soul around. "Under the bridge," she shouted.

They cut to the right and sped down a shallow slope to the canal. She heard the bus's engine, louder and closer, and leaned to the left to turn under the bridge. The bike went over, spilling her to the ground. She landed hard on her hip, but managed to keep hold of her bag. She scrambled to her feet, righted the bike, and ran after Rusty, pushing the bike as she followed him under the bridge. *Crazy fucker thinks he's gonna mow us down.*

When they were directly under the bridge, they pushed their bikes into the water, into what she hoped was the grassy part of the shallows. The bikes sank and they scurried over to the concrete pipe that carried excess water into the canal during the rainy season. Lucky for them, it hadn't rained in months and the pipe was nearly bone dry inside.

But it was totally black in the pipe and they were still in their stocking feet and the floor was slippery with slime, algae, moss. Her feet crunched over things— *snails? Were those snails?*—and she stopped long enough to run her hand over the bottom of her socks, cleaning off the bits of snail and shell, and pulled on her shoes. She passed Rusty his sneakers, then they moved deeper into the pipe.

She heard the bus as it drove over the bridge, the thunder of the tires, the echo of the engine. The pipe, set into ground that had been fortified with soil hauled in from the mainland, amplified every sound, even their ragged breathing. Lydia pressed her hands over her ears, squeezed her eyes shut, but she could still hear the tires, the engine.

When the bus had gone over the bridge, the silence returned. Beyond the silence she heard the *plunk, plunk* of dripping water.

"I've got some matches," Rusty whispered.

"Listen," she said.

The bus, coming back. It was definitely the bus, she heard that odd ticking of the VW engine.

"Move," she hissed.

They crawled farther, then Rusty stopped and lit a match. The light of the tiny flame bounced off the walls of the pipe, allowing them to see that it curved just ahead. They moved quickly toward it, the flame winked out. She didn't hear anything at all in the outside, up-top world. But in here, in the pipe, the dripping noise got louder and she heard a rustling, a sound like that of the wind through saw grass.

They made it around the curve and pressed up against the cold, damp wall of the pipe. Seconds later, a beam of light shot through the mouth of the pipe and struck the floor just beyond them. Lydia pulled her feet in as close to her body as she could get them, her eyes fixed on the beam, following it as it darted from one side to the other, poking into crevices of darkness. Light spilled like liquid down the sides of the pipe they had just come through and glimmered against the puddles of water just beyond them. Ripples spread across the surface of the largest puddle.

Ripples from what? Water bugs?

"Hellooooo, anyone home?"

Wheat's voice boomed through the pipe, echoing and bouncing like a Ping-Pong ball against the concrete walls. Lydia sucked in her breath, wrapped her arms around her legs. The beam of Wheat's flashlight climbed the wall where the pipe curved, then dropped to the floor. The surface of the puddle rippled again. A snake, startled by the light and the sounds, whipped out of the water and froze in the glare of the light, its tongue flicking. A skinny snake with red, yellow, and black rings.

Coral or scarlet king snake? She stared at it in horror, struggling to recall the rhyme about coral snakes. Was it *Yellow and black, a friend of Jack*? Or *Red and black, a friend of Jack*?

Rusty touched her shoulder; he saw it, too.

The beam of light moved again, slid away, went out. Had he given up, left? And where was the snake now? Was it a coral snake? To realize a snake shared the darkness with you was bad enough. But to occupy that darkness with what might be a coral snake was unimaginable. Rusty was now gripping her arm, warning her not to move, not to do anything.

Now, the rustling again. The snake was moving. An elemental fear gripped her. She couldn't scream, couldn't move, could barely think. *Do something*. She slid her bag off her shoulder, set it on the floor in front of their feet, a barrier against frontal attack. "Give me your matches," she whispered.

"The light will draw it to us," he whispered back, but pressed the matches into her hands.

"I'm making a fire."

Using her teeth, she ripped the sleeve off her shirt, wrapped it around the visor of her baseball cap, and lit three matches that she held to the fabric. It caught fire, burning slowly, brightly. And there, not two feet from them, the snake coiled, its red, yellow, and black rings clearly visible. *Red and yellow kills a fellow.*

That was it. The rhyme. If the red and yellow rings touched, it was a coral snake. These rings touched.

Lydia waved the flaming cap, thrusting it out as she and Rusty moved along the curve of the wall. The snake stayed just as it was, coiled tightly, tongue flicking. Lydia blew on the flames, stoking them. The fire burned more quickly, racing over the top of the cap, devouring the fabric. The heat singed her knuckles and she hurled the cap toward the snake.

It sprang, striking out at the flaming cap, and she and Rusty scrambled forward on their hands and knees, her bag banging against her hip, the stink of the burning cap filling the pipe. They shot out of the mouth of the pipe, sprang to their feet. She stumbled, Rusty caught her arm, and then he waded into the shallows of the canal and retrieved their bikes.

Moments later, they pedaled madly across the bridge, through the moonlight that filled the empty road.

2

Kids, Wheaton thought. Just a couple of kids on bikes up to no good. Pranks, petty theft, no telling. He had spooked them badly and they were probably still hiding down in that big old rain pipe.

As soon as he thought this, a memory surfaced, of that night in June—*this* night, thirty-five years in his past—when he and Eva had gone skinny-dipping in the lagoon. That part of the memory was so clear he could still taste her skin. But the rest of the memory felt new. They had hurried into the house, Eva entering the kitchen first . . .

. . . and she gasps. "My God, what happened?"
He shuts the door, comes up behind her, and looks slowly around the room, at the red shit on the walls, at the letters on the fridge, the cabinet, the pantry door. PERVERT.

Wheaton slammed on the brakes. His breath exploded from his mouth. The kids were in the house, the kids he had chased had done this *But who are they?* Macon was behind it. Sure, Billy Macon. Had to be. He wouldn't dare come into the house by himself, that wasn't his style. He would pay a couple of his friends to do it, the townies who clung to him like moss to rock. *Go trash the house.*

He was sure this memory was new, that it was another deviation from the past, like Eva waitressing at the lodge. If the past deviated too much from his memory of it, something might go very wrong. Death might come looking for Eva sooner or in a different way and all of this would have been for nothing. It had to start tonight.

Wheaton pressed his foot against the accelerator and spun right onto the highway. Twenty minutes later, he reached Big Pine Key. He turned at the intersection where, in his time, there was a shopping center with a Winn Dixie, a pet store, a Cuban coffee shop, and other retailers. Now, the area was covered with pines. Everywhere he looked, there were pines and within these pines, the population of key deer flourished. In his own time, signs were posted along the road, warning motorists to watch out for the deer, and other signs gave the current number of deer fatalities for the year.

He drove for several miles, up and down dirt roads, his mind busily plotting, planning. He pulled over once to get out his map and to roll the cane out from under the backseat. It was metal covered in wood, this cane, another one of his pity props, like the cast, that never failed to create the impression that he was harmless. He changed his glasses to a pair with thick black frames. He mussed up his hair. From the duffel bag on the floor of the car, he pulled out a T-shirt and jeans and quickly changed into them. Now he looked more like a nerd than a college professor

The Macons, like his own parents, were rarely home. When they weren't out playing bridge, they were with their country club group. Their other children were grown, he remembered, so Billy got all the teen toys he could possibly need to amuse himself.

Sure enough, his red Mustang was parked in the area under the house, the hood up, a bright work light shining down, music playing from a nearby radio. It was the only house at this end of the street. On the other side of the canal, trees filled the empty lots. In thirty-five years, this part of Big Pine would be well developed. But Billy Macon wouldn't live long enough to see it.

Wheaton slowed, a perplexed tourist who had lost

his way. He drove past the house, made a U-turn, then approached the house again and pulled into the driveway, behind the Mustang that, on July first, Eva would be driving. She would be blasted and would plow the Mustang into a gas pump that would explode. She would be catapulted from the car and die instantly of head trauma. Macon would be burned over 60 percent of his body and would linger in a coma for weeks, his skin charred to a crisp.

Billy came out from behind the hood, wiping his hands on a towel tucked into the waistband of his filthy jeans. He wasn't wearing a shirt and was more muscular than Wheaton remembered.

He picked up his cane, the map, and got out of the bus. "Hi," he called. "I seem to be lost." He leaned on the cane as he made his way to the front of the bus.

"What address are you looking for?" asked Macon, the good Samaritan.

"Ferry Lane." *What'd she ever see in you?* "I'm not sure if there's a house number or not." He spread the map on the windshield of the bus. "I'll show you where I need to go."

"I've never heard of Ferry Lane. You sure you're on the right key?"

Wheaton laughed. "I'm not sure of anything."

Macon frowned. "You look familiar. Have we met before?"

"I don't think so. I live in Miami." He pointed at a spot on the map. "This is the place I'm trying to get to. My brother marked it on the map."

Macon leaned forward, studying the map, and Wheaton stepped back slightly, checking the street for cars, witnesses. But the road was dark and empty. Ironic, he thought, that on Macon's time line the incident with the hammock had happened only several days ago. *Adios, Billy.*

"Do you remember what I told you the night you and Eva tumbled out of the hammock, Billy?"

Wheaton spoke softly and Macon's head snapped up, shock seized his eyes, and then Wheaton whipped the cane upward and slammed it across the kid's throat, shattering his Adam's apple. Macon stumbled back, eyes bulging, hands clawing at his throat, his breath a pathetic wheeze.

He struck Macon once more across the throat, then across the back of the neck, and he was dead before he struck the ground.

Exhilarated now, Wheaton worked quickly, expertly. He dropped the cane, grabbed Billy's hands, a disgusting sensation. So many germs. He began to pull him toward the space under the house. The bastard was at least a hundred and sixty pounds of dead weight. His feet scraped against the driveway, a sound like fingernails across a blackboard. Sweat streamed from Wheaton's pores, his heart hammered.

He pulled him around in front of the Mustang, dropped his arms, pulled a handkerchief from his pocket, and wiped Macon's hands. He wrapped the handkerchief around his fingers and turned off the overhead lights. With any luck, the body wouldn't be found until his parents rolled in later tonight.

Wheaton ran down the driveway, swept up his cane, wiped it clean, grabbed the map off the windshield. Then he got into the VW bus and drove away.

Part Three
Shifts

"There is no meaning to the past of an event except
the set of of events that caused it. And there is no
meaning to the future of an event except the set of
events it will influence."

—Lee Smolin, *Three Roads
to Quantum Gravity*

Twenty-three

Sheppard and Goot pored over satellite photos of the black water mass that had been taken every four hours since Mira and Annie had disappeared. Goot had picked them up early this morning from Tina Richmond and now they were spread out on a table in Mira's office at the bookstore, their unofficial headquarters.

They arranged the photos chronologically, then separated the ones for the last three days from the others. The eighteen satellite photos for the last seventy-two hours showed a startling consistency for the mass's position, almost as though it had grown roots and stabilized. Its position now, in fact, was nearly exact with where it had been the night that Mira and Annie had disappeared. Even though it had broken into smaller pieces, the two larger pieces, floating like dark continents in the photos, remained within an area that was about four miles square. Granted, he was no marine biologist. But when you considered the rise and fall of tides, the gulf currents, winds, temperature, and the vagaries of the weather, this consistency struck Sheppard as downright strange. His opinion was echoed among some of the scientists studying the mass, who had described it in metamorphic terms, when they ventured to describe it all. *Like a living entity with a will of its own,* said one marine biologist.

In some of the satellite photos, it *did* look like an entity of some kind, Sheppard thought. In fact, when they used the computer to set the images in motion over a period of twenty-four hours, the smaller mass, the one into which he and Goot had ventured the night Mira and Annie had disappeared, had two very dark areas in it that resembled erratically shaped eyes. Set in motion, the eyes seemed to blink, to laugh, sometimes narrowing to slits, other times opening wide.

"I say we take a boat into this area," Goot said, tapping the area with the eyes. "We've got the coordinates for it, we've got a plane and pilot from Ross Blake, and we definitely have the time. And no Dillard is breathing down our back."

That wasn't quite true. Dillard was still very much a presence on Tango, but neither Sheppard nor Goot had to deal with him. Sheppard had requested a two-week leave, a combination of vacation and personal days. Such requests usually went to Baker Jernan's secretary, bypassing Dillard altogether, so Sheppard had faxed her, gotten Jernan's e-mail address in Europe, and told him what was going on.

Thanks to the CNN coverage on the discovery of the children's bodies, Jernan already knew the broad strokes. When Sheppard filled him in on the rest of it, Jernan approved his leave, suggested that Goot also take time off, and said he would e-mail Dillard to that effect. *Do whatever you have to do to find this bastard, Shep.* In essence, he had given them carte blanche to pursue the investigation. Sheppard would have done it regardless, but at least now he wouldn't forfeit a paycheck and his job.

"I'd like to duplicate the conditions that existed when Mira and Annie disappeared. In other words, start out from Little Horse around seven in the evening, in a boat similar to hers, and head into the geographic area that Nadine pinpointed."

Goot, standing with his hands on his hips as he stared down at the map, now raised his eyes. "Which just happens to be very close to the location of these two eyes or whatever the hell they are in the smaller mass."

"Right. If I'm wired with a portable radio receiver tuned into GPS, you can track my location."

"We need to test it to see if it works in the mass. We'll have to test weapons in the mass, too. And flares. We need to know the parameters."

Nadine strolled in with a manila envelope under her arm and three smoothies on a tray. She set the tray and the envelope on Mira's desk. "Strawberries, bananas, mangos, and pineapple. *Salud.*"

They clinked glasses, then Nadine walked around the table, looking at the satellite photos. She ran her fingertips over several of them, then picked up the one that showed the eyes most clearly. "Start here. In the eyes."

Sheppard and Goot glanced at each other. "You're spooky, Nadine," said Goot. "Sometimes you're really spooky."

She turned, smiling. "Here's something else to add to the spooky repertoire. After you told me that my new memory and the note from Mira were an *anomaly*, Shep, I tore apart the attic in the house to see if I could find anything else. And I did."

She held up a manila envelope like an attorney presenting evidence. "This was in a box I don't remember packing." She removed the items from the envelope and set them on the table with the satellite photos, as if to say they were as incontrovertible. Sheppard's knees cracked as he stood. When he moved toward the table, his body felt as unfamiliar to him as an ill-fitting suit he had borrowed for some special occasion. He picked up the first item, a note scrawled in Mira's handwriting.

> Shep, the man who took Annie should be visible on the digital camera. Look up Lydia Santos, who checked me in at the colony. My intuition says she's still alive in our time. A guy named Jake Romano who owns a bar called Rum Runners got me a car through his friend, Janis Joplin (yes, THE Joplin). Jake, I believe, is also alive in our time.
>
>   I love you.
>   Mira

His hand shook as he laid the note down and moved on to the next item, the same photo he had seen at the artists' colony, of Mira with Janis Joplin, the two of them standing near a VW Bug with a psychedelic hood. His brain couldn't wrap itself around this any better now than when Nadine had shown him the note, because way down deep a part of him balked at what his gut knew to be true. The skeptic in him couldn't allow the believer to spell it out. And in that moment, Sheppard understood this always had been his dilemma. Not so long ago, his debt had distracted him from dealing with the dilemma. But when his aunt had died and left him enough money to indulge himself, he had spent six months on the road and the traveling had forced him to confront himself.

He was the gringo who witnessed miraculous healings by shamans in the Peruvian Amazon—and later attributed it to good luck and placebos. He was the guy who spent three weeks with a tribe of Indians who had lived their entire lives at fourteen thousand feet in the Andes, sustained by their rich spiritual lives. And when he left the tribe, he deemed them to be kind and caring people whose lives were governed by superstitious nonsense. PSICOPS, the contemporary sentries of the mainstream belief paradigm that said the world and everything in it was like some well-oiled *machine*, had nothing on him. A skeptic was the easiest thing to be and he had made it an art form.

Goot read through the note. "Let me get this straight, okay? We're talking about time travel. That's what all this evidence points to. Somehow, Wheaton knows how to move through time and that's where he's been taking the children he abducts. And, somehow, when Mira gave chase, she ended up back there, too. Do I have it about right?"

"Exactly right," Nadine replied.

Goot howled with laughter. "Give me a break."

Nadine glared at him.

"Nadine, I believe you can see things the rest of us can't," Goot said. "I believe that Mira has that talent, too. But with all due respect, time travel is the *last* thing we should consider. I agree that something strange is happening out in that black water and that we need to investigate it. I agree that there're a lot of inconsistencies in this case, but—"

"You have a better theory, Goot?" Sheppard asked. "Maybe a conspiracy theory you'd like to share with us?"

Goot took umbrage at the remark. "Even a conspiracy theory would make a hell of a lot more sense than time travel, for Christ's sake."

"Yeah? How?"

Now Goot looked shocked. "*You're* buying it? Mr. Skeptic himself? Seconds ago, you were telling Nadine it was all some goddamn anomaly."

"Because just the idea terrified me. But it all fits, Goot. Annie's scrawled message. The forensics results on the children's bodies. Mira's note to Nadine. Nadine's dual sets of memories about a single event. This second note from Mira. The photo of Mira with a singer who has been dead for more than three decades. Jesus, how much clearer can it get?"

Goot slid his fingers through his hair and paced restlessly around the room. "Look, there's one big problem. Even if your theory is true, Shep, just how the hell do you propose to get back to 1968?"

"Through the black water mass, just as Mira said. She gave us coordinates, she described a place of total darkness within the mass . . ."

"Yeah, great. So you get into the mass and what do you do? You and I were *in* that mass, Shep. And the only things that happened to us were problems with the compass, the radio, and the engine. We didn't get whisked off anywhere. So what do you do when you get there? Pray? Visualize? Hope? How the hell does the whole thing *happen*? What momentum propels you into the past?"

"We don't know."

"I've given it some thought," Nadine said. "To a psychic, time is very much like a river. You step into the river back here, and you're in a client's past. You step into the river up there, and you're in the client's future. But the river doesn't flow in just one direction. In fact, many times through the course of our lives, the river goes off to the right or the left and, depending on what kinds of choices we make, the flow moves in and out of probabilities."

Goot looked like he was about to roll his eyes. "So?"

"If you know the coordinates of the various events in a person's life, past, present, future, and all the probabilities in between, then you can step into that flow anywhere and come back with information. It's what the government's remote viewers did in the Stargate program. Targets were assigned random numbers or, if the target was a geographic location, they were sometimes assigned geographic coordinates. The remote viewer was given a number—rather like an e-mail address—and then zeroed in on it."

Excitement stirred in Sheppard. He had a strong intuitive feeling about where she was going with this. But he kept quiet, letting her finish.

"Mira mentioned coordinates. Let's say that these coordinates correspond to the heart of the mass in both our time and on this particular date in the past. In other words, in June 1968, its location was exactly where it is in June 2003. Since Wheaton apparently had gone back and forth a number of times, then perhaps he has a way of calculating the precise coordinates for each of his trips. Once he has those coordinates, it's just a matter of moving into the black water, finding those coordinates, and letting the mass do whatever it does."

"I get the theory, Nadine," said Goot. "But the science doesn't bear out."

"Not as we now understand science. But we're dealing here with something science doesn't even know about it. A natural phenomenon. Nature's time tunnel."

He sensed Nadine was close to the truth, but felt something was still missing. "You don't have to worry about it, Goot. I'm going, you're not."

"He's having a crisis of faith, Shep." Nadine said this as though Goot weren't in the room. "All his life, he has been surrounded by *santeros*. He knows the world is steeped in mystery. He accepts this idea intellectually. But viscerally, in the deepest part of himself . . ." And now she looked at Goot. ". . . he can't quite make the leap." She smiled then, smiled as though Goot were some young child whom she loved dearly, but who just didn't get it yet. "He'll come around eventually."

She winked at Sheppard, and for the first time since he'd met Mira he felt like a full-fledged Latino brother and not some gringo bastard son, hovering at the edge of the in-crowd.

Sheppard's laptop beeped, indicating he had e-mail. He went over to Mira's desk to check it. Since this story about the children had broken in the media, Sheppard's in-box had been inundated with e-mail. Some were from well-intentioned people expressing their horror or offering leads. *I believe I saw Patrick Wheaton on the corner of . . .* Others were from nutcases who offered their theories about what was really going on. These theories ranged from alien abductions to ritualistic killings by satanists. Sheppard forwarded all of these e-mails to Dillard.

He had twenty-one new e-mails. He glanced through each one, then forwarded them to Dillard. The last e-mail, though, was different.

From: jhe@hotmail.com
To: sheppard@usgov.fbi.com
      Tomorrow night @ 10:10, the mass will be positioned precisely at the coordinates that facilitate travel through the corridor. On 7/1, @ 6:30 A.M. it will be @ that position again. If you don't return then, you'll have to wait for another two years. The coordinates are: 81W0510, 24N5010.
      The children whose bodies you discovered were killed by the time sickness. This is not a hoax, Mr. Sheppard. Events have been set in motion. Please look at the attachment and you'll understand.

Sheppard clicked on the attachment.

From The Key West Courier Archives
June 30, 1968
      BIG PINE KEY—Sometime on the evening of

June 26, Bill Macon, 18, was murdered by an unknown assailant. His parents, Dr. Hans Macon
and his wife, Gretchen, found their son's body in
the carport of their home shortly after midnight.
He apparently had been working on his car when
he was brutally attacked.

So far, police haven't got any suspects and aren't
releasing many details about the murder. If you
have any information, please call Lt. Grendetti
with the Monroe County Sheriff's Department.

Sheppard went into the newspaper archives on-line,
found this article in the archives, then requested more
information. He received a message saying that the
archive site was still being constructed and to please
get in touch with the newspaper directly.

"What is it?" Goot asked.

"Tell me what we found out about Bill Macon, Goot.
What your memory is."

Goot gave him an odd look. "He was in a car accident with Wheaton's stepsister on July first and died a
few weeks later from burns. Supposedly he was ar-
ranging for Eva Wheaton to have an abortion in the
Bahamas."

"And the e-mail says?" Nadine asked.

Sheppard read it and the article on Macon's death
aloud. "So if Billy Macon is dead, Eva Wheaton won't be
in the car with him on July first. Therefore, she won't
die. Or, at any rate, she won't die the way that history
said she did. If Patrick Wheaton is back in 1968 and
killed Macon, that tells us that Patrick Wheaton figures
he's going to prevent his stepsister's death. Brilliant."

"What do the abductions have to do with any of it?"
Goot asked.

Nadine looked stricken. "Dear God," she whispered.
"To save his sister—to undo the past, in other words—

he figures he has to have something to give in return. Another life."

An intense cold seized Sheppard, covered him, permeated him. When he spoke, his voice sounded small and scared. "A sacrifice."

Twenty-four

Mira stood at edge of the woods on the colony's eastern ridge, determined to see the sun come up this morning. But it seemed to be behaving like a teen who wanted nothing more than to embrace sleep for another ten minutes, another hour, the rest of the morning. In her time, the teen would hit the snooze button; she didn't know if teens in 1968 even had a choice. Their clocks weren't digital, she doubted if they even glowed in the dark.

She had awakened an hour ago, rested but restless, discouraged but still hopeful, the noise in her skull gone and the internal silence eerie and unsettling. She had showered, made coffee, had a slice of grapefruit, done some yoga stretches. Then she had gone outside to watch the sunrise.

At home, she disliked getting up early. Nadine was usually up before she was and opened the bookstore every morning by nine. Mira usually arrived an hour later and closed up in the evening. Late mornings, dusk, and darkness fit her body rhythms. But this morning, she needed the familiar, the mundane, something that linked her to her own time, and that was the sun.

Now here she stood, waiting for something that would expose the bridgeless bay, the dark shape of Key West twelve miles distant, the endless churning of the ferries. She was homesick for her own home, her own life. She wanted to be with Annie, to feel the familiarity of her own house gather around her, the company of Shep and Nadine, her cats and books. She missed her bookstore, the days that Annie worked there after school. She missed the smell of the books, the feel of their covers, the emotions that certain books evoked, the scent of freshly ground coffee in the café. She missed the yoga classes, the music, the rhythms of it all.

Around her, birds twittered and sang. A soft, salty breeze strummed the branches of the trees. The water below her lightened, turning from lead to dove gray to some color that actually looked blue. A year ago she and Shep had flown to Virgin Gorda for a week, just the two of them, and had camped out on beaches where the rocks were huge and the water, an indescribable blue. In her time, the bay waters would never turn that shade. They were too polluted. But maybe in 1968, they still had a chance, she thought, and sat against a tree and watched as light claimed the sky.

She heard voices beyond the woods, other residents out walking, jogging, or stretching for their yoga class on the green. Sunrise Yoga, it was called in the colony brochure, vestiges of pagan rituals that probably dated back to ancient India.

"Mira?"

She glanced around as Lydia came through the pines. She was decked out in her sixties equivalent of exercise clothes, her plaited hair gathered up in back. "Hey, you figure you're going to get lost back here or what?" She brushed pine needles off her white shorts, removed her tennis shoes, positioned them carefully on the ground, and sat down on them. "You had your coffee yet?"

"Just one cup. Why? You have some brewing?"

"Hon, I got the best Cuban coffee beans outside of

Havana. But I'm asking because I think you're going to need some really good coffee to jump-start your day. The sheriff's waiting outside your cabin."

"Sheriff Fontaine?"

"The one and only."

Mira got up and brushed off her shorts. "Pretty early for a social visit."

"You know him?"

"Sort of. I read for him the other day."

"For *Fontaine*? He believes in that stuff?"

"He does now."

"Then I guess there's hope for the man. Anyway, I told him I'd come looking for you."

"What're you doing up so early?" Mira asked.

"Got a friend moving into my cabin today and I need to shuffle stuff around and make some space for him."

"A love interest?"

Lydia laughed. "No. Too young. He's just a guy who needs some help right now."

As they reached a fork in the main path, a flock of wild parrots lifted suddenly from the trees. Mira and Lydia stood there watching them. One of the birds separated from the flock and swept in low over the path, squawking, "Hello, hello." Then Dusty flew upward to rejoin her friends. Mira had the feeling she had seen the last of the conure and wondered if it meant that her own time here was drawing to an end. If that was true, it meant that she was close to finding Annie, since she wasn't leaving here without her.

She hurried on toward her cabin, puzzled about Fontaine's visit. Maybe he'd found out that she had lied about her last name. Maybe he just wanted another reading.

He was sitting on the hood of his car outside her cabin, smoking a cigarette, and smiled when he saw her. "Sorry to barge in so early," he said, dropping the cigarette and grinding it under his foot. "You have a few minutes?"

"Sure, Joe. What's up?"

"After the things you told me the other night, I was, uh, wondering if you've ever done any of that for the police."

Uh-oh. "Yes, I have. I don't like to do it, but I have."

"Would you do it for me?"

Her first impulse was to tell him no, forget it, she couldn't do it. But she had promised herself to act upon whatever came her way, regardless of how removed it appeared to be from the reasons she was here. And there was the other fact to consider: Fontaine was, at the very least, acquainted with her daughter's kidnapper.

"What's it concern?"

"A murder. There was—"

"That's all I need to know, Joe. Let me grab a mug of coffee first."

Relief defined his smile. "The department will pay you for your time, Mira."

She suspected the payment would be coming straight out of Fontaine's pocket, not the department's petty cash. "Buy me lunch and we'll call it square."

"That's a deal. Hey . . ." He rapped his fingers against his chest. "I took your advice. Got the vest on. Front *and* back."

Mira scribbled a note to her clients, explaining that all readings would be postponed until tomorrow, and ten minutes later she and Fontaine were boarding a chopper at the Tango Airfield. It was just the two of them and the pilot, jammed into a chopper that lacked the space of choppers in her time and also many of the bells and whistles. But she had the backseat to herself and as the chopper lifted off, a vastness opened in the pit of her stomach.

This was the first time she'd been off the island since she'd awakened on that beach more than two weeks ago. The landscape a thousand feet below was beyond anything she had imagined, the islands strung together like delicate jewels, pale green surrounded by a practically infinite blue. There were more mangroves, more beaches, more sky and water, more of everything except buildings. Thirty-five years of rabid development would bring unprecedented pollution, traffic, and crime.

From here, she could also see an area that resembled an oil spill. It drifted several miles north of Tango, between it and Little Horse Key. The black water mass. "Joe," she called over the din of the rotor, "what's that black stuff down there?"

"No one knows."

He said it as though the black water was just one more impenetrable mystery in a universe of such mysteries, best left to philosophers and marine biologists. *No one knows.* But she knew. She hoped it would be her and Annie's ticket home.

The pilot flew just offshore, following U.S. 1 north. Mira kept her face turned toward the window, drinking it all in. Somewhere down there, a monster held her daughter captive and thirteen-year-old Tom Morales was living out a full summer.

As the pines below them thickened, the chopper descended and circled a vacant lot at the end of a street. Mira didn't see any police cars or a horde of reporters or even a crowd of curious onlookers. She leaned forward and tapped Fontaine on the shoulder. "Where're the cops?" she asked.

"They've come and gone. The body was discovered around midnight last night."

She sat back and a few minutes later the chopper touched down. "I'll need something of the victim's to touch," she told Fontaine as they started up the street.

"Not a problem. He was at home when he was killed."

It was a quiet street, barely populated, most of the vacant lots covered in pines. Although it was still early, the morning heat promised a scorcher by noon. Already, the sun baked the asphalt and waves of heat quivered like a mirage just inches above the pavement. Gulls swept eastward from the gulf, their cries echoing in the humid stillness.

Tom lived just up the road a ways.

Don't.

"How much do you want to know about what happened?" Fontaine asked.

"I'd rather not know anything."

Her breathing shifted and she heard the humming rising up from deep inside her skull. She tensed, terrified that it would explode into that horrid shrieking, a level four beyond her ability to control. Instead, it settled in, there but not there, and she felt herself adjusting to it.

Fontaine nodded at the two cops parked in front of the house and stopped at the end of the driveway. "This is the place. That's his car in the carport. Everything's just as we found it."

No crime tape, she thought, and wondered about that. Maybe it wasn't used in 1968. Maybe it had been removed. *And maybe you'd best get started.* Her reluctance to move forward was now so huge that it loomed in front of her, an invisible wall, and she realized that she needed something that belonged to the victim.

"I need a personal item from the victim."

"Oh, right. Sorry about that." He reached into his pocket and withdrew a set of keys. "They've been dusted and entered into evidence. They're his." He dropped them in her upturned hand, her fingers closed around them. "Okay if I follow you?"

"That's fine."

"Is there anything special I should do?"

"Listen, but stay out of my way."

She worked off her sneakers and walked barefoot up the driveway to the Mustang, the keys clutched in her left hand. When she reached the car, she placed her right palm against the lid of the trunk, paused, walked along the left side of the car, her fingers trailing across the door. She waited for images, impressions, sensations, a rush of information, but nothing came to her. She got to the front of the Mustang, to the raised hood, and looked down. Chalk marks: the body had been found here. But this wasn't where he died.

Mira turned slowly in place, her eyes skipping across the radio, the tools, a shirt hanging from a hook on the back wall. Something was missing. What?

She walked toward the other side of the car, stopped, shut her eyes.

Mom and dad aren't home, won't be home till later, have a couple brews with the guys and then get laid.

The air smelled of metal, oil, and a woman's skin.

Who was the woman?

Hammock collapsing, the cocksucker.

Mira backtracked now, moving swiftly out of the carport, down the driveway, and into the street. She glanced right and saw the chopper in the vacant end lot, the water behind it. Didn't come from that way. "He came from the south. Drove a VW of some kind, I can hear the tick of the engine, you know that tick VWs have? It's a newer car and he takes good care of it, hasn't driven it much. He likes the way it smells, how clean it is, the seats so . . . so *unsoiled.*

"He's ready, he's so goddamn ready, and he knows just how to play it. The innocent question. Who would suspect? He's good at details, he's got them down pat."

Now the killer's energy seeped into her, an insidious poison, and suddenly Mira couldn't breathe, her lungs refused to move, to draw in, to inhale. It was as if she were three hundred feet underwater sucking on an empty oxygen tank. The air just wouldn't come. She clawed at her throat, her knees buckled, she went down.

In her peripheral vision, she saw Fontaine flying toward her, saw the world tilting, and she was *there*, inside the killer.

"Some day you'll leave me," he says. "I know you will."

"You're so silly, you know that?" and she tickles him in the ribs and they laugh and laugh and roll across the bed and off of it and hit the floor.

They come to rest against the wall, her body on top of his. He gets lost in her eyes, in the beauty of her skin, in everything that she is and is not. "Truth or dare," he says.

"Fuck you." She laughs, and rolls off of him.

He rolls, too, and pins her arms under his. "C'mon, truth or dare."

"Dare."

"Have you screwed Billy?"

"Billy who?"

And then she could breathe, the air rushed into her lungs, and they pumped wildly, frantically, and Fontaine was shaking her, saying her name.

"Okay, okay," she said crossly, and flung his arms away. "I'm okay." She got up and hobbled up the driveway, leaning heavily on her cane.

What cane?

Mira stopped, turned, looked at Fontaine. "He used a cane."

"A *cane?*" Fontaine repeated. "You mean, a cane was the weapon?"

It irritated her that he'd said that. It was a leading

question, not a mistake that Sheppard would ever make. "I mean he . . ."

Across the throat, the back of the head. "Yes. A weapon. He hit him across the throat and the back of the head. But he also walked with a cane."

Why? Is he old? Hurt? Why's he use a cane?

The humming suddenly escalated in pitch and lit up the inside of her body. *Pity ploy, pity ploy, pity ploy.*

Like a cast.

Uh-huh.

Hey, hello, my engine conked out. Can you give me a hand? Hi, I seem to be lost.

Different crime, different day, different time zone. But same guy.

Mira knew she was falling and groped for Fontaine's arm. The moment she touched it, she was immobilized on a table, watching as a nurse prepared to administer an electroshock treatment. Fontaine was open-minded enough to call in a psychic, but not so open-minded that he would buy the truth.

She hit the ground, he landed beside her, and for brief moments there in the hot light she thought she was going to collapse and sob. Instead, she started laughing, laughing so hard she couldn't stop. Then Fontaine started laughing, too.

"We're nuts," he said, wiping his eyes with the backs of his hands.

"Joe, was the victim named Billy?"

"Yes."

"He was killed out of jealousy, over a girl. She was sleeping with Billy and the killer."

"So the killer is around Billy's age?"

She didn't know. "He seemed to be both older and younger." Mira frowned. "The girl. She's a knockout. Eve? Eva? Something like that."

"That'd be Eva Wheaton." He seemed surprised to

realize he was on the ground, next to her, and he got quickly to his feet and helped her up.

"She was his girlfriend?"

"Down here, in the summer, these rich young northerners form alliances that are good only when they're here. Once they get back home . . ." He shrugged. "No more. She was that sort of girlfriend."

"Does she know that Billy's dead?"

"No. Right now, only family and relatives know. His parents gave us a list of his friends and we're checking that out today."

"I'd like to see this woman, Joe. Is that possible?"

"You're up to it?"

"Definitely."

"Great. Let's go."

Fontaine spoke briefly to one of the cops parked out front and he got out, handed Fontaine the keys to his cruiser, and off they went. "If this guy is young, why's he use a cane?" Fontaine asked.

"It's a pity ploy. He did it to appear nonthreatening. He has other props that he uses, too."

"He's done this *before?*"

Careful. "I don't know if he's killed before, but I think he's done other things where he used similar props."

They drove on in silence.

The gate to the Wheaton home stood open and Fontaine drove in and parked behind a white Mercedes. The house was the only one on the street that was elevated on concrete pilings, a style that would become mandatory in the near future. Part of the area under the house had been converted into a screen porch, the rest of it looked to be for storage. The yard was magnificent, a spread of beach sand and tropical plants, with a private dock and a canal that fed into the lagoon, which the house faced.

"This cost a pretty penny," Fontaine murmured.

"What do the parents do?"

"They're scientists up in Boston, come down here for summers and holidays."

As he opened the screen door for her, she immediately felt uneasy, she wanted to . . .

Run, hide fast before it's too late.

But it was already too late. Fontaine had rung the bell, and a pretty woman in tight capri pants—pedal pushers in 1968—and a sleeveless shirt tied at her waist peered out at them through the screen. Her curly hair was pale blond and tumbled around her shoulders. "Yes?"

"Mrs. Wheaton?"

"Yes, I'm Katherine Wheaton."

"Ma'am, I'm Sheriff Fontaine. Is Eva home?"

"She's still sleeping." She pushed the screen door open, stepped out onto the deck, her arms clutched to her waist. "What's this about?" Her dark eyes flickered to Mira, then back to Fontaine.

"Was your daughter dating Billy Macon?"

"She's my stepdaughter, actually, and yes, she's been dating Bill. Why?"

"He was murdered last night, ma'am, and we'd like to ask her some questions."

"Murdered?" Her hand flew to her mouth and her eyes filled with the horror that all decent people felt when murder happened practically in your backyard. "But . . . but . . . Eva doesn't know anything about it."

"I'm not saying she does, ma'am. We'd just like to speak to her. She might know something about Billy's life that would provide us with some leads."

"Yes. Of course." The horror receded. "Come in, please."

Mira's unease deepened as she and Fontaine followed Katherine Wheaton upstairs to a spacious living room. She invited them to sit down and said she would wake Eva. Mira felt too restless and uneasy to sit. She wandered around the room, not touching anything, just looking. She paused in front of a lineup of family photos. Mom, Dad, Eva, and a young man who was probably her brother.

Something about the young man disturbed her. She leaned closer. His eyes? Was that it?

"She'll be down in a few minutes," Mrs. Wheaton said, returning to the room.

"Is your son home? We'd like to speak to him, too," Mira said.

"He's out in the lagoon fishing. He should be in shortly."

Eva Wheaton came downstairs in tight shorts that showed off her long, tan legs, and a T-shirt that was two sizes too large. She was breathtakingly beautiful, with the kind of face that graced magazine covers, TV screens, Hollywood lights. She also looked scared shitless, Mira thought, noting how her eyes darted to Fontaine, then to her stepmother.

Fontaine introduced himself, his southern voice paternal, comforting, a voice that said, *Trust me.* Mira was introduced by her first name only, as his assistant. "We'd like to ask you some questions about Bill Macon."

"What about him?" She sat down at the edge of a chair, her body language suggesting that she might bolt at any second.

"You've been dating him?"

"Yeah, so?"

"For how long?" Mira asked.

"We see each other every summer and holidays." She twisted her hands in her lap. "Why? Has he done something?"

"He was murdered last night," Fontaine said bluntly.

"Mur . . ." Her hands gripped her knees, her eyes flooded with tears. "But . . . but . . ." she stammered, and then broke down completely, sobbing into her hands.

Katherine Wheaton hurried over to her with a box of Kleenex and stroked her hair. Eva didn't seem to find any comfort in her stepmother's touch and wrenched away, grabbed a handful of tissues, and wiped her face. Mira heard the door open, someone coming in through the kitchen.

"When did you last see him?" Fontaine asked.

"A . . . a couple days ago. We went out, then came back here. I . . . I . . . Who would do something like this? Just about everyone liked Billy."

"Patrick thought Billy and his friends were the ones who pulled that prank last night," Katherine said.

"That's *ridiculous,*" Eva snapped.

"What prank?" Mira asked.

"Spaghetti sauce all over the kitchen," said the tall young man in the kitchen doorway. "The walls, the counter, the stove and fridge."

The center of Mira's chest exploded with heat and the heat raced like blood through her arteries and veins. *It's him.* She nearly shot out of her chair and lunged for him, nearly screamed, *Where's my daughter?* But the humming spiked into a deafening shriek inside her head and the agony pinned her to the chair.

"And you are?" Fontaine asked.

"Patrick Wheaton."

"This is Sheriff Fontaine and Mira, his assistant," Katherine said.

Patrick Wheaton smiled, a bright, vibrant, cocky smile. In the few moments it took him to stride across the room in his bare feet, Mira could do nothing more than watch him, measure him against the picture in her mind of the man on the beach. *Peter.* This was Peter's younger self.

He shook Fontaine's hand. "Nice to meet you, sir." Very polite. Very amiable.

When he turned to Mira, she met his gaze and his smile evaporated like moisture in a desert heat. Everything inside her rebelled against taking his outstretched hand, but she did it because she had to see what he saw, to know what he knew. He was a conduit to the monster he would become. "Nice to meet—"

It was all she heard. A roaring filled her skull, multiple paths exploded open in front of her, and her nervous system blew apart, the pieces scattering like motes of dust in a freak wind. And then the information rushed into her at the speed of light, frying synapses, melting circuits, scorching new afferent pathways through her brain.

Seconds, that was all it lasted, no more than a quick blink in the cosmic scheme of things, but it was seconds too long. By the time he stepped back from her, his face seized up with puzzlement and fear, sweat poured from her, and heat surged from the center of her chest and raced up her neck and into her face.

Patrick Wheaton knew something strange had happened, she could see it in his eyes. But no one else knew. No one else had noticed. Fontaine picked up his line of questioning, Eva kept sniffling and wiping at her eyes, and Mira struggled to process everything she had seen and felt in the seconds after her head had exploded.

Wheaton watched her, she noticed, a sly, careful scrutiny, the eyes of a predator, and when she asked Katherine if she could use the bathroom she felt his eyes on her as she walked down the hall. She shut the door, locked it, and sank against it, hands over her face.

Think it through. The adult Wheaton had killed Billy

Macon, but that didn't make the younger Wheaton cul-
pable. But the younger Wheaton was infected with the
same malignancy, the same evil. If she could stop him
now, did that mean Annie's kidnapping wouldn't happen? That all of this would be canceled out somehow?

She had glimpsed the faces of other children whom
the adult Wheaton had kidnapped, tasted their
tragedies. If she stopped the younger Wheaton now,
would those kidnappings and deaths never happen?
Would Annie's kidnapping be undone? Would she
wake up in her own bed, in her own time, in the life
this man had stolen from her? It seemed unlikely.
These events had happened already on this time line,
and if she stopped the younger Wheaton now, a new
time line might open up.

Or everything will collapse.

She took a towel off the rack, ran it under the faucet,
pressed it against her face. In her vision, she had seen
the crash of a red Mustang, Billy Macon's car, and
knew that on one time line, both Eva and Billy had
died in that crash. But Macon had died last night.

And then it hit her. The adult Wheaton had killed
Macon to save Eva. *But why?*

She was family.

No. A monster like this . . . No, family wasn't the
reason.

Some day you'll leave me . . . Are you screwing Billy?

"Dear God," she whispered, and dropped the towel.

Young Wheaton and Eva were lovers, Macon was his
competition. Maybe the adult Wheaton had some sick
notion that he could now live happily ever after with
his stepsister.

But that didn't explain why he had kidnapped
Annie.

A knock at the door. "Ma'am? Sheriff Fontaine says
he's ready to leave."

The young Wheaton. *Go away,* she thought. "Thanks, I'll be out in a minute."

She stabbed her fingers through her hair, dabbed her face dry, opened the door. The young Wheaton stood there, leaning against the wall, arms crossed, that cocky smile turning one corner of his mouth slightly upward. "I know you," he said quietly. "I can't figure out where or when we met, but I never forget a face."

Even when it's passed down from the future. Well, hey, guess what. Maybe it works both ways. "What's your point?"

"Don't you recognize me?"

"Should I?"

He jammed his hands into the pockets of his shorts and rocked forward onto the balls of his feet, leaning in so close to her she could smell the salt and fish on his skin. "You tell me. Something happened when we shook hands." He reached out and curled a strand of her hair around his index finger.

A sixteen-year-old kid coming on to her: what audacity. It might have been outrageously funny, too, except that it was Wheaton. "I'll tell you what happened, Patrick, and I want you to remember this. I want you to carry this conversation through time. You hated Billy Macon because Eva was sleeping with him. He excited her in a way that you didn't." His face had gone white. She had his full attention now and plunged ahead. "As I think you found out during the hammock incident."

His jaw fell open, he released her hair, and the rest of it came to her, a large piece sliding effortlessly into place. "She's pregnant with your child and she doesn't want it. She can't wait to get rid of it and away from you. She doesn't love you, never did. You're an amusing distraction, an—"

"Shut up," he hissed, and grabbed her arm, pinning her to the wall. "You don't know what you're talking about. You—"

Mira's knee jerked up and sank into his balls. He gasped and doubled over and stumbled back into the opposite wall. "Here's a message for you, Wheaton. I came through the corridor and I know what you're up to. If you hurt my daughter, I'll follow you to the end of the fucking universe. Carry that one through time."

"What happened back there?" Fontaine asked once they were in the car.

"That girl is in danger, Joe."

"From?"

"Macon's killer."

"Does she know him?"

Did she? Had the adult Wheaton risked such a thing? "I don't know. She might. But I don't think she has a clue that he killed Macon. She's also pregnant."

"By Macon?"

"No. By her stepbrother."

He made a face. "Christ almighty. So they were rivals."

"To her complete delight."

"That kid reminds me of someone."

She fought to keep her voice interested, but neutral. "Who?"

"Don't know. Can't place it. You think Patrick killed Macon?"

Yes. "It's possible." *But not the Wheaton you just met.* "I can't say for sure." Her hope was that the adult Wheaton would remember the message she had given to his younger self and do something careless, something that would tip the odds in their favor. "Joe, would you do me a favor?"

"Are you kidding? After what you've just done today? I'd consider it a privilege."

"I need to go to Marathon. I have friends who live there and I need to deliver something to them."

"Done. What's the address?"

She gave it to him, rested her head against the seat, and shut her eyes.

Twenty-five

In her time, the house where Tom Morales had grown up looked worn and neglected; in this time, it looked as hopeful as a young bride.

It was a simple concrete block painted a pale yellow, with a yard enclosed by a wire-mesh fence. Dozens of fruit trees provided shade, and beneath them hardy plants flourished. No garage, just a carport with an old Pontiac parked inside.

"This it?" Fontaine asked, pulling over to the curb.

"Yes."

She stared at the house, drinking it in, her heart filling with love and wonder, hesitation and fear. Two bikes were parked just outside the fence, one of them a gleaming silver. Tom, she knew, had gotten it for his thirteenth birthday. She remembered his description of it, his first brand-new bike, and there on the polished chrome were his initials: TM. Mira reached into her pack and withdrew the envelope with Tom's name on it. She had written it over the last three days, as a kind of therapy for herself. It had begun with a single burning question one night while she had lain in the cabin, unable to sleep. If she could tell Tom anything about what his life would become, at least from what she knew about it, what would it be?

She knew she couldn't just come out and tell him never to step foot in a convenience store, especially in

1992. It wouldn't mean anything, he wouldn't remember it. So she had phrased everything she'd written with that warning in mind but had never come out and said it.

Mira opened the gate, stepped into the yard. The scent of citrus from the orange and grapefruit trees hit her. She inhaled the sweetness of ripened mangos, the cloying perfume from a lone gardenia bush. The hot sun beat against her back. She rang the bell and moments later a short, plump, and pretty woman opened the door. Mira had never met Tom's mother, she had passed away several years before she knew him, but Mira knew this was she.

"Buenos días. La Señora Morales se encuentra?"

"Soy Iris Morales."

Mira introduced herself as an employee at the local high school and asked her to give the envelope to Tom. "It concerns the reading list for next year," she went on in Spanish. "It was supposed to be handed out at the end of school, but . . ." She shrugged. "You know how it goes. So I'm going from neighborhood to neighborhood."

Iris Morales took the envelope, Mira thanked her, the door shut, and she continued to stand there, her feet rooted in the concrete, her muscles frozen up. Suddenly, two boys ran out from alongside the house, shouting and squirting each other with hoses. They stopped when they saw Mira and the tallest one, the boy she knew was Tom, dropped the hose and just stared at her.

She didn't know how long the eye contact lasted, certainly no more than five seconds, but to Mira it seemed like a lifetime. His dark eyes shone like wet streets, the sun kissed his smooth, beautiful cheeks, and she suddenly saw him lying on the floor of the convenience store, twenty-four years in his future, a pool of blood beneath him, and her feet uprooted from the porch. Her legs moved her across the yard and he now came toward her, the two of them drawn together by the same inexplicable force that would attract them to each other years from now, while they each stood in line at the courthouse to pay for speeding tickets.

They stopped a foot away from each other and everything else vanished for her. It was just the two of them, a boy who was Annie's age, and a woman who was forty-one years old, staring at each other across the incomprehensible continent of the human heart, and trying, at some level, to make sense of what they felt.

"I . . . I gave your mother an envelope, Tom," she said. "I told her it's from the school, but it isn't. I hope you read it and keep it with you for many years."

He didn't say anything. The silence stretched on so long that she now felt foolish and turned to walk back through the hot light, to Fontaine's car.

"Wait," he said suddenly, and caught up with her. "Who *are* you?"

"Mira. My name's Mira."

"Habla español?"

"Claro que si."

The instant she said it, she realized they had—or would have, depending on the time line—this exact conversation on the day they met. Tom had bumped into her accidentally as they waited in that long, slow line at the courthouse and she looked around, annoyed by the wait, the bureaucracy, and he blurted, "Who are you?" Did that mean he remembered these moments now, in this backward, messed-up version of events? Was that why he later told her that those moments in the courthouse confirmed his belief in the miraculous? "For years, Mira, I had this mental image of a woman and that day in the courthouse when I saw you, I knew that woman was you."

It came back to the old, familiar riddle: *what comes first, the chicken or the egg?*

"How do you know my name?" he asked.

"It's complicated. Just read the note, okay? And always believe that you can be anything you want, anything you can imagine."

His friend called to him, but Tom didn't look back, didn't acknowledge him in any way. His dark eyes remained fixed on her face, filled with questions, wonder, bafflement. "You want to hear something weird? Once I had this dream where a lady who looks just like you talked to me about my life, about my future. Are you real?"

Mira laughed. "I'll tell you a secret. I had a dream where a kid who looks just like you asked me that same question. You're going to become a lawyer, Tom. You'll have a daughter named Annie and a wife who loves you and she'll always tell you to never shop in convenience stores."

He grinned. "Why does she tell me that?"

"Because it's really important. Remember it. I need to get going."

She hurried away before he could say anything else and nearly ran toward Fontaine's car. *Will this save you? Will this prevent your death in 1992?*

And Mira suddenly knew this was what she and Wheaton had in common. They both loved someone who had died and now that they found themselves in a time before those deaths, they couldn't resist the temptation of trying to change that—she, in her way and he, in his. Tom had been murdered; Eva was supposed to have met her death in Billy Macon's car. Mira had glimpsed it when she'd shaken hands with the younger Wheaton. In other words, both had died as a result of someone else. No simple heart attacks here, no strokes. These were deaths that might be prevented.

Wheaton's first step in prevention had been to eliminate the kid whose car his stepsister was in—or driving?—the night she was killed. His second step in prevention would be to snatch Eva with the same ease he had snatched five other children, and to have someplace to take her where they could be together. It didn't matter to the adult Wheaton that he would be fifty and she, only seventeen. In his mind, he and Eva and their baby were already living in paradise together, somewhere in a new life and maybe in a new time as well.

And that, she knew, was their primary emotional difference. She couldn't even begin to image herself at forty-one living intimately with Tom at thirteen. Although they recognized each other at a soul level, they wouldn't have any more in common in real life than animals of different species. Wheaton seemed to have overlooked that part of his equation. She doubted if he had even considered the ramifications of saving Eva's life.

How would the abduction and disappearance of Eva affect the younger Wheaton? How would it shape him? What impact would it have on his later decisions? Would the older Wheaton have his younger self's new memories? Would a new time line be created? If so, how would that time line affect the one that she and Annie were on now?

Her head ached when she slid inside Fontaine's car. She felt small, stupid, depressed, afraid, all those horrid adjectives that amounted to one big fuckup. "You okay, Mira?" Fontaine asked.

"I need lunch."

"I know just the place."

Not once did he ask her about her exchange on the lawn with a young kid, an event that might have looked strange to him, might have looked strange to anyone on the outside. He didn't push her to talk in the car on the way to the restaurant, just left her alone to brood and sulk and mourn on her own. But over lunch, he questioned her about Wheaton. So she told him her bottom line.

"You need to watch the girl, Joe, and I mean *really* watch her. If you can get her out of that house and to a safer place, then do it. If you can keep her in her home but safe, even better. He's going to come for her and it'll go down in a way you can't even imagine."

He sipped noisily at his Coke, lit a cigarette and puffed on it a couple of times, then stabbed it out. His eyes didn't leave hers. "What else?"

"Don't take that vest off."

Fontaine nodded. She had a feeling that he knew she wasn't at all what she claimed to be—Mira Piper, stalked by an ex-hubby and stranded here. But she suspected that he was intrigued enough by her hits to overlook her inconsistencies, her small lies.

"I want her home and guarded, but I don't want her family to know." He paused, looked up at her. "Even if Patrick killed Billy Macon, he won't hurt her. He's crazy about her. It's there in his eyes. I could see it. It's the same way my son looks at his girlfriend. You feel it. So if she isn't at risk because of Patrick, then you're talking about someone else, right?"

"Yes." *The adult version of the same young man, but a separate physical entity.*

"Who is this guy? What's he after?"

"He wants to save her."

"From?"

"Herself," Mira replied.

Twenty-six

As Sheppard drove toward Nadine's, he went through a mental checklist, just as he did before any trip. In fact, if he didn't think about his destination, his preparations for this trip weren't much different than the preparations he made for dozens of other foreign trips in his life.

He had called the number Ross Blake had given him and asked for a plane and pilot for eight tonight. Not a problem, Blake had told him. Someone would be there. In lieu of a passport, he had genuine ID from 1968: a federal badge straight out of the Hoover era and a driver's license registered to Wayne Sheppard, born in 1926. He even had an insurance card issued in his name. To get this stuff, Goot had called in just about every favor they were owed from the boys at the Miami bureau.

His duffel bag, made of a lightweight waterproof canvas, wasn't so big that it would attract undue attention, but was sufficiently large enough to accommodate most of what he needed. Packs like his actually existed in 1968, and Sheppard and his backpack were very old friends. It had traveled with him through South America, Europe, and Asia. He considered it to be his good-luck charm; it was going wherever he went.

His P226 Sig Sauer and extra ammo and a Baretta were also going with him. His laptop, a superthin model that weighed less than two pounds, was packed as well, loaded with everything he had been able to find on Patrick Wheaton, his stepsister and parents, the colony as it had existed in 1968, and anything else that might prove useful. His clothing was circa 1968, as authentic as it got except for the New Balance running shoes and the marine sandals with ribbed rubber soles and Velcro straps.

Since money had changed dramatically since 1968, obtaining old bills had been a problem. But Goot, endlessly inventive, had managed to get five hundred bucks and change. With any luck, he wouldn't need more than that. The GPS locator that he would carry would be useful only as long as he was in the here and now; the satellites that made it possible hadn't existed in 1968. Cell phones, compasses, and radios didn't function in the black water, but these items and flares would be in his pack nonetheless.

The Zodiac raft that would carry him into the mass would have emergency food rations and water to last him three days. It would also have a first-aid kit that contained a five-day supply of broad-spectrum antibiotics powerful enough to lick most bacteria, both liquid and spray Benadryl, a cortisone ointment, Advil, and a host of other remedies that seemed like overkill. Sheppard had finished packing this afternoon and dropped everything at the dock, as Blake had instructed. He was up to date on his shots, which covered the basics—typhoid, tetanus, yellow fever—and, thanks to 9/11, the more exotics, like smallpox and anthrax.

If he had been taking this trip under the official auspices of the FBI, the list of supplies would be longer, the bureaucracy would be intolerable, and truth be told, he thought, the trip probably wouldn't happen at all, because who would believe it was possible? He still had moments when he pictured himself drifting aimlessly out in the black water, waiting for something to happen. But in those moments, he thought of Mira and Annie, of the incontrovertible evidence, and his skepticism went south.

He pulled into Nadine's driveway promptly at seven and saw Leo Dillard sitting on the porch steps, smoking a cigarette. In the evening light, he looked strangely peaceful, unhurried, like a man for whom time had never been an issue. Definitely an illusion, Sheppard thought, a trick of the light. Adjectives like peaceful had never applied to Dillard. Never would. The words that described Dillard were usually sharper, uglier, and tended to be verbs that were used as adjectives. *Pissed off. Fucked up.*

As Sheppard got out, Dillard stood, flicked his cigarette down the driveway, and strode over, his body language shouting that he had a bone to pick. Many bones, no doubt. Sheppard regarded him as just one more obstacle that loomed between him and Mira and Annie.

"Hey, Leo. What brings you out here?"

"You said you were leaving town, but here you are."

"Actually, what I said was that I was taking some time off. Jernan approved it. Goot and I are leaving tomorrow."

"I was informed that your pal Gutierrez had some fake ID printed up and that he's been scrounging up old currency. What's going on, Shep?"

"Goot's got some strange hobbies."

"That may be true, but I have this gut feeling, see, that all this shit is related to you, not to Goot, and that you're in direct violation of my orders."

"Leo, Leo. Your gut feelings and a quarter will buy you a little card with your daily fortune on it at the video arcade. Now, if you'll excuse me, I've been invited for pizza."

Sheppard started past Dillard, hoping he would grab his arm, that the stupid shit would give him a reason to deck him. But Dillard sensed Sheppard's mood the way other people might sense a minute change in temperature, and didn't touch him. "Shep, once I prove that you know more about these abductions than your files indicate, I'll have your ass fired."

"Instead of pouring all that energy into hating me, Leo, put it where it should be, into finding Wheaton."

"I'd like nothing better. But there're some weird inconsistencies with this whole thing that weren't mentioned in your files. Like why the bones in those graves were more than thirty years old."

"You removed me from the case before I got the forensics results. All I know is that Annie wasn't buried there."

Dillard came over to Sheppard, worry carving new lines across his forehead, deeper crevices on either side of his nostrils. "Let's rewind the last few days, Shep. I'm putting you and Goot back on this investigation."

"What about that rule?"

"Screw the rule. Like you said, it's not official."

"Love to help you out, Leo, but Goot and I are headed to Bimini to do some fishing."

"While your girlfriend and her daughter are still missing? I rather doubt it."

"*Very* good, Leo. So let's apply that logic. Just because you tell me I'm off the investigation, why would I do that when Mira and Annie are involved? I'm pursuing this my way and I have Jernan's blessing. So get lost."

Sheppard left him stammering in the hot stillness.

Goot peered out the side of the living room blinds. "If he's got the house under surveillance, then all he's got so far is the pizza delivery guy and Nadine and me arriving."

"And directional mikes," Sheppard added, softly.

Nadine came in with the pizza and a large bowl filled with a tossed salad. "We should invite him for dinner." She set the bowl on the table, then turned on the TV, the volume loud. Cover noise.

Goot spoke quietly now, the three of them huddled over the coffee table, helping themselves to food. "The pilot will be on the dock at eight. I say we split up and head out in two cars. You'll be in Nadine's backseat, Shep. I'll drive your car, lead them away, lose them. I'll meet you at the dock."

Sheppard considered this, then shook his head. "Won't work. Dillard will have both cars followed. I say we head out of here on foot and then on bikes."

"You two head out on foot and bikes," Nadine added. "I'll lead them to the bookstore, go out the back, and meet you at the dock. We'll stay in touch by phone."

Thirty minutes later, Sheppard and Goot walked their bikes out of the garage. To the west, the sun looked like a curve of flaming grapefruit as it sank into the gulf. Its light tipped the trees that covered the hillside below them, turning them to fire. The light made Sheppard feel vulnerable and he quickly walked his bike into the trees and started down the steep, rocky trail, Goot behind him.

The trail twisted through the dense growth, and about two hundred yards down it intersected a second trail. This trail was more level, cutting neatly back and forth between the trees, then finally straightening out to run parallel to the beach, but thirty feet above it. It fed into the bike path, where they paused so Goot could call Nadine. He spoke rapidly in Yoruba, a language that Dillard and his boys, if they were eavesdropping, certainly didn't know.

"She was just turning into the bookstore lot," Goot said as he disconnected. "Two cars were tailing her. She spotted a third car parked in the trees across the street from the lot. She'll wait until it's completely dark before she leaves the store."

It would be a long night for the third man, Sheppard thought, as he sat out there in the dark, watching the TV's light flickering against the blinds.

They mounted their bikes and pedaled fast. Sheppard hadn't heard anything from Lydia Santos, Nadine's contacts hadn't been able to locate Jake Romano, and Rusty Everett apparently had vanished after he'd inherited Wheaton's property. So Sheppard would have to go on the information he had, which left him feeling like an astronaut hurtling through space who knew next to nothing about the solar system or the planet where he was headed.

When they turned into Tango Sea and Air, stars were popping out against the tight, darkening skin of the sky. They left the bikes propped up against the front of the building. While Goot headed off to use the rest room, Sheppard went on out to the dock, anxious to check his supplies and get under way.

The pilot was nowhere in sight, but the plane bobbed in the water, the passenger and storage door open. The key was in the ignition, the pilot's flight book lay in the seat. His plastic supply container rested on the dock. He set his pack down and looked in the back of the plane to make sure the outboard engine and Zodiac were there. Everything looked to be in order. He started checking through the items, determined to keep his mind on the immediate task so he wouldn't have time to speculate about what lay ahead of him.

A boat approached from the northeast, a small fishing boat with a noisy inboard engine. It seemed

unlikely that Dillard had figured out where he and
Goot were headed, but just in case the man was
smarter than Sheppard thought, he kept an eye on
the boat.

There was one person on board, a silhouette against
the last of the twilight. Sheppard expected the boat to
chug on past, but when it began to turn toward the marina, he replaced the lid on the container, set his pack
on top of it, and loaded it into the back of the plane.

The boat, engine idling now, came up alongside the
dock. It stopped and a tall black woman tied it up and
got out. She wore jeans, sandals, and a turquoise shirt.
A straw bag hung from her right shoulder. Her hair,
cut very short, was beginning to gray.

"The marina's closed," he said as she approached.

"I'm looking for Wayne Sheppard."

Right then, he knew. "I'm Wayne, Ms. Santos."

Her smile, though hesitant, seemed genuine. "I got
your note, Mr. Sheppard."

"Not too surprising. You were in the house the whole
time."

"Yes, I was. I had to think things through. You have
to understand I had decisions to make. I made them."

"So it's true? You knew Mira in 1968?"

"And checked her into cabin eleven. And yes, I
treated all of the children that Patrick Wheaton
brought through the corridor. Only Rusty Everett and
Annie survived the time sickness."

"You knew about the graves?"

"Of course I knew about them."

"And Annie? Mira? What happened?"

"I don't know, Mr. Sheppard, and that's why I'm here.
My memories of that time seem to be . . . shifting, rear-
ranging themselves, with new memories forming even as
we are standing here. It's the only way I can describe it.
I feel displaced."

Like Nadine's new memories, he thought. "What are your older memories?"

"If I go into that now, we'll be here all night. I'm not being evasive. It's just that our time is somewhat limited. As I understand it, the corridor will be in place at ten-ten tonight. But you need to be in the mass before that. You'll only have one chance to get there and one chance to get back, because early on the morning of July first the corridor moves again. I can help you, but even what I'm able to do may not be enough."

"Help me how?"

"To counteract the time sickness." She reached into her straw bag, brought out a small, dark bottle. "This is a concentrated version of what pulled Rusty and Annie through. It'll give you the edge you need, Mr. Sheppard."

Sheppard held the tiny bottle between his thumb and forefinger and held it up to the light from the lampposts along the dock. "What's in it?"

She smiled then, a quick, beautiful smile. "Centuries of secrets."

"Did you send me that e-mail?"

"No. Rusty Everett did."

"He's *alive?*"

"And doing quite well."

Goot and Ross Blake hurried up the dock, Blake in shorts and running shoes, a pack on his back. Sheppard introduced Lydia to Goot and started to introduced her to Blake, but just then his pack slid off Blake's shoulder and he caught it in his left hand. The hand, Sheppard realized, that he had kept in his pocket when they had met several days ago. His little finger was missing.

"You're Rusty Everett," Sheppard blurted.

"I haven't been Everett since 1973." Then he leaned forward and hugged Lydia. "Good to see you, *mí amor.*"

Sheppard and Goot looked at each other and then

both of them spun around as tires squealed somewhere beyond them. Two cars raced into the parking
lot and six men leaped out, Dillard in the lead.

"Shit," Goot hissed. "Dillard and his boys. We'll stall
them. *Go, go.*"

Blake ran over to the plane, Sheppard on his heels.
Goot untied the plane, Blake scrambled into the pilot's
seat, and Shep buckled himself into the passenger seat.
Goot slammed the door, stepped back.

"Clear," Blake shouted, and the engine started up
and the propeller began to spin.

Moments later the plane sped across the surface of
the gulf, water flying back against the windows, and
lifted smoothly into the air. As Blake banked the plane
steeply to the right, Sheppard looked below. Goot,
Lydia, Dillard, and his boys looked no larger than the
characters in *Toy Story*.

As soon as they were in straight and level flight,
Blake handed Sheppard a set of headphones with a
mike, so they could talk without shouting.

"Why didn't you come forward before now?" Sheppard asked.

"When would you have believed me?"

Good point, Sheppard thought. "But you could have
prevented Annie's kidnapping."

"Maybe. But I would have had to kill Patrick. And
quite honestly, Mr. Sheppard, I was afraid to do it because I didn't have any idea what it might change in
1968. Even after all these years, I don't really understand how it works. Some things seem to change, other
things don't. New memories form or old memories either wither up and die or they exist alongside the new
memories, like phantoms."

"Does Annie survive?"

"I don't know. In the time line of events that I remember, I tried to free Annie and Patrick caught me

and chopped off my little finger and I ended up in the hospital and never saw either Patrick or Annie again. In that version of events, Lydia was arrested for theft because Patrick accused her of stealing money from him, and Mira—your Mira—and Jake Romano bailed her out. She beat the rap and left Tango shortly after that."

"What happened to Mira on that time line?"

"She disappeared."

"Disappeared. What the hell does that mean?"

"It means she disappeared. I never knew what happened to her or to Annie."

"I know that Wheaton intends to save his stepsister. But how do abducted children fit into that?"

"I think, in the beginning, Patrick was lonely. So when I survived the trip through the corridor, I became his son. But by the time he brought the second child through, there was something sinister about his motives and I think it had to do with rules. He was big on rules. When you broke one of his rules, you had to sacrifice something to earn forgiveness or to balance the books. If you apply this idea to Patrick's life, it goes something like this. On his original time line, Eva was pregnant with his kid and she didn't want the baby. Billy Macon had relatives in the Bahamas who could help her obtain an abortion. The night she died driving his car, they were on their way to a boat that would take them to the Bahamas. She died, therefore, it was Patrick's fault. To undo that event—in other words, to balance the books—he believed he had to sacrifice something and that something was going to be—"

"Another life," Sheppard finished.

"Exactly. But Patrick was a very careful man. He knew that if he was going to save Eva—pregnant with his younger self's child—then he would have to raise the child with her and do that elsewhere. After he disappeared—"

"With Eva? He succeeded in saving her?"

"Let me put it this way. When I got out of the hospital and returned to the house, Patrick was gone. The place had been cleaned out of all his personal effects. A few days later, I heard that a young woman on Sugarloaf had disappeared and the police were calling it a kidnapping. That young woman was Eva Wheaton. It wasn't until years later that I realized the man I'd known as Peter Wheat was actually Patrick Wheaton. And then it all began to make sense. So, see, I know that Patrick had another identity, another life set up somewhere else, and that's where he went with Eva."

"Then which time line are *we* living?"

"Beats the shit out of me."

"Why didn't you ever go to the police back then?"

"And tell them what, Mr. Sheppard? The truth?" He laughed. "No one would have believed me. The man I knew as Peter Wheat was wealthy and respected. Even if I had taken the sheriff to the graves and not told him about the corridor—and I nearly did that a couple of times—I knew what that would mean for me. I was under eighteen and would have ended up in a foster home. As it was, the only person I told about my situation—a girlfriend—disappeared. After that happened, I knew I could never risk confiding in anyone again. My plan was just to live there until I was old enough to leave and then turn him in."

"Why didn't you ever come back through the corridor?"

"I didn't know how. Right before I sold the property, I found a notebook Peter had hidden in the attic and apparently forgotten about. It was his theory about how the corridor worked. In the place of blackness, reality seems to exist in an in-between state, as both a particle and a wave, and correlates to a probability field in the brain. As soon as an observer is present and on the correct coordinates, the wave collapses and the corridor becomes the equivalent of a stream of particles that emerges into a location where the black water mass and the corridor exist in another time. The pull of your natal time line is very strong and the more he went back, the deeper the groove of that time line."

"What's to prevent me from emerging earlier in June 1968?"

"My understanding is that you'll lose a few hours on either side of the time you go through, but it will be in the same general vicinity, just thirty-five years ago."

"So there're no guarantees that I'll make it there, but if I do, it will be easy for the three of us to make it back here?"

"I don't know about easy, but as long as you're in the corridor at six-thirty on the morning of July first, it's unlikely that you'll end up somewhere else."

"And if we aren't there?"

"Then look me up."

The plane began to descend and Sheppard quickly downed the stuff in the bottle Lydia had given him. *Centuries of secrets.* "On the morning of July first, make sure you're in the water well before six-thirty. I'll be waiting for you on the beach here, in this time line."

"Where will I come out in 1968?"

"You should come out on the western shore of Tango. Rum Runners will be a couple miles up a dirt road. I've drawn you a map of the island as I remember it. You know where Patrick's house is, right?"

"I found it. A burned-out hulk."

"I torched the place myself. It was the only way to cut loose the horror of those years. There's something else. The sheriff I mentioned? His name's Joe Bob Fontaine. He's still alive, pushing ninety now. He's in a nursing home in Miami. He has memory slippages, too, and I'm not talking about those related to age, okay? He remembers Mira. She tuned in on Billy Macon's crime scene for him, but everything else is hazy for him. Tell him Rusty Everett sent you and did so with Ross Blake's blessing."

"But in 1968, he hasn't lived the part of his life that includes Ross Blake."

"It's all the same soul, Mr. Sheppard, the same self, just in different time zones. Memories work both ways."

With that, the plane touched down and Sheppard climbed into the backseat to prepare the raft.

Blake helped him and did it with the quick, economical movements of a man who was accustomed to efficiency and did whatever he did well. When the Zodiac was in the water, tethered to a strut, Blake turned off the raft's running lights and switched on one of the large hurricane lanterns that Sheppard carried.

"Once you're in the mass, this won't work. Use the kitchen matches and candles I packed in with your provisions. We'll stay in touch by cell phone until those don't work, either. The GPS probably won't work in there, either."

"You never ventured in?"

"Nope."

"Not even curious?"

"Hey, once was enough for me."

Not exactly what Sheppard wanted to hear right now. He stepped down into the raft and Blake passed him the supply container.

"What time do you have?" Blake asked.

"Eight-fifty."

"You've got a wait of over an hour. As long as you're in the black water, Dillard's people won't see you."

"They'll spot your plane."

Blake grinned and passed Sheppard the lantern. "As soon as you head out, I'm leaving."

"Thanks very much for your help."

"Sheppard?"

"Yeah?"

"Just get the fucker."

Sheppard mounted the hurricane lantern and started the engine. Within minutes, he heard Blake's seaplane taking off and suddenly he felt very much alone.

And scared.

At 9:26, the engine sputtered and died, his compass spun wildly, and then the lantern went out.

He dropped his head back and looked up. Total darkness. Not a star in sight. No stars, no planes, no moon, just impenetrable blackness. It was as if he drifted in a black cosmic soup way back at the dawn of time. He got out the kitchen matches and one of the glass containers that held a candle and lit it. The flare of the little flame soothed his nerves until he realized it wasn't moving. It just stood there, erect, unmoving. Like the air.

Sheppard tilted the engine back out of the water, picked up the paddles, and started paddling. He deviated slightly to the left, then the right, testing the compass, but it just kept spinning. And the blackness didn't end. The air became oppressive. With every breath, he felt as though he were inhaling a glutinous substance that was accumulating in his lungs, filling them. His body got heavier, more lethargic. He kept paddling.

Suppose it's all bullshit?

The compass suddenly stopped spinning. His course now read 81W0508, 24N5008. He dropped the engine back into the water and it started without so much as a hiccup. The hurricane lantern came on, casting a pall of light across the raft and the black water immediately around it. He tried the cell phone, but it was dead.

He kept the speed low and steered the raft slightly to the right, until the coordinates both ended in ten. He didn't know what to expect, but had visions of the raft suddenly shooting upward and then forward or sideways or backward, rather like the car in *Back to the Future*. The raft seemed to bump up against what felt like a wall, an area of air impossibly dense. Sheppard cut the engine back to idle and extended his hands in front of him. He could *feel* the denseness. His fingers sank into it, as if into a sheet of foam. Sheppard opened the engine up wide and the boat shot forward, pressing against the denseness.

His ears began to ring.

It was annoying, but not painful until the ringing abruptly rose in pitch and seemed to whip from the top of his skull to his feet, again and again, creating a vibrating cocoon of sound around his entire body. And then he was doubled over on the floor of the raft, gasping for breath, his skull exploding, his brain on fire.

It was his last sensation before he lost consciousness.

Twenty-seven

Wheaton bolted awake at just past 1:00 A.M., knowing that something was wrong. But what?

He listened to the house, but heard nothing irregular or unusual. The noises that broke up the silence were the usual ones—the click of the AC as it came on, branches scratching at the windows, and the wind skipping through the pines. Wind meant that rain was on the way.

Then it hit him. He didn't hear the tap of Sunny's claws against the floor. The dog often wandered around in the middle of the night, nibbling at the dry food in the kitchen, scratching at fleas, getting up on the furniture where she wasn't allowed. Even when Rusty was out late, as he was more and more frequently, he usually left the dog here. But not tonight.

He finally threw off the sheet and went down the hall to Rusty's room. The kid had been locking his bedroom door whenever he wasn't home, and Wheaton, believing it was some teenage phase, didn't violate his desire for privacy. But the door wasn't locked now and as soon as he nudged it and turned on the overhead light, he realized how foolish his respect for Rusty's privacy had been. The room had been cleaned out.

Gone, everything was gone—the CD player, computer, CDs, software, radio, alarm clock, posters, music, calendar, everything. The walls were bare, the closet was empty. An abrupt, visceral dread opened up inside him. *Gone where, Rusty? To the cops? To Fontaine?*

Wheaton went over to the bed, yanked the quilt off the bare mattress, stripped off the sheets, grabbed the pillow, and tossed everything into the hall. He jerked open the top desk drawer. Empty. He yanked open the other drawers, empty, empty, empty. "Goddamn ingrate," he spat, and pulled the top desk drawer out and hurled it against the wall. "Goddamn traitor." Out came another drawer. And another.

He kicked aside the pieces of the broken drawers and went into the closet. He ripped hangers off the bar, swept shoe boxes to the floor, and suddenly grabbed the bar and tore it out of the wall.

Left without a word.

Wheaton turned, swung the bar, slammed it against the bed frame, the mattress, the frame. He went after the walls, the desk, the closet door, the bedroom door. And when he was done, he was breathing hard, sweating, and the beast of his rage was spent. He surveyed the appalling mess—*the germs, dear God, the germs loose in here now*—then backed out of the room and shut the door behind him.

That was when the memory swept over him, through him, claiming him, a memory that seemed to be from long ago, yet also seemed fresh, almost new. *How can it be both?*

In this memory, whatever it was, Mira Morales had been to young Wheaton's house with Fontaine to question Eva about Billy Macon's murder. And in the bathroom hallway, as young Wheaton had wrapped a tendril of her hair around his finger, Mira had kneed him in the balls. *Here's a message for you, Wheaton. I came through the corridor and I know what you're up to. If you hurt my daughter, I'll follow you to the end of the fucking universe. Carry that one through time.*

How the hell could this have happened? How had she followed him through the corridor? And how had she met up with Fontaine? *I know what you're up to.* How?

My mom's psychic . . .

How much had she told Fontaine?

Anything was too much.

Wheaton ran into his bedroom, threw open the closet door, picked up two of the suitcases he had packed in preparation for the final phase. And the final fucking phase was here.

He hastened downstairs and loaded the suitcases into the van. Next, he packed his computers, the TV and VCR from his own time, the Nintendo set, the games, the DVDs. Even though the house in Miami was furnished with just about everything he, Evie, and the baby would need, he couldn't leave incriminating evidence behind.

He collected phones, computer supplies, video camera, and tapes. He had withdrawn most of his money from the bank and had been transferring it gradually to his Harvey O'Connor account, but he still had quite a bit of jewelry. He needed to retrieve it and then go for the girl.

And the gas, don't forget the gas. For the boat, for the bus, for the end.

It was now 1:17 A.M. Five hours before the sun rose. He wanted to be off the island long before then.

He stood now in the kitchen, looking slowly around, taking a mental inventory. He didn't need things like dishes, silverware, glasses. But he needed his guns, a 30-06 rifle and a Beretta 9mm. He opened the pantry and reached back behind the dishes for the Beretta. He dropped it in a beach bag and pulled the fridge away from the wall and brought out the rifle. Every room, he thought, had to be inventoried.

As he started into the living room, he passed the

control box for the shed and realized Annie hadn't been fed since the day before yesterday and that the power was still off in there. Well, too bad. In a few hours, he thought, the shed would look like paradise to her.

He moved quickly into the living room.

2

Annie had tossed and turned for what seemed like hours. She was hungry, hot, scared, and pissed off. She had managed to get the storage door open and had the mop and broom handles at her disposal and a bucket she had filled with various types of cleansers. But so what? Peter hadn't come down to the shed, and unless he did, all she had were useless tools, not weapons.

She already had beat the broom handle against the windows, but the glass wouldn't break, didn't even fracture. She had rammed the cart into the metal door, denting it, but it hadn't broken through the multiple locks. She tried to lift the cart to smash it through one of the windows, but it was too heavy.

She couldn't just sit here and do nothing. Sooner or later Peter would come down here and she had to be ready for him.

Annie made her way toward the bathroom. Her eyes were accustomed to the dark now and she reached the bathroom without tripping over anything. She pulled her towel from the rack, then got down on her hands and knees and crawled over to the linen closet, the towel draped over her shoulder. She opened the door, spread the towel out on the floor, and reached inside the closet.

How many tiles were there? She'd never counted

them. But she counted them now as she picked them up and set them down on the towel. Three to a stack, four stacks across on the first row, four stacks on the second, four stacks on the third. Thirty-six tiles in all. She folded the corners of the towel in toward the tiles, bunched the corners together in her hand, and lifted her little terry cloth bag.

It was heavy.

She crawled back to the bathroom door, pulling her terry cloth bag beside her. Maybe it would work, maybe it wouldn't, but she had to try. She couldn't stand it in this place anymore. When she reached the door, she pressed her back to the wall and stood slowly. It was the only way she could maintain a point of reference in all this darkness. She wrapped the corners of the towel securely around her hand and moved quickly into the front room.

Now: the windows. No light to speak of. She had to go over to the window, set her bundle down, and feel her way across the glass, learning the topography through touch. When she found what she believed was the center of the glass, its potentially weakest point, she picked up the bundle again and took three giant steps back.

Mother, may I?

You bet, kid, go for it.

She swung the bundle way back, swung like some hot-shit player who was up to bat, and the tiles crashed into the unbreakable glass. Something shattered. But it wasn't the window.

Annie dropped to her knees, the shattered tiles struck the floor, and she started to cry. She should have experimented first with just a few tiles, to see what would happen. How stupid, stupid, stupid could she be? She pushed to her feet and went over to the window, ran her fingers across it. As smooth as a baby's butt.

She pressed her nose against the window, this moon glass, this *stuff* from her time that he had brought back with him. A time thief, that was Peter. He was able to live thirty-five years in the past only because he had the toys of the future. The PCs, VCRs, DVDs, CDs. Acronym technology. He stole other things from the future, too, Advil and antibiotics that hadn't been invented in 1968. And people. Kids. He stole kids.

Annie squeezed her eyes shut, rested her forehead against the flawless glass. She was so exhausted, hungry, scared, angry, frustrated, desperate, and every other adjective she could think of, that she couldn't even cry now.

Then she heard it, a sound like noisy crickets in the wind. Her eyes snapped open and she strained to see through the flawless but filthy glass, through the starless night, past the wall of trees. A beam of light brushed up against the window and she saw Rusty. Her palms went to the glass—and so did his.

"Annie?"

"Rusty." The word rushed from her.

He pressed his hands to the other side of the glass exactly where her own hands were. She felt the heat of his hands seeping through the glass and into her own palms. She felt their sorrow, their tragedy, their apology.

"I'm going to get you out of here," he said.

3

A dream woke Lydia, the one about the white men dragging her granddaddy out into that clearing in the woods. It was so real and vivid that her heart was racing, her sheets were tangled around her feet, her damp T-shirt clung to her.

She sat up and saw some of Rusty's things piled in the far corner of her cabin, stuff he had been moving in gradually. The little computer, CDs, DVDs, VCR, whatever they were, all alien artifacts of the future, were hidden in her closet. The couch she had made up for him earlier tonight was empty. Lydia leaped off the bed and ran to the window. When she'd gone to bed, his car had been parked next to hers. Now his car was gone and she knew what that meant. She knew he had gone back up to Pete's to free Annie, something they were supposedly going to do together, around five this morning.

"Goddamn fool."

She dressed quickly in dark clothes, found her keys, her flashlight, and headed for the door. She wished that she owned a weapon. She knew that a rifle was kept in the colony office, but the office was locked now, and Diego—who had a set of keys—was probably sleeping over with one of his women tonight. Forget a weapon.

The night was warm, windy, and smelled of rain. Clouds scudded across the moon and began to swallow up the stars. Thunder rumbled in the distance, the storm was moving in from the gulf. She got in, slipped the key in the ignition, turned it. *Click.*

"C'mon, c'mon, you shit-ass car." She turned the key again and again. *Click, click.*

Dead battery, dead starter, what the hell did she know? She wasn't a mechanic. She got out and ran over to the closest electric cart, plugged in at one of the pole outlets. She looked inside for the key. Residents who rented the carts rarely took the keys inside with them. They hid them under mats or in the glove compartment or under the seats. She searched, but couldn't find a key. She searched two more carts without any luck. Since she was close to the office, she loped to the front door, hoping the last person out had forgotten to lock up, but the place was as secure as a military base.

"You'd better be home, Diego," she muttered, and took off down the path at a swift clip.

4

A resounding boom was Sheppard's first clear awareness that he wasn't dead. Seconds later, lightning burned through his lids and his eyes snapped open just in time to see a jagged bolt of horizontal lightning undo the sky. He scrambled out of the raft and pulled it up through the sand, the wind at his back, shoving him forward. He stumbled along like a drunk. His head felt as if it had been stuffed with straw, his throat was parched, his body movements were jerky, erratic, like a puppet's.

Lightning seared through the darkness again and was followed a second later by thunder that rumbled across the water, the voice of a discontented god. He knew he had to get off the beach before he was struck by lightning and fell to his knees in the sand, next to dunes covered with tall sea oats. He shrugged off his pack, threw open the lid of the supply container. He couldn't take everything, there was simply too much, so he selected some of the food items, water, and essentials from the medical supplies.

He grabbed his poncho from the raft and put it on, slammed shut the lid on the supply container, and slung his duffel bag over his shoulder. His legs felt foreign to him, as though he were a double amputee who had been fitted recently with a pair of prostheses. It was an effort to stand, to drag the raft over the dunes and through the sea oats. He didn't allow himself to think about where he might be, whether he actually had made it to 1968 or whether he had drifted off course to one of the nearby uninhabited keys. His only thought was to hide the raft and get off the beach to make himself a less likely lightning target.

He paused briefly under the gnarled branches of a sea grape tree to remove his running shoes and put on his sandals with the Velcro straps. He checked his compass, his watch, his flashlight. Everything was working again. He pulled out his cell phone, turned it on. The battery was good, but when he punched out Goot's cell number, nothing happened. There wasn't even any message telling him he was out of range.

Does that mean I made it?

Lightning flashed again, turning the beach to the brightness of midday. A tremendous crackling sound reverberated through the air and a tree about fifteen yards from Sheppard suddenly toppled over. Then the heavens opened up and the rain poured down in slanted sheets, blown eastward by the wind. He quickly set the supply container in the sand, put the raft over it, then scooped up leaves and branches and covered it.

He turned on his flashlight, darted out from under the shelter of the tree, and raced through the sea oats and up a shallow incline to a dirt road. It was raining too hard for him to tell where the hell he was. He took a compass reading. If he was on Tango's western shore, then he needed to head south and that would hold true whether he was in his own time or in 1968. If he had ended up someplace else, then it wouldn't make any difference where he headed.

He dug a bottle of water out of his pack, sipped at it, and began jogging to the south, the voluminous poncho keeping him relatively dry, except for his feet. The lightning kept up its show, the thunder got louder and closer. The beam of his flashlight moved from side to side, seeking people, cars, buildings, anything that would tell him where he was. He passed pastures, cows huddled under trees.

Then, half a mile later, he spotted a motel on the left side of the road and another building on the right. The motel looked abandoned and although he didn't see any lights on in the other building, its lot held half a dozen Harleys and at least as many cars. He shone his flashlight across them: all looked to be from the fifties and sixties. It didn't mean he'd made it, though. Maybe there was a classic car meeting inside.

Sure, at this hour of the night?

Sheppard jogged up to the door. SORRY, WE'RE CLOSED, read the sign.

But he heard music and laughter coming from inside.

He turned the knob, pushed the door open, and stepped inside. The music didn't stop, but it seemed that everything else did. Men and women turned to stare at him. The four guys playing pool turned to look at him. The people at the bar, the bartender, two of the waitresses: everyone stared.

Sheppard shut the door, slid the hood off his head, went over to the bar. "Place is closed for the night," the bartender said.

He looked like a hippie, but that didn't necessarily mean this was 1968, either. "Is this Rum Runners?" Sheppard asked.

"The one and only," the guy said, wiping down the bar. "And we close at one."

"I'm looking for Jake Romano."

"And who are you?"

"Wayne Sheppard, a friend of Mira's."

The man's hand stopped moving. He glanced up. "Took you long enough to get here."

"Excuse me?"

"You're the friend who's bringing her money, right?"

"Uh, yeah. That's right. Look, this is going to sound like a weird question. But what's the date today?"

Romano rolled his eyes and laughed. "You even talk like she does. You want to see my driver's license, too? It's June twenty-ninth, 1968."

Holy shit, Sheppard thought, then sank onto one of the stools and started to laugh.

5

Annie paced back and forth in front of the window as Rusty used a hammer on the locks. The chain had broken apart on the first blow, the padlock had popped on the fourth blow, but the dead bolt wouldn't give. Even though he had wrapped the hammer in a towel to muffle the noise, every hit made her wince. It was too loud, too loud despite the wind and the rain that now pelted the windows.

"The window," she shouted in between hits. "Try the glass."

"Stand back."

He struck the windowpane a dozen times, hard, decisive, and powerful blows that reverberated through the glass, but didn't break it. He went back to work on the dead bolt, wedging the pronged part of the hammer under the doorjamb in an attempt to pry it loose. He held the flashlight in his mouth as he worked, going after the door as though it were a living thing, and she kept her face pressed to the glass, watching him, silently urging him to hurry up, please, oh God, hurry up.

He tore away two long strips of wood, then shouted for her to stand clear of the door. She backed up and, through the wet, dirty glass, saw Rusty running away from the shed, turning, and tearing toward it. A moment later, he slammed into the door and it gave with a great wrenching heave and swung inward on two hinges.

Rusty rushed in, Annie lunged toward him, and their arms went around each other. He held her close, against his sopping raincoat, his hands combing through her hair. Over and over again, he apologized for not doing this before, for being such a coward, and then he pulled back slightly and cupped her face in his hands and kissed her.

Her heart leaped, her body melted, the rest of the world went away.

When he finally pulled back, he grasped her hand and she slipped the spatula from her pocket. "Here's the stupid weapon I was going to use on him."

"I've got something better." He slipped a switchblade out of his pocket, showed her how to open it, then pressed it into her hand. "Keep it someplace you can get to easily. We're not outta here yet. Let's get going. My car is parked in the woods."

Annie put the switchblade in the pocket of her jeans, Rusty lifted his poncho so she could get under it, and they ran out into the rain.

The wind whipped up over the edge of the cliff like something out of a sweeping Gothic romance, and they pressed together under his poncho and hurried through the dripping woods. The thick pines bent in the wind, branches snapped back at them.

"I'm going to take you to the artists' colony, where Lydia is," he said loudly. "We'll hide you there until we can figure out what to do."

"Does he know Lydia lives there?"

"Yeah, but he won't come there looking for you. Not there. Too many people." He tightened his arm around her. "I've been moving my stuff out a little at a time, so he wouldn't notice. Last night while he was sleeping, I got the rest of it. Stuff's still in my car. Once you're on your way back through the corridor, I'm going to turn him into the cops."

"You said you don't know where the corridor is."

"Not yet. But I will."

As they neared the road, she heard Sunny's frantic barks. "She hates being left cooped up in the car," Rusty said. "But she hates the rain worse."

Annie was no expert on dogs, but she knew a lot about distress cries, and this one didn't sound like a complaint. It sounded like a warning. "Rusty, I think we better—"

And suddenly the car's headlights came on, blinding them. A shot exploded through the wet air, startling sleeping birds from the trees, and Rusty pushed her away from him, shouting, *"Run, Annie, run!"*

She stumbled forward, the wind hurling rain into her face, her eyes. Another shot rang out and Rusty shrieked and she knew he'd been hit. Annie heard the monster behind her, lumbering like a giant through the woods, his voice booming, the wind seizing it, scattering it. Annie ran and ran, zigzagging through the trees, the darkness, her terror whipping her forward, faster and faster.

Her T-shirt caught on a branch and ripped and she toppled over something on the ground. It moaned— *oh my God, it's Rusty*—and she dropped to her knees beside him. "Go, Annie, get out of here. That shot hit me in the leg. *Just get outta here!*"

A bright light impaled them and the monster stood there, the barrel of his rifle jammed against the back of Rusty's neck. "Get up, Annie, or I'll blow his head off. Get up and come over here to me."

"Don't do it," Rusty screamed.

"Shut up," the monster said, and moved the rifle off Rusty's neck, to his hand, and shot off one of his fingers.

Rusty's eyes rolled back in his head and he passed out. Blood gushed from the stump, and for the space of a heartbeat Annie just stood there, staring, numb. Then she dropped to her knees, grabbed the hem of her torn T-shirt, ripped a strip off with her teeth, and wrapped it around his hand, covering the stump. The monster let her do that much before he grabbed her by the hair, jerked her to her feet, and took her over to Rusty's car.

Sunny, tied up to the back fender, went nuts, snarling and growling and trying to break free to get to the monster. Wheaton kept a safe distance away, but pushed the barrel of the rifle into Annie's back. "Untie the goddamn dog and swat her on the rump so she doesn't come toward me. If she does, I'll shoot her."

Annie spoke softly as she approached Sunny and the dog whimpered and licked at her hand as she untied the knot. "Get out of here!" she shouted, and slapped Sunny's butt. The dog shot away from them and Peter grabbed her shoulder and pushed her toward the front of the car. He threw open the passenger door, hand-cuffed her to the handle, shoved her inside.

He kicked her door shut, hurried around to the driver's side, got in. Peter tore up the road and screeched to a stop next to a VW bus. He transferred her to the bus, cuffed her to the handle like before, and just then, a car pulled into the driveway, headlights piercing the rear window of the bus, revealing all the stuff inside.

"Joe Bob," she heard Peter say.

Annie shrieked, shouted, threw open the car door, and stumbled out, one hand still cuffed to the handle, the other waving in the air. In the backwash of the headlights, she saw the man—*a cop, he's a cop*—pull his gun, but he wasn't fast enough.

Peter blew him away.

Twenty-eight

The girl was shrieking hysterically, jerking on the cuffs like a dog in chains, her soaking hair flying out around her head as she struggled to get away. Wheaton ignored her, stepped over Fontaine's unmoving body, and peered into the cruiser. He killed the headlights, the engine, and smashed the radio with the end of the rifle. He stepped back and blew out two of the tires.

As he hurried back to the bus, he had a bottle of chloroform in one hand, a kerchief balled in the other. The girl saw him moving toward her and screamed, *"You killed him, you fucking freak, you killed him!"*

Wheaton struck her so hard with the back of his hand that she fell back into the bus, her legs kicking as she tried to get up. He poured the chloroform into the kerchief and slapped it over her nose and mouth and held it there even as she struggled, kicked, and clawed at the air with her free hand.

When she finally went completely still, Wheaton tied the kerchief behind her head, unlocked the handcuff, and put her in the back of the van. He snapped the free cuff to a metal bar on the floor where the middle seat usually locked into place. He covered her with a blanket, so it would look as if she were sleeping.

He slid behind the wheel and took one last look at the house, his past. He was now headed toward the future.

Wheaton couldn't back up without hitting the

cruiser, so he went forward and turned in front of Rusty's Chevy heap and sped down the driveway and out into the road. The wipers whipped back and forth across the windshield, the rain poured down. He was soaked to the bone and would have to stop to change clothes before he took the ferry. But in the overall scheme of things, this seemed a minor inconvenience.

Although he already had his ticket for the ferry— he'd bought six of them the other night on his way back from Macon's—he would still have to pull into the booth and give it to whoever was there. And then he would have to get through the ferry ride. At this time of night, there would be a handful of travelers, misanthropes, and wayward teens, couples out for a romantic evening, couples cheating on their spouses, the usual hippies. He wouldn't attract any attention.

Once he reached Key West, he would be practically home free.

So he drove faster and found a sort of comfort in the storm; it made him feel protected somehow, invisible, just another car traveling through the wet dark.

2

Mira drove the VW out onto the road in the blinding rain, an agitated Lydia perched at the edge of the passenger seat. She kept wiping frantically at the inside of the windshield to clear it, first Mira's side, then her side, but the defogger didn't work and the glass quickly fogged again. Mira finally cracked her window and the rain blew in.

Lydia had pounded on her door thirty minutes ago, practically in tears as she begged Mira to give her a ride. A friend of hers was in trouble, she said, and her car wouldn't start and Diego wasn't around so she couldn't get an electric cart and please, Christ, please, would Mira do her this one small favor? Mira threw on some clothes and they dashed outside to the Janis mobile only to discover that the VW leaked and the backseat was soaked and water had seeped down under the seat to the battery, which wouldn't work. They had to remove the backseat and then spent twenty minutes drying the leads with towels. They tucked more towels down around the sides of the battery and taped towels around the edges of the back window where the leaks were the worst.

Given the brutality of the storm, Mira doubted their work would last very long. She just hoped they didn't stall out in some remote part of the island. No cell phone, she reminded herself.

"Can you go any faster?" Lydia asked.

"The tires are nearly bald, the brakes are mushy, the steering is sluggish. No, I can't go any faster. Tell me about this friend of yours who is in trouble."

"Rusty. He . . . oh Christ, it's too complicated."

"What kind of trouble is he in?"

"His stepfather is fucked in the head, okay? He . . . Rusty . . . moved out of the house and left his stuff in my cabin. He was on the couch when I fell asleep. He wasn't there when I woke and I   I know what he's doing and it's . . . not safe."

"What's he doing?" Mira rubbed one of the towels across the glass, clearing it.

"Take a right."

Mira downshifted, repeated her question. Lydia lit a cigarette and cracked her window to let the smoke escape. "He . . . he's keeping a kidnapped child in his shed. There are other graves behind the shed. Children's graves. He's . . . oh Jesus God, he's such an evil man . . . three of the five children died. I done what I could for them, but I'm no M.D., it wasn't enough. Just

Rusty and Annie survived, that's it, two outta the five, and we—"

Mira swerved to the shoulder, slammed on the brakes, and the Bug died. "Annie?" She could barely say the name. "The girl he kidnapped is named Annie?"

"Yeah, why'd you stop?"

"How old is she?"

"Thirteen."

"Does she have long dark hair?"

"Uh, yeah."

Mira pressed her fists into her eyes. "Oh Christ. The man. Does he go by the name of Peter?"

"You *know* this fucker?"

"Annie's . . . my daughter." She found it difficult to speak, to even form words. "He . . . he kidnapped her when we were on Little Horse Key." She swallowed, swerved back onto the road. "How far do I go on this road?"

"A mile, then turn right by a white church. Annie can't be your daughter. We can't be talking about the same Peter."

"Of course we are."

"No. It's impossible. Peter . . . he's . . . sweet Jesus, this is going to sound really strange. But he's a time traveler." She laughed as she said it, a laugh like hiccups, then brought her fists down hard against her thighs. "Peter Wheat is a time traveler. Every kid he's brought through has been from the future. Rusty, from 1997. Becky Sawyer, Antonio . . . they all had the time sickness, they . . . ." She stopped. "*You* were sick right after you arrived at the colony. Sicker than a dog."

Mira felt even sicker right now. All this time, the answer had been right there in front of her, in cabin 14. And all along, she'd been right that everyone she had met was significant in some way to what had happened to Annie. She had lost weeks. "I live thirty-five years in your future, Lydia. On June eleventh, 2003, Annie and I were on Little Horse Key. A guy showed up with a cast on his arm." She pressed the accelerator to the floor, shifted into fourth gear, swept her hand across the glass, clearing it. "He claimed he was having engine trouble. He . . . he knocked me out. Took Annie. I could feel her psychically. I followed that feeling and . . . and ended up on a beach in 1968."

Lydia sat back hard against the seat. "That's the God's honest truth, isn't it."

It wasn't a question. "Is . . . is Annie alive?" Mira asked.

"Yes. But Peter . . . he's got a plan, something to do with a girl named Eva Wheaton, who lives up on Sugarloaf."

What she felt just then was a strange mixture of horror and awe. She had followed the cues that had come to her and had come full circle: Peter Wheat, Patrick Wheaton. "How much farther?"

Lydia rubbed at the windshield. "Another quarter of a mile." She reached out and touched Mira's arm. "You got a weapon of any kind?"

"No. Do you?"

Mira shook her head and realized it didn't matter. Nothing short of a nuclear blast would stop this man. She took the turn just beyond the white church, and the Bug slammed through potholes large enough to swallow it and chugged up the hill.

"What drug cures a time sickness? What did you treat Annie with?"

"No drug, not in the normal sense. My people, since way back, have been healers. What I gave Rusty and Annie is a soul drug. We all get to a point where life and death become the soul's choice, you know what I'm saying? I gave them the remedy and their souls chose. Can't explain it any better than that. If the soul's done what it came here to do, then the body passes on. Otherwise, the soul and the body stick around and you get whatever you get. Go left."

Mira sped into the turn. The headlights skipped across pines, a forest of pines. In one long spot, the pines formed an effective barrier that took some of rain and most of the wind, and Lydia told her to turn off the headlights. With the wind quieter through here, she could clearly hear the distinctive voice of the Bug's engine and knew the headlights were beside the point. Wheaton would hear the engine before he saw the headlights. She could either pull to the side of the road and go in on foot or race to the finish line.

She turned on the brights and gunned the accelerator.

She came out of a curve and saw something crawling across the road, a bedraggled dog trailing behind it. Mira slammed on the brakes, pulled up on the emergency brake, and she and Lydia leaped simultaneously out of the car. They ran over to the thing in the road, and the dog snarled and started barking to keep them away from it.

It was human.

It was male.

He had long wet hair and wore soggy clothes and a poncho that was three sizes too big, like a big balloon. A bloodstained cloth was peeling away from his left hand, blood still pouring out of it, running in rivulets through the water in the dirt. His leg was also bleeding. Lydia fell to her knees beside him and the dog began to whimper, to lick Lydia's hands, then it plopped down beside her, watching. She ran her hands over the young man's wet face, and when he tried to speak she shook her head. "No, no, stay quiet."

"Who is he?" Mira asked.

"Rusty. Rusty Everett. The first survivor. Help me carry him over to the Bug."

Mira lifted him by the feet, careful not to touch his skin for fear that she would take on his injuries. But in the brief time it took for her and Lydia to carry him over to the Janis mobile, images flashed through her, of this young man and her daughter. *He freed her, but not soon enough.*

The dog ran after them, barking, and Lydia pushed the front seat forward with her foot. "Go on, Sunny girl, get in there." The dog scrambled into the back and even though the seat was missing, she settled down, panting. They had to put Rusty in the front seat, his legs draped over Mira's lap and his torso and head resting against Lydia. He had passed out and Lydia fussed with the sopping bandage on his hand and Mira felt the warmth of the blood from his leg wound against her thighs. The humming in her skull was back, loud and steady, but not intolerable. Not yet.

She turned into a driveway and stopped behind a police cruiser. "Stay with Rusty," she whispered, and got out.

She moved fast through the rain, reached the steps, the porch, and slipped inside. There, in the dim glow of an overhead light, Joe Bob Fontaine paced back and forth in front of the kitchen counter, a phone mashed to his ear, his fingers rubbing at his chest.

"Joe."

He spun when he heard her voice. "Mira." His eyes held hers as he said a few more words to whoever was on the other end, then he dropped the receiver back into the cradle. "What—"

"Rusty is outside in my car, bleeding to death. Get an ambulance."

"Rusty? Sweet Jesus." He made the call, not a simple 911, either, but through an operator. Then he slammed down the receiver. "Ever since we met that young Wheaton, I'd been trying to place his face. Tonight it clicked into place. Peter Wheat is young Wheaton's real father."

What? But of course he would think of it like that. She didn't correct him. "And the girl he has is my daughter," she said, and her voice broke and she began to sob.

Fontaine took her by the arms. "Listen to me. He had her in the bus. She was shouting, waving her arms. Then he shot me. I was wearing the vest, like you said, but the shot knocked me clean out. When I came to, they were gone. A chopper's coming. We'll get him, Mira, we will. Let's go check on Rusty."

Mira scooped up some towels from the counter and ran after Fontaine.

Lydia sat in the passenger seat of the Bug, Rusty's head in her lap. "He's lost a ton of blood. He got shot in the leg, too, but it's not as bad as his hand. Tear up those towels for me, Mira."

Mira tore the towels into strips, Fontaine paced, and Lydia unwrapped the soggy bandage from Rusty's hand. "My God," she whispered, and asked for matches or a lighter and some light.

Fontaine handed her a Zippo lighter and turned on his flashlight. She wrapped a strip of terry cloth around her index finger, tightening the fabric, then held the Zippo to it, setting it on fire. She let it burn for a moment, blew it out, and held the glowing embers to Rusty's shattered finger. He came to, screaming, his body lifting slightly off her lap, then fell back down onto her thighs, groaning.

"That'll stop the bleeding."

"Where the hell is that ambulance? And the chopper?" Mira asked.

"The rain may be delaying the chopper," Fontaine said. "I'll run up to the house and call again."

He took off toward the house and Mira glanced back, saw headlights reflected against the wet trees. "Here they come." She ran down the driveway, past the cruiser and into the road, waving her arms and shouting, *"Here, we're right here!"*

The Pontiac screeched to a halt and two men leaped out. In the backwash of the headlights, she saw Jake Romano—and Sheppard.

3

To say that the moment was surreal for Sheppard didn't describe it. He felt as if his entire life had been distilled to precisely this instant, in this rainy patch of light, thirty-five years in the past. He ran toward Mira, moving against the wind, splashing through puddles, and threw his arms around her, hugging her close, terrified that if he released his hold on her, he would wake up in his own bed in 2003.

"You're real," she breathed, pulling back slightly to peer up at him, her wet hair plastered to her head and the sides of her face, raindrops standing out like freckles against her cheeks.

"Got your message," he said. "Came as fast as I could. Is Annie—"

"Not here. He took her. He's headed—"

"To Sugarloaf," he finished.

Romano halted alongside them and threw open the passenger door. "Hop in."

Sheppard and Mira piled in, Mira sandwiched between the two men, and moments later he pulled in behind the Bug. They ran over to it and a kind of shock shuddered through Sheppard when he saw Lydia, thirty-five years younger than the woman who had stood on the dock of Tango Sea and Air last night, and Rusty

Everett, his head in Lydia's lap, his hand wrapped in bloody towels. "What kind of injury is it?" he asked.

"Gunshot. Blew off his little finger and shot him in the leg," Lydia replied.

Blew off. But the adult Rusty had told him that Wheaton had *chopped* off his finger. The time line was already shifting. Sheppard dug out the first-aid kit and removed a syringe with penicillin in it. "Is he allergic to anything that you know of, Lydia?"

"Don't know of anything."

"You know how to give an injection?"

"Yes. Do I know you?"

"Not yet," he replied, and handed her the syringe.

Her eyes flicked to Mira, who stood at the other door, peering in. "He's from your time."

She nodded.

"Shit," Lydia murmured. "It's like Halloween, people pourin' through the corridor."

She gave Rusty the shot, then handed Sheppard the spent syringe.

An ambulance came tearing up the road, siren shrieking. Romano ran out to the road to wave them into the driveway, and a man hurried out of the house. "Who's that?" Sheppard asked Mira, as they took refuge on the porch.

"Sheriff Fontaine."

"Joe Bob?" he asked, and Mira looked at him quizzically. "Long story," he said.

The paramedics appeared with a stretcher, and police backup arrived sixty seconds later, two cruisers roaring in, lights spinning, sirens crying, radios crackling. "I'm going with them in the ambulance," Romano called, and trotted alongside the stretcher, a dog racing along in front, howling, barking, and leaping up, trying to reach Everett.

Lydia paused long enough to run over to the porch.

She hugged Mira and gave Sheppard's arm a quick
squeeze. "Seems like I got a memory of you and me
meeting on a dock somewhere, which I know didn't
happen. How's that possible?"

"How's any of it possible?"

"Does Rusty survive?"

"Rusty flew me into the black water in my time,
Lydia."

"Thank God," she said softly, then ran down the
steps and scrambled into the back of the ambulance
with Everett, Romano, and the dog.

While Fontaine talked with his men and used their
radio to communicate with the chopper, Sheppard and
Mira went inside the house. She didn't get very far. She
dropped his hand and stood in the mouth of the hallway, shaking her head. "I can't stay in here, Shep. He's
. . . he's everywhere."

"There's a shed down through the woods. That's
where he kept her. She left us a message, carved into
the bathroom wall. When I found this place, it had
been burned. Rusty eventually torches it."

Mira rubbed her hands over her face. "Shep, we
need to get going, to go after him, to—"

"The chopper will be faster. We know where he's
headed."

She backed out of the hallway. "I . . . I can't stay in
here."

Sheppard didn't want to let her out of his sight, but
he remembered the strange sensation that had swept
over him when he and Goot had been in here. He
went into the kitchen and looked slowly around. He located the power box that, in his time, had triggered the
déjà vu he'd experienced. He opened it. The bastard
had turned off the power to the shed. He flipped the
main switch and hurried outside to find Mira.

The other cops were spreading out into the woods,

apparently following Mira, and Fontaine trotted over to Sheppard. "You're Mira's friend."

"Wayne Sheppard," he said, and showed Fontaine his badge.

"Joe Bob Fontaine. Good to have a fed here."

He remembered what Ross Blake had said to him about Fontaine, but given the situation, decided to put his own spin on it. "Ross Blake sends his regards."

Fontaine frowned, as though he understood, at least at some level, what this meant, then shook his head. "Look, I know some pretty weird shit is going on here, okay? But I don't have time to figure it out right now. Mira read for me a few nights ago, told me to wear a vest. I did. It saved my life here tonight. You're a friend of hers, that's good enough for me. She ran down to that shed, following something. Let's go."

"When's that chopper getting here?"

"It's en route now. Had to fly in from Key West. It's going to land in the church parking lot at the bottom of the hill."

The woods seemed infinitely darker than the night Sheppard and Goot had been here in his time. His shoes squished against wet leaves and pine needles and the trees shuddered in another gust of wind. "Sheriff, behind the shed there are three graves, the other children who were abducted."

Fontaine looked baffled, but shouted at one of his men to contact forensics. Sheppard had been through this horror once and didn't need a repeat performance. He hurried on to the shed, wondering how this would effect events in his own time, the events he already had lived through. He didn't want to think about it.

Two lamps were on and although cool air now poured from the vents, the air inside the shed was still stifling, oppressive. Mira was moving silently around the large room, her hands extended, touching this, that. He didn't interrupt, didn't intrude. He just stood there and watched, waiting for her to say something.

At the couch, she crouched and ran her hands over the cushions. Tears flooded her eyes and rolled down her cheeks. She moved toward the bathroom and ran her hands over the door, the sink, the tub, and crawled across the floor to a storage closet, her hands always moving, absorbing, *reading*. A bruise appeared on her upper arm, materializing like some optical illusion. Her lower lip split, opened, swelled. He had seen this before, too, the way she took on other people's injuries. These injuries, though, started to fade, to transmute, he thought, as she made her way back into the main room. That was new, something he had never seen happen before.

She finally stopped and looked up at him, noticing him for the first time. Her eyes glistened. Her face was horribly pale. "That kid, Rusty. He helped her, Shep. He freed her. And he gave her a knife. She can defend herself." Her voice caught. "She has a chance."

Twenty-nine

Annie was awake, conscious, and had been for some time. Maybe when she turned her head in her drugged sleep, the kerchief had gotten rolled up off her nose and mouth or maybe the chloroform had evaporated. She didn't know. The only thing that mattered was that when she inhaled, she breathed in fresh air. With every new breath, her head got clearer.

She ached everywhere, her arm had fallen asleep. She could hear the rain, the wipers, and felt the bus moving. She could see the back of Peter's head, too, and as long as she could see it, she was safe. She felt the switchblade in her right pocket, her savior, her redemption. But she couldn't reach it with her right hand because it was cuffed to something metallic, a bar of some kind. She inched her fingers across her belly, careful not to move her right hand, terrified that Peter would hear the slightest noise, and slipped her fingers into her pocket and withdrew the switchblade. She tucked it under her left thigh, where she could reach it quickly.

Now: the kerchief. She rolled it up onto her forehead, careful not to roll it completely off; she wanted to be able to pull it down over her face if she had to. There, better.

And don't think about Rusty, bleeding in the rain.

But she couldn't help it. That image was permanently etched in her brain, fueling her hatred for Peter and her determination to stay alive.

Annie knew that she wouldn't be able to sit up all the way, the cuff was too short. Even if she could sit up, she was on the right side of the bus and Peter was too far away to stab. The switchblade wouldn't be able to cut through the metal cuff, but maybe she could dig this bar or whatever it was out of the floor on one end and slide the cuff off. *And maybe not.*

She picked up the switchblade and rolled onto her right side, her back to Peter. That made her nervous because she couldn't see him, but he couldn't see her, either. From where he sat, it would look as though she rolled onto her side. Annie set the switchblade up close to her chest, the blade still folded in, the blanket up around her shoulders, and felt around with the fingers of her left hand, defining the metallic shape.

A bar, definitely a bar, probably part of what the middle seat fit on when it was in place. The carpet on either side of it felt like it had been cut away, and when she worked her fingers under it, her heart leaped. A loose screw seemed to be the only thing holding it in place. She pressed the button on the switchblade and the blade snapped out. With great deliberation and care, she slipped the blade under the carpet, cutting away at it a little more so that she wouldn't have to work with her fingers under it. She paused, turned her head to glance back at Peter.

His head was still facing forward, the bus was still moving, the rain still falling, the wind still gusting, howling, whistling. She felt the moment when the wind slammed into the bus on either side simultaneously and knew they were on a part of the highway where there were no trees, no buffer, where the only thing between the gulf and the Atlantic was a narrow strip of asphalt.

Quick, don't stop. With the carpet cut away, she

pressed her index finger down against the screw and tried to turn it counterclockwise, to remove it. But her fingers were damp, the screw was probably stripped, and she didn't dare jerk on the cuff to try to wrench it loose because Peter would hear it.

The wind shook the bus and it suddenly veered sharply to the right, the tires bouncing over ruts, pot-holes. Pebbles pinged against the hubcaps, the brakes whined. He was stopping. She quickly closed the knife, tucked her chin in close to her chest, and rolled the kerchief down over her nose, but not her mouth. She slid her left hand between her legs, the switchblade tight against her palm, held in place by her thumb.

Because her face was pressed down against her shoulder, chin tucked in against her chest, Annie didn't think he would be able to tell that the kerchief didn't cover her mouth. As long as she breathed in through her mouth, she would be okay.

The bus stopped, he turned off the engine, the headlights. Annie shut her eyes and waited, her heart hammering. She heard him open his door. The rain got louder, the wind swept into the car, he shut his door. She figured it would take him between five and eight seconds to get to the right side of the bus, to slide open the door. She began counting, very slowly, and was at fifteen when she realized he had gone else-where.

She rolled the kerchief up to her forehead again and lifted up on an elbow to peer out the rain-smeared window. All she saw was the darting beam of his flash-light, a distant beacon in the unforgiving darkness. He was far enough away so that he wouldn't hear her carv-ing on the metal rod, jerking the cuff, trying to wrench the screw free from the floor. She braced her left hand against the floor and pulled as hard as she could on her right hand. It hurt like hell, the cuff biting into her skin, her bone. And nothing happened. She opened the knife, touched the screw until she could trace the groove on the top, then pressed the tip of the knife into it and began to turn. *Counterclockwise, up and out, please, please, come loose.*

It started to give and she thought, suddenly, of the life the monster had taken from her. Okay, so it hadn't seemed all that great when she was in the middle of it. She had been lonely, she hated the in-between of her body, suspended somewhere between childhood and adolescence, but not a part of either, and most of all she had hated the endless monotony of it all. Now she would gladly return to it. She would embrace the whole package, would revere it, would live entirely in the moment, forever and ever, amen.

Annie glanced out the window again. The glass was fogged, the rain still smeared across it like thick spit, but she was pretty sure the darting beam of light was coming toward her now. *Shit, shit, shit.* One last wrench, she thought, and jerked her right hand upward, biting her lip against the pain, straining with whatever strength she had, and felt it, a slight give, a low scraping sound.

One more violent jerk might do it. The screw would be out and she would be able to slide the cuff off the bar. *If he opens the sliding door, snap upward, the blade extended, and hope the bar snaps loose.*

But even as she thought this, she knew she wouldn't do it, that she couldn't risk it until she was completely free of the bar. Three times before, she had made her lunge for freedom and each time, the monster had caught her. There wouldn't be a fourth time. If she tried and failed again, she would die.

Annie quickly lay back down on the floor of the bus, the kerchief covering her nose but not her mouth, her chin tucked in against her chest, her left hand—and the switchblade—sandwiched between her legs.

2

Mira could feel Annie now, her energy like a soft, bright light against her heart. Alive, she was still alive. And as long as she was alive, there was hope.

The chopper flew high and well offshore so that to anyone on the road, it would be almost invisible. Wheaton might hear it, but she hoped he wouldn't connect it to the police. He probably had no reason to. He thought Fontaine was dead.

"Here's the deal," Fontaine said. "I can put out an APB for the bus and have the local cops surround the Wheaton house."

"No," Mira said quickly. "If he's trapped, he'll kill her. He wants Eva and I feel that he's going in by water. He'll park the bus elsewhere."

"A boat," Fontaine repeated, nodding. "There's a marina across the canal from the house."

"How close to the house can the chopper come down?" Sheppard asked.

"We can land almost anywhere there's an opening and no power lines, and if he sees or hears the chopper, he's going to know we're on to him. We've got three cops in unmarked cars at the Sugarloaf Lodge who are standing by, ready to get wherever we need them or to get us to wherever we need to go."

Mira shut her eyes and let the various options play out across the inner screen of her eyelids. She suddenly knew what to do, but it would be difficult to explain to Fontaine because he didn't realize that the young Patrick Wheaton and Peter Wheat were the same person. And he didn't know that she and Sheppard and the man he knew as Wheat came from thirty-five years in his future. But he trusted her and knew there was something strange about all this, so perhaps he would go along with it.

"I think the chopper should drop us off at the Sugarloaf Lodge. Sheppard goes to the Wheaton household, with backup in the event that he needs it, and arrests Patrick Wheaton for the murder of Billy Macon. He also gets Eva out of the house, since that's who he really wants. You and I go to the marina, Joe. We're waiting for him when he shows up. When he leaves the bus to get to his boat, we move in and take Annie."

"You stay at the lodge and I'll move in with one of my men," Fontaine said. "I can't take you in."

"We need her feedback, Joe," said Sheppard, one lawman to another.

"If she comes, she has to stay out of the way." Fontaine said this as though Mira weren't there.

"That's fine," Mira told him, knowing it wasn't fine at all.

"We've got one big problem, though. We don't have any conclusive evidence that he killed Macon."

"I know that he did," Mira said. "I realize that's not conclusive evidence, but you can take him in for questioning, can't you?"

He thought about it, glanced from Sheppard to Mira. "I get the feeling there's a lot you two know that you aren't saying. I need to know whatever it is."

Shit, Mira thought. *Now what?*

But Sheppard was ahead of her. "It's like this, Joe. The man you know as Peter Wheat and young Patrick Wheaton are the same person."

Fontaine looked at him as if he'd lost his mind. "Sure. Of course. What the hell are you talking about?"

"Just trust us on this. They're the same person. The young Wheaton has to be handled carefully because whatever he experiences will pop into Wheat's mind as a, uh, new memory," Sheppard said. "It'll tip him off."

"The timing has to be exactly right," Mira went on. "As soon as your men at the lodge spot his bus, they radio Sheppard and you and me, Joe. Sheppard goes in and arrests Patrick and gets the girl out of there."

Fontaine didn't look convinced. "You're telling me to take this on faith, right?"

"Something like that," Sheppard replied.

"I'll do it your way on one condition. When it's over, I want a full explanation."

Sheppard nodded. "You got it."

"Okay," he called to the pilot. "Take us down in the lodge parking. Radio the guys on the ground that we're ready to move."

Please let this work, Mira thought, and turned her head toward the window and stared below as the chopper started to descend.

3

Two more bridges to cross, Wheaton thought. The first would take him onto Sugarloaf and the second would take him across the canal to the marina. He would still have plenty of time until daylight, and by then he and Eva would be halfway to Miami.

But the rain worried him. It already had screwed up his timing. The ferry had taken fifty minutes instead of thirty-eight and he had gotten delayed another fifteen minutes on his way out of Key West because of a car accident. The wipers on the bus were slow and sluggish and when he took the bus over forty, it reduced his visibility to zero. Worse, he lost another five minutes when he stopped to take a piss.

He glanced back to check on Annie. She had rolled onto her side, but was still out cold. Just as well. Before he left the bus, he would soak the kerchief once more so that she wouldn't regain consciousness before she died. A painless death was still a fair exchange for Eva's life. If you broke the rules, you were required to make a sacrifice. The universe didn't give a shit how Annie died, as long as she did.

As soon as he had unloaded the bus, he would saturate the inside of it with gasoline and leave the inside light on so that he could see it from across the canal. Once he had Eva in the boat, he would fire two shots—one at the bus's window and another at the gas tank, and it would blow sky high, just as Billy Macon's car had. A fitting exchange, one life for another.

Cars and several trucks passed him in the other lane, headed for Key West or Tango. Two cars pulled out from behind him and sped by, tires kicking up a virtual waterfall that the bus's wipers struggled to vanquish. He downshifted, wiped his hand across the glass to clear it, and crossed the bridge to Sugarloaf.

He could feel the future rushing toward him now, the life that Billy Macon had stolen from him and Eva. Almost there. Almost home.

4

Sheppard got the word: the VW bus had been sighted. He got out of the police cruiser and opened the gate to the Wheaton property. The two cruisers pulled in side by side, effectively blocking a way out in case anyone in the Wheaton household decided to run. Two of the detectives from the Monroe County Sheriff's Department accompanied him onto the porch.

He was acutely aware of the hundreds of small details that his presence in the past already had changed. And he had been here only a matter of hours. No telling what all Mira's presence here for more than three weeks had changed. But all of that was beside the point now. He was entering an unknown country and speculation about what might come out of this was anyone's guess.

Sheppard unscrewed the porch lightbulb, then rang the bell and pounded on the door. Moments later, a man in pajamas opened the door, blinking sleepily.

"Yes? What is it?"

"FBI, Mr. Wheaton." He flashed his genuine 1968 badge and the elder Wheaton glanced at it. "And the Monroe County Sheriff's Department. We would like to speak to your daughter and Patrick."

"Now? It's the middle of the night."

"Right now," Sheppard replied.

The elder Wheaton opened the door wider and Sheppard and the two cops followed him into the house. Mrs. Wheaton, wearing a robe, stood at the top of the stairs with a beautiful young woman wearing cotton shorts and a halter top. Eva, a young, seductive goddess who was pregnant with Wheaton's kid.

"What's going on?" Katherine Wheaton demanded.

"One of you wake Patrick," Dan Wheaton told her, and reached to turn on a light, but Sheppard stopped him.

"No lights. All of you are in danger and need to get out of here as quickly as possible. Please go with the detectives."

"We're not going anywhere until we know what the hell is going on," Katherine announced.

"Think again," her husband snapped, and took her firmly by the arm.

"I'll get Patrick." Eva started for the stairs that led to the second floor, but Sheppard stopped her.

"I'll get him. Go with your parents."

"It's the second door at the top."

Sheppard took the stairs two at a time, his weapon out, his gut telling him that something was very wrong. Wheaton's door was shut and Sheppard didn't bother knocking. He threw the door open and moved cautiously into the room, both hands clutching his weapon. Wheaton's bed had been slept in, but it was now empty and the wind blew through the crack in the sliding glass door.

Shit. Sheppard slid the door open and stepped outside onto a balcony where the wind blew hard and fast. There, just below him, Patrick Wheaton climbed down a wooden trellis with the tenacity of a spider. *He knows, somehow he knows.*

Sheppard spun around and hit the stairs at a run.

5

Mira and Fontaine stood behind the marina's office, a building that looked as if it might blow away if the wind got any stronger. From here, they had a view of the parking lot, lit by a lone, very dim sodium streetlight that gave the wet air a nicotine-tainted cast, and of the docks, four boats tethered to it, rocking and rolling in the choppy water. They had beaten Wheaton here, but not by much. He had been sighted by the cops at the lodge.

Mira stepped back from the corner and disengaged the safety on the 9mm that Sheppard had thrust into her hand before they had separated. The clip was fully loaded. "You know how to shoot that?" Fontaine asked.

"Yes." She had learned during the Lauderdale investigation and hadn't touched a gun since. She hated guns. But she would use it now if she had to.

"Then we're going to cover each other," he said. "Climb that ladder to the roof. You'll be safe up there, but with a bird's-eye view."

He darted out from behind the building and into the high weeds and brush that grew along the end of the seawall closest to the road. Once he sank into the weeds, he was invisible. Mira quickly climbed the wooden ladder that led to the roof of the building.

The roof was flat and the marina sign jutted up enough to provide a hiding place. She was grateful for the poncho that Fontaine had lent her, but it was beside the point. Her clothes were so wet that they squished with even the slightest movement. She peered over the top of the sign and took in the panoramic view of the parking lot, the canal, and the road.

She spotted headlights, headed this way, and quickly stretched out flat on her stomach on the roof, and watched from the edge of the sign.

The VW bus was turning in, circling the lot, prowling it. Then it began to back up slowly so that it would come in alongside the building. She knew that Fontaine wouldn't jeopardize Annie by taking a shot at Wheaton before he was out of the car, but beyond that, she didn't know anything for sure.

Suddenly, across the canal, a boat roared to life. . . .

6

Sheppard raced across the yard, headed for the dock that jutted away from the seawall. But young Wheaton was already in the boat, a long, sleek powerboat that would take him out of here so fast he would be gone before they ever found the means to follow him. *Shoot or keep running?*

Floodgates opened inside him, adrenaline poured through him, and he hurled himself the last yard and slammed into the boat just as the engine bellowed, an explosion of noise that nearly rendered him deaf. He tackled Wheaton and the kid fell back, away from the controls, and they rolled across the floor.

The boat whipped away from the dock, a powerful beast turned loose. The rain poured over them as they struggled, filling the runaway boat as it pitched violently from one side to the other. Wheaton sank his teeth into Sheppard's arm, scrambled to his feet, spun the control wheel to the right, and the boat turned sharply, headed for the dock, the seawall. Then Wheaton leaped over the side and Sheppard jumped in after him.

7

No no no. Wheaton's head felt as if it were exploding, his lungs refused to draw air, and a new memory leaped full-blown into his consciousness. *Sheppard, cops, young Patrick, wrong, everything going wrong, I can't breathe, I'm underwater, the boat's going to hit the seawall, swim, swim, faster . . .*

Then, the explosion that released him, an explosion that catapulted a fireball through the air and lit up the parking lot. Wheaton slammed his foot against the accelerator and the bus shot forward, but he wasn't quick enough. Behind him, someone fired. The rear window shattered, the wind and rain blew through.

The bus slammed over the wooden bridge.

Water. Got to get to water. To the black water. To the mass.

8

When the boat exploded on the other side of the canal, Mira leaped from the roof of the building, her poncho filling with air, like a parachute, and landed hard on the roof of the bus. Her gun flew out of her hand and now she clung to the top of the bus, terrified that the next turn would throw her off.

Wheaton drove very fast, seventy or eight miles an hour. The wind bit into her eyes, the rain lashed her face. She realized he was headed north, toward the next bridge, a bridge higher than the others, and panic filled her. Mira pushed herself forward with her toes, pulled herself with her fingers, held on to whatever she found, and inched her way to the front of the bus.

She pulled the poncho off over her head with one hand, intending to fling it across the windshield, but the wind tore it out of her hand and carried it off. Desperate, she shoved herself back along the roof, toward the shattered rear window.

9

Annie bolted upward, the screw snapped out, the cuff slid off the bar, and she crawled frantically toward the driver's seat, the switchblade open. A violent turn to the left threw her off balance and she struck the far wall of the bus, the air rushed from her lungs, but she didn't lose her grip on the knife.

She sprang onto the balls of her feet, reared up. *This one is for Rusty, you shit.* And she brought the knife down, aiming for the back of his neck. But he must have glimpsed her in the mirror, because he suddenly moved and the knife plunged into his shoulder and sank to the bone. He shrieked, the bus spun crazily to the left. Annie was knocked back against the side door. She groped for the handle, pushed down, but it wouldn't give. It was jammed, dear God, it was jammed. Her only chance was the back window.

She crawled frantically toward the rear of the bus, over

the supplies, the broken glass, the bus still careening across the road. She pushed herself through the window, the jagged shards tearing at her hands and arms, her legs, and suddenly hands grabbed her arms and her mother shouted, "Hold on to me, Annie, hold on!"

Then the bus plowed into the bridge's guardrail and kept right on going.

Her mother swept her up in her arms and leaped off the bus.

10

The bus sailed through the windswept darkness and Wheaton yanked the knife from his shoulder, hurled open the driver's door, and jumped.

It seemed to take him a long time to fall, although he knew it was only a matter of seconds. And in those few seconds, he reached out for his younger self and found him still alive, escaping, on a boat, headed into the gulf. This wasn't so much a new memory as it was a living, breathing connection, man to boy, boy to man, one soul, and he gave him everything that he knew about the black water, the corridor, and time.

He hit the water hard, water closed over his head. *Run*, he screamed to his younger self. *The black water is yours.*

11

The sky was turning the color of volcanic ash when the chopper touched down on the bridge where Wheaton's bus had gone over. Sheppard scrambled out and ran over to what remained of the railing and looked down. Shadows eddied beneath the bridge. He didn't see the bus, Mira, Annie, or Wheaton.

Like the younger Wheaton, it seemed they had disappeared.

Desperate and fearing the worst, Sheppard loped down the bridge to the prayer rug of sand that ran under it. He shouted, but the wind took his voice away as it whistled around the struts and howled on back out to sea. Then he spotted them, huddled together on the sand.

Sheppard ran toward them and suddenly realized that the thing lumbering out of the water was Wheaton, clutching something in his right hand. He moved swiftly toward Annie and Mira, but they didn't see him. Sheppard raced up the beach, not daring to shoot for fear he might hit Mira or Annie and unable to shout because Wheaton, who hadn't seen him, might hear him.

Now he was ten yards from Mira and Annie.

Seven yards.

Sheppard knew he would never close the gap in time. He dropped to his knees, aimed, fired. The shot exploded through the wet grayness and echoed under the bridge. Wheaton stumbled back, turned, stumbled again, and collapsed to the sand. Sheppard ran over to Wheaton's body, the Sig aimed at his back, and kicked the switchblade out of his hand. Mira and Annie reached Sheppard and he motioned for them to stay back. Annie did, but Mira didn't.

She came over to Wheaton, crouched, and rolled him over. His eyes were open, he was still alive, but barely. Blood oozed from the corners of his mouth, from his nostrils, his breathing was labored. "Lost young Patrick . . . didn't you, Sheppard?"

"My hope, Wheaton, is that he dies with you."

Wheaton's bloody mouth twisted into a terrible grin, then he died.

12

As Mira touched her hand to Wheaton's head, his spirit, his soul, his phantom self, sat up out of his body and looked around. She wrenched back, her eyes fixed on it, on him, then he stood and turned. He leaped back when he saw her, his eyes darting from her to Sheppard, to Annie some distance away.

"What is it?" Sheppard whispered.

"Him. Wheaton," she whispered back.

Wheaton finally looked down at his own body and an expression of profound horror seized his face. "You're dead," Mira said aloud.

She knew that he heard her because his head snapped up, his mouth opened, and she heard a resounding *Noooooo*. He lunged at her—and passed right through her. A chill filled Mira, the kind of bone-splitting chill that you might feel in graveyards on dark nights. The hairs on the back of her neck stood up, goose bumps raced over her skin. Mira whirled around, saw his vague, shimmering shape moving toward Annie. She saw it, too, and scrambled to her feet, shrieking, "You're dead and you can't hurt me!"

She ran toward Mira and Sheppard and threw her arms around them both. He swept her up in his arms, and Mira watched Wheaton become less dense, less visible, and then he just faded away.

"Is it gone?" Sheppard whispered.

"Yes," Mira managed to whisper.

"Then let's go home."

Thirty

July 28, 2003

Her mom stopped at the curb of the large house in Pirate's Cove. Annie looked at it. "You sure this is where he lives?"

"Lydia gave me the address. She should know. Go on, hon. I'll wait."

Annie got out of the car, her bag over her shoulder. The July heat felt like a weight against the top of her head. Crickets sang from the shadows. Butterflies swooped around the bougainvillea vines that spilled over the concrete wall. She opened the metal gate, paused, glanced back at her mother.

Her mom gestured her forward and Annie continued up the walk. She thought of the many things she wanted to tell him, how she and her mother and Sheppard had kept checking the newspaper archives for how the time line had changed, and had found some pretty significant changes. Eva Wheaton, for instance, had vanished four days after the younger Wheaton had escaped, and her father and stepmother had died several years later, a double suicide. The bodies of two of Wheaton's other victims were discovered in 1968, but one was discovered in her time, by Sheppard. The second note that her mother had written Sheppard had been delivered to Sheriff Fontaine, who had given it to the younger Nadine after Annie, Mira, and Sheppard had gone back through the corridor. So many contradictions, so many dichotomies. Time had rewritten the details of their personal histories.

But she knew she wouldn't say any of this to him. That wasn't why she was here.

Annie rang the bell before she could change her mind. A maid in a crisp white uniform answered the door.

"Is Mr. Blake home?"

"He sure is. Come on in."

"No, that's okay. I'll wait right here." She didn't want to enter the world he lived in now. She just wanted to thank him and leave.

The man who came to the door was tall, just like the Rusty she knew, but everything else was different. He was old. Older than her mother. Older than Shep. "Hi," he said, and blinked, then frowned, almost as if he recognized her.

For her, the phantom sensations of his kisses had happened only a few weeks ago; for him, they were thirty-five years in the past. It took her a few moments to find her voice. "I have something that belongs to you." She reached into her bag and brought out the Jimi Hendrix CD that he had played for her that day in the shed. "Here."

He looked at it, his eyes swept up to her face. "Annie."

"I just wanted to thank you for saving my life."

Something tragic happened to his face, his eyes. He gazed past her, at the car parked at the curb, then brought his eyes back to her. "I was going to meet you on the beach the day you returned through the corridor, but I just . . . I couldn't do it. I knew what it would be like for you. I knew what it would be like for me. So Nadine took my place."

Annie knew that he was apologizing for what he saw

as a failure on his part, that the monster had left this deep void inside him that he always would try to fill with apologies because he thought he didn't measure up. "Screw the rules," she said, and put her arms around his waist.

His long arms came around her and they stood like that for what seemed to be a long time, neither of them speaking.

"It's unfair," she said softly.

"I know."

Then she stepped back, reached for his maimed hand, the injury long since healed, and pressed it to her cheek. "See you around, Mr. Blake."

She turned and ran back down the walk to her mother's car.

More Books From Your Favorite Thriller Authors

More Nail-Biting Suspense From Your Favorite Thriller Authors